David Boyle is the bestselling author of *Alan Turing: Unlocking the Enigma* and other titles; fiction and non-fiction. He has stood for Parliament, run an independent review for the government and worked for a number of thinktanks. He has also edited a range of magazines and newspapers. He lives in the South Downs.

PRAISE FOR DAVID BOYLE:

'Exhilarating' – Roger Lewis, *Daily Mail*

'A book that is engagingly sensitive' – Dominic Lawson, *Sunday Times*

Also By David Boyle

Broke: Who Killed the Middle Classes?

Give and Take: How Timebanking is Transforming Healthcare

The Tyranny of Numbers: Why Counting Can't Make Us Happy

Scandal: How homosexuality became a crime

V for Victory: The Wireless Campaign that Defeated the Nazis

THE XANTHE SCHNEIDER ENGIMA FILES

DAVID BOYLE

LUME BOOKS

LUME BOOKS

First published in 2019 by Lume Books
85-87 Borough High Street,
London, SE1 1NH

ISBN 978-1-83901-160-3

www.lumebooks.co.uk

For Grace and Tom, Penny, and my brilliant cousin,
Xanthe Louise.

Contents

“Never shall a young man,
Thrown into despair
By those great honey-coloured
Ramparts at your ear,
Love you for yourself alone
And not your yellow hair…”

W. B. Yeats

BOOK ONE

THE BERLIN AFFAIR

PROLOGUE

Cambridge, February 1939

Xanthe had always felt a bit of an outsider, especially in England. She never knew which fork she was supposed to use or how to greet people with that very English reserve. But of all the moments where she had struggled as an American in Cambridge, she never felt so out of place as when she walked into a philosophy lecture at King's College, in the rooms of Dr Wittgenstein himself. It wasn't just because she was from the Midwest, which she felt had been wearing her like a veil since she had arrived as a very young student the previous Autumn. Or really because she was a woman – that was always a factor, but she recognised it and tried to ignore it. It was being in the secret hiding place of a man who seemed almost as out of place as she felt herself. There he was, sitting in a deckchair next to a huge black stove, with his head in his hands. For one horrible moment, she wondered whether he had been put out by her obvious lateness.

Xanthe was certainly late. She had been invited by a slight acquaintance and turned up trying to look more than usually demure, only to find that the friend had gone down with a chill – everyone in Cambridge seemed to have one in those dank, dark February teatimes some months before the war broke out.

There had been no reply when she knocked at the door and absolute silence from inside. She stood there for a moment wondering whether she should just give up, then she thought she would just peer around the door – and then she found she was stuck. They all craned their necks to look at who had arrived, as if she was somehow more interesting than the slight, wizened man thinking before their very eyes. Perhaps they hadn't seen a woman before in King's, she wondered. It is quite possible they had never seen a woman at all. They had certainly never seen an American woman. She stood there, frozen to the spot by sheer embarrassment, wondering what *faux pas* she had committed and desperately checking and rechecking the fifteen wooden chairs to see where she might sit down.

She could hardly sit on the bed or the floor. Could she? She was about to escape in confusion out into the damp air again, never to return, when a slight voice attracted her attention. She saw that even this bold soul seemed unable to actually look her in the face, and his eyes focused on a spot somewhere near her feet. As he cleared his throat, nervously, she wondered whether he was about to ask her to leave.

"Here we are," he said. "Have my chair. I can perch over here."

"I am *real* grateful," Xanthe whispered as she passed him. He had short brown hair and a round face and what seemed to be a sort of twinkle in his eye. She glanced down and saw his trousers were held up with a bit of string, and gave him as big a smile as she could manage – we do big smiles in Cincinnati, she thought to herself. Then suddenly the professor was off again. "No, no, no," he said in a heavily Germanic accent. "Words do not stand for themselves. You can only understand them in context. They mean different things to different people. Language is not an objective truth. It is a *code* and we have to interpret it differently according to who we are… Yes?"

"Professor, does that apply to mathematical language – I don't think it does?"

To Xanthe's surprise, she realised this was her rescuer. He was not actually uncertain at all – at least not about mathematics and philosophy. He and the professor crossed swords throughout the meeting – more like a dialogue than a lecture. He couldn't have been shy after all, unless it was perhaps with women. That was not so unusual, after all, and especially somehow in Cambridge.

She hung around afterwards to thank him for rescuing her, and overheard Dr Wittgenstein asking one of his colleagues out to what he called the 'flicks'. By the time she had turned around to look for her rescuer again, he had gone. There was something about him she had found fascinating. There were so many pale young English men, nervous perhaps because they all knew war was coming but so innocent of life, it seemed to her – though she realised she was just as innocent in her own way. So awkward in their voluminous Oxford bags. This one had been just as shy – if not more so – but she had sensed something determined in him. He hadn't cared what anyone had thought of him.

She described him to her friend afterwards and asked who he was.

"Oh yes," he said. "I know that one. He's a real oddball. I should steer clear of him if I were you. He's called Dr Turing."

Only a year later, they would meet again in very different circumstances.

CHAPTER ONE

Bletchley, 22 March 1941

My baby girl/boy,

I can feel you kicking inside me, but I still don't know who you are. I don't even know if you're a she or a he yet. But I'm writing to you as if you were already grown up and the war was over, and you're fully grown and safe. Above all, safe. Mostly I am hoping that I will be there with you, so you won't have to read this at all – because I will have watched you grow up and can tell you everything myself. But the air-raid siren is sounding, and I am going to take you with me to the basement. It reminds me that none of these hopes can be taken for granted.

In case I am not there to be with you when you grow up, and that seems to be a strong possibility now, I wanted to let you know something about your mother in my own words. It is hardly as good as hearing it from my own lips, but perhaps you'll consider it a consolation.

That is why I am defying all regulations that prevent those of us on active service from keeping diaries. I do what I am told most of the time but, in this case, I am rebelling. I tell myself that it isn't my war at all – that I don't know how I became involved in it as an American citizen, and don't see why I should keep to their rules any more than I keep to their stiff upper lip.

So I hope you will forgive the informality of this letter. The truth is I am writing this at a time when I feel like I know you very well. I can feel your every move inside me, yet I don't even know your name (though I have an idea of what it might be). They used to call that a paradox in the days when I studied philosophy at Cambridge before the war. I've always liked paradoxes. And you are the greatest paradox of them all.

But I must stop talking in riddles. If all goes well, you will be twenty-one years old in 1962, so far in the future that I can barely imagine it. But I can imagine you – perhaps a little like myself and so close to the age I am now – holding this letter in your hand, and begging me to get to the point. I suppose I am dodging around because I am trying to avoid the full, unvarnished truth.

There is no point in this letter unless I tell the whole truth and I have already strayed from the narrow way long enough. I do know how I became involved in their war and how it became my war. Indeed, I understand very well why, even with you to come home to, I will do as I am asked and risk my life again, as so many others are doing all around me.

*

It was Xanthe's father who first introduced her to crossword puzzles, when she was fourteen, and had entered her – as a joke as much as anything else – into the under-twenty-one crossword championship for Ohio. She had been terrified and practised every evening when she got home from school, a little ashamed of her growing obsession. She certainly told none of her friends. Even so, she was astonished that she not only won, but was hungry for more. There she sat, evening after evening, with her thesaurus and encyclopaedias next to her, solving clues like "*Arrange a trunk call to the panel*".

What can it be, what can it be? "Arrange" implies I need to change the word order or letter order – there are 8 spaces for 3 Down. Must be an anagram. She grabbed her pencil and scribbled "*the panel*", then a flash of inspiration. Trunks? Could it be? Yes, it's "elephant". Yes, the thrill of the chase and the satisfaction of an answer, and then the pretence – on no account must her friends know, or she risked, well, ridicule at least.

So when she won the regional youth heats for the Midwest – Xanthe was born in Ohio – apparently without effort, along with the embarrassment, she gathered an extraordinary reputation for effortless intelligence, which she carried with her in later years. As she discovered, when the boys began to cluster around her a little, blondes were not supposed to be clever. "I'm not clever either!" she would assure her friends when a nervous look crossed the faces of Buck or Brad. "I've just got a knack, that's all."

Xanthe had been born in Cincinnati on 2 December 1919. Her father, Douglas Schneider, had been back from the war almost exactly nine months before, with a facility for languages and a smattering of German, and had taken up his job as a sales representative at Procter and Gamble, a middle-sized firm of washing powder manufacturers. Her first memory was sleeping against the comforting tweed of his shoulder.

"Sleep tight," he used to say. "Don't let the mice bite."

"What mice?" Xanthe would ask when she was old enough to be worried about it. "Where are the mice?"

"Oh, don't you worry, my sweetheart. There are mice."

There were stages in her life when she lived in such fear of the mice, with their little toes. It was only in her early twenties, in war-torn Europe, that she found there were bigger fears, and more terrifying ones, and she finally stopped worrying about the mice. In fact, there have been times when the thought of the mice in Cincinnati were actually comforting.

Douglas loved philosophy. He wanted her to study as he never did. He gave her a Greek name in honour of Plato, he said, and also the distinctive colour of her hair. That is why he called her Xanthe. It was to her a blessing as well as a curse: she found that people expected something from her that she feared she was not old or unusual enough to give. The crossword triumphs in her teens continued and she began to fear that, far from extraordinary, she was actually some kind of freak. She would catch herself solving clues on sunny afternoons, or attempting to read Kant in the original German, and tell herself very firmly to get a grip. "I'm a pretty ordinary yellow-haired girl from the Midwest," she said to herself, "but without a mother."

She used to ask her father about her mother, who she knew had been called Daisy and had come from England. One reason for going to study in England was that she hoped, at the back of her mind, that she would run into her one day out shopping in Harrod's or buying a new hat in one of those London emporiums she had been reading about at home for so many years. Xanthe had a fantasy that Daisy would sweep her up in her arms like a princess.

Her father always replied to her questions about what happened to her mother the same way. "I don't know, sweet pea," he would say. "She just went out one day and never came back."

Xanthe's aunts, her father's sisters, told her that Daisy never really settled down to bringing up a child. They told her she loved her daughter, but... The sentence was never quite completed. When, some years later, during air raids in the darkest parts of the night, listening for the bombers overhead, she found herself trying to conjure her mother again, as she had done when she was a child, as a talisman that might protect her.

When she was living in England in those days, writing a letter to her unborn child, waiting for the sirens to sound the All Clear, she struggled to tell the absolute truth. Because, in fact, she did know what had involved her on the British side in a war that was not her own. It was partly that youthful enthusiasm for crossword puzzles, which never quite left her. But it was also a chance encounter at a cocktail party in London in those final weeks of what they called the Phoney War. It was there, fatefully but somehow inevitably, that she met Ralph Lancing-Price and that led to everything else.

*

Xanthe had always loved the sheer idea of England when she was young. Her friends aspired to be cheerleaders; she wanted to be a princess and see the Crown Jewels. She wanted to walk down Knightsbridge or live in the Dorchester or, better still, spend the weekend with Ivor Novello or Noel Coward. So when her father came up with the idea that she should study there, it was a source of enormous excitement – not to mention enormous fees. Xanthe was unsure later if he had understood that Simonetta College was really a kind of glorified finishing school, in Cambridge but not really *of* Cambridge in the way they had both imagined. But for him, as it was for her, it was also an attempt to recapture the elusive spirit of her mother.

Either way, she crossed the Atlantic in the old liner *Aquitania*, in August 1938, loosely attached to a number of Cincinnati ladies of a certain age who were acting as kinds of chaperones. Then suddenly, there she was. She had expected England to be a fairy-tale place of royalty and castles, and maybe even knights and ladies. It was something of a shock to find herself at Southampton docks, a transient hole dedicated to efficiency and modernity.

At first she was obsessed by how differently she made her hair up to all the other girls around her. Xanthe imagined she could see them watching in their powder compact mirrors. She imagined they could see what she saw in herself, an absolute innocent from the world of

Little Women, who happened to be good at crossword anagrams. But she did at least know where she was going, via a long, cramped and smutty train and an underground ride to a peculiarly warren-like station called Liverpool Street. From there, she headed out towards the damp of Cambridge and the Fens.

She had found herself involved with King's College students through acting and they began to phone her at her college. Every so often she would be studying *The Tempest*, or something similar. "Come on now girls," Miss Moorehead used to shout – she had a voice like the *Aquitania* – say after me: "Full fathom five, thy father lies…" Then, always at inopportune moments like this, there would be a knock on the classroom door and the school secretary would enter.

"I am so sorry to interrupt, but I'm afraid Miss Schneider is wanted on the phone again."

On one occasion, the man on the other end asked her to a party in London. He said he wanted a bit of glamour with him so, rather vainly, she said she would go. She regretted the decision immediately: Jack Blenkinsop had a bulbous nose and a scrawny neck and his English confidence was only skin deep, and sometimes not even that: an undergraduate with a very long woollen scarf and collars that were carefully ironed and clearly fixed in place by someone else. She did not fancy spending a whole evening with him. On the other hand, the war had been going by then for more than six months and she was worrying that she should really go home, despite the closure of the Atlantic because of submarines. And if she was going to need to leave, she should see life a bit. That was how it began, the set of events that culminated in everything else.

CHAPTER TWO

London, April 1940

Two weeks later and Xanthe was walking down the Strand – her first visit to London in the spring – and looking at the barrage balloons in the distance, and the black-and-white stripes painted along the kerb for the blackout, and watching out to see what else might have changed since she was there last. It was the weeks before the Dunkirk beaches, during the early days of the German offensive in the west, and she expected to see worried crowds waiting for newspapers, tearful farewells outside Charing Cross Station – but there was little or no sign that London was anything other than a little bored by the whole thing. Some windows were boarded up but the theatres seemed to be open again: she passed Robertson Hare at the Strand Theatre and then crossed the road to find the Savoy Hotel.

It wasn't hard to find, with the taxis drawn up outside in the half-light, and the big black curtains being drawn as the blackout began. She had wondered if the Savoy, which seemed to be immune from rationing regulations and the sheer drabness of war, would perhaps be immune from blackout regulations as well. It was a relief to see that the natural order applied even there. She had been staying at the flat of her friend Moira in Maida Vale but a short journey on the Bakerloo Line to

Trafalgar Square had delivered her, clutching a gold-edged invitation, to Lady Colefax's At Home at the hotel. It was cold, but her hand was shaking for a different reason: she had never been to anything of the kind before and her affection for Jack – never exactly strong – was dwindling by the moment. Why on earth had she allowed herself to be partnered at such an event by a dull fish with an "honourable" before his name?

From the start, the Savoy evening refused to go right.

Jack was about a quarter hour late as the guests streamed inside, dressed in their pre-war frocks and finery, past the chandeliers and the functionaries who seemed to reach back to a kind of pre-war deference. They barely glanced at Xanthe in the black dress she had borrowed from Moira, who was rather taller. A voice in her head kept struggling to quote the line from the novelist Morgan Forster, who she had met in King's, about how charm was "just decoration", and wondering what it meant. She was going to just drift away from the Savoy in shame when a flustered looking Jack appeared looking a little the worse for wear for drink.

"I'm so sorry, my dear. Just getting up a little Dutch courage. Don't often take girls out, you see."

"Honestly, Jack, it isn't your wedding night or anything. And please don't call me 'my dear'. I'm nearly as old as you are."

Not for the first time, she wondered about these poor English men; so tentative, so callow, yet she knew many of them who were already in uniform.

"Sorry, Xanthe." He tittered alcoholically. "Some of them thought I needed a bit of strengthening medicine." He reddened around the gills. "Shall we go up; I expect the fellows will be there by now."

*

The rest of the evening was little better. Jack's strengthening regime continued and his friends either didn't like Xanthe or they were as frightened of her as he was. It was not the first time that she had been confronted by the strange reputation of American girls among English men. In Cambridge, they had just assumed she was stupid; in London, they also assumed she was some kind of vamp.

She came to the conclusion that it must have been a little of both because Jack and his friends largely ignored her. She kept catching sight of them behind the pillars, usually with a bottle of champagne to the lips. She found herself wandering around the room with a feigned air of purpose. It worked for half an hour or so before she began to feel too conspicuously inconspicuous for comfort. The string quartet was grinding out Handel and there was that upper-class English smell of champagne mixed with sweat that reminded her of Cambridge.

It was then that she met him. To be completely accurate, he met her.

"You look like someone I could get to know," said a voice behind her. She swung round. For a moment, there seemed to be nobody there at all.

"Come over here. You can't hear yourself think out there. I'm hiding away. Come and join me."

It took her a moment to see where the voice was coming from, and to make sure it was directed at her. Then she saw him, looking languid in a little alcove, with a glass of what must have been whisky. She was impressed with him, partly because he was not drinking champagne, and partly because he was clearly not properly dressed for the occasion. Jack and his friends wore wing collars and evening suits, the kind of outfit of tuxedo and black tie they very rarely wore in Cincinnati. This man, whoever he was, wore nothing of the kind. In fact, he had a collar and tie and a black charcoal business suit, graced by a necktie that looked vaguely regimental.

"Sorry, I don't generally speak to strange men…" she was irritated with herself that this would sound as if she was flirting. But, then again, perhaps she was.

The man smiled to hear her accent. "Aha, you're one of our American cousins. Tell me, what brings you to this corner of the doomed world? This sceptred isle, this demi-paradise, this seat of Mars, blah blah blah. I was just wondering what on earth had brought me to this party."

Xanthe laughed. He had an infectious smile – it was the first element about Ralph that she really liked. She caught Jack and his friends out of the corner of her eye a few times and he seemed pretty oblivious, so she carried on talking. The stranger was a good listener and seemed to know everything, but carried the knowledge lightly.

"So, let's sum up, shall we? Your name is Xanthe and you come from Cincinnati, and you are studying in Cambridge until the end of this summer? Am I right? After which you are not sure what to do – but you want to be a journalist of some kind..."

"Bravo!" she pretended to clap.

"I can understand that going home right now is not an obvious choice what with all those U-boats."

"Sure. Quite right. But what about you? You haven't told me anything about yourself?"

"Well, you haven't asked – but perhaps I should say that I am betrothed to my constituents, the good and very sensible people of Chanctonbury in the county of Sussex."

"Your constituents? You're a senator of some kind?"

"A member of Parliament? I am, and I have been for what seems like decades, but it has actually only been for five years." He sat back with a mild air of self-satisfaction that Xanthe found unexpectedly attractive. He was the first grown-up man in England who had really looked at her in quite that way, confident and unabashed. She loved it.

"Look, Xanthe, if I might call you that so early in our acquaintance. I had been hoping to talk to you..."

She giggled a little, heard herself and then stopped. "What nonsense: you didn't even know me."

"Yes, but that was exactly why. You were the only person here I couldn't place. I've got a pretty good idea who the others are, but I had no idea who you were, at least the only one I wanted to talk to. I don't get out much these days, what with the war and everything. So I wondered if you might have dinner with me next week. Do you have a telephone number where I can reach you? Perhaps you could write it there?"

He produced a small pocket diary filled with spidery hieroglyphics, and a little pencil. As she was writing down the number of Simonetta College office again – she had no access to a telephone line in the dormitory where she was staying – she was suddenly aware of a flurry of activity behind her.

"Mr Lancing-Price? You're wanted urgently on the telephone."

"Really? Who is it? My mother?"

"No sir, it's the Admiralty. They asked if I could send you straight round if I found you."

"Ah yes," he said with an air of exhaustion. "The fleet calls."

"Yes but, what…?"

"I fear I omitted to tell you about my day job. I am among a couple of parliamentary undersecretaries to the First Lord of the Admiralty. There are only two of us but Winston requires the services of whole charabancs of undersecretaries to satisfy his restless soul. We are kept busy."

*

She flushed as he left, and was furious with herself for doing so and, later, looked back on that flush as a sign of innocence which she would never quite manage to rediscover. But the truth was that she had liked him, had basked briefly in his attention, and assumed she would never hear from him again. It was sad, but there it was.

But she did hear from him. The irritated face of the college receptionist sought her out in the philosophy class – actually a glorified exercise in sex education and morality – and knocked on the door.

"I'm sorry for disturbing, Miss Bright. But there is yet another telephone call for Xanthe Schneider." Then, with great disapproval, she said: "They say it's the Admiralty." A titter went round the room.

That evening, Xanthe found herself in the lobby of the House of Commons, staring up at the garish mosaic of St George and wondering what to do next. She had come down in a train full of troops and it had exhausted her. Three of them had offered her a seat but the journey had been squashed and stultifying. She felt nervous, once again in a place where establishment figures dashed busily to and fro which made her fear she looked conspicuous. Conspicuous again by her own attempts to stay inconspicuous.

"And who are you waiting for, miss?" said a man in a black-tailed coat.

For a horrible moment, she realised she had forgotten his name. "Um, Ralph…" her mind went blank. "Lancing-Price!"

The man consulted his desk. "I'm afraid, miss, that…" Then suddenly, there he was. She was afraid for a moment that he would see her intense relief. He stared at her for a moment, then he took her arm and marched her off to one of the innumerable restaurants around the Palace of Westminster.

It was the start of a peculiar friendship. The two of them would meet at weekends. She spent more and more time at Moira's flat in Maida Vale. She was aware that Ralph had a lady friend, a raven-haired society beauty, and had seen her photo in the magazines. Maybe even a fiancé. But he never seemed to talk about her, let alone see her. Xanthe feared it was her own sheer innocence that attracted him. And the parks were full of couples walking in the spring sunshine, as they wandered through Kensington Gardens. They saw *Gone with the Wind* at the Empire Leicester Square. They saw *Me and My Girl* at the Victoria Palace.

Occasionally, he would have to leave earlier than expected and, naïve as she was, three things began to worry her after they had met a few times. First, he had some peculiar opinions – he had a visceral hatred of bankers, which Xanthe thought strange for a Conservative. It also worried her that he never asked her about herself. And third, of course, although he did kiss her somewhat half-heartedly and not very often, he seemed less than fascinated by the idea of getting her into bed.

It was not that she actually intended to or wanted to sleep with him, but there was a recalcitrant part of her that wished *he* wanted to and was a little affronted that he so clearly did not.

"I know I have nothing of interest for you," she said, petulantly, as they had tea before an early goodbye at Baker Street Station. She had been a little jaded all evening and was irritated that, even on a Sunday, the Admiralty called. "I can't imagine why you want to be with me."

"Ah, Xanthe. You see, you are a human code, and I love codes. It is one of my responsibilities, in fact."

"I don't think I'm really that complicated."

"Well, there you would be wrong. It is quite true that I can't quite read you, but I nearly can. Do you know why? Because I'm a member of the Anglo-Saxon race and we are pre-eminent in the world when it comes to cracking codes. So I'm close to cracking yours."

"Really?" said Xanthe hopefully. There were, after all, many things she would have liked to know about herself, feeling she was some way still from cracking her own codes. But Ralph did not expand. Instead, he began to give her a lecture about naval codes and how the British

Admiralty had succeeded in cracking the German naval codes in 1914 and had to crack them all over again every night.

"And now? Can they still?"

"Well that, my dear Xanthe, is classified information and I have already told you too much. But I will make a small wager with you. Within a few weeks, I will myself have made a small contribution to the art of code cracking. My lips are sealed until then."

He reached inside his jacket, pulled out a silver flask and poured himself a generous helping of whisky. Xanthe had never seen him drink so early before.

"Other races can't do it. I don't know why it should be but, if you're British, the whole code world comes easier to you. If you're American or Jewish or Russian, well good luck to you."

Had he been drinking all day, she wondered? This seemed to be a whole new arrogance that she had not noticed before.

"All the Jews I've met have seemed pretty clever to me."

His face darkened. "Don't you believe it. It's a cleverness that's entirely concerned with making money, like your own countrypeople – not the Russians, of course. They don't seem to have the first idea how to make money. Otherwise, it's a cleverness that drives the great, tyrannical plutocratic machine, this great alien force that moves the markets and puts all the poor people out of work…"

"Heaven's Ralph," she said innocently. "You're beginning to sound like Herr Hitler."

"Well, I know we are at war and all that, but Herr Hitler, as you put it – I haven't heard him described like that now for some months – is still right about some things. Part of the tragedy of this war is that we're in some ways fighting the wrong side. It's hard to tell isn't it. The Soviets, the Americans, are also threats to the way the world is."

"You don't mean that, do you?"

"No," he said, as if suddenly coming to. "I don't mean anything. I'm being a little silly, which is what comes of being tired, and especially tired of my boss."

*

She was upset when she heard nothing from him for a week. She realised she didn't even have a telephone number for him. She had an address of course, and – after agonising about the decision for a couple of days – she used it. She wrote to him. She composed a short note apologising for being too forward – she had also agonised about exactly what she should apologise for – and sent it to the House of Commons. There was no reply.

Six weeks later, she saw the letter again, by which time she had come to regret sending it and the memory of Ralph had begun to recede a little from everyday consciousness. Most people don't expect to be confronted by their little missives begging for some man or other to go back to paying them some attention, especially when there was a war on and their friend is busy organising it. But Xanthe was.

She had been hauled out of an end-of-term exam – where she had been writing about Shakespeare's morality in *Othello* – by the long-suffering school secretary, Miss Beale. When she got to her office, there was a man waiting for her in a dirty mackintosh. He looked a little like a child molester who had seen better days.

"Miss Schneider. I am sorry to disturb you from your studies."

"Oh, no trouble." She could hear Miss Beale sniff disapprovingly.

"I have a message from you, which I would like to discuss with you on the way."

"On the way where?"

"To Scotland Yard," he said, as if the answer was obvious. "I have a car outside."

Xanthe blanched. "What? Are you saying I've done something wrong?"

"I don't believe so, no, miss, but I'm not at liberty to tell you now. Except to say that I believe the purpose of the meeting is to enlist your help."

*

She was aware – how could she not be? – of just how scarce petrol was at the time. It unnerved her that they were prepared to spend so much of it just driving her to London, but apparently they were. There was little traffic on the main road through Hertfordshire and, an hour or so later, they were speeding along the Victoria Embankment towards Big Ben.

They turned right just in front of it and a London policeman in a helmet saluted them as they went by. Moments later, Xanthe was being taken upstairs to a cosy office with ancient leather armchairs, a pot of tea and all the atmosphere of a gentleman's club. It also seemed to be full of people.

Closer inspection revealed that there were only four of them, and none of them seemed very friendly apart from the old gent behind the desk.

"Miss Schneider." She was announced.

"Come in, come in, Miss Schneider. Please make yourself at home. Would you like some tea? Now these gentlemen have asked if they can, how shall I say, borrow my office for the purposes of meeting you, so I am going to hand you over to them, and I believe Commander Fleming here has some questions for you – that's right, isn't it, Fleming?"

"Thank you," said a tall, aloof-looking man with wavy stripes on the sleeve of his naval uniform. "As my colleague said, my name is Fleming,

Commander Fleming, and we are all extremely grateful to you for giving up your time to help us. You're not a British citizen I understand?"

"I'm American. Could I ask what this is all about? I don't think I have done anything wrong."

The old gent gave Xanthe a reassuring nod and it was then that Commander Fleming opened the file in front of him and, with a disdainful air, picked up her letter to Ralph Lancing-Price.

"May I ask, did you write this?"

She got up for a closer look. Her heart sank as she recognised the childish handwriting. She began to shake involuntarily.

"Yes, was it very wrong of me? Don't tell me, he's married or something. I promise not to write again, if that's the problem."

"Please don't upset yourself, my dear," said the elderly police superintendent whose office they were in. "My colleagues here would like to talk to you about it, that's all. Mr Liddell here and his colleague have some responsibilities for counter-espionage and I work for a department we know as Special Branch. These are serious matters, but you are not under investigation, I absolutely promise you."

"We simply want to know how well you knew Mr Lancing-Price," said Liddell.

She began to tell the story of their somewhat one-way relationship, the first meeting and their conversations since. She told them about their small tiff and how Ralph had failed to contact her again. When she had finished, she was asked to leave the room and, about ten minutes passed as she stood in the corridor, then she was invited back in. Why had they used the past tense about the relationship, she wondered – why did they say "knew" not "know"? Was there something they knew about Ralph that she did not?

"Now, Miss Schneider," said the old gent. "We have a few questions for you and I would like to ask you to be as honest as you can."

She nodded uncertainly.

"Did you tell him much about yourself and your plans?" Fleming hardly looked up from his notes.

"Not really. He didn't seem very interested. He knew I wanted to get into journalism someday. We did talk a little about how I would like to go home – to Cincinnati, I mean."

"Fine," said Fleming. "Now, I can't ask this one delicately. Can you tell me what kind of relations you had with him? I mean sexually."

Xanthe reddened. The men looked pointedly downwards. "We kissed I think three times. No more."

"Are you sure?"

"It isn't the kind of thing a girl forgets."

Fleming grinned at her for the first time.

"Look," she said. "I might be able to help you more if you could tell me what this is about. I'm sure Ralph, um… Mr Lancing-Price, could confirm what I say."

The men exchanged glances and Fleming gave a little nod.

"No, you see," said the superintendent. "That would be a bit difficult, because he's in Berlin."

CHAPTER THREE

London, June 1940

How do you get from one side of London to the other without being followed? It's a useful trick and it is one that Xanthe decided she was increasingly proud to have been taught. She also learned it the hard way, between Paddington and Whitechapel, being followed and then following her fellow trainees, over and over again. It was hardly that she believed it would ever help her much in civilian life, if she managed to survive to take part in it. It appealed to her fondness for puzzles. It reminded her of the winter, snowbound evenings she spent with her father wrestling the latest crosswords and drinking cocoa.

But then it was a severely foreshortened training. She had been recruited to a branch of naval intelligence for one purpose alone, and it was apparently an urgent one, though she was not told why. There was no time to train her in unarmed combat or marksmanship or any of the skills the other recruits on her course were being taught in an old office in Gloucester Terrace. But she passed and she was proud of herself. There were two Canadian women, but she was the only other person from the USA. They were not encouraged to socialise and, in any case, there was very little time. She had to learn, not just the skill of being inconspicuous and how to use a dead letter box, but she also had a crash course in German. She had picked up some from her father, who had taught her when he had nothing better to do, but she needed a serious upgrade.

By the end of four weeks, Belgium and Holland had surrendered, the British Expeditionary Force had been rescued from the beaches and Winston Churchill – Ralph Lancing-Price's erstwhile boss – had ascended to the top job. And Xanthe could get by in conversational German. It wasn't entirely unfamiliar to people brought up in the north European atmosphere of the Midwest.

When those three men in Scotland Yard had asked her to help them, it seemed to Xanthe to solve two immediate problems simultaneously – it allowed her to escape Simonetta College and it enabled her to earn some money. If she was stuck on this side of the Atlantic then, sooner or later, she would have to support herself. But she realised later that she had given remarkably little thought to precisely what they would ask her to do, though they promised to tell her if she managed to progress on the course. She guessed that, if she had struggled in any way, she never would have heard from them again. But she didn't sink – she had managed to escape those following her by the time she had reached Great Portland Street.

She had been told she would be attached to the Government Codes and Cipher School but, when she asked if she could meet some of her colleagues, she was told that the information was classified. When she complained to her extremely reticent instructor, she was told how unusual it was for a foreign national to be involved in the war effort in this way. "To be frank," she said. "It might be a good deal easier if you would just tell me what it is you want me to do, so that I can go and do it."

"May I advise you, Miss Schneider, that signs of impatience can be fatal and would lead to your expulsion from this course and from government service."

Finally, there was a week in Scotland on the moors, and she had hoped for conversation with the older men and women who were being tested along with her. But the other trainees kept themselves to themselves. They didn't seem to talk to anyone. They certainly didn't want to know Xanthe.

*

At first, she had refused to accept that Ralph had gone over to the enemy. It was hard to believe. So when she was told later, in a more comprehensive meeting, that he had left behind an alternative explanation, she was quick to believe it.

Commander Fleming told her this in a small interview room in the Admiralty; strange because it seemed to have been fitted with a bath. Nobody mentioned this, so Xanthe pretended it was not there.

"Miss Schneider, sorry to keep you waiting," he said. "You have completed our foreshortened training course very successfully, I am told. So the moment has arrived for me to take you a little into our confidence. You must understand before I do so that you are now in His Majesty's armed forces and are bound by the same laws and regulations that we are. Furthermore, any careless talk by yourself about anything you hear now from me would mean not just instant dismissal but probably also imprisonment. Do you understand?"

Xanthe nodded. She was feeling numb, unable to comprehend exactly what she was about to do and why, and aware that she was not thinking as clearly as she should.

"And if you're wondering why there is a bath in here, then your guess is as good as mine – but I can tell you that it allowed our chief codebreaker in the last war to think more creatively. He used to spend his nights in it."

"Well, I didn't like to ask."

"There's a lesson here," said Fleming, in a schoolmasterly tone. "Anything odd – you notice it. You don't have to mention it, but you have to notice and file it away."

"Thank you," she said. More of the blasted obvious, she thought.

"Now when Ralph Lancing-Price went to Berlin, he did so via Switzerland, I understand, where he went as part of a small parliamentary delegation to talk to the Swiss codebreakers. But he left behind an explanation which would, if it were true, make him less culpable – brave and probably insane, but less culpable."

She nodded nervously.

"He claimed that he was going to do a Zimmerman. Have you any understanding of what that meant?"

This time she shook her head.

"The Zimmerman Telegram brought your fellow countrymen into the war in 1917. It was from the German Foreign Minister, one Zimmerman, who wanted to carve up the USA with Mexico – I expect you've heard about it. Anyway, the point was that it was encoded with a range of different codes and, when you do that, it's like the Rosetta Stone. It meant that we could then crack others too. Lancing-Price plans, or so he claims, to persuade the Nazis to send telegrams to their embassies and the army, and the navy, at the same time. We will intercept them all and it will – as the saying goes – provide us with an admirable clue. Now, does that ring any bells?"

It didn't really ring anything to Xanthe, if she was honest, but she didn't want to admit it. She was horrified that Ralph, who she had liked and trusted, would go over to the other side, and she was already nervous about meeting Fleming again.

"I know he was fascinated by codes."

"Yes, but nothing else? Fine. Now, listen carefully, because this is the critical bit. He claims that he'll find some opportunity to broadcast a message about opposition to the war in Britain, and in the navy in particular, which will have to be explained also to the Kriegsmarine, the navy that is."

Her head was spinning a little. So Ralph's plan was to create some kind of event, or campaign, that would allow the same signals to go out on different networks. It sounded clever but almost impossible.

"Now, as you might realise, this is a high-risk strategy, and not just for him. You're aware of the Nazi radio broadcasts and their 'P for Peace' campaign. You may not know that somebody – and we don't know who – painted out all the letters from the sign at Paddington Station last week, and they just left the 'P'. We think that's significant. There will come a moment when these forces that want peace will be urged to stand up here and be counted. Maybe in the next few weeks, given that the BEF is now home – most of them – and without weapons. Oh, by the way, would you like a cup of tea?"

This seemed to be either extraordinary egalitarianism on the part of Commander Fleming or they were about to tell her to do something difficult. It proved, pretty quickly, to be the second.

"So this is what we need you to do, if you agree of course. We have procured your accreditation on the staff of the *Chicago Tribune*, who have been very helpful to us in the past. As an American citizen, you can come and go around Berlin. That means you will go there as a journalist, quite legally, find Lancing-Price, as if by accident, and work out for yourself whether his story is true and what his motivations really are. You will then let us know, and I'll tell you how to do that if you agree to go."

Xanthe realised suddenly that there was someone else behind the desk, and he looked a little familiar. She was unsure why she hadn't noticed him before. He seemed painfully shy and still had not spoken.

"It's a risky venture," Fleming was saying, "but you are the perfect man, that is to say person, to do it. You're not British and you will blend in perfectly with the American press corps in Berlin, of which there are rather a large number. I think you will do a brilliant job and we certainly need a brilliant job at this juncture in our history."

She stared at Fleming's companion, wondering why he seemed so familiar. As she did so, she was wondering vaguely whether Fleming was being jaunty, with a dry sense of humour, or whether humour was entirely alien to him.

"As I say, you're not British. You're under no obligation to go, but we would have the most enormous gratitude if you did. Ah, here's the tea!" He rubbed his hands in anticipation. "Miss Schneider?"

Rather naively, she thought later, she had been congratulating herself on her good fortune. The war had begun in earnest. The beaches of Dunkirk had been a recent triumph, Italy had entered the war and a great silence seemed to have fallen across most of Europe. It seemed unlikely that she could safely sail home any time soon. More urgently, Simonetta College had closed for the duration, and she was staying temporarily in Moira's flat. She badly needed to earn some money. This seemed a solution. One thing worried her more than the rest.

"Why do you trust me?"

"Well, the truth is, Miss Schneider, that we have taken the trouble to know a great deal about you..."

Xanthe felt a rush of fear and then an almost uncontrollable urge to giggle. She managed to prevent herself – it would hardly do to lose any kind of control at this crucial moment.

"We know about your parents, about your father at least. We know about your friends, here and back home. We know what you ate for lunch most days since the war began and where you buy your undergarments..." He snickered a little.

"In Marks and Spencer?"

"Quite so. We also know you speak a little German and are no friend to the Nazis."

"And we know about the crosswords!" said the other man, with a note of triumph. Xanthe had forgotten him again. "I say, I have a feeling that we know each other. Do you perhaps have some connection with King's?"

Fleming looked daggers at him.

"Turing, I don't think this is the right moment."

"I thought you knew all about me!" she said with a little laugh. Then she remembered who he was – Dr Turing, the man who had given up his seat to her in that strange philosophy lecture. "Oh yes, you saved my life once. In Dr Wittgenstein's room!"

"Of course! I remember. Good to see you again – glad we'll be working together. If you are in agreement?"

"I look forward to it," she said, but the news was disconcerting. She could not imagine herself working very closely with anyone quite so philosophical. Also, as she realised, walking to Strand station to get the underground back to Moira's flat, that they appeared to have employed her on the basis of her very short career as a crosswords enthusiast. It is strange where the most mundane details will redirect you, she said to herself, watching the balloons hanging in the sky. Even more worrying what it said about their confidence in other facts they clearly only half understood.

CHAPTER FOUR

Berlin, June 1940

Some weeks later, Xanthe filed into the Propaganda Ministry in Berlin for her first press conference as an accredited foreign correspondent. "Just come along and listen. I'll handle the news bit for now. Just get your feel of it, ok?" said Sigrid, the head of the *Chicago Tribune* office in Berlin. But, however friendly they were – and they all seemed friendly and pleased to have another woman – she felt a fraud. As she sat on the leather upholstered chairs and waited, she realised this was because it was exactly what she was. She had been trained to avoid being followed and about dead letter drops and conversational German. She had been told how to make contact in Berlin – simply by going into the American embassy and saying the words "Uncle Sam" at the front desk, then heading to the bench opposite the elephant house at the zoo. But she had been told nothing at all about how to actually be a journalist. One of the peculiarities of the English, as she discovered, is that they think professional skills magically emerge just with a bit of practice. But where was the magic?

She had asked about this, but was told that "journalists are never trained in this country. They just pick it up".

"Hello," said a burly man next to her in English. "So where have you wafted in from?"

"*Chicago Tribune*," she said, without much conviction. She felt unhappy and doubly homesick, part for England and part for Ohio.

"Great!… What happened to Frank?"

Xanthe had a cover story for this one. "Frank got ill on the crossing and had to go back home. I'm a last-minute replacement, I'm afraid. I'm a bit of a beginner."

A big smile seemed to cover his face. "Don't you worry, kid. Just stick with me and I'll show you the ropes. Big morning: their chief is addressing the foreign press. Hans Fritzsche. I expect he'll go big on the French. How's your German?"

"A bit threadbare, to be honest."

"Same here. But we get by don't we… What I usually do is ask Bill at the end – where is he, now?" He searched the faces around the room.

"Bill?"

"William Shirer from CBS. There he is at the front."

There were not that many of them in the big conference room with comfy chairs and a large platform like a stage. It looked like it was designed for a good harangue. There were now none of the belligerent press there – the British and French had gone. TASS was there from the Soviet Union: she could see a dull little man in the corner. There were a few excitable men at the back whom she took to be the Italian reporters. Otherwise, it was mainly Americans, a little like her. And sitting draped across two chairs was a balding man with a high forehead and a small moustache. In his wire-framed spectacles, he looked like a bank manager. That must be Bill.

"My name's Bob, by the way. Yup, we Midwesterners must stick together – what was your name again?"

"Xanthe. How did you know where I was from?"

"Oh, you can always tell. Listen, I'll introduce you to Bill at the end. Great guy – great name, by the way!"

Fritzsche came in quietly, looking shorter than Xanthe had expected, and then produced a monumental rant against the British and French, how they were both finished. The word "heroic" was bandied about generously, applied exclusively to the German forces. The word "cowardly" was applied to the British, who had apparently sacked Louvain and burned the library. Even to Xanthe, a novice and without experience, this seemed extremely unlikely.

She had been in Berlin only a few days. She had arrived via a journey by ship to Lisbon and then a train to Italy, and with every mile south she went, the terrible sense of loneliness gripped her further. She felt utterly alone and utterly unprepared for what she was about to do. What had she been thinking when she agreed to go to Berlin? Why on earth had she volunteered to go, friendless, unsure of her purpose, of the language, with no knowledge even of her adopted cover profession? How stupid, she thought – just to get a little excitement? Had she been feeling left out? By the time she had landed by plane in Lisbon and taken the ferry to Italy, she began to feel seriously frightened. But there was no turning back now, and somehow the fear was crystallised when she had been met at the station by Sigrid, who seemed to disapprove of her youth.

"Listen, the editor suggests you get into the life of ordinary Germans at war, women, rations and so on," said Sigrid. "Stick to the facts. Look out for a guy called Bob, who will guide you around. You'll meet him at the first press conference. And trust nobody. Not even me. And definitely not Bob," she added with a meaningful look.

The sunshine was bright outside in the street. There were fewer cars than there were in London, but there were the distinctive yellow-and-white trams, and their bells, which zipped past her ringing their excited notes. The office girls were out to enjoy the heat at lunchtime as Xanthe went to her tiny office. Sigrid had arranged a press pass, a ration card of bizarre complexity – clothing, food, washing stuff and so on. There was a pass that allowed her to live in Berlin and a key to the lodgings to which she had been assigned and a letter to the landlady Frau Menschler. There was a very great deal to take in. She could hardly believe she had been, within a few short weeks, living in the capital cities of both warring powers, but then this was the reality for foreign correspondents. The fear remained but, as she got busier, she also found herself thanking the fates that she had, entirely by accident and not attributable to any skills of her own, found herself in a profession she had actually aspired to join.

Bob also directed her to the Hotel Adlon, a luxurious dive past its prime, with strange curved ceilings and plasterwork, where so many foreign correspondents spent their evenings and, in some cases, much of their nights. These were mainly Americans, so much of their conversation was in English, around the strange dark, Germanic wooden chairs and over-ornate marble pillars. It smelled of pipe tobacco.

Xanthe was determined at least to start work before making any attempt to find Ralph, though she had been told he often drank in Adlon and spent time also in the Rundfunk offices where the wireless broadcasters were based. She realised she needed to master something of her new profession, even for a few days, before she pretended to run into him.

During her first evening at the Adlon, a particularly charming American sidled up to her. He had pockmarks and a centre parting which seemed to involve a little too much oil. “I happened to overhear, so sorry if I’m intruding.” The two reporters she had been talking to visibly stiffened. “Where are you from?”

"Cincinnati," she said.

He laughed. "I mean, what paper do you represent? Or are you a broadcaster. They have all kinds here..."

"They certainly do," said Sigrid. She stumped off to the bar.

"Sorry," said Xanthe, in rather an English way.

"Don't worry yourself. Happens to me all the time. I take it you're a newspaperwomen?"

"I try to call myself a reporter," she said, with proper immodesty.

Sigrid was suddenly back. "Go fuck yourself, Fred..."

There was a delicate moment when a flush went over his face. Xanthe watched him struggling with himself. Then he smiled and raised his arms in surrender.

"I was just going to offer your friend a drink," he said, innocently. "Another time perhaps." And he was gone inside the press of people.

"It just goes to show how careful you have to be," said Sigrid, as soon as he had gone. "That was Fred Kaltenbach. From Iowa. He hates the Jews so much, he has gone over to the other side. I know, it isn't exactly treason but it isn't friendly either. Sorry to be so tough. But you know how it is..."

*

Xanthe felt she had learned precisely nothing at the press conference. It was hard not to find yourself suspicious of the daily bombast on these occasions, she told herself. Mostly Fritzsche and his colleagues were enraged by their collective failure to report the news precisely as the Nazis wanted. She soon discovered that press conferences were mainly rants about their inability to tow the party line.

She began to do as suggested, investigating the impact of the war so far on ordinary people. There was hardly any soap to buy, and to buy a dance record you had to hand over an old one for melting down. It was also now practically impossible to buy toilet paper anywhere. Those all might make stories, she thought.

There was a poster everywhere around the parts of the city that she tended to go in daylight which said that "*NOBODY SHALL HUNGER OR FREEZE*". She had it pointed out to her by a large man who sidled up to her in the Hotel Adlon. "They've forbidden being hungry or getting cold now," he said. "What next!" Then he gave a great guffaw and he went on to tell her that all the foreign correspondents get regular off-ration eggs and bacon from occupied Denmark.

"Really? I seemed to have missed out on that."

She mentioned the joke to Shirer when she was finally introduced to him, and he seemed gracious and helpful, though Xanthe knew he was also terrified about how to get his wife and child out of Italy before the French capitulation that now seemed inevitable. He had no idea where they were.

"I have no idea who to trust, when I ask people about their ordinary lives," she said. She told him about the poster.

"Well, as you may have been told already…"

"I know – don't trust anyone."

"I mean, for example, who told you the joke about the poster?"

"It was a German guy in the Adlon. I know it sounds silly but I was inclined to trust him because he bowed to me so formally."

"Was he a big guy, large?"

She nodded.

"We call him Fatty. He is definitely in the pay of the Nazis, or he wouldn't be allowed to talk to us. That doesn't mean that what he says is all lies – just that somebody up there wants us to be aware of what he tells us. I wouldn't dismiss it; just check it out."

She began to despair of ever cracking the Berlin code that would lead her to any kind of unambiguous truth. She must have looked a little crestfallen because Bill perked up too, and made her an offer.

"Listen, I've been asked to go up to Kiel tomorrow. They want to show us how little damage the RAF did a few days ago. Do you want to hitch a ride? I can probably get you permission to come. We fly out at six a.m. if you can face that?"

*

It was a fateful visit in more ways than one, and it certainly was for Xanthe. But ostensibly it was for the press to assess the Propaganda Department's report of a recent RAF raid on the naval facilities there – but also perhaps also to let them boast about the damage they had inflicted on British warships during the Norwegian campaign, now that it was clearly at an end.

Bill kept his word. They met the next morning, some hours before breakfast, arranged a pass for her, and soon they were swooping low in a light plane over the German countryside, heading north-west. A junior official was there as well, fussing away like a duck with ducklings at the small brood of accompanying reporters from the foreign press. It was a military plane and the seats had no cushions. Bill complained to anyone who might hear, but Xanthe kept her discomfort and nerves to herself.

They drove in a small fleet of cars through the morning into the naval base and most of the navy appeared to be there, under battalions of barrage balloons. The base was busy, with many ships under camouflage netting and others behind huge screens. There were sailors and shipwrights everywhere. The sunlight reflected blindingly off the sea and Xanthe watched the little tall-funnelled tugs busying themselves around the grey-painted ships. There seemed to be a great deal of construction, including what looked like a half-built aircraft carrier. "Keep your eyes skinned," said Bill. "The fact that they want us to come at all implies that the British claims are a little, shall we say, over-optimistic – but who knows."

"I expect they've had time to do a bit of spring cleaning," she said.

"Well, some things can't be cleaned in a day or so. Look for funnels and masts sticking up out of the harbour…"

"Do you know, I have about as much naval knowledge as I need to tell if a ship is afloat or not – so I'm just the right reporter for this task."

Bill laughed. "Keep your ears skinned too – the navy is not a place where Nazis find life that comfortable for some reason."

They wandered hopefully around the biggest ship in harbour, which they were told was called *Gneisenau*, and she was immediately impressed by the rapport her colleagues managed to maintain with the officers and men.

"So you can see, no damage – despite what they say," said one of the ship's officers. Their minder had wandered off to find the rest of his brood.

"Quite right," said Bill. "But the British said one of their submarines torpedoed and sank a cruiser. It couldn't have been you could it?"

One of the officers tapped his nose and winked and took them over to the side. "Over there," he said indicating a ship in dry dock with a huge hole in the side. "It was the *Leipzig*. Not sunk but damaged."

"Aha," said Bill. "Not sunk, I see. I can certainly report that."

It was pretty clear that, in this case, the RAF raid had caused about as much damage as Dr Goebbels had said they had. "It's pathetic," said Bill under his breath, as they watched the evening come down in the harbour. "I mean, how can they expect to hold the Nazis at bay if they're that incompetent?"

"Practice makes perfect," they said, thinking of Jack and the other young men she had known in Cambridge. "Give them a chance." She wondered how many of those youths had given their lives for this botched raid. They looked sadly at the intact docks and bridges.

It was when they were being shown around below decks on the *Gneisenau* – technically, it was a battlecruiser, she was told – that the officers began to relax. They were taken into their mess room, with a smell of oil and alcohol, and Xanthe found herself talking to a good-looking lieutenant about the sinking of the British aircraft carrier *Glorious*. The schnapps was flowing quite freely – they were all feeling a little confessional.

When she was sure nobody was listening, she dared to ask the question she had been formulating in her mind.

"I know that, in the last war the British navy was able to read most of your wireless messages and signals to the fleet," she said. "It is pretty well known that they were able to. I don't really understand how they did it. Are you – that is to say – how are you going to make sure they can't do the same this time?"

Once she had made herself understood, what she saw was a mixture of triumph and nervousness on his face. "I don't want to get you into trouble," she smiled, reassuringly. "But is there anything you can say about that? I apologise for my German."

"Your German is excellent. But, as you must know, Fraulein, this is a subject on which I must not speak. It is summed up in one word – Enigma. That is our weapon in the naval war this time, and I think you will find it is an effective one. Now I must say no more."

By the look on his face, he clearly wished he had said nothing. Strange, thought Xanthe: it isn't a word she had heard before. Neither Fleming nor Turing had allowed it to pass their lips. Her mind reeled. What could this Enigma be? Was it the name for a code or for some piece of technology?

But she hardly had time to think any further about it because there was a clatter of footsteps on the metal deck outside, the door to the wardroom opened and – judging by the reaction of the naval officers there – a very senior officer, followed by a man in the kind of leather trench coat the Gestapo were renowned for wearing. She was staring at the officers and trench-coat man while, all around her, the ship's officers were leaping to their feet. Bill joined them ("Force of habit," he said later). Then, all of a sudden, in came Ralph.

She stared at him, incredulous. She had been wondering how to run into him without raising suspicion in Berlin and here they were, falling over each other by genuine coincidence in the bowels of a battlecruiser on the northern coast, though – as Bill and Sigrid had warned her to – she checked her own credulity to believe that coincidences were quite what they seemed. Perhaps she had failed the test at this point, she wondered.

The officers soon realised there was a lady in the room and were clicking their heels at her in a most disconcerting way. She raised her arm in an apologetic half acknowledgement, then – realising it might be interpreted as a Hitler salute – she put it down again and just nodded her head.

The man in the leather coat, with a rather bulbous nose and very small eyes, took her hand and kissed it. Then Ralph saw her.

She had been wondering what his reaction would be when they met – suspicion, rage, indifference, snobbery? It could have been any or all of them. When it came to the point, he actually burst out laughing. "I don't believe it! Xanthe! What on earth are you doing here?"

She found herself laughing too. It was infectious. The naval officers around her were laughing without understanding why.

"I don't know what you mean!" she said. "I'm with the American press – what on earth are *you* doing here?" She glanced to the two officers with him. "Have you been captured?"

He translated – "*Sie haben gefangen genommen worden*?" – and the two roared with laughter.

She was so used to the idea that traitors – if indeed he was a traitor – were furtive, secretive people, that this show of extraordinary confidence wrong-footed her. Bill and the other reporters were looking at them in astonishment. Ralph was so obviously British, so overwhelmingly relaxed, that it was hard to read the situation.

Ralph said: "We knew each other in London. How are you, Xanthe?"

The man in the trench coat stood expectantly. "Herr Lancing-Price, would you please introduce me to your friend?"

"Oberleutnant Gustav Stumpf, let me introduce you to my old friend, Xanthe… um… Schneider."

"Charming. And a good German name too. Now, may I say, young lady, and to our colleagues in the press – that nothing about this meeting must be reported. I will inform the censor. You are welcome of course to tell the story of our fleet and their indomitable work in Norwegian waters. But this conversation I fear we must be discreet about. Do I make myself clear?"

"Xanthe, where are you staying?" said Ralph in her ear. "I will call on you tomorrow, if that is ok."

"Very well," said Stumpf, a leer creeping down his face. "Fraulein, I *also* will call on you – but perhaps at a different time…"

She stared at their departing backs as the door to the wardroom closed behind them. There was a silence and she knew she would have to be ready with some answers once the questions started: unaskable questions irritate reporters, she knew. She also had to be as honest as she possibly could be.

They were driven back to the airport and were soon in a tiny plane flying over the German countryside in the early evening. It was just as uncomfortable and this time also freezing cold. But it also looked idyllic as they passed over small farmhouses and great dark woods, casting long shadows on the fields. It seemed to be magically untouched by war and Xanthe compared it in her head to Poland and France where, even now, the refugees were drudging under dive-bombers, pushing their few possessions in a pram.

"Who was that guy, Xanthe? He seemed to know you well. I've seen him around a bit too." Bill was the first to voice the questions.

"Well, I knew him a little some months back in London. The thing is I can't really understand it. He was a politician. A member of Parliament, with links to the navy. I suppose he must have defected over here or something – or wants us to think he has."

"As I say, he seemed to know you well." There was a slight edge to his voice that she recognised but dared not respond to.

"We met a few times after we ran into each other at the Savoy. I hadn't heard from him for weeks and weeks – perhaps that's the reason: he was here."

"So whose side is he on, do you think? I mean really?"

"I just don't know, Bill. But I'm going to find out…"

It was as much as she was going to say and it seemed to satisfy him. She would need some more answers later if her new press colleagues were not going to think more closely about the issue than would be entirely comfortable. The oddest thing was that, if Ralph had gone over to the other side, it was strange that neither side was admitting it. Perhaps the stakes were too high and neither were quite sure yet about whose side he was really on, apart from his own.

CHAPTER FIVE

Berlin, July 1940

The Berlin blackouts seemed deeper somehow than the London ones, though as far as Xanthe knew, there had been no bombing so far. It was dark beyond dark, and made all the more difficult to navigate by the fact that German lamp posts were usually in the middle of the pavement, rather than on the edge, as they were in London. That meant she was constantly colliding with them as she made her way home to her small room, and she found herself counting them – twenty-four to the end of Unter den Linden, and four fire hydrants too.

Apart from that, Berlin seemed remarkably untouched by war. She found herself wishing the city had been a little damaged so that she could explain something about ordinary life there. There had been occasional raids, as there had in Kiel, but either they were hugely inaccurate or they just confined themselves to the usual diet of propaganda leaflets. Also, unlike the local population, she had access to the news wires which included broadcasts from London as well. There was claim and counterclaim and there seemed to be little strict regard for the truth on either side, though the Propaganda Ministry sank the *Ark Royal* a number of times in her weeks in the city. This was disappointing.

Yet the German news also appeared to be so wholly partial, and their lies seemed overblown somehow, as if they were bound to be found out. Perhaps that hardly mattered in a totalitarian state where what the leader says is true becomes true by definition. Except that it doesn't actually become so, at least not while the foreign press is there.

She decided the outright lies were for Sigrid, Bill and their more experienced colleagues to skewer (Sigrid kept up a close link with Goering, despite her ferocious views on the Nazi system). Xanthe herself concentrated on the lives of Berlin people in wartime and, because of that, she attracted peculiarly close attention from the censors. Sigrid explained that they were sensitive because the last war ended with revolution thanks to the same naval blockade that was already causing some deprivations again. Xanthe knew from her history lessons that it had been the civilians who had given up in 1918, helped by the sailors of the High Seas Fleet who had risen in revolt, partly from sheer boredom, partly because they were afraid their families were starving back home.

Even that was important to pin down, she felt. She knew from so many conversations from Cambridge and London that the prevailing view there, especially on the political left, was that Germany could not endure war for more than a few months. Yet, judging by what she was seeing every day, just on the streets and in the shops, they were wrong.

It was a vital message to get across, she told herself. If they were there in the war cabinet in London, taking decisions based on the idea that Germany was about to implode economically, then they were deciding things on the wrong basis. She talked to Sigrid about this, but was told this was the 'wrong motivation'.

"You see Xanthe, you're new to all this. The idea is that – whatever the reason is – we tell the truth. Nobody appears to have any kind of commitment to the truth, and when we do pinpoint it, then the censors stop us writing it. When John Dickson wrote that Hitler and Stalin would divide Poland between them, that was worth it, not because it helped them take decisions in London – and it didn't seem to – but because it was true. The world needs the truth, that's all."

"Who's John Dickson?"

"Oh, well, that was me – I needed a pseudonym."

They laughed. Sigrid had hidden depths. "Can people see the truth now? Can people even recognise it when they see it?"

"I don't know," said Sigrid, a little sadly. "I guess so. I hope so. But even if they can't, I need to believe they can. Otherwise I'd have to go home and be a ploughgirl."

After the attentions of Stumpf and a few like him, mainly Nazis who had lost control of whatever used to restrain them, Xanthe felt she needed advice from a tough woman. "Listen Sigrid, can I ask you something else? What can you do when they hit on you – the Nazi ones, I mean?"

Sigrid looked suddenly concerned. "Are you having trouble with anyone? If so, we can tell Boris. He's our senior government handler, a lugubrious type who I don't trust at all. But he probably has the power to haul someone off to the concentration camp if we ask him nicely..."

"Heavens no, nothing like that." The last thing Xanthe wanted was to attract any kind of attention. But there was a worryingly intense element to some of the men she had met, something frenetic, almost frightened. She was unsure quite how to conduct herself as a foreign correspondent. The men never received this kind of attention. It made her nervous. And on one occasion, she was forced to slap a young army officer who had tried to pull her, quite literally and bodily, out of the hotel foyer with him.

"No," said Xanthe, attempting to reassure. "Just want to be the best reporter I can."

"Listen honey, I know what it's like. The thing is to cultivate a formidable hide like a rhinoceros and not to look anyone in the eye except to spit in them, if you can possibly avoid it. Then no blushing, no intense gazing, no smiling, just tough rawhide. With me? Attagirl."

Xanthe thought about this conversation as she headed down to the hotel bar in the Adlon, hoping that Ralph would keep his word and come and find her later in the evening.

"Fraulein!" said a voice as she steered through the large wooden revolving doors. It was hardly the greeting she had expected, and the usual impromptu American party was already well under way. The alcoholic noise was rising. In the corner were the usual crew from the *Herald Tribune*, with their correspondent Barnes in his habitual spot, holding court. For a moment, she could not see where it came from.

It took her a moment or so to recognise Gustav Stumpf, in his party uniform with black armband; he carried a cap under his arm and was wearing what appeared to be glorified riding gear. Xanthe blanched a little, wondering what she would have felt if she had seen someone dressed in this way in Cincinnati Main Street. Might she not have felt he looked a little ridiculous?

"Oberleutnant. I didn't expect to see you."

"The pleasure is all mine, Fraulein Xanthe."

She realised she had to think swiftly. Why was Stumpf there? Was it the usual reason – basically lust – or was it some other reason? Was he actually suspicious of her or was he trying to impress her in that insane get-up? She had done nothing to engineer the reunion with Ralph in Kiel, apart of course from becoming the accredited correspondent of the *Chicago Tribune*. Still, she had to assume the worst.

Now he had pushed his way through the Americans and was there before her. "Fraulein," he said. "Let me say how delightful it is to be in the same city as you."

She felt stupid, aware that – if she had been older, or more sophisticated – she would have known how to reply to this. She um-ed and ah-ed.

"Let me immediately explain my reason for trespassing upon your time. I would like to invite you to the theatre next week."

She searched for a valid excuse but the time elapsed before she had one.

"Thank you, I very much appreciate it," she said.

What would an experienced foreign correspondent do? Play for time…

"Listen, Oberleutnant, as I'm sure you understand, I haven't been in Berlin long and I want to do the best I can. I don't want to appear ungrateful. But I am unsure how best to…"

Then she had a brainwave. Of course she wanted to go to the theatre: what reporter would fail to seize the chance to forge a relationship with a contact at a high level?

"I tell you what. I will come with you on two conditions," she said. "First, that it will be partly work for me, that you understand that and don't mind it – I want to write about life in Berlin in wartime. Second, that you don't mind if I bring a friend."

"A friend! Why of course. And I will bring one too. We shall be a foursome. Do you Americans not have a phrase, 'double date'? I shall meet you here on Tuesday, if that is agreeable. That is excellent news – at six thirty?"

"You want to be a little careful of that one," said another voice in her ear, as Stumpf clicked his heels and withdrew with a punctilious bow.

She swung round and found that Ralph had sidled up behind her. The bar was now extremely full and it was possible to move around unnoticed. Then he kissed her, full on the lips.

"Listen, Ralph. I'm a working reporter now – I can't go round kissing men like that." She smiled as she said it to soften the criticism.

"Oh yes, I know and all that. Now, where shall we go? We have a great deal of catching up to do. I tell you what, we'll go to Horcher's – we don't need coupons to eat there!"

*

"So," said Ralph after they had ordered their off-ration meal. "Like the Savoy, this place seems immune to wartime deprivations. What on earth brings you to Berlin? I remember you wanted to be a journalist."

They had walked through the Tiergarten. It was a warm summer evening, and old gentlemen were walking slowly home from the park now that the sun was beginning to go down. It occurred to her that, whatever reason he was here, he may have been lonely.

"Well, I was in touch with the *Chicago Tribune* in London and wrote some things for them. Then one of their reporters got ill on their way out to Germany and they couldn't find anyone nearer, so they asked me to replace him. It was a huge piece of luck. I think even foreign correspondents think twice about crossing the Atlantic right now."

"I expect they do. The U-boats are pretty effective."

It was time to take the plunge.

"Look, Ralph, isn't the real question what *you're* doing here. Have you gone over to the Nazis?"

He glanced over her shoulder and then tentatively over his own. Then he lowered his voice.

"Do you believe that?"

"Well… You *are* here…"

"Well," he said, grinning. "You can't believe everything you hear, now can you…"

Xanthe felt irritated. He was teasing her.

"You're still on the same side?"

Ralph breathed a long, somewhat exasperated sigh. Then the pork arrived. It was hard to believe they were eating real meat. He waited until the waiter had gone.

"Xanthe, Xanthe – still a lovely name, by the way – it isn't that at all. I think I said something about what I was planning to you once before. I expect it to be a masterstroke. Don't let's talk about it now."

"You mean about codes?"

He made frantic hand signals to keep her voice down. "Well, what do you think, Xanthe? You don't think perhaps everything hangs on what happens next in the west?"

For a moment, she wondered what he meant. France was now divided and ruled. Belgium, Holland and most of Scandinavia were so-called protectorates. It was hard to see what else could happen – unless he meant the invasion of Britain.

Xanthe said nothing. But she began to wonder about the strange paths that had brought them both to this foreign city in such unusual circumstances. She knew she must not leap to conclusions. She would meet him again, either because he wanted to or she ran into him somewhere, and in the meantime she would be instructed by her contacts.

She also had work to do and she asked Ralph what he thought about rationing, about the non-availability of soap, and the strange behaviour of Berlin taxis. The band began playing something that sounded remarkably modern. Was it swing? Was it actually American? It wasn't jazz exactly, which she knew had been banned from the Reich, but it had a certain jaunty air about it. She began to relax a little.

"Ralph, can I ask – what did your colleagues think when you left? They must think you're some kind of traitor. They must be wondering about you at least?"

Ralph stared at her for a moment as if he had not quite considered this possibility. For some reason – it can't have been a surprise – the question seemed to trouble him. "My real friends will know whose side I'm on," he said. It was obviously the formula he used to reassure himself, yet it seemed to give him little relief.

"Because codes are different now aren't they – I mean compared to Zimmerman and all that, last time round? What about Enigma?"

She was unsure how he would react, but this time he fell about laughing. One tear ran theatrically down his cheek.

"Enigma. Of course, Enigma. You're well informed, my love. I should put the same question back to you – what do you know about Enigma?"

"Almost nothing," she admitted. "Except the name, of course."

"Well, I shall enlighten you. Enigma is the coding system used by all the German armed forces and diplomatic services here and has been for decades now. It's like a typewriter. You set the system for the settings of the day, you type in a code that allows you to set their machine the right way at the other end. Then you type your signal and – hey presto! – you get a code which they can read the other end. But nobody else can read it, because they don't have the same settings. It is actually completely uncrackable."

He explained about the permutations. She immediately forgot the huge number of possible solutions, but it was big. Clearly the old idea that you just find a clever crossword puzzle expert and arm him or her with a great deal of coffee and a hot bath at the Admiralty, was hardly going to work this time. It was fascinating. They both knew, without having to say, that this could hardly be an exercise in journalism – it would need permission from the censors to write anything and no end of trouble from people like Stumpf – but it was useful deep background, or so she told herself.

But there was a contradiction here and it bothered her, because of his obvious belief in the sheer sophistication of the Nazi code system. She wondered how to raise it.

"Ralph, listen, I keep thinking about one thing and it worries me – can I ask you?" He nodded generously. How could he not? "You worked at the Admiralty – you must have known this then, mustn't you? And the story you told me in London…"

She deliberately lowered her voice again and he leaned a little closer.

"You remember, the story about comparing texts? How will that help them in London to crack Enigma?"

He smiled enigmatically and, for the first time, she wondered if Fleming's assessment was correct and that the man was insane.

"That, my dear Xanthe, is going to have to wait. Now, I find myself at something of a loose end in the evenings, and I very much enjoy your company. Would you perhaps have dinner with me again? Not tomorrow night – I have a dinner with the German Admiralty – but the day after tomorrow, if I meet you same time, same place?"

*

Xanthe lay in bed that night, listening to the noises of the city, waiting for the telltale roar of the arrival of the RAF on one of their leaflet distribution visits. It sounded remarkably like London, with its traffic hum and the occasional honking of horns or bass sirens. She could hear the footsteps of people walking home below her window in Charlottenburg. It sounded like a great city breathing in and out, going on its way regardless, which in many ways is what it was. The smell of sausage wafted over from the cafés in the next street – a poignant smell since, as Xanthe knew very well, the sausages would not be real. The evening with Ralph had been frustrating, because he really came nowhere near telling her anything, but also rather lovely. It almost felt like it had been in those afternoons in London, except that this time he had been engaged in a different way.

She could not get Ralph's laugh out of her head. It was free and infectious. It seemed in some ways the very antithesis of Nazism and everything she knew about it.

She knew she also had to finish the story she had been researching the previous day, so her mind was already cluttered with details of agricultural statistics. There was also a press conference at eleven the next morning at the Propaganda Ministry which she didn't want to miss.

As it was, Dr Goebbels himself strode, with a slight limp, into the room on the dot of eleven. Xanthe had not seen him before in the flesh and he would have seemed wizened and pathetic were it not for his sheer self-belief, and his rather public rages.

He was pretty furious this time, mainly with Shirer, who was still on his way back from France having been the only radio journalist to have been an eyewitness to Hitler's armistice signing with the French in Compiègne. "I gave specific instructions that German radio was to have priority. Yet one of you allowed himself to use unofficial transport to a forbidden area and to have broadcast uncensored reports. And let me tell you…"

He dropped his ranting style to a fierce monotone.

"Let there be no doubt," he said. "There will be the severest consequences for those who helped him. As members of the foreign press, you get considerable privileges. It would be most unfortunate if they were to be withdrawn because of the actions of a few irresponsible individuals."

The flow of fury began to abate. Xanthe noticed Sigrid putting up her hand to ask the first question. Goebbels glanced up, saw her stand up in her place, went a kind of beetroot colour and stormed out.

"What privileges did he mean?" she asked Sigrid as they all filed out again, suitably battered.

"Oh, didn't you know? We have been designated as heavy labourers. It means we get double the rations."

She had not quite understood this. She still thought the eggs and bacon from Denmark delivered in little packages were just a friendly gesture, now they had begun to arrive in her pigeonhole at the Adlon. The packages made her feel a little uncomfortable before; now they felt like a bribe that is forced upon you. For some reason, the discovery frightened her – it made her realise how much she was living this peculiar life under false pretences. She had always claimed to hate pretence – *now* look at yourself, she said quietly and under her breath.

"Remember what I told you," said Sigrid. "Trust nobody. Not even yourself."

*

The whole experience of being shouted at, along with the rest of the foreign press – most of them Americans – was, she felt, deeply radicalising. There was something about the ferocious arrogance of Goebbels which made her want to dig her heels in and resist. It was not exactly that she had been trying not to take sides; she felt she was trying to see things clearly without getting her various and obvious bias in the way of the truth. She now saw that was wrong.

It was also nonsense, given that she was pursuing journalism as a means of gathering the information her real employers needed. It was silly to pretend otherwise, at least to herself. She had already chosen a side and her priority had to be to survive and find out what she was supposed to do.

In fact, perhaps she had been wrong to act out the role of an open-minded journalist. She was anyway beginning to suspect that Dr Goebbels may be a threat to human civilisation. Ironically, that gave her renewed respect for Bill whose journalism was absolutely committed, but who was still tolerated by the regime because he and his censor genuinely respected each other – and because of his influence back home and on world opinion. She decided that there were powerful reasons why even the Nazis needed to respect someone like that.

Xanthe was thinking about this the following night, a couple of days before Stumpf was due to come round. She asked around their tiny office for someone to come with her, but the truth was she knew too few of her colleagues in that way – and it was too embarrassing to ask Sigrid. Both of her office colleagues were busy and looked at her a little oddly. In the end, she asked Mathilde, a girl about her own age who worked next door and who lodged with her.

Was her German adequate to the task? "You want me to come to the theatre with you?" said Matilde, as if Xanthe had asked her on a date on her own account.

"Well, there are two others, both men," she said, a little embarrassed.

Her face lit up. "Ah, *doppeldate*!" said Mathilde.

*

On the morning of the impending theatre visit, she made her first trip to meet the man who was to be her contact in Berlin. She had no idea what his name was but she had been given detailed instructions about how to find him. In fact, it was almost the only area of her life in Berlin where she had been given detailed instructions about anything.

She had registered with the American embassy back in June, when she had arrived in the city, and she had gone there also to talk to the consular department to get her ration books and the paperwork accrediting her as a journalist and a foreign national in the city. But this was her first visit in earnest.

It surprised her slightly that there were links between diplomatic channels in the USA and the naval intelligence division of the British that she had been working for, but apparently there was at least some co-operation. She assumed it was not something that either side was entirely comfortable about. The American embassy was, after all, supposed to be neutral territory. She had asked Fleming the last time they had met why she was able to go into the American embassy and effectively leave a message for him and he had refused to tell her.

"Xanthe, you really don't need to know," he had said. "And if I tell you more than you need to know, it doesn't just put us at risk, it puts you at risk too. So don't ask so many questions…"

Follow the instructions, she was always being told. Just follow the instructions. Her instructions in this case were, luckily, pretty unambiguous. She was to go to the reception desk inside the embassy and have a conversation with the uniformed man at the desk, during which she was to mention 'Uncle Sam'. This was the sign, when she was ready, that would trigger a meeting with her contact at a specific spot in the zoo, in the first instance, by the elephants.

It stretched Xanthe's credulity to believe that they would happen to overhear her or that, somehow, the man at the desk would note down if a blonde American woman used the phrase – but she put these worries to one side. It was time to do what she was told without thinking about it too much.

It was a beautiful July morning when she set out to walk from their tiny office to the Pariserplatz. The air was alive with early summer and the birds were singing as she crossed the Tiergarten. It was hard to imagine that there was war now from one side of Europe to the other, with fighting in the English Channel. There was the embassy ahead, a little back from the road, a huge Renaissance-style edifice, a palace among embassies – though she knew that the ambassador had been recalled and the staff had been run down.

As she approached, she could just see the huge letters "*USA*" painted in white on the roof, presumably in a vain attempt to warn the bombers overhead that this was a neutral building.

Inside, there were people milling around in the foyer and the queue of desperate, demoralised-looking people snaking around very slowly towards the visa department. She marched straight up to the man in uniform at the desk, wondering how to begin a conversation.

"Excuse me, is it possible to read the American papers anywhere?"

"Yes, ma'am. We have a copy of the *Herald Tribune* over there at the table by the bench if you'd like to read it."

Then she said it. "I just wanted a touch of Uncle Sam," she said, with a toss of the hair.

"That's right, miss," he said. Xanthe looked for a flicker of recognition, but there wasn't one. For form's sake, she went and glanced at the *Herald Tribune*. The news was irredeemably bad. The Channel Isles were being occupied; the German army had reached the Pyrenees.

Then, desperately trying not to look back, she took her handbag and walked purposefully out onto the street. She had an hour to kill and she didn't want to sit drinking at the Hotel Adlon again. She decided to scout out the particular bench in the Zoologischer Garten next to the Tiergarten where she was then supposed to meet Uncle Sam, or whoever it was used his code name.

It was obvious when she got there. There was a bench outside the front of the elephant house and, after a pleasant wander through the trees and past the lions and antelopes, she sat down with about five minutes to spare.

The time ticked by. She kept glancing at her watch. People walked by enjoying the Berlin lunch hour in the sunshine. The smell of elephant dung wafted over them. By the time her contact was ten minutes late, she began to worry. Had she not been explicit enough? Was he perhaps absent today? What was the point in being in Berlin at all? She looked at her watch again.

"Are you late for an appointment?" asked the elderly gentleman next to her as she did so. "I couldn't help wondering because you keep looking at your watch. I mean it is a lovely city, isn't it?" he said, in German. "It isn't Cincinnati, of course."

Xanthe breathed a huge sigh of relief and said her designated reply: "No, but I expect the Reds would find it hard here." It was a reference to her baseball team back home. Not her idea – she had never really followed baseball.

She was shocked at herself for hardly noticing the man, dressed in black in the fashion, perhaps of the 1890s, and looking every inch a local. He dropped his voice: "Now please don't look at me or smile. Or tell me more than I need to know. What is your message?"

"Could you tell Uncle Sam that I have made contact with…" – for a moment she had forgotten the code name they had agreed to use, then a flash of inspiration. "I have made contact with the editor and will work up the article in the next week. No conclusions."

"Excellent," said Uncle Sam. "I will see you in precisely one week, by the antelopes. And you will bring your report wrapped in a newspaper for the letter drop, right? I will see you then, good day to you."

Xanthe sat for a few moments without him on the bench with the sun in her face and the rich smell of the elephants from across the way, and marvelled at the fact that she had become a spy. It was hardly a word she had used about herself so far – she had thought of herself so far as just helping out – but, for the first time, she now felt that was what she actually was. And so extraordinary in the kind of world she lived in to find the best-laid plans actually working. She remembered that, in England, they used to say: "Don't you know there's a war on?" to cover up the fact that things did not work very well anyway. Certainly they never worked very well back home in Cincinnati. Yet there was she, following instructions and making things happen. Who would have thought it?

That moment of elation would so easily have been her undoing, as she realised at the time. She was by then late back at the office.

CHAPTER SIX

Berlin, July 1940

Stumpf met them at the Hotel Adlon that evening and hailed a taxi – an impressive touch, given that ordinary Germans were no longer able to hire them – and whisked them off to the theatre, where Xanthe and Mathilde were introduced to a shy and nervous naval officer. Carl seemed to be iron deficient. Either way, he was as pale as a corpse, but seemed to have a little more life in him than that, and they made polite and gentle conversation in English, for which Xanthe was grateful.

"What brings you to Berlin, *leutnant*?" she asked him during the interval. "It isn't known for its sea!"

"My ship still requires repairs, after a little spat with the British navy off the coast of Norway." He gave her a big grin. "Perhaps I should say the same to you, Fraulein. What brings you to Berlin?"

"Oh me – I'm a reporter…"

"And yet you have some powerful friends – Oberleutnant Stumpf, who I know only a little, and I understand you are a friend of our British guest."

It was so tempting to ask more but she thought it best not to press her advantage.

"Well, I was – I'm not so sure we are friends now." How do you change the subject? "Tell me about your ship."

"My ship is a cruiser. It is called the *Admiral Hipper*, after the celebrated hero of the Battle of Skaggerak."

Xanthe pricked up her ears. The British had reported that the *Hipper* had been badly damaged in an encounter with the British destroyer *Glowworm*, but the Propaganda Ministry had denied it.

"Really? I understood your ship had only suffered slight damage?"

He laughed heartily. "Oh no. We nearly sank. Don't you believe everything you read about us. The destroyer was courageous. We battered away at it from point blank range and it just came on until it had rammed us, and damn nearly took us to the bottom with it."

"Why did they not tell the truth?"

He looked pained.

"There are ways in which we have more in common with our enemy at sea than either of us have with our governments – as I believe your British friend will tell you."

She tried to look understanding. She had noticed already one of the peculiarities of good reporters – that the more people talk to you, the more they trust you. A strange and rather dangerous paradox.

"Should you be telling me this? I can't believe your friend would approve."

"Nonsense, Fraulein. I am a sailor not a politician. Anything you want to know about the navy, you just ask your friend Carl."

It was extremely tempting, but she approached it from sideways.

"Ok Carl. This badge you're wearing with the lightning coming out – what does it mean?"

"It means signals, of course!"

"So you operate the codes? Exciting!"

Carl seemed to relax. He laughed again.

"Yes, and since our naval codes are completely impregnable, I'm going to defy our friend Stumpf and tell you just how impregnable it is. Have you got a bit of paper?"

She had a copy of *Frankfurter Zeitung* in her bag. She handed it over. He got out his pen and wrote a series of letters along the margins on the outside as he explained it.

"Army Enigma, they just choose their own three letters to start with, let's say EAX. We look ours up in the book of the daily settings and we put two of these on top of each other, like this:

E A X

D C B

"Then you add a letter at random to the beginning of the first line and the end of the second like this:

P E A X

D C B G

"So that gives us four pairs, PD, EC, AB and XG. Then we look those up in the tables and see what their equivalents are. Then you arrange their equivalents again in the same way, on top of each other, with me? Like this, say:

Z D G H

B G R T

"That is then sent just like that, without being coded. Then the receiver at the other end knows what settings you're using. Simple – well, actually, not very simple – but there we are!"

"Gosh, Carl, should you really be telling me all this?"

He was suddenly serious.

"In fact, it may be you who should be a little careful, I think, not me. Just some advice about our friend Stumpf. Whatever Stumpf wants, I know from past experience, Stumpf gets."

Stumpf came back a moment or so later, and so did Matilde and the play was soon off again. Xanthe folded the newspaper and put it in her bag, marvelling at what men will tell women without apparently thinking.

The play was called *Einsiedel*, and appeared to be totally without humour; certainly nobody laughed. The first half seemed to involve most of the protagonists losing their memories. Towards the end of the second half, a First World War memorial service or patriotic songs revived the memory of the hero. In the final minutes, he appears to die of a stroke.

With difficulty, the sheer lugubriousness of the play threatened Xanthe with an attack of the giggles. She managed to resist, just as she had halfway through when she began to feel a slight pressure on her thigh and realised Stumpf's hand was attempting to make some kind of entry. She moved out of the way and, when it began to again, she gave it a good slap.

She glanced at him a few moments later and saw him completely impassive, staring at the stage, where the hero was trying to remember where he was.

"There is no need to be so distant, Fraulein," he hissed during the applause. "Otherwise we may just have to ask about your meeting yesterday in the zoo. Then we might find that it is you who have something to be ashamed of."

CHAPTER SEVEN

Berlin, July 1940

When Stumpf referred to her clandestine meeting by the elephants, Xanthe had no guilty conscience, but she also knew all too well that she had something to hide. What she did not know was whether Stumpf actually knew anything or whether he was just supposing. A cold feeling ran down her neck. She reassured herself by reminding herself that he was having her followed – as he clearly was – on the off-chance of finding something on her. She tried hard to ignore it. Any reply, beyond a kind of interrogative look, would simply confirm his suspicions.

"My conscience is pretty clear," she said, challengingly. "I'm just asking you not to paw me during the play."

"Listen, Fraulein Schneider," said Stumpf suddenly, and rather too close to her face. "You may have reason to be extremely grateful to me, and if you don't realise that, then you may find yourself in a rather – how do you say it in English? – sticky situation."

"Now," he said, drawing himself up again and changing the expression on his face. "Let me give you another chance – let us both give each other another chance, yes? I fear the play left something to be desired – perhaps we could try again next week. I am free, as it happens, on Saturday night, and this time, let it be just the two of us."

*

"What should I do about Stumpf?" she asked Ralph over tea the next day – Ralph insisted on tea in the English upper class style. It was not a familiar meal in Berlin, any more than it was in Cincinnati. "He doesn't seem to have any, well, inhibitions. But I don't want to cross him – and you clearly don't want to either. But equally I don't trust him, and I don't like the way he touches me the whole time, as if he was sort of – treating me like Poland, I suppose. I mean, who does he think he is?"

Ralph smiled. "Oh, I don't think we need to worry about Stumpf, either of us. He isn't nearly as important as he thinks he is. I think he'll just calm down in the end – but I agree that it makes no sense to irritate the man. Can't you just go to the theatre with him and then beat a hasty retreat?"

"I don't know. He's beginning to give me the heebie-jeebies."

"Hah! I know what you mean." He looked thoughtful, as well he might; she stared at him, and not for the first time, wondered what kind of game he was playing. "I tell you what. I will run into you after the play and tag along. It will annoy him intensely, but I'd like to look after you."

It was said with a kind of sincerity that she had barely heard from him before. She felt pathetically grateful.

"The thing about Stumpf is that he has so little role, you know," said Ralph. "All that uniform, that liaison position between the Propaganda Ministry and the navy, it is what he makes of it. If it wasn't for the uniform, I'm not sure he would be anybody."

It reminded her of the strange conversation she had enjoyed with Carl and his open gossip about Enigma. It haunted her since, even after she had hidden the newspaper with the notes on under a wobbly floorboard in her bedroom. She did not expect this place would survive more than a few minutes if Stumpf's friends arrived to do a proper search, but it made her feel safer.

She decided to say nothing about it to Ralph. Instead, they found themselves talking more broadly about life in Berlin and she told him about another article she was hoping to file. She imagined that, as long as she praised some aspect of German wartime supply, then maybe she might get away with telling the truth about some of the other deprivations. She explained that she had therefore chatted to as many people as she could in bars, sometimes putting up with the inane news broadcasts that nobody dared turn off. It was when she was chatting, in rather broken German, with the owner of a bar around the corner from where she was staying in Charlottenburg, that another woman she knew by sight began to join in. It was not clear what had reminded her, but she told a story which seemed extraordinarily grotesque – and Xanthe retold it to Ralph.

It had concerned one of her neighbours, and so much of the conversation was taken for granted. Reading a little between the lines, she had realised she was trying to say they had received a telegram informing them that their son Wolfgang had been lost at sea when his submarine U-33 went down. They were busy planning a memorial ceremony and a wake with all the relatives when, guess what – the family heard on the wireless from London that he had been rescued and was a prisoner in England.

"The woman said she never listened to the broadcasts herself, and of course we were not necessarily intended to believe her," Xanthe explained. "Then she took a big slurp of ersatz coffee. So what should they have done, she asked? If they cancelled the ceremony it would look as if they had been listening to foreign broadcasts and that would get them into big trouble. But if they carried on with it, they would feel like idiots."

"You understand, Fraulein," the woman had said. "We don't listen to broadcasts from our enemies. You can get sent to prison."

"What a dilemma," said Ralph. "What did they do?"

"They went ahead with it anyway. What else *could* they do?"

As Xanthe had listened to the story, she knew it was hardly one she could use. The pathetic element was too obvious, not to mention the revelation of what it was like living in a totalitarian state in wartime. But it was still fascinating background.

"You know Frau Schultz?" the barman had asked his friend. She nodded. "Three-year sentence for listening."

"No!"

"Her daughter let it slip at school." His friend had pursed her lips as if to say she had opinions but could not express them.

Xanthe was happy to tell Ralph all this because, for once, she could talk to him about her professional life, and he listened, raising his eyebrows here and there. Then she asked him what he thought.

"Desperate times. Desperate times," he said.

This seemed strangely bloodless. She had expected something more visceral, perhaps because she was now aware of him in an increasingly visceral way. She felt him as a physical presence as she had certainly never done before, even in their brief flirtation in London. He was a good fifteen years older than her but somehow in this great equality, of living in wartime, away from home and under such a government, she felt they had something in common. Both had risked everything to be there. And neither was apparently able to tell the other. Rather perversely, this made her fonder towards him.

"Ralph, it's time now. Come on, tell me why you're really here. I don't believe you've turned your back on your own country…"

"Not here. I'll tell you later. Promise." And he stood and kissed her lightly on the lips. "Come on now, the film's going to start."

*

The film was a dreadful trash, though they knew it had been popular. It was called *The Great Love* and it was a little hard to follow – lots of suffering women on farms, separated from their husbands and overcoming hardship like heroines. It was odd that the war, presumably the reason for the separation, was never mentioned.

Of rather more interest was the newsreel, which showed the Luftwaffe attacking the coast of Britain, and some painful stuff about Marshal Pétain taking absolute powers over the section of France he was still allowed to rule.

Afterwards they strolled through the Tiergarten in the evening, among the flurry of unidentifiable uniforms from black and brown to blue and grey. She could not stop thinking about the strange reaction of the audience in the news feature – they had laughed when Goering came on the screen. He was clearly almost as much of a figure of fun in Germany as he had been in England. What was different was the way that the audience was addressed – everything was always expressed as a kind of rant involving overblown words like "cowardly" (about the RAF) or "glorious" (about the Luftwaffe), spiced up with martial music and extra bombast. How could people stand it, being spoken to continually by their government as if they were idiots? Perhaps that was the only major difference between the warring nations – but, then again, perhaps it was symptom not cause. In any case, as far as she could remember, only the intellectuals and the politicians ever took a blind bit of notice of the news in England, apart from the sports pages and racing results.

"Well, that was a strange business," he said. "Honestly, what a film! Were there any jokes at all? I apologise for cluttering your mind with it."

"It's all good research, I suppose."

"I tell you what. All these uniforms remind me of a strange story I heard yesterday about a British airman who bailed out over Berlin. Got rid of his parachute and tried to give himself up. But there are so many uniforms around that nobody realised he was British."

"I'm not sure I believe that one," she laughed.

"In that case, I won't believe yours… Anyway, I gather that all the RAF aircrew get given a twenty-pfennig note, just in case, and he used his to go to the cinema, like we just did."

"Do you think he saw the same film? It might have encouraged him to escape!"

They both laughed. The mood had lifted.

"Listen, Xanthe. Why are you *really* here?"

For a fleeting moment, she wondered whether she might just come clean and relax in his company, as she now longed to do – to sort of sink with relief into his arms. The temptation seemed overwhelming, but she reminded herself that it was not really her secret to divulge.

"I told you. I wanted to be a reporter and I happened to be at the right place at the right time."

There was an agonising silence for a moment.

"Mmm. I suppose the one thing to be said for war is that it throws up opportunities like this all over the place. The man who has to take over a platoon or who always wanted to fly – or the girl who dreams of being a foreign correspondent."

She relaxed again and we walked on in silence.

"The thing is that I love my country," said Ralph suddenly. "You know that, don't you?" She nodded supportively. "It is just that I saw an opportunity to help it and I have been completely open with everyone about what I am intending to do. The beauty of it is that both sides want me to do it – they just see the advantages to them differently. I just can't tell you now. You will have to trust me."

She had thought it best to stay silent and let his plans develop, but it would need a nudge and that meant taking a risk.

"I know what you're planning because you told me in London. You're going to do a Zimmerman."

A cloud went across his face.

"I've never said that to you. How did you know that term?"

"You're just forgetting, and you forget that I'm not the young know-nothing you knew back then – I hear things and I understand more than you think. I'm not an idiot, Ralph!"

He stared at her, unblinking. Her heart began to race. Had she made a mistake?

"I know that. I know that. I'd just forgotten using the term, that's all. But tell me what else you've heard, why don't you?"

Careful now, Xanthe told herself.

"Well, I don't know – but you told me it had something to do with codes. I imagine that you're going to broadcast using more than one kind of code – that's what a Zimmerman means, doesn't it?"

Ralph began to relax. "It's true that I've never made a secret of what I was planning, nor made a secret that I want peace. That isn't such a sin, is it? All I'm going to do is try to make common cause with the peace movement back home."

"So, let's see if I've got this right," said Xanthe, feeling more confident with every moment. "You're going to help the Germans to broadcast simultaneously on all their networks about how to make common cause with the peace people in England?"

"That's right, up to a point. I just want the diplomatic service, army units, Luftwaffe squadrons and the navy – I want them to know that British forces are likely to lay down their arms in support of Hitler's peace offer. It's an open secret that he's going to make one in the next week or so. I have the draft already, telling them to expect demoralised ships and units to approach them, and explaining what they must do."

Now it was Xanthe's turn to go quiet. Was the man insane?

"Are you actually listening, Xanthe?"

"Absolutely. Every word. I'm just trying to understand what you're saying. Because, really, there is no peace movement in England. At least, it's ever so quiet if there is."

"Let's talk about that in a moment, shall we? Whether there is or not, I will be providing the British eavesdroppers with exactly what they want to carry on the war – the same message in three or four different versions of the same coding system at the same time. If they carry on fighting, then England will have the means to crack the Enigma code."

"So why don't the Nazis realise what you're doing?" she asked in a whisper.

"Because they really believe in the British peace movement. They think our forces are demoralised and, above all, they think that no power on earth – no matter how many versions get sent out – will ever crack Enigma." For a moment, he looked a little pleased with himself, almost smug. "So it works for both sides. Both sides know what I'm intending to do and both sides are happy for me to do so. What I have to do is to draft the scripts – and of course draft the signal telling the various forces what to expect and when. All we need to know – if you're working for British intelligence which seems possible but very unlikely – is the date, which will be four days exactly after the Fuhrer's peace offer."

She chose to ignore the probing assumption. She carried on walking next to him, astonished at his arrogance – or was it insanity – that allowed him to believe he could move freely between warring regimes, like the member of the aristocracy that he took himself to be.

"I have to say, Ralph: it sounds a bit mad. It does, doesn't it…"

He laughed again and she found herself smiling. She had a suspicion that he was one of those bizarre, fatal kinds of Englishmen who think that war is an almighty jape. But she thought no less of him for it. Then to Xanthe's surprise, he gave her a big hug.

She was delighted for a moment, as he brushed her hair out of her eyes, but then just a little disappointed. It felt a bit too brotherly to be really exciting.

"Look we're nearly at my hotel. Would you like me to get you a car – or would you come up for a nightcap?"

"Not tonight," she said. "Perhaps another time." This was a little too bold, she thought, given what she wanted by now, but she felt she could not go on with the evening. She had too much to take in.

"You know…" He stared into the middle distance as if dreamily choosing his words carefully. "I don't think the British would have carried on fighting even as long as they have without the encouragement of your countrymen – I mean Roosevelt, of course. Perhaps because he's Jewish."

"He isn't Jewish. I don't think he is."

"Of course he is; basically just look at the name. Anyhow, I will see you shortly, I hope. Maybe after I rescue you from Stumpf?"

His fingers lingered in hers as they said goodnight.

*

When it came to be time for her to meet Uncle Sam again, by the antelopes this time, she prepared carefully. She brought a copy of the *Berliner Tageblatt.* She put inside it the page of the newspaper on which Carl had doodled his Enigma code example, and a full note about her conversation with Ralph, couched as if she was discussing the Dow Jones Index. "Market is fluctuating but rising," she wrote. "Expecting major statement within weeks, and results exactly four days following. Market still spread and will coincide with share offer."

Would that make the case? She felt disloyal passing on what he had said to her in confidence, but confident also that she would be helping to clear his name back home in the long run.

She was doing Ralph a favour. She believed it. She had to, because she liked him – more than liked him, she realised. In a world of angry men, he was an idealist. He might be quite mad, but perversely he made her feel safe. He was also by far the best-informed, most fascinating person who had ever taken an interest in her. Of course she was doing him a favour.

CHAPTER EIGHT

Berlin, July 1940

The summer was becoming idyllic. Xanthe was enjoying her job and also rather enjoying the male attention, aware that it might not be exactly for herself alone or just – as Yeats put it – for her yellow hair, which seemed to her to have become a particular focus for attention in this city, at least at this time. She was beginning to settle into a rhythm and could not see how events were coming to a head for her.

In particular, she had become fascinated by the way the Nazis regarded women, and realised that this could make an article or two for the women's pages back home. She had not grasped before that journalism could cover just about anything. Then, looking at one of those Nazi propaganda posters of a blonde-haired woman with big childbearing hips, sowing grain, she suddenly realised how to go about having ideas in her adopted role.

She had been worrying about her own inexperience covering issues around Europe and foreign affairs and what Molotov had or hadn't said, or what would happen to Pétain and Laval in France – but her colleagues in the American press corps knew what they were doing and had been following those issues for years. They could do battle with the censors in the way that she did not yet have the authority to do. But, as Sigrid had suggested at the beginning, she could do human interest stories about Germany at war. The piece she wrote about rationing had gone down well and the editors had asked for more, and seeing the poster gave her an idea.

She asked Mathilde about the clothes women wore in Berlin. She had heard her American colleagues talking in disparaging terms about German women – Bill Shirer said they were ugly – and it was true that they did not seem to take care of their appearance in the way that they would have done back home in Ohio.

"Well, it is so," said Mathilde. "I know my friends would like to use make up as we used to do, but…"

"But what? Is it forbidden?"

"No, no," Mathilde was very keen to make sure Xanthe didn't think it was anything of the kind. "But it is, how shall I say, a little discouraged. Not that I have any complaints. No complaints at all," she said loudly, in case anyone was listening. "But you know – they want us to be producing children all the time. They want us to be pregnant. And – well, I have no man – I'm not married. And I don't see why I shouldn't wear trousers, if I want to."

The last sentence was spoken in such a confidential whisper that Xanthe realised she should press for more information. But Mathilde obviously felt she had said too much. She resolved to pursue the trousers story when she had the chance, and began asking anyone she met about trousers – in cabs or on street corners if she could summon up the right words, certainly in shops and in the Hotel Adlon.

So much of the foreign correspondent's life seemed to take place in and around the Adlon, just across Pariserplatz and the palatial splendour of the American embassy, and within sight of Hitler's Chancellery. The

RAF so far had left them alone, and confined themselves to dropping their leaflets. Xanthe wondered whether they ever saw the letters USA on the roof of her embassy at all.

She asked Mathilde again in the morning about wearing trousers and Mathilde sniggered meaningfully. "They don't want us wearing men's clothes. Anything that gets in the way of childbearing or something."

"Do trousers get in the way of childbearing? I suppose they do if you're actually giving birth." They both laughed.

"No, but have you read the papers? There was something in yesterday's." She dug in her bag. "Here we are – letters page… '*Trouser-wenches with Indian war paint*' – I ask you! And that's just about women doing air-raid duty," said Mathilde with a meaningful look.

"Listen, would you bring in a couple of friends who might chat about it? I could get them tea at the Adlon Hotel?"

*

In the event, Mathilde's friends came in on the day Xanthe was supposed to go and dine with Stumpf, which made her nervous. They drank fake coffee, made from acorns and chicory roots – Xanthe was fascinated that they called it *muckefuck* – and they sat together in the corner and laughed about what they felt about trousers. She gathered that Goebbels himself had intervened in the trouser controversy on the other side – "*It is a sad state of affairs that actresses, dancers and singers have to be exempted from the Reich Labour Service by a special decree*," he had written.

"Well, he would say that, wouldn't he?" said Mathilde. Her friends guffawed. Goebbels' reputation with women had passed Xanthe by until that moment. No wonder he wanted them to be allowed to dress more enticingly.

Xanthe was feeling pleased with herself for suggesting this as an idea for a story. She began to write the intro in her head – "*There is another war going on behind the scenes in German life and it doesn't involve bombs or bullets: it's about pants and whether women should wear them…*" Yes, that sounded right.

But when she said goodbye to the three friends, the one called Valerie hung back nervously.

"Fraulein Xanthe, is there somewhere we can talk privately?"

Xanthe was flummoxed. She had nowhere and the tea room and bar at the Adlon were pretty public. She assumed this kind of request happened to journalists all the time. Then she saw Bill by the bar, having just returned from his trip covering the French armistice, and to see his family in Geneva. She sidled up to him. "Bill, can I borrow your room for a few minutes? Someone says they want to talk privately."

"Ok, Xanthe. Here, Bob, can you hold this for me without drinking it? I'll be back in a jiffy. Come on then, I'll bring the key."

She beckoned over to the woman, who was looking uncomfortable by the door. They slipped up to the third floor. Bill opened the door.

"Valerie, this is William Shirer, a friend of mine, from the American CBS wireless network. You can trust him completely."

She shook hands shyly. "Thank you. Could you stay? I have something to tell you both."

Bill disconnected the telephone and checked behind the curtains and up and down the corridor, made sure there was nobody listening through the crack under the bathroom door, and switched on the wireless.

Valerie promptly burst into tears.

"I have been working with Pastor Bodelschwingh at the big hospital not far from here," she said. "Where we look after children, who – I don't know how to say it – cannot learn. I happen to know he was refusing to hand over some of the children to the secret police. It is said that the police are putting them to death because they say they are a 'drain on our resources' – can you believe it? Now I'm afraid because the Pastor has been arrested and the hospital has been bombed. I am very scared, but I want people to know."

Bill and Xanthe exchanged glances. "I thought there had been no bombing," she said.

Valerie just looked at Xanthe pathetically.

"You will know what to do about this. I do not. Just make sure that you never mention my name."

"Thank you, Valerie. I'll take you down the back stairs."

*

Xanthe only had an hour to get back to her lodgings in Charlottenburg and to change before meeting Stumpf at the theatre. The traffic swirled around her and the summer sang in the air with the smell of exhaust. She felt proud of herself, excited to be alive, but apprehensive. She told herself she would write about German wartime theatre and that this was her excuse – at least to herself – for her continued association with Stumpf.

The incident with Valerie, far from making Xanthe nervous, had emboldened her – she was feeling elated. She checked herself constantly and reminded herself to be careful.

In the event, Stumpf was charming. "I fear our German theatre is not quite as uproarious as your American musicals, but I fancy there is some interest still, is there not?"

"Definitely. I'm very grateful to you, Gustav."

In the event, the play had even fewer laughs, if that was possible, than her previous night at the theatre. *Christa, I Await You* was an unhappy mélange of blood, soil and womenfolk who would not have been seen dead in a pair of trousers.

"You know what your name means, Xanthe?" Stumpf asked as they ate through a meal of potatoes and vegetables – the meat was now impossible to come by, and even now they had to hand over a small part of their ration cards for butter, apparently, because the potatoes were cooked in grease. Stumpf had an unnerving habit of running his fingers through her hair, though they were sitting opposite each other.

"Something about blonde hair? People usually know what their own name means."

The implied criticism slipped out and she bit it back. This wasn't a moment for cheek, but Stumpf took it well.

"It does indeed. Yellow-haired. And you are right – forgive my assumptions. I forget sometimes, because you are so beautiful, that I am in the presence of an intelligent woman."

"Thank you, Gustav, I think… It's a bit of a backhanded compliment, but I accept it."

"You know we venerate blonde hair, especially in the Reich. We see it as a sign of good breeding, passion and—"

"And fertility? I'm writing an article about whether women should wear trousers."

Stumpf was delighted. "Ah, now you have the most important issue before us. You will be glad to hear that I am very liberal on the subject… Now, perhaps I can persuade you to a little coffee or nightcap around the corner?"

She had assumed they would go to the Hotel Adlon, where she would be relatively safe and among friends. Instead, the taxi stopped outside the front door of the Kaiserhof and she was increasingly nervous. Not only had Ralph agreed to run into her that evening to head off the inevitable pass that Stumpf was clearly steeling himself to make, and would not know where they were, but this was also the hotel much frequented by senior Nazis. She would feel extremely alone. She began reminding herself that, although she was American, she was a British spy – not just technically either – and was liable to the death penalty if she was too bored or perhaps forgot herself for a second. She was playing a dangerous game, and she reminded herself that the consequences of being caught were terrifying – death and probably torture, both elements that nobody had really emphasised in London.

"Gustav, do you mind? I have an important story to write up tomorrow and was hoping for a relatively early night."

"I promise you shall have that. Just one drink, then away..."

They turned off the Wilhelmplatz and under the canopy of the Kaiserhof, just as a Transylvanian folk band in traditional costume was filing past them in a subdued mood. They were shown to a corner of the bar, on the kind of carpet pattern most likely to induce a migraine, and a waiter glided over. She peered nervously around. There was an unnecessary supply of gold braid on display on strange, almost outlandish uniforms with the regular blacks and reds of the Nazi style. Nobody seemed to be looking their way. Stumpf tipped the waiter with a fifty-pfennig note.

"You must show me what you write about trousers," he said. "You see, Xanthe, we enjoy blonde hair. It is one of our little weaknesses but it is also a great strength." She could feel some fumbling under the table in the direction of her knees. This is the moment, she thought to herself – what should she do?

Then, as if she had conjured him up herself, there was Ralph. Stumpf was on his feet greeting him, with some magnanimity, she thought, given what he had just interrupted.

"No, do stay seated," Ralph was saying. "My apologies for interrupting, only I am the bearer of a request from the British contingent at the Adlon – Joyce and Norman Baillie-Stewart, Frances Eckersley and the rest – and we knew you might be here, and I promised I would pass it on if I saw you. Would you both like to come?"

She felt overwhelming relief. She was so grateful to Ralph that she had not registered surprise that there *was* a British contingent at the Adlon. She had realised, of course, that there was a group of misfits who had found their way to Berlin at the outbreak of war. She knew that Bill was an acquaintance of the broadcaster William Joyce, the distinctive voice of Lord Haw-Haw. The surprise was that they had organised themselves together at all to meet at the Adlon, if indeed they actually had.

There was also the surprise that Ralph had guessed where Stumpf would take her. For a moment, she loved him for his intelligence and courage.

Either way, by the time Ralph had finished speaking, she was on her feet, had thanked Stumpf for a wonderful evening and picked up her handbag and was about to walk out onto Wilhelmplatz.

*

Joyce had organised the get-together as a sort of launch for his book *Twilight Over England*, which had just been published. His wife Margaret was there too – Shirer used to call her "Lady Haw-Haw" – and both were in great spirits. Joyce looked a little frightening, like a menacing version of Stan Laurel, but he gave Xanthe a big smile, and the scar on his face twitched into a different shade of red as he signed her a copy.

"Go on, give it a read. You might learn something," he said. Shirer and the others were there on the fringes. Sigrid regarded them with a frosty stare from the other side of the bar.

She opened the book and read the first paragraph:

"*Our only purpose is to show how England's historical development contributed to the fateful and fatal action which her government took on September 3rd, 1939. There is a certain dramatic irony in Mr Chamberlain's choice of the date. For September 3rd was the date of Oliver Cromwell's birth and also of his death…*"

"Purple prose," said Bill in Xanthe's ear.

"On the contrary – I don't really understand what he's on about. What's Cromwell got to do with it?"

Xanthe enjoyed the occasion, so confusing in its loyalties and diverse in its company. For a brief moment, in their extraordinary mixture of different nationalities and political affiliations, the war seemed forgotten – except of course that none of them would have been there without it.

Ralph drank whisky a little apart from the rest. She was thinking how extraordinary he was – perhaps the only person in the whole city who remained unafraid of anything: not the Gestapo, not the RAF, not the Nazis, and not his own side, pursuing his own war in his own chosen way.

What she should have been wondering perhaps was how he had become so intimate already with these people, mixed up in the whole tragedy as flyblown traitors.

CHAPTER NINE

Berlin, July 1940

She handed the draft of her article about the "pants" controversy to the censor with some satisfaction. Xanthe felt pleased with herself. She had told the truth, but had not compromised her ability to get it passed by spelling out her conclusions – but she confided quietly to herself that any regime that seemed to disparage the clothes that women wore was probably not competent to fight a world war. She knew from her time in London that there were women in trousers even then driving buses, operating radar, making shells, and this must give them some advantages. She did not spell this out, though of course she wished she could have done.

"Now Fraulein Schneider, this is an interesting piece but it is somehow a little – er, pointless, is it not? It is not very important."

She had not expected this kind of angle from the censor. "Well, I leave the military stories to the experts," she said defensively.

"Very well, I will pass it with just one deletion. I should like to remove the word 'unfeminine'. I would not want you to give the impression that German women were unfeminine, even in wartime."

"Ok," said Xanthe, with relief. "How would you describe it then – why the fear of pants, I mean trousers?"

"Perhaps we could use the words 'dressed as they should be' or 'appropriately' for their vital role."

"How about 'dressed correctly'?"

"Very well. We agree. Thank you, Fraulein. A fruitful negotiation."

*

Should she be having "fruitful negotiations" with Nazi officials, she wondered as she asked Ralph about the pants controversy again that evening as they walked again in the park? Berlin matrons were enjoying the evening sun. There was even a military band playing in the distance. She recognised the notes of *Gott Strafe England*. They talked about the strange contradictions in Nazi society – worrying about the word "unfeminine" while a naval officer happily reveals the truth about damage to his ship in action (not to mention what he confided about Enigma, but she kept that element to herself).

"It's true that the naval officers you meet are enjoyably open and free of pomposity, rather like our own navy back home," said Ralph. "They are also supremely confident in their own way of doing things, the U-boats, the uncrackable code system."

This time, she could barely resist.

"If Enigma is really uncrackable, then what are you doing here? I don't completely understand, you know Ralph. Sorry to be so direct."

He stopped walking and looked her full in the face. His smile had vanished.

"Xanthe, it is time for the truth. The most important truth."

She feared she was in for an accusation. But it wasn't one.

"I think I'm beginning to fall in love with you."

"You too?" she wailed. "What is it about this country? They can't all adore blonde hair!"

He looked cross.

"Well, that's a bit flippant, after what I've just told you."

She found she was breathing faster than she felt she should. There was something about Ralph's sheer defiance which really attracted her. It was as if everything she had ever wanted had been given to her. A great feeling of excitement and happiness was wafting through her, like the waves of a storm.

"Oh Ralph, I don't know. I mean, how can we? We're in such a peculiar and dangerous place…"

"That's enough of an answer for me," he said. "Now I'm sure you feel the same. Come here." He pulled her into a shadowy corner in the trees, bent over her and kissed her.

When they drew breath, she nestled into his chest. Xanthe said: "Let's just leave this city. Together. They give you so much freedom, Ralph; you could just escape and go home."

"Yes, and be hanged as a traitor."

"But you're not, are you? You have plans. We both know that. How can we love each other here?"

"Well, I don't see – listen, Xanthe, tell me now. Who sent you here? Did you really come for the *Chicago Tribune*?"

She could feel the immense relief, almost physical, that she was about to come clean. The words even came into her mouth to say. But at that moment, she saw Sigrid on the other side of the path. She leapt apart from Ralph just before she was seen.

"Come on, Xanthe," she said. "You'll miss the press conference. Remember? Or didn't you hear – at the Propaganda Ministry?"

By the time she had recovered and excused herself, promising to meet Ralph later that evening, the moment had passed.

*

The press conference was too hot, as they invariably were. Almost everyone Xanthe knew in Berlin seemed to be squeezed into the heated room to hear Hitler's ideologue Alfred Rosenberg make an extremely verbose statement about how Sweden would now have to apply to join the Nazi Scandinavian protectorate.

As soon as he said it, some civil servants rushed out to report – presumably to the Foreign Office – and came back in time to pass notes to the shadowy man who was chairing. As soon as Rosenberg had sat down, the chairman was on his feet explaining that these were simply "Herr Rosenberg's personal views".

"Why did they do that?" she asked Bill. "Was it because they don't really want an absolute domination of Europe, or is it because they don't want us to know yet?"

"Good question. I think everything really points towards the latter, doesn't it?"

She was pleased that he had replied kindly. She had realised her press colleagues disapproved of her growing closeness with Ralph when she found herself excluded from key conversations. Of course they were reporters, and quite able to stab each other in the back in pursuit of the right story, but as foreign correspondents – and particularly with such fearsome hosts – they knew they also stood or fell together. If one of them sloped off for an event, the chances are that the others would follow, knowing they risked losing their job if another paper got a key story they had missed. So they organised their lives in such a way as to minimise the chances of that happening.

Reporters like Shirer went their own way, but he was anyway a broadcaster with different technological needs. Otherwise, they stuck to each other like limpets – particularly when one of the censors proved particularly intractable, or when one of them was threatened with deportation because of the tone of their reporting.

When that happened, there would be little clusters of American journalists in the bar at the Hotel Adlon, hammering out joint approaches or simply listening to each other's sob stories. Xanthe first realised she had become an object of suspicion when she ambled over to join one of these clusters and the hubbub of voices hushed; people looked at her, irritated. She waited for a moment and then slipped away. It was mortifying, but what could she do? She was in reality not quite one of them, and they seemed to sense this.

"Why are people avoiding me?" she asked Cynthia, an American Associated Press stringer she had become friendly with.

"Oh come on, honey. It can't be a surprise. Because you're such pals with that Brit – they don't know whose side you're on."

"That's ridiculous. I'm *supposed* to be friendly with people on the other side. We all are – you are, Bill is, every journalist is. That's how we get our stories."

Cynthia put down her drink and turned to face her. "Xanth, I like you. Really do. So don't make me spell it out. Of course we're friendly to people, even in the regime. But generally speaking we don't fall in love with them. We don't sleep with traitors."

Cynthia saw the look of shock in Xanthe's face. She wondered how best to deny it.

"I'm not sleeping with him. I am *not*."

But the truth was that it was becoming untenable resisting his advances. She may not have been sleeping with Ralph, but she could certainly imagine herself doing so. He seemed to her to rise above the whole business of war. She still could not grasp quite what it was he was attempting to do. She had made no real decision about his sanity. She understood the challenge of the naval codes and how vital it was to find a clue, any clue – let alone a key that would unlock Enigma, if only to keep the trade routes open so that Britain could feed her people. But she could not quite see how he was planning to provide it – and despite all that, she admired his sheer aplomb, his *savoir faire* in the face of what was a clear case of tyranny. How often in life do you meet someone so courageous, or so insane, that they can rise above complexity and tyranny with good humour? She may not have been sleeping with him, but she certainly loved him.

*

The conversation upset her, partly because it struck an obvious nerve. What was she doing? Who was she actually betraying? It had all seemed so simple to start with when Commander Fleming had briefed her. She stayed awake in her little room, listening to the sounds of a typical Berlin boarding house, the running water, the banging doors, as she wept. The air-raid warnings went again, and she pulled the covers over her head and listened for the telltale cracks of bombs which never came.

She felt she could hardly confide in Ralph. In fact, there was nobody she could confide in; who would forgive an agent who falls in love with her subject? A horrible suspicion began to grow in her that this was precisely what Fleming and Turing had intended all along, though she could think of no proper reason. Why would they want her to fall in love with Ralph? What advantage would it give them? And if they had not considered the possibility, why had they not? Did they not understand the way that men and women were, especially when they were a long way from home?

She began to resent their involvement in her life. She decided again that she would throw herself on Ralph's mercy and tell him everything and ask him to forgive her. She still had not understood his plan or its purpose, and she no longer really cared enough. She was giving up, handing in her spy's licence, if there was such a thing. Not publicly, of course, but in her own understanding of her main purpose. She was due to meet Uncle Sam this time next to the reptile house, and she would fail to show up. She knew now what was most important.

She was seeing Ralph as usual that evening. They saw each other most days when he had time – and, this time, she told herself, she would come clean. Once she had used the phrase to herself, she knew it was an appropriate one – her very small secret smelled; it made her feel dirty. She no longer really minded *whose* side Ralph was on.

"I've got something to tell you," she said sheepishly as they passed the Hotel Adlon.

"Well, hold on," he said, steering her across Pariserplatz, taking her arm as they dodged the military vehicles which seemed to be crowding through the Brandenburg Gate.

"I tell you what," he said. "I will walk you round to my hotel, we'll have a night cap in my room, and you can tell me there."

She knew what this implied and a warm feeling of nervous anticipation flooded through her down to her toes. But in the event, the anticipation was too strong for any conversation.

"Weren't you going to tell me something?"

"Oh, don't worry – it wasn't important…" She was hardly thinking any longer.

She leaned back towards him as they went in through his door and she felt his arms come around her body.

"It's hard not to, isn't it," she said.

"It certainly is."

She was not a virgin. But sex in Cincinnati had not really been more than a few smutty fumbles after a dance. Or once in Cambridge after a foreshortened May Ball in a borrowed dress that previous summer. This was somehow grown up and luxurious in Ralph's huge bed. She had wanted to feel the weight of him on top of her, wanted the smell of him on her and around her. It was a moment of fulfilment for which she had no regrets at all. Wartime makes for unlikely conjunctions: here was she, a girl from Cincinnati, Ohio, in the arms of a former parliamentary undersecretary for the Crown, up to heaven knows what combination of selfishness and heroism. He was flawed, she knew. He was arrogant and pompous sometimes, and maybe not even entirely sane. She couldn't see into his mind or his thoughts, but somehow his sheer bravado, his very madness, made him exciting. The rank male odour that emanated from him, under his carefully pressed aristocratic collars, made him feel different. But then again, she had never really been in love before.

There was only one peculiarity about the night, the strange habit that made him cover his face at the moment of climax. She took it for shyness at the time, or vulnerability. It was only as she stared up at him, his face flushed, his fringe flopping down over his eyes, that she realised she had still not made her confession.

CHAPTER TEN

Berlin, July 1940

"What are you so busy doing?" Xanthe asked Ralph the next morning. The sunlight was pouring through the net curtains.

"Well, you know; I've got things to do."

"What things?"

"Oh, come on, Xanthe. You know what I'm doing. I don't need to spell it out. Time's getting on. Everything's kicking off in the next few days."

She got up in bed and wrapped herself in a sheet as a robe. She had stayed with him that night right through until breakfast. His bedroom smelled of sweat, whisky and eau-de-cologne.

The moment had passed for her confession, at least like that, but now that they were actually talking about it, she realised she wanted to know a great deal more. Why the preparations? Why the meetings with Stumpf? Why, in fact, was he being looked after in some comfort by his Nazi hosts? She still did not quite understand.

"I know I've asked you this before, but I don't understand why you need all these meetings. What are you preparing for?"

"You'll know in two days," he said enigmatically. "We are invited to a party, in fact, if you would come. In the Rundfunk building."

"Of course..."

"Weren't you going to tell me something important last night?"

She had barely articulated these questions to herself before. Perhaps she had been too preoccupied with her changing feelings for the man that she had not asked herself these things with quite the objectivity that was required. Where did he actually go in the daytime?

Of course, Xanthe knew he had hardly come to Berlin to retire. He had not come to get rich: she knew he had been on the verge of inheriting a tidy sum when his mother died. So what was he doing, apart from the fantasy he had portrayed to her about winning the war somehow single-handedly? Every day he was with Stumpf or at the Admiralty or the Propaganda Ministry. But then she was at the Propaganda Ministry herself most days, for press conferences or to talk to censors.

*

It was 19 July. The long-awaited party was due that evening.

"How are we going to be together?" Xanthe asked Ralph that lunchtime. It had been weighing on her mind and she asked him as soon as she reached his room.

"I hadn't really thought about it."

She decided to control her response.

"What do you mean? I've been thinking about it the entire time. If you can't go to England, maybe you could come with me to the States? At least we're neutral."

"Oh, we'll be able to go to England and quite soon if my calculations are right. I said we had been asked to a party at the Rundfunk Building tonight. Because tonight, the Führer will make his peace offer to England."

Things began to fall into place a little.

"You mean his speech tonight. Of course. But they'll never accept it, will they?"

"They won't to start with – but you are misunderstanding the politics in London. If I may say so…" Ralph was getting excited, but he calmed down, took a visible breath and reached into his briefcase, pulling out a strange circular metal contraption, about the size and shape of a bicycle gear.

"Now. Do you know what this is?"

"Don't change the subject," she laughed.

He waved it at her.

"What is it then?"

"It's a rotor for a naval Enigma machine. There are a number of these in each set, and they go into the machines in different orders, according to the settings for the day."

"Amazing. Show me."

Xanthe held the rotor in her hand. It was heavier than she expected.

"It's the pass that will get us into the party tonight. It's a kind of joke really – and the Admiralty would be horrified – but I said we'd show one to get in. The only thing is, I can't really put this great lump of metal in my pocket. It would stick out. Could you put it in your bag for me?"

"Yes, I'll rescue your flawless lines," she said with a grin. "But I've only got this." She had brought a small pink canvas bag where she kept her keys and notebook and lipstick and most of her papers, but not much else. She stowed it away anyway.

"Now, please explain how this is going to end the war when Churchill will never accept Hitler's peace offer."

A flash of irritation crossed his face.

"Oh, he will do given time. You see there are so many people, in the government and his party who think the way I do. In the civil service, in parliament, in the Lords. Certainly in business. As soon as Hitler makes a reasonable offer of peace, they will make their feelings felt. Britain can't carry on a war without an army, without equipment or an effective air force. Especially when the real enemy isn't Germany at all, it's Stalin and the Soviets."

Xanthe stood silent, listening. It was the first time he had really explained his thinking to her in any depth. She had not realised what his priorities were before.

"Let me tell you what will happen after tonight. Hitler will make his offer. The British government will start to unravel as they debate it. People will call for peace. My messages will go out. I am expecting whole units, ships and squadrons, to declare themselves for peace. The British can't survive and they know that all too well. The war effort, the war party, will unravel – and, yes, they'll come to the conference table, you'll see. Then you and I will be able to go home."

She stared at him.

"Is that your plan then? Has that always been your plan?"

"Always," he said.

"Yes, but… But you said you were helping the British crack the German codes?"

"Well, it will help them, but by then it won't matter. Sense will have prevailed."

It slowly began to dawn on her what this meant. "So – well, you are a traitor then. To your country." She felt close to tears. "There are people, friends of yours, dying now because they're standing up to Hitler."

He went bright red, and was suddenly enraged.

"Don't you dare tell me I've betrayed my country. Don't you dare!" He waved his finger in her direction. "And don't be so sentimental. Even Halifax has been talking quietly to the Italians. Is he a traitor? The

Foreign Secretary? I'll tell you who betrayed my country. It was those people who insisted on fighting a war when they were so unprepared, that was the real betrayal. Who listened to the Jews and financiers and your Jewish president when they wanted us to fight the one force in the modern world capable of resisting the Soviet menace. No, I'm on the *side* of my own country and on the side of history, dammit. And I am going to do my *damnedest* to stay on the side of history."

She was weeping by now. She felt a fool, an idiot, a dupe. Partly because she felt betrayed herself, partly because she also still loved him.

"Now, for goodness sake let's get dressed and go to this party. But first, I'm going to give you a surprise."

*

"What are we going here for?" she asked him, struggling to keep up. She noticed he was in a double-breasted suit that made him look a little like a Chicago gangster.

"I don't believe it, I don't believe it," said a voice in her head, round and round and round.

She had been into the Reichstag before, of course. There were Nazi armbands everywhere they looked. Ralph swept in and showed a pass to a functionary, indicating that she was with him, and they were beckoned on to follow. They went quickly up some back stairs, which smelled of urine and paint, as the back stairs of public buildings tend to. "Just in time," he said.

It was a few minutes before six o'clock as they came out at the top of the stairs above a huge array of people. There must have been a couple of thousand squeezed in there, many of them in uniform, the luminaries of the regime and those who wanted to be like them, all gathered in the well of the building in great black and red rows. It was a wonderful position they were in, way above the auditorium.

She could see the Nazi leaders on the platform, Goering, Keitel and poor old Field Marshal Halder, who Hitler was supposed to hate. Himmler, dressed in grey, was fussing in the background and muttering. Ralph pointed out Quisling, the new Norwegian leader.

"Who's that?" she asked Ralph, nudging him towards a small man who appeared to be chewing gum on the edge of the platform.

"Ciano. Italian foreign minister. Can't seem to sit still, can he?" Ciano kept on leaping up to salute. It was most disconcerting.

There was an electric atmosphere of expectation. It was the moment they had been waiting for after nearly a year of war. The room hushed and everybody rose in their seats, as Hitler himself marched in. She had only glimpsed him once before in the flesh. He was a small man, but there was an aura of power about him as he flashed his arm in a kind of half salute to acknowledge the cheers.

He marched quickly and seriously down the red carpet, which matched the red fabric draping all the walls. As Hitler stood quickly in front of the huge German eagle and swastika at the back of the hall, for a split second she saw the red drapes like blood. It seemed like a visionary flash. She wondered whose blood it represented.

The silence gathered. It was a peculiar feeling watching him in real time, not on a black-and-white newsreel, as if Mickey Mouse had come unexpectedly to life. He checked his notes as he stood before the audience, and Xanthe glanced quickly around them in the visitors' gallery. There was Shirer, there was Sigrid. They glanced back at her.

Then he began.

"Deputies, men of the German Reichstag! In the midst of the mighty struggle for the freedom and future of the German nation, I have called on you to gather for this session today."

It was just a little Shakespearian, full of the kind of rhetorical vanities that would have been too much even for the Senate back home, but with none of the histrionics that they had come to expect of the man.

"The purposes for today are these. To give our people an insight into the historic uniqueness of the events we have lived through. To express our thanks to our deserving soldiers. And to direct, once again and for the last time, an appeal to general reason."

It was a clever speech, humble at the right moments, demanding sometimes, and he gave the performance of a lifetime, ironically putting his head on one side – his timing was perfect. Then came the crescendo…

"In this hour I feel compelled, standing before my conscience, to direct yet another appeal to reason in England. I believe I can do this as I am not asking for something as the vanquished, but rather, as the victor. I am speaking in the name of reason. I see no compelling reason which could force the continuation of this war. I regret the sacrifices it will demand. I would like to spare my people. I know the hearts of millions of men and boys aglow at the thought of finally being allowed to wage battle against an enemy who has, without reasonable cause, declared war on us a second time. But I also know of the women and mothers at home whose hearts, despite their willingness to sacrifice to the last, hang onto this with all their might…"

There was absolute silence in the hall. You could feel the weight of longing, willing the British to accept the offer.

"Come on!" Ralph was pulling Xanthe to her feet.

"Where are we going?" she whispered, aware the handful of other press representatives were also leaving.

"We're going to the party. Didn't I tell you?"

"I don't believe it, I don't believe it," said the voice in her head again. A feeling of misery, in a round ball, seemed to be growing in the pit of her stomach.

As they ran down the steps outside, she could hear behind her the shouts of "Sieg heil!" from a thousand throats in the audience inside. Hitler had reached his conclusion.

She saw Bill in front of them looking for the CBS car. "Can we join you?" asked Ralph.

"I'm going to broadcast."

"The Rundfunk? That's where we're going too…"

"Ok, jump in."

*

"And now it begins," said Ralph as he led Xanthe upstairs past offices full of uniformed censors, discreetly pointing in her bag to the smiling officers on the doors. They grinned and clapped Ralph on the back. Clearly the joke was understood. She saw other people making similar gestures towards bulging pockets.

Bill had gone to a different entrance to do his own broadcast and they had braved the main one, with a soldier in a helmet guarding the door.

Then in they went to what looked like a wood-lined boardroom on the top floor, with a view of the city beyond, and – for the second time in the evening – she found herself in the strange world of the Nazi in-crowd, this time a melee of officials, broadcasters and a few foreign journalists. In the corner, she recognised some of the British contingent. There was Mildred Gellars, also from Ohio, as she had discovered recently, an American announcer on German radio. On the other side of the room were Lord and Lady Haw-Haw: she was talking to a young blond German man and they seemed deep in conversation. The radio was blaring away in English.

"It's the only place people can listen to foreign broadcasts legally," said Ralph.

"I suppose you're enjoying all this," she said, close to tears. "What have you led me into?" There were champagne bottles doing the rounds and canapés.

"Hello, Xanthe," said Fred Kaltenbach. "Exciting, isn't it? We're going to be in at the end after all."

"Are we?" she said. She was feeling sick.

"Radio London on in five minutes," said a man who appeared to be acting as master of ceremonies.

"Right," said Ralph. "This is the moment. I can't imagine what the first British reaction is going to be. They are going to be thrown into an almighty funk by that speech. Churchill will be on the back foot. Halifax will be pushing hard for a negotiated peace; the whole establishment will be pushing hard. They will either negotiate or capitulate and I must say I'm going to enjoy the chaos while they try and battle it out. I can't believe they will be able to accept quite this soon, though."

"I want to go back home," said Xanthe. "I really can't stand this. You are enjoying your country's discomfort. You're *enjoying* it."

"It isn't your country. I don't know why you're so upset about it. I never made any secret about what I was going to do."

She hissed back: "Yes, but I never thought you were going to enjoy it so much."

There was hush as the volume of the wireless was put up and they could hear the BBC loudly and clearly and the familiar sound of Big Ben.

"This is London," said the announcer. "This is the BBC German service. And this is Sefton Delmer speaking."

There was a ripple of recognition and amusement around the room. "Big Sefton," someone said with a giggle.

"Delmer was here for the *Express* for some time," explained Ralph happily.

Sefton Delmer started his commentary as a direct reply to Hitler's speech, which he must have listened to live on Berlin radio. He started deferentially, speaking directly to Hitler, who he had clearly met and conversed with. Then he built up towards a crescendo of rudeness.

"Herr Hitler, you have on occasion in the past consulted me as to the mood of the British public," said Delmer. "So permit me to render your Excellency this little service once again tonight. Let me tell you what we here in Britain think of this appeal of yours to what you are pleased to call our reason and common sense. Herr Hitler and Reichkanzler, we hurl it right back at you, right in your evil-smelling teeth."

This time, the silence was one of shock. Nobody spoke.

"I don't believe it," said Kaltenbach, standing next to Xanthe. "They *can't* have decided yet. Delmer must have gone out on a limb."

"How could he have?" said another one of his group. "They would never let him broadcast his own line on something as important as that. We know the most powerful people in Britain don't want the war."

Ralph still hadn't spoken.

One of the German diplomats was suddenly shouting at Shirer. "Can you make it out? Can you understand these British fools? Turn down peace now? They're crazy!"

Then Ralph exploded. Turning to the window, he smashed his fist down on the sill, knocking two champagne glasses into tiny shards of glass on the floor.

"I don't believe it. I don't fucking *believe* it! Those stupid fucking traitors!"

"Ralph...," Xanthe said quietly to him, holding her hand out towards him. But he turned on her.

"Oh, don't touch me. You're as bad as the rest of them. Weak, weak, weak. Don't you all understand the direction history is taking? Don't *you*? What am I doing wasting my time with you and the Jews. Get away from me!"

He turned around, white with fury and stormed out of the room, upsetting a chair as he went.

By now the room was in uproar, with officials and journalists talking animatedly to each other, bitter disappointment all over their faces. Xanthe stared after Ralph, tears pouring down her face.

"Xanthe, are you ok? Can I get you a driver? I'd drive you home myself, but I'm on the air in five minutes."

"No, no, thanks, Bill," she said to him as she headed for the door. She stumbled into the street, ran across the road and sobbed against the balustrade. Not only had she fallen in love with a traitor and a fascist, she had fallen for one with such a temper that he could reject her so brutally in front of all her colleagues – who could take her heart and crush it into pieces. She had to get out of there, not just out of Berlin but out of Germany. She had to get away.

CHAPTER ELEVEN

Berlin, July 1940

There was a knock on Xanthe's bedroom door, abrupt and demanding. Her make-up was streaked with tears and she felt drained. She decided to ignore it.

She had flung herself on her bed when she had got back to her lodgings and, between bouts of uncontrollable misery, had been trying to work out what to do. The streets of Charlottenburg around the Rundfunk building had been full of people celebrating the peace that they imagined was now inevitable. Perhaps they had not heard the news from London that the peace offer had been spurned in such graphic terms. Once she had reached the street, she had breathed as deeply as she could. Then she stood up and tried to work out how far she was away from her room. Less than a mile, but it was suddenly a frightening walk and for a few minutes she felt unable to face it. But she had to and, anyway, she badly needed the air.

Across the street, three soldiers without their helmets were staring at her. She set herself in the other direction with determination and tried to put them out of her mind.

What was she to do? She had torpedoed her career in journalism, or so she assumed. She had let down Fleming and Turing and her employers in London. She had failed miserably to see clearly what Ralph was actually doing, purely because she had blinded herself to the truth. She had made what her friends in London used to call a complete pig's breakfast of things, and everyone she knew in Berlin would soon know about it. But worst of all, she still loved him. Yes, she despised his opinions and she could not forgive him for what he said to her, nor the way he said it – humiliating her so publicly – but she could not quite expunge her original feelings. In fact, they added an extra layer of misery.

There was no doubt at all that she would have to leave and as quickly as possible. She could hardly go to the American embassy now. It would be shut and the reception desk closed. No, she would ask Sigrid what to do the next morning though, after her disappearance in the evening, she was not at all sure Sigrid would speak to her.

As she walked, she had thought back over the extraordinary events of the night. Was it possible that Sefton Delmer had taken it upon himself to reject Hitler's peace offer, on his own authority? From the little that she knew of the inner workings of governments – mainly from talking to Ralph – it seemed extremely unlikely that he had been told what to say, one way or another. He would have needed to get instructions from the cabinet in less than an hour. It was a great weakness of authoritarian governments – she realised now – that, not only did they never dare to take a bold initiative like that, but they couldn't imagine anyone else doing so either. Maybe Delmer had very cleverly forced Churchill's hand, just by saying no all by himself – maybe Ralph had stormed out too early.

By the time she had turned off the main road and into her immediate neighbourhood, she had at least the outlines of a plan. She breathed just a little more freely. That was when she heard the steps behind her.

She stopped and turned around. The street was deserted and almost impenetrable in the blackout. She stopped and looked around again. Nothing. But when she started again this time, she could hear the echo of someone there. Was it a real echo? She varied her pace, but the echo did not change. She speeded up, but this time the footsteps went faster. She thought back to her training in London, remembering Baker Street, turned sharp left and doubled back. The steps seemed to disappear.

Now she was in her own street. She fumbled for the key to her room as she began to run as fast as she could. A man stood outside the front door. As Xanthe got closer, it was clear that he was in military uniform.

"Excuse me," she said as she flung herself against the front door. It was unlocked as usual. She slipped straight through and upstairs to her room, where she threw herself and her handbag down heavily on the bed. There were none of the usual sounds. Mathilde must have been out. It was only a few minutes later that she heard the peremptory knock.

"Open please," said a voice outside the room. Then another bang, more insistent than before.

"Who is it?"

"It is Gustav Stumpf. Open now, if you please."

Xanthe's heart sank. He was about the last person she wanted to see, and there was more than an element of risk.

"Oh please, Gustav. Can I talk to you later? I'm very tired and rather upset…"

There was another bang on the door. "I am afraid I must insist."

With a sigh of irritated frustration, she got to her feet and walked a little giddily to the door. She turned the key in the lock.

There was Stumpf, in full uniform.

"Thank you, Fraulein Xanthe. Now, if you please…" He pushed past her and into the room. "Sit, please," he said.

She sat on the bed, her apprehension growing.

"It is my duty to inform you that you are under investigation for espionage. So are a number of your American press colleagues. The investigation is in its earliest stages, and yours in particular may take some time."

"Oh, for goodness sake, Gustav. They – we – are accredited correspondents. We're not spies. You know that."

"On the contrary, Fraulein, I know nothing of the kind. May I remind you of the punishment for espionage."

"So, throw me out of the country. Nobody would be happier than me."

"I regret that things are a good deal more serious than that. The punishment for espionage is death – and the courts tend to do what we tell them."

She was not feeling emotionally strong enough at that moment and the news that Stumpf was assuming the power of life or death over her was just too much. She buried her face in her hands.

"This is not an admission, Oberleutnant. I'm just tired."

"On the contrary, most agents break down sooner or later. It does not matter how well your American spymasters have prepared you."

Perversely, the news that Stumpf had no idea who she had actually been working for cheered her enormously. She felt a little determination seep back into her will.

"We have arrested your friend Carl. It is sad; he has been a good naval officer, but he should not be so garrulous. Luckily, we have complete faith in our Enigma system. But that does not mean we can tempt fate."

It was truly a devastating night, and now the news that the gentle Carl had been arrested and all because he had gossiped to her. Was it possible that the police had intercepted her note to Uncle Sam and put two and two together? Or was Stumpf just fishing again, because he had overheard them talking about Enigma on his way back to his seat?

There was silence in the room as Stumpf stood against the fireplace and Xanthe sat on the bed. Then he moved towards her and sat down next to her.

"Luckily, there is a way out for you, Fraulein Xanthe, you and your blonde hair. I can certainly find a way to delay the investigation. But you have to co-operate."

"Oh, godammit, Gustav. I'm not a spy so how can I co-operate?"

"I think you know."

He took off his cap and leaned back on the bed confidently.

"If you mean I need to sleep with you and you'll promise not to have me shot, then it isn't a very good method of seduction."

"For goodness sake, you Americans are so melodramatic," he said, undoing the buttons of his black tunic.

She could see a nervous and exultant glint in his eyes in his anticipation.

"Sorry, Oberleutnant. Please go. You're out of luck."

His face went red. For the second time in the evening, she was confronted by a man in incoherent rage.

"What is it about you that makes you think you can resist me?"

"Oh, I think…"

He pushed her backwards onto the bed. She screamed with anger and fear. In the moments afterwards she listened for signs of help as she resisted, but the house remained as silent as night.

"Over my dead body," she said as she began to push.

"Don't tempt me. That can be arranged too, if necessary…"

He hit her in the eye and she fell back. Then he was heavily on top of her, fiddling with her skirt, fumbling as she pushed him away. She could feel her strength ebbing. She realised she was about to faint. She felt on either side of her for some kind of weapon and her left hand grabbed her handbag. Was it heavier than it should have been? Then, with all her remaining strength, she slammed it against his head.

He fell back and, this time, she swung the bag by its handle and hit him again. Blood spurted from his temple and he fell awkwardly across the bed.

She struggled to get her breath back, once more listening for signs that they had been overheard.

"Now, *please* – please will you leave me ALONE!" she whispered, breathlessly.

There was no response. There was a great deal of blood all over the sheets and on her bag. His eyes were open with a glassy stare. It occurred to her that she might have killed him, and desperately searched for a pulse on his wrist. The blood was beginning to congeal on his head already. There was no pulse. He was still staring at her, but the look of tyrannical expectation had given way to one of blank, horrified surprise. She sat down trying to collect her thoughts. A mirror, that was what she needed, rooting around in the bag until she found a powder compact. She put it up to his nose. Nothing.

He was dead. She had killed an official of the Nazi party, and apparently with a piece of their top secret Enigma machine. She had to act, if she was going to survive. And she had to do so quickly.

*

She shook uncontrollably. You are a trained agent, she told herself. I'm not defenceless. I have resources. I can deal with this if I just breathe. If I just breathe calmly and slowly I might just stop shaking. Don't let the mice bite, she said to herself as her father used to – don't let the mice bite.

She had only a few minutes. Stumpf obviously had some men outside and they would seek him out shortly, though they had clearly heard no signs of the struggle – or if they had, they must have assumed she was on the losing side. They would be suspicious if he did not emerge triumphant pretty soon. There was no time to pack, and it would anyway make sense to leave her suitcase behind. Packing it would imply that she intended to leave the country. It would give them a clue about what she was planning to do. She lifted the wobbly floorboard and extracted her notes. It was hardly a very good hiding place anyway.

She took some make-up and some dark hair dye she had been saving just in case. She dumped the bloodstained bag, transferring everything in it to a loose canvas holdall. She took her passport and papers and her notebooks, shoving them all in, with some clean underclothes and a different-coloured top, and the Enigma rotor.

She looked at herself in the mirror, the black eye where Stumpf had hit her was coming up beautifully, but there was nothing she could do about that. On a sudden impulse, she closed her eyes and shut Stumpf's staring eyes, taking a rug from the other end of the bed and covering him as if he was asleep. It might give a few minutes delay. All the time, she was trying to imagine a way out of the house without being seen.

She knew there was a back door to the yard if she could get past Frau Menschler in the kitchen. She must have heard them upstairs and would be nervous, perhaps listening terrified next to the stove. But she tiptoed downstairs in her stockinged feet, carrying her shoes and with her bag over her shoulder, and there was no sign of her. Frau Menschler must have felt that discretion was the better part of valour.

Outside in the courtyard, there was another gate into the next-door street. Mercifully it wasn't locked. She peered through it. Stumpf had clearly not imagined an ending to their encounter along these lines. There seemed to be nobody in sight. She slipped through and out into the blackout.

I'm a murderer, she said out loud as she felt safer in the pitch dark. I killed somebody, just because they wanted my body. I *killed* them.

Breathe, she told herself. You are just an ordinary foreign correspondent, out a little late. That's all. She forced herself to put one leg in front of the other in rhythm. Don't let the mice bite. One, two, one, two, three, four…

Turn left and then towards the Tiergarten and the zoo. People were driving past honking horns every so often, following the prospects of peace, but there was no real joy in the street. The news must now have spread that the British had rejected the offer. It was also getting late. The streets were darker than ever. The cars went by as black shapes and disappeared quickly into the gloom.

Then the sirens went. There had been no bombing so far – and in fact Hitler had promised there would be none. But the RAF still sent bombers over Berlin, still dropping leaflets, perhaps just to show that they could come at all. There was no panic, but people began to file out of the houses and into their basements just in case, this time, it was for real.

The cold air on her face was beginning to calm and revive her. Up ahead, down Unter den Linden, she could see the shape of the Brandenburg Gate and knew she was getting near the only place that could help her – the American embassy. How stupid she had been to fail to keep her last appointment with Uncle Sam.

She could see the shape of the Hotel Adlon now etched against the night sky, and imagined her colleagues descending into the air-raid shelter underneath the hotel. But she could not go to them for help. Not now Stumpf was dead.

The starlight caught the letters USA on the roof of the enormous embassy. No lights shone. Did everyone go home at night? She didn't know.

Her heart was in her mouth as she crossed the expanse of tarmac outside the building and up the steps. The door was locked. The long queue of people begging for visas, there every day, would have been moved on by the police. The cavernous entry hall was empty. She rattled the door, tears rolling incriminatingly down her cheeks. Then she thumped on it.

"Uncle Sam!" she whispered, then louder in English: "UNCLE SAM! Help me – for goodness sake, help me!"

She felt the panic rising in her and fought to keep it down. What else could she do? She had to get out of Berlin.

It was then that she heard a small voice from her right. She looked round and there was a man beckoning to her. She hurried over.

"May I help you miss?"

She panted and fought to keep down the terror. He stood by her patiently, and said: "Perhaps you could come in here. I'm just the duty officer. I will find the First Secretary."

"I will deal with this," said a man in the shadows. "Miss Schneider, please come with me."

"I came to see Uncle Sam," she said, pathetically.

"I know who you have been looking for. I'm afraid he has been sent home during the election campaign."

"The election?"

"As you may know, President Roosevelt is fighting for re-election on a keep-out-of-the-war ticket. You will understand what that means in practice."

Xanthe nodded. She knew what it meant. It meant practical support for the British war effort would have to be suspended for some months.

"Now, if you would come with me to my office and, if you can be scrupulously honest with me, then I may be in a position to help you."

Saying nothing and miserably grateful to this man, she followed him and sat in a hard chair beside his desk. The lights were off. An occasional searchlight lit up the sky through the window.

"I know who you are, Miss Schneider, and have some idea what you have been doing, which is why I would be grateful if you don't compromise me by saying anything about it. What I want to know is what brought you here at this hour. I have some idea about that too, but would like the confirmation from you."

She breathed deeply again and began to go through the story of the evening, starting in the Reichstag and Ralph's fury when the British showed no signs of agonising, still less falling apart over the peace offer. She explained something about Stumpf. When she described his arrival at her flat, the official said: "Right, now we are getting to the nub of things."

She told him what had happened.

He was silent. "Let me think a moment or two, Miss Schneider, if you would."

She sat and stared out at the blackout through the window, at the searchlights, feeling numb but even so her heart was ricocheting inside her chest.

Then he got up.

"Right, Miss Schneider, we have very little time and we need to get you out of Germany if we possibly can. Excuse me while I make some arrangements."

She waited in the dark for about ten long minutes, watching the big round clock face as the hands clicked round, before there was a flurry outside and he was back. With him was a young man in a black suit.

"Now, my car's outside the back. I want you to go with William here. He will drive you out north of the city as if you were going to

Sweden. We will then take you to a house out of town where you will be safe for a few hours, and where you will change your appearance to look like this." He produced a passport with a photograph of a young lady about ten years older than Xanthe, with dark hair, called Shirley Johnson. She was also given various permits made out in her name.

"Listen, I don't even know your name," she said as the three of them walked quickly down the corridor. "I am more than grateful and I don't deserve it. Why are you helping me?"

"Have you heard of an organisation called British Security Co-ordination? I understand my government has been co-operating with the British on various intelligence projects and you are, after all, an American citizen."

This seemed peculiarly generous. Xanthe had never really known her own government to be *generous*. Imaginative, maybe. Inexorable, definitely, but generous?

"More to the point, I have strict orders not to allow – if I can possibly avoid it – our relations with the Nazis to become part of the election campaign back home. The accusation and arrest of an American citizen on a murder charge, with strong implications of intelligence involvement – and I fear your story of attempted rape would not reach the press – would not be, shall we say, helpful to the US government right now."

She understood. It was coincidental but helpful that she would embarrass her own government if she was caught. It was a very subtle balance but, as a result, they were therefore helping her.

"What I should also say is that we can't risk being caught with you. So we will leave you by the Elbe in Wittenberge with enough money to get to Geneva, and onwards, and suggest that you leave there by train as soon as possible tomorrow morning."

"And who is this Shirley? I ought to know."

"Shirley, as far as she exists at all, is a secretary at the embassy. You will have limited diplomatic immunity, as this pass explains. Just keep your head down, stay inconspicuous, and hopefully I will see you again in Washington one day."

*

She enjoyed talking to William as they drove out through the northern suburbs of Berlin. The All Clear sounded as they drove out of the embassy gates and onto Unter den Linden, the searchlight still played in the sky searching for the RAF, but they either had not come or had disgorged their cargo of propaganda leaflets already and left.

"I don't know why they bother," he said. "Have you read the leaflets? They're pretty dire. They seem to have no idea of conditions here. They seem to imply that everyone is on the brink of starving to death."

"I did see them. I agree with you. They're not starving – though the coffee is repulsive."

"Did anyone tell you the joke I heard in one of their music halls down south?" said William. "We are from Berlin and we are quite happy eating rats – but now we are being forced to eat *ersatz* rats!"

They both laughed. It relieved the tension. A little.

"I am normally part of the consular staff – I deal with visas – but I'm allowed out occasionally."

There were suddenly soldiers ahead.

"Now we have to be seen here," he said. "Just in case. This is the northern checkpoint in the city. We want them to look back at their records and see that an embassy car went north. Now, quick, put the scarf to cover your hair…"

The car was flagged down by two stormtroopers. Xanthe's heart seemed to stop. William wound down the window.

"Papers..."

They inspected their passes, William and Shirley out for a drive.

"And what brings you both out here tonight?"

William winked at them and leaned out of the car window. "Between you and me – you understand, a man has certain recreations..."

The soldiers guffawed and handed back the documents.

"You can't do it anywhere in the city then?"

"We're diplomats," said William, spreading his hands.

"Ok, ok. On your way – and have a good one." The leering laughter continued as they drove on and she breathed again.

"Sorry," he said. "I thought that was the best approach."

"Honestly, you do as you think fit," she said. "They should remember, which makes sense."

"Quite."

*

They sped north on Autobahn 44, with the signs indicating Hamburg in the far distance, and then turned west. There was hardly any other traffic. When William fell silent, the picture of Stumpf's staring dead eyes began to haunt her. When she managed to push it back down, what emerged instead was the rage in Ralph's face at the Rundfunk party. As the dawn seeped into the sky, they headed through the narrow streets of Wittenberge and along the river, which became slowly visible, glinting in the morning light. William drew up outside a nondescript front door.

"Here we are, thirty-three Dorfstrasse, black front door, see? You can get out at the end of the road – here's the key – and I'm going to put the car somewhere less obvious. This is our safe house."

Five minutes later, William was back. But he hardly stayed long.

"Right Xanthe, may I call you that? I'm going to leave you here. You will see that there's an express train southwards which leaves the station round the corner at eight thirteen a.m. and I suggest you get on it if possible. Did you say you had some dark hair dye? The colour doesn't matter – it's only a black-and-white photo. You just have time to use it."

Xanthe gathered her bag and papers together. She had been dreading this moment as they had driven through the night.

"Oh, and I have been instructed to give you this." He handed her a small parcel. Inside was a wad of banknotes.

"William, how can I thank you enough?" she said.

"That's an easy one to answer. By getting home safely."

*

The train was an hour late. It was packed and, by the time she had changed at Leipzig and reached Munich, it was running at least five hours behind and almost a whole day had gone by since her disastrous awakening at the hands of Ralph. The various uniforms on board made way for her to sit down but the delays and the lack of refreshments made her tired and tetchy. There were grunts of protest when anyone else tried to squeeze into her apartment or when the ticket collector tried to check their papers.

The train to Zurich was no better. Then the police checked everyone on board. Had the soldiers at the checkpoint noted down her new name when she was with William or would they still be searching for a blonde called Xanthe Schneider? She had no idea and this was the critical moment. But they checked her pass, stared into her face and passed on.

There was a clanking as the locomotives changed and then the Swiss border guards came on board. Xanthe burst into tears of relief.

The plane from Geneva airport took off that evening, swinging and wobbling into the sky. They touched down once in Barcelona before they reached Lisbon. She was utterly drained, feeling desolate and wracked with guilt, but she went straight to the British embassy and asked them to send an urgent telegram to Commander Fleming at the Admiralty in London to verify her identity.

"I don't think that'll be necessary, Miss," said the official. "If you would come with me, please."

She followed him behind the desk, down a short corridor in municipal paint, down to a small office. There, standing in his full naval uniform, was Fleming. He was grinning.

"I'm sorry," said Xanthe. "I'm so, so sorry."

*

"I'm sorry to ask you this, miss, but we're at action stations. Could you please go below?"

"Ok, Jack," Xanthe said, and the petty officer indicated a ladder downstairs.

She had been holding onto the rail on the quarter deck of the destroyer HMS *Harvester*, speeding across the Bay of Biscay with the spray in her face, staggered to be alive and away from the horrors of Berlin.

"The chaplain suggested you join him in the wardroom," said Jack.

"I'm afraid you'll have to direct me."

There was some discomfort about having a woman on board, and an American woman at that. Fleming had spent most of his time on the bridge, claiming that she was unnerving the crew. This seemed to her to be highly unlikely, though there had been some obviously raised eyebrows as they had been transferred quickly onto the destroyer from a Portuguese fishing boat. It was explained that British vessels could not use a neutral port like

Lisbon. The destroyer could not come to them, so they had to go to the destroyer, which had been redirected from convoy duty up the coast of Africa.

"You can't be doing all this for me," she said to Fleming. "Not when I've let you down so badly."

"Nonsense. If you had let us down, I would hardly be here myself. Our American friends tipped us off about what you were doing and I took the plane to Lisbon yesterday morning, probably just as you were crossing into Switzerland."

"I don't understand. I messed up everything. I didn't warn you about Ralph. Worse, I even *liked* him. Maybe too much."

"Oh, we don't worry about things like that. I have to say, Xanthe, that your notes on the bigram were absolutely invaluable." He saw her blank face. "On the numbers that set up the code every day – we call them bigrams in the trade. You made Turing's blood race and his colleagues' too. We thought we had understood before, but it is good to confirm our thinking. But the *pièce de la resistance* is this," he produced the rotor which she had used so unexpectedly to kill Stumpf. "We have managed to capture these before but this one is invaluable: we haven't seen one like it before. I have to congratulate you on a mission accomplished – not quite as planned, but then they never are. If you would like to continue to work with us, nobody would be more delighted than me."

*

"You have met before, I believe?" said Fleming. They were at the Admiralty a week or so later. She had slept for what seemed like days, but still had the nightmares about Stumpf, both waking and sleeping. She shook his colleague's hand.

She knew they had indeed met before but, for a moment, she could not place the man with the Hitler fringe and the faraway look in his eye.

It was only when she saw that his trousers were held up by string – an unexpected touch for Whitehall – that she remembered. It was Turing.

She shook his hand and he avoided her gaze.

"In fact, we've met twice before, haven't we?" she said gently.

"We have indeed," he said, giving her a shy smile. "And once with Dr Wittgenstein of all people. Please call me Alan."

"Thank you, Alan."

Turing sat back in his chair.

"Now," he said. "I have been given permission to tell you this. What really helped me were your bigrams, which you included in your second report, on a piece of old newspaper."

"Really, I thought you knew all that stuff already."

"No, well, yes, that is to say – we did, but we know – thanks to you – that the example had been given to you by a serving naval officer. So we theorised that he was actually using the settings for that day."

She could not quite grasp what he was saying.

"Ok, I get that, but I never told you what day it was, did I?"

"Ah no, no you didn't. But we had your newspaper and we guessed that it was the day's paper when you had the conversation. And we were right – we have therefore been able to read signals, all the signals in fact, sent that day. Which was the third of July, as it happens."

"The first day we have been able to do that," boomed Fleming. "No other days so far, but we read that day, some weeks late I'm afraid, but it is all great practice until we can read every day *on* the day. And you made it possible."

EPILOGUE

Bletchley, March 1941

The baby was due. The weather was improving by the day. Xanthe was bored; bored with England and her friends and most of all bored of being pregnant, of her weight which she heaved around her room at Bletchley Park in the pale English sunlight. She had written to her still unborn child, aware that Fleming wanted her to undertake another mission when she felt ready – if indeed she ever did.

The dark streets of Berlin already seemed a lifetime away. But at night, she would relive Stumpf's staring eyes, and her panicked, desperate journey across the city. It seemed extraordinary to be where she was – still cut off from her family back home, but looked after at a secret government research station in the last stages of pregnancy.

Despite the despair, she had no regrets. She was surprised when she missed a period, and assumed it was because of the strain – but it was soon clear that she was, in fact, pregnant. The father could only be Ralph. She told her few friends that she had fallen in love, and slept with a pilot who had been killed defending London, as so many had been that summer. If the truth was a little different, it was not different in what she felt. Now her life had shrunk down to the chintz in this bedroom, having given up her new job on the *New Yorker* magazine, and she had come to regard Ralph as a hero in a similar way: he believed in something and he risked his life for it. The fact that she profoundly disagreed with him about it hardly detracted from that. Her baby had been conceived in love. She had loved and believed she had been loved in return, and her account would – she hoped – be able to help the baby understand later where it had come from.

Turing and Fleming were neither of them conventional people and they knew what had happened as soon as they saw her expand and offered their support, without judgement. That is what brought her here, to a place she could refer to only as "Station X."

The invasion of England now seemed less likely but, if it happened – and if it worked – she told herself that there was a part of her that welcomed the fact that she, the baby and its father would be reunited at last.

BOOK TWO

THE ATHENS ASSIGNMENT

PROLOGUE

Bletchley, April 1941

Xanthe breathed deeply, as she had been told to do. She blew out rhythmically, panting like a desperate steam engine, impatient to leave the station. Breathe, breathe.

She felt like she was being torn in two. It hardly seemed possible that she could survive such red pain. She gripped the bedpost ferociously and hated the doctors standing around as she lay, spreadeagled on the bed like a specimen on a dish. How long was this going to take? How much could *she* take? She had heard that sometimes it could take days and nights, and she doubted whether she could live through it and remain the same, down to earth, crossword puzzling, Cincinnati girl.

In the intervals between contractions, she let her mind shoot back to her weeks in Berlin, that she had spent as a foreign correspondent in the first months of the Nazi assault on the West, the year before, and her ordeal at the end of it, escaping from the country in disguise, chased by the Gestapo, and all the time feeling desperate about her lost lover – lost to the Nazis, in more ways than one.

Yes, she had escaped the prospect of her body being broken by the Gestapo torturers, but there was an irony here which she could not quite grasp – driven out now by another wave of pain. And here it comes again: remember, breathe, breathe, breathe.

"That's right, Miss Schneider," said the doctor patronisingly. "Nearly there. I can see baby's head."

She felt supremely sorry for herself. About five thousand miles from home in Ohio, in some kind of clinic in an alien landscape, missing her father and her friends in Cincinnati and missing, missing, missing Ralph, who had rejected her so publicly and had, in some ways, put her where she was now, trying to expel or extract his baby from her body. Where were they all when she needed them? She just wanted someone to hold her hand, not these clinical instructions and bright cheery midwives and the excruciating scarlet pain.

Why, why had she involved herself in a mission of such questionable sanity, a whim of a middle-ranking enthusiast in naval intelligence, and now look at her – breathe, breathe and now: "PUSH! There's a good girl, now… yes, it's coming! It won't be long now. Ready…"

Once more, Xanthe had lost herself in the journey she had made through Berlin, on the night of Hitler's peace offer to the British, having fought with her ferocious Nazi acquaintance in her small room in Charlottenburg – and apparently struck him such an unusual blow to the head that she escaped intact. The process of giving birth had put her into a semi-conscious dream where she relived every step of her journey across the blacked-out city, and down Unter de Linden, finally to the American embassy and another long and exhausting ordeal. Like this one, this tearing birth, it had been fearful and largely alone.

She summoned up all her strength again for a great heave. She gritted her teeth, imagined she was gripping the bag with the Enigma rotor once again, as she had that fatal evening, about to whack her attacker over the head for the second time. Then she pushed…

The English wouldn't think this noise at all ladylike, she guessed as she groaned. But fuck them, she said, fuck them – SOD THEM ALL!

"There! The baby is out and, yes, you've got a little boy. Oh, and he's absolutely lovely."

Xanthe lay back, utterly drained, aware of the nurse bustling around with a pile of flesh in her arms. Would he look like Ralph, she wondered, too tired to find out?

"Do you want to hold him?" she heard the nurse say.

Xanthe ignored her, too exhausted to speak. She was not just physically exhausted, she was emotionally overloaded. She now had a son, for whom she was solely responsible, and – despite all British types wishing her all the best, as they put it, she was unsure what she was supposed to do now. Tied down in the prime of life. She had written to her father on the other side of the Atlantic, and begged his forgiveness for being pregnant for some months, without telling him – and explaining very little, and certainly not the full truth, that her lover had been in Berlin and had revealed himself as a Nazi rat and a traitor. Nobody seemed to tell the truth anymore, now that real war had taken hold – and she feared she only had a tenuous hold on the truth herself – and her beloved dad had sent no reply. Probably the U-boats had sent his loving letter to the bottom of the Atlantic. But whatever the reason was, she felt more alone than she had been in her life.

Then suddenly there was a burst of noise cutting into her reverie. The baby was crying, like a siren, and Xanthe emerged again into the present. She could hardly believe that out of her small and vulnerable body had come life. And now that it had done so, she felt the surge of an overwhelming need to protect it.

"Yes, yes, please, give him here."

She no longer cared what the nurse thought of her, another unmarried mother among so many, a raucous swearing American reporter – involved in goodness knows what. Just a bit loose, perhaps. Well, really, who gave a toss any more what people said.

Her experience in recent months, and especially as an undercover agent in wartime Berlin, had convinced her – personally and politically – that you could not just wait around for things to happen. You had to *act.* Well, it was time to act again, starting with holding onto the new life that her love for Ralph Lancing-Price had somehow managed to create, in the sickness of the Nazi capital.

The bundle of life, writhing a little, with its eyes closed, nestled into her, with a shock of untidy black hair and tiny fingers clutching at nothing. Xanthe's heart went out to him. She felt his future pain, so alone in the world, so young, he had hardly lived at all. And yet somehow she had agreed, hadn't she, and with some enthusiasm, to go back to the war.

But not now. She would call Commander Fleming as soon as she was up and about and would say that she could no longer help him. How could she leave her vulnerable, pitiable son, with his mewing and desperate hunger for the milk that was now filling her breasts?

From now on, she said, it was going to be somebody else's war. It was quite clear where her duty lay, and it had nothing to do with codes at all. The only code she was prepared to help crack was the one which would help her understand her newborn son and his needs. It was going to be difficult, it might even take a lifetime, but she was going to work it out.

*

She woke with a start and for a moment she thought she was back in Berlin, with the constant underlying threat and fear. Where was the baby?

She felt torn and bruised and exhausted beyond words. Her bottom hurt intensely. The fear was strong; what was she afraid of now? Had she dropped him already or rolled on him, or something awful? She looked around in the pale daylight, unsure what the time was, uncertain exactly where she was. The insipid April sunlight was falling across her face. There was the baby, asleep, next to the bed. She noted the good colour with a huge sense of relief. Yes, now she remembered where she was, at the nursing home in Bletchley. Yes, she had given birth. She now had a child to look after.

"Just for a few minutes," she heard the nurse explain firmly outside the door. "She's very tired."

There was a knock on her door.

She tried to say, "Come in," but almost nothing came out except for a kind of croak.

The door swung open slowly, and a small bunch of roses slid through, followed by a shy-looking man peering out from under his fringe.

Xanthe recovered her voice. "Alan! How lovely of you to come!"

"Well, you know…"

"No, it is lovely of you. I've no idea what the time is, but I know you ought to be doing something else. Well, something more important than seeing me."

As she lay there, the feeling of gratitude to Alan Turing, for remembering her, began to grow. Tears sparked in her eyes. Get a grip, Xanthe…

"Not at all. Um, these are from everyone in Hut Eight."

"They're beautiful, Alan. Maybe…"

The nurse had come in soundlessly behind him, like Jeeves, and swept the flowers up into a vase and fiddled with them expertly, before putting her head on one side to look critically at her arrangement and plonk them down next to Xanthe's bed.

"Is it a…?"

"It's a baby!"

They both laughed.

"No, it's a boy, of course."

"Why of course?" said Alan, always able to ask a question that melts away social niceties.

"I don't know. I always said it was going to be. Perhaps because of Ralph."

"You mean, because his father's a boy, then he has to be a boy? I hate to tell you this, Xanthe, but all babies have fathers – even the girls. Do you think we should tell him?"

"You mean, tell Ralph?" Xanthe lay back in exhaustion. She had forgotten that Alan was one of the very few people in on the secret. "Oh, let's worry about that another time, shall we?"

"Sorry," said Alan. "Not very tactful sometimes, um, I'm afraid."

"Nonsense, Alan. You're lovely. It's just that…"

She paused, searching for the right word.

"Just what? I'm usually the tongue-tied one, not you."

Come on, out with it, Xanthe…

"Well, I just feel sorry that I can't help you any more. I'm going to have to look after Indigo."

She indicated the bundle in a white shawl next to her bed.

"Indigo?"

"Yes, do you like it? I thought it went with my mood."

"Really?" said Alan, humming a bar or two of *Mood Indigo*. "I don't know, maybe. Um, maybe yes!"

"I have to look after him now, you do see that don't you? I know we had plans and stuff, but I just can't."

She felt tears pricking the back of her eyes. Why was she feeling so emotional at the moment? She hated to let Alan down, and everyone else who had been so supportive – but she could hardly let Indigo down either…

She hummed a little to herself.

Always get that Mood Indigo,
Since my baby said goodbye…

CHAPTER ONE

London, November 1940

Xanthe walked into the small office off Fleet Street, six months before the birth, through the torn newspapers of yesterday's editions, strewed across the alleyway. The windows were still broken from the raid a week before. The smell of burned brick dust and plaster hung in the air.

She had been working for the *New Yorker's* London office since her return from Germany, and there was a great deal to be done. There were letters to answer on behalf of Mollie Panter-Downes about her column. There was A. J. Liebling to cajole into writing something about Paris, though he was now back in New York, and there was her own writing as an anonymous correspondent. She had been lucky to get the job, organised again with a little word from Commander Fleming at the Admiralty.

Yes, she was pregnant – as the handful of rather dusty staff were beginning to notice as they looked up from their ancient Victorian desks – and getting more pregnant by the day, but she desperately wanted to keep her hand in. More than that, she guessed that her brief period as a *Chicago Tribune* reporter in Berlin had been somehow a little compromised. She had loved the work but feared that she would have to give up to give birth and would therefore crash out of the assignment, just as she had crashed out of Berlin. The name Xanthe Schneider was no longer useful in that respect, and she would now continue writing – on the rare occasions they gave her a byline – with the identity she had been given in Berlin.

So as far as the readers were concerned, she was Shirley Johnson, a former clerk in the US diplomatic service. Because of all that, she felt she still had things to prove as a journalist.

So when she was not chasing down details for Liebling or Panter-Downes, she had begun thinking up story ideas of her own, in the hope that it might impress Harold Ross, the proprietor of the *New Yorker*, enough that she might grace the pages alongside the names of Vladimir Nabokov, Dorothy Parker, James Thurber and E. B. White.

In search of a story, the strange English way of toilet paper had begun to fascinate her, especially during the crisis. And while the Blitz had begun, and London was thrilled to find itself besieged from the air, she began collecting anecdotes about how people wiped their bottoms in wartime and began thinking how to communicate this in an amusing way to her generally prudish fellow Americans.

In fact, toilet paper was getting increasingly scarce. People were reverting to using old newspapers cut into strips and hung in the loo – she was fascinated to see how often it was the *Daily Mirror* or the *Daily Sketch*. Failing that, there was always a roll of Bronco, shiny on one side, like wiping your bum with corrugated iron. "*Deluxe tissue*," it said, "*for the bigger wipe*."

The difficulty was writing it. It required a pen more deft than hers. She began to worry about it.

But by the time Xanthe had begun to grow and feel the baby kicking inside her, she had become adept at being a magazine sub-editor and writer, putting together or editing copy on her knees in Shepherd's Bush underground station, out of the sound of the bombs falling but with the sound of so many babies echoing in her head, wondering at the same time what it would be like to be responsible for a small human life at such a moment in history.

It was a peculiar but exhilarating life. The disapproval with which people saw a pregnant woman struggling into the wreckage from the raid the previous night surprised her, the way people avoided her eyes – perhaps for fear that, in the face of danger, they would become responsible for rescuing her. People behaved unusually once the raids had begun, with great fortitude but also great care. But it was thrilling too; one of those moments in life when you look back and realise that suddenly, and despite all the carping, bitterness and disagreements, and all the doubts and anger about how the nation around her had been treated by its leaders, everyone magically seems to be on the same side – pushing away useless official jobsworths, making do despite the mess.

It was heart-warming, if only she could relax into it.

It was just that she was nursing not only a dislocated relationship with her family back home – she had been getting the occasional clipped and disapproving letters from her father, though she had not had a reply to any of her letters telling him she was pregnant – but also a broken heart. She had loved Ralph, or so it seemed to her, with everything she had. Though they had only acknowledged this towards the end, and she now had to assume – since he had stormed off in a rage after the rejection of Hitler's peace offer – that he had not really loved her at all. It rendered the Blitz nights and the dogfights and the charred, dismembered bodies all the more difficult to bear, given that they were being delivered by Ralph's new friends and allies.

She knew she should not take the bombs personally, but sometimes it was hard not to. There were days when she felt so miserable that she could hardly force herself out of bed, except for the sheer exhilaration of the battle in the skies that was going on overhead. Then, one day, just as she was leaving her friend Moira's flat, she suddenly noticed a man who, in the bright sunlight of a Double British Summer Time, looked exactly like Ralph.

She stood there, staring, not sure what to do.

"I'm looking for Xanthe Schneider," said the apparition, who was in RAF uniform.

"Yes. I mean, that's me."

"Listen, I know this is an unfair question, but I'm on a mission for Lady Maidenhead – who, as you may know, is Ralph Lancing-Price's mother. I was wondering if I could be very cheeky and buy you a cup of tea? I'm his cousin Hugh, and you may be the only person I know who can help me."

Xanthe urged herself to keep her presence of mind.

"Really, why is that? I mean, how can I help?"

"Because I've been trying to find out where he is, on behalf of my aunt. I know that you knew him in London because I've talked to some friends of yours. I also know you have been a correspondent for the *Chicago Tribune* in Berlin and wondered if it was possible that you could confirm that he's there. We – the family I mean – think that's where he is, but nobody will tell us anything. Perhaps not surprisingly."

Xanthe's mind reeled. She could see how this man had managed to track her down from Simonetta College where she had been studying when she had met Ralph. She could see how he might have recognised her name in the *Chicago Tribune* and put two and two together. But, if so, it was a lucky shot. She dared not confirm too much.

"Listen, Hugh, I will certainly have a cup of tea with you, but I'm not sure I can go much beyond that. Yes, I knew Ralph in London before Dunkirk. As for the other rumours, I just don't know. And if I did know, I'm not sure I would be able to say."

Hugh stared for a moment, thinking and perhaps wrestling with himself.

"That's good enough for me," he said. "Have a cup of tea with me anyway. It's taken weeks just to find you."

Rather against her will, Xanthe found herself melting before this young man who looked so like the man she had loved.

"Are you a pilot? Where are you based?"

"Touché," said Hugh with a grin. "Careless talk, and all that… Sorry."

"Of course. Silly of me. Tell me, if you don't mind, what you know about Ralph. I was as surprised as anyone when he… when he disappeared. To start with, I wondered if he'd been detained under the law which arrested Mosley."

"No, he went before all that. Come with me and I'll explain."

They wandered up the Uxbridge Road. Xanthe noticed the looks of approval, even envy, as she walked alongside a man in RAF uniform, apparently next to his pregnant wife. That must have been what people must have assumed. It seemed poignant and touching. She saw people's eyes soften at the sight.

They sat down at a table at a Lyons' Corner House, and he told her how Ralph's distraught mother had begged him to find out where her son had gone and why. Ralph had left a letter behind him, telling her that he was going away and that he would see her soon, but not explaining when or why. She had assumed initially it was on some kind of mission for the British government, but there had been rumours of a former British minister in Berlin, and hurtful remarks passed by her neighbours in Marlow. The whole affair had upset her terribly. And she missed her son too.

"Ralph was always the apple of his mother's eye," said Hugh. Xanthe looked to see a hint of irony. The English middle classes seemed quite immune to any reluctance to use clichés, she thought.

Hugh had promised his aunt to help, but then the Blitz happened – was still happening – and his squadron was on the front line, and he had been too busy to do more than send a few letters. But Ralph's pocket diary had been left behind, and it had been found to include the name Xanthe Schneider, in an unknown handwriting – her own, she remembered. From there, it had been an easier journey, with help from a private investigator who had tracked her to her college in Cambridge, had turned up something about her crossword past, and from there, via her college friends, to Shepherd's Bush.

Xanthe found herself warming to this duty-bound young man and reminded herself not to be too helpful. It would hardly do to say where and when she had last seen Ralph. Certainly not that, at that very moment, she was carrying Ralph's baby.

"Sorry to go on about it, Miss Schneider, but I know you've been working in Berlin. I mean, can I ask? Did you happen to hear anything about him there?"

A surge of emotion went through her. Ralph suddenly seemed awfully close.

"Listen, Hugh. I can tell you I knew him in London. But I was in Berlin for a short time and I just can't help you with that one. I have wondered myself, many times, what has become of him."

That last sentence was so much the truth that it brought tears to her eyes.

Hugh looked disappointed.

"Very well then, can I ask you something else? When is the baby due? I hope you don't mind me mentioning it..."

Not for the first time, Xanthe was taken aback by the strange middle-class English reserve – as if noticing she was pregnant was somehow tantamount to asking how it happened. Indelicate.

"Is your husband… I meant, what does he do?"

"He *did*, I'm afraid. He's no longer with us."

It was her standard explanation. It was an all-too-common situation, especially with RAF wives.

"I'm so sorry. Was he in the RAF? Where was he based?"

Xanthe apologised. Now it was her turn to mumble something about careless talk.

Hugh reddened.

"Of course, of course."

"Listen, Hugh. I wish I could help you more. Can you let me know if you find out anything?"

She rose from the table.

"But you haven't even drunk your tea. I'm afraid I've upset you."

Xanthe was, it was true, afraid she was about to break down. The juxtaposition of this man, who looked so like Ralph but was not Ralph, at the same time as knowing herself to be carrying Ralph's child, was nearly too much for her. One day, one day, she told herself, I can tell this sweet man the truth. But not now, not given what she had been asked to do. Right now, the truth could only hurt both of them – all three of them…

She stumbled out and down the street, struggling towards Shepherds Bush. Hugh followed behind.

"Miss Schneider, I'm so sorry I upset you – may I see you again?"

She nodded, unsure what else to do, and then he was gone. She went back to the flat to weep on her pillow, where only the barrage balloon hanging outside the window could see, as she had done so many times before.

*

She cried herself to sleep, aware that so many real pregnant widows were doing the same, those who had not been stupid enough to fall in love with people with divided loyalties or people with doubts, or semi-fascists, as she had done. People who had not been there for her when she really needed them.

And yet, and yet, meeting Hugh, so like Ralph physically and yet not him, had made her imagine that she knew him after all. It had brought back some of her precious, overwhelming feelings for the man she had loved and lost and left behind.

The next morning, feeling bleary-eyed and exhausted, she had to force herself to go to work, because otherwise, she feared she would just stay in her bed until a bomb "with her name on it", as they said, fell, and that would have been that.

Then it was down to the Central Line, and out at Strand station, and then over towards Aldwych, a quick walk down towards the battered City, and into her office. There was Bob, rocking back on his chair, its legs bowing under his considerable weight.

"Hi, honey," said Bob. "You look like you haven't slept much. Was there a raid last night? I must have slept through it."

The *New Yorker* office was still preening itself on the success of Joe Liebling's articles, though Joe himself had now gone – first to Paris and then, via Lisbon, home to New York. That left Bob and sometimes Xanthe to man the office, plus the occasional grand arrival of Mollie Panter-Downes, up from Surrey for the afternoon.

"Say, what's up today, then Shirley?" Bob asked, since she was now using that as a pen name for anything she wrote.

"Blitz damage for Mollie," she said. It was always fact or atmosphere collecting for Mollie, for her to weave into her famous phrases – was it not Mollie who had coined the phrase "Phoney War"? All that seemed a little uncomfortable given that there was now nothing phoney about the war at all…

In fact, if she had seen the war from the point of view of Mollie Panter-Downes and the *New Yorker* office, she might have understood it all in a way different to how she understood it now. She might have imagined it to be a clash of civilisations, as Churchill's rhetoric suggested. She might have seen it as a huge battle between the Luftwaffe and the people of London and the other European cities. But actually, she was beginning to see it instead, as a clash between competing signalling systems, between coders and cryptographers. Because at weekends, she took the train down to Bletchley Park.

CHAPTER TWO

London, November 1940

On Friday afternoons, Xanthe would pack up the office, take a small holdall she had packed that morning and make her way to Euston Station, through the great classical arch, streaming in alongside all the Tommies and Jacks in their uniforms, and the Johnnies in the grey colour of the RAF.

It was astonishing, she thought to herself, how the status of the RAF had risen in just a few months. From the nearly men of Dunkirk, failing to protect the troops, they had become the semi-mystical "Few", the saviours of the nation, the fabulous weavers of a whole new wizard slang. Perhaps she should write about it.

From Euston, she took a train to Bletchley, usually along with a number of other dusty, nondescript academic types, who studiously ignored each other on the train, such was the secrecy of Station X.

She had begun going to Bletchley at Alan Turing's invitation, after her full debrief following the Berlin adventure – the Berlin debacle, she called it herself. Turing used to collect her from the station, but she had recently offered to take the bus, which deposited her along a leafy walk, now in the wintry last of the sunshine. It always invigorated her to wander up to one of the ugliest red-brick country houses she had ever seen, past the somewhat lax security of the gatehouse, showing her pass and identity papers. She was now recognised as a habitué and her entry was a little easier every time she made the journey.

Her understanding of Bletchley was extremely limited, and she believed that was a situation shared by most of the people who worked there, the crossword puzzle experts and linguists, the prep school German masters and the geographers and mathematicians. She had even met a seaweed expert – and most of them were kept willingly ignorant about anything that happened outside the orbit of their own huts, the rickety structures in the grounds, scaldingly hot in summer, freezing cold at this time of year.

Turing had welcomed her into Hut 8 and introduced her to most of the members, including Peter Twinn and Hugh Alexander.

"Can't you really tell them anything about why I'm here, Alan?" she asked him one afternoon. "I feel I stick out like a sore thumb."

"Well, you know…"

"I don't want them to feel like I'm an interloper."

"Interloper? We're all interlopers in one way or another. I stick out like your sore thumb too. Do you hear me complaining?"

They both laughed. They knew he complained rather a lot.

"We're all attached to a hut for no obvious reason. You're no exception. Everyone just assumes there's a highly secret reason why you're here," he said. "And there is!"

"Ok, I see. Fair enough."

"Security is so obsessive here, thanks to Old Man Denniston. Nobody comes here by accident. Everyone knows that."

"What about that man who's an expert in seaweed?"

Turing thought for a moment.

"Well, he's an exception, but he's still a valued part of the team. Actually, he dries out codebooks which have been thrown into the sea."

The truth was that Xanthe had serious doubts about whether or not she had the right to be included, despite what she had done or not done in Germany.

"Of course you're one of us," said Alan supportively. "You know about the Nazi codes in… um… practice."

"Well, I've killed a Nazi official with an Enigma rotor, if that's what you mean."

The relief of having one person she could talk to about her time in Berlin was absolutely invaluable. It was an extraordinary relief, in fact. Turing knew, as nobody else knew, apart, of course, from Fleming, who remained a somewhat aloof figure.

Turing and Xanthe swung through the rickety door of Hut 8.

"Here we are, teatime I think," he said. "Hold on! Which of you, b… b… buggers has taken my mug…?"

The handful of people in the hut, mostly men with wide trousers and relaxed weekend shirts, collapsed with laughter.

"Come on, Prof," said one of them. "Are we cryptographers or are we not? If someone padlocks their mug to the radiator, then we are duty bound to crack the code which holds it in place."

"Ok, where… where is it, then?"

"I've got it!"

A girl with dark hair and round glasses popped up from behind one of the screens with maps on, dividing the oceans into arbitrary sectors.

"How do you do," she said, shaking hands confidently with Xanthe. "I'm Joan. Welcome to our humble hut."

She smiled engagingly.

"I was just saying to Xanthe that it was, um… her hut, um… too," said Alan.

"Really, are you a linguist or a mathematician?"

There was a heartbeat of embarrassed silence. Those in Hut 8 or any of the other huts were not supposed to ask questions about each other.

"Oops, sorry!" said Joan, looking embarrassed. "New people are too intriguing!"

"None of those anyway," said Alan. "She works in the field."

"But not at the moment," said Xanthe, indicating her obvious pregnancy.

"Remember, careless talk," said Alan. "All we need to know from Xanthe is where she's lodging this time."

"Pfff. I hate it when you go all official…" said Joan, prodding him.

"I'm lodging in my usual digs in Bletchley, just near the cinema."

"Not Mrs West?"

"How did you know that?" said Xanthe laughing.

"We're paid to know things here," said Joan with a grin, putting her finger to her lips.

*

"You realise you know more about this stuff than the First Lord of the Admiralty," said Turing as they walked outside.

"I don't believe you."

"Really. He's a big trade unionist. And, after Lancing-Price, I think they make sure they tell their ministers nothing about codes."

Xanthe's eyes began to fill with unbidden tears.

"Oh, for goodness sake," she said, whipping out a hanky. "Sorry, Alan, you're quite right."

Turing stood, rooted to the spot in horror.

"I'm sorry, so… so sorry, Xanthe. I didn't, um, mean to… I mean…"

"Really honestly, Alan, I'm just being silly. I'm more hard-headed than that. I just can't stop weeping at the moment. I think it's the pregnancy or the baby, or maybe I was always a bit like that."

"I tell you what? Let's go to the cinema this evening. I'm coming to the end of my watch in about twenty minutes, then we can have a drink in the Eight Belles. They've got *Snow White* on again in town."

Xanthe breathed a deep sigh of relief that she was foreign and was therefore allowed the occasional emotional outburst. She wiped her eyes and suppressed the sad thoughts about the baby she was carrying, and what might have been. At least she no longer felt like she wanted to vomit all the time.

*

"It's just that we need to talk about your future," said Commander Fleming, looking sophisticated in his uniform with its gold, wavy stripes. That's why I've asked you to come in."

This was only the third time in her life that she had been in the ever more untidy, disorganised and crowded office in the Old Admiralty Building in Whitehall, the anteroom to the hub of naval intelligence, and from there to the small office with the bath again. Exactly the same, except that this time, Xanthe knew – because Alan had told her – that the bath had been used by Dilly Knox, now Alan's legendary boss, during the First World War to help him decipher the new ciphers used by the German navy. They were launched each day at midnight and, after hours in the hot water, Knox had more often than not thought through some kind of breakthrough. It was an extremely productive bath.

Xanthe had even met Knox, though he had been a somewhat aloof figure. She would have liked to have told him that, on this visit, there had been a spider in his bath, but she knew she wouldn't dare.

What a strange mixture I am, she said to herself. Brave enough to go stupidly to Berlin during a war, but not brave enough to banter with Dilly Knox.

But now, clearly, Fleming was waiting for some kind of response.

"I was trying not to make any decisions until the baby's been born," she said.

"I know, I know. Only there *is* a war going on and we do need to plan ahead a little."

Xanthe detected more than an edge of sarcasm.

"Listen, Xanthe. You have unique knowledge and some expertise, and I really don't want to waste you. Turing has, I gather, integrated you into the Station X set-up – though I had advised him not to. He's not a great one for obeying orders."

Xanthe felt a little weak. Why was he addressing her so? It wasn't as if she had really done a good job in Berlin.

Fleming stared unrelentingly at her. Then he reached a decision.

"All right. Let me just say this. I know you're working at some American magazine or other."

"The *New Yorker*."

"Good, good. And you're learning something about the way Enigma works. And if you're not, I've asked Turing if he can find someone to instruct you. That's all I want. Just to be ready. Because of the… after the… um… birth – is it possible we may ask you if you can help us again?"

"That's fine, Commander. Just as long as you understand I'm making no decisions now."

Fleming ignored her.

"Right, last thing I wanted to talk about. Where are you giving birth?"

"Well, I'm registered with a maternity clinic in Shepherd's Bush, but they've made it pretty plain that they don't think I should be in

London. At least, not with the Blitz going on – and it shows little sign of letting up, does it?"

"No, and I agree. That's why I have what I think is a somewhat unconventional solution. Not yet, but when the time comes, I've asked Dr Bush who is the senior medical officer at Station X whether he can accommodate you there. There are many medical staff there with training in obstetrics, I've made sure. There are so many unused bedrooms upstairs in the big house. I've asked Deniston's permission, and, well, actually he's not that pleased. But I anticipated no great opposition if Admiral Godfrey is behind it. And he is."

"Who's he?"

"He's my boss, the DNI. Director of Naval Intelligence. He was so keen that we accommodate you, I thought he was about to offer up his own flat in Curzon Street…"

"God, no!"

They both laughed, but Xanthe wondered what on earth he was talking about.

"I just thought you'd be more comfortable in the countryside and where the action is too. I know it sounds a bit odd. I'm not sure anyone has given birth there, but there's always a first time for everything!"

*

The days of sickness had given way as winter came, to a more elysian period of happiness for Xanthe. Having felt so guilty about feeling sad before, given what everyone else seemed to be going though, she now felt guilty about feeling a twinge of happiness – and for exactly the same reason.

She loved coming and going in Hut 8 and learning about the Enigma machine with a small working model that some of the Bletchley technicians had provided for her. She still felt something of a fraud – as if maybe she had been chosen for the role because of some misunderstanding about her crossword skills in her teens. But she felt at home there and sat for hours with Peter or Alan, thinking about the practicalities of using an Enigma machine, and what slivers of information they could glean from it.

"I know this is actually somebody else's business – how you actually use the darn thing is really down to Hut Six, but we need to think about it too."

And then there was the continuous ache in the back of her mind: the treachery of Ralph, and his rejection of her, so public and so cruel, and her father back home. She had heard nothing more from him, though she wrote every week. She knew the Atlantic was treacherous for things like mail, but she had sent so many, and she longed to hear from him – a small note of forgiveness would have transformed her life, but it didn't arrive.

At the end of the year, struggling to keep warm, she was given soap for Christmas, like everyone else. Bananas were now a distant memory, along with most imported fruits, like oranges.

From Hugh Lancing-Price, there was a small gift too, addressed to her room in Shepherd's Bush, and that turned out to be a bar of soap too. It was the kind of jocularity people appreciated at Christmas: intimate without being rude, personal without being impertinent. Hugh had become something of a friend. She saw him regularly, and he no longer asked her about Berlin, sensing perhaps that there was some constraint that prevented her speaking of it. But she told him about her work at the *New Yorker*. They laughed about her job, researching toilet paper.

"There's this stuff I found called 'Bronco for the Bigger Wipe'. Can you believe it?"

"Believe it – I've felt it! That's the stuff we've got on the base. 'Only the biggest wipes for the pilots,' said the squadron leader."

"The thing is, I now can't find any of it anywhere. There's stuff called Jeyes on sale, but it's like wiping your bottom with a piece of cardboard."

"Cardboard lined with razor blades! What do people use in your household – my aunt uses the *Daily Herald*, 'The Thinking Woman's Toilet Paper!'"

"Really, I think Moira's landlady buys the *News Chronicle*."

It was a few days after Christmas and Hugh had to go back on duty.

"You know, old thing, I worry about you," he said. "Who is looking after you these days?"

Xanthe could not tell him the truth: that she appeared to have been adopted by the academics of Hut 8 and much of the Naval Intelligence Division."

"That's nice of you, Hugh. How is Ralph's mother, I mean your aunt?"

"Well, not too good actually. She says she's always cold. She's been bombarding Churchill with letters demanding him to supply her with coal. I was wondering, would you like me to ask her if she would give you somewhere to stay outside London, I mean when..."

He tailed off. It really was extraordinary, the English sensibility, she said to herself. They would happily have a good laugh about toilet paper but then, when things really matter, that involve less everyday bodily functions, like giving birth – they became all tongue-tied.

Then it struck her. Had Hugh guessed something? Was he really suggesting that she move in with someone he'd guessed was the baby's grandmother?

"That's so kind, Hugh. But I'm fine, really. Keep safe, won't you?"

They said goodbye. He took the train down to Biggin Hill to carry on the war. She hurried back to her office to meet Bob and answer more letters addressed to Mollie Panter-Downes.

She was sad to see Hugh go. She was finding walking more difficult now, but the buses were so cramped. There were few, if any, taxis, even if she could have afforded one. As she slogged up the Embankment, looking at the barrage balloons hanging over the Thames and the anti-aircraft battery opposite parliament, she sent a small and tentative prayer for Hugh. "God keep him safe," she said and closed her eyes for a moment.

When she opened them again, she told herself that on no account was she to fall in love with another member of the Lancing-Price family. She just could not. Still, there was something so heroic about Hugh – he had his cousin's looks, but none of his cynicism.

God, keep him safe, she prayed again.

*

Easter was late in 1941 so it was not until Palm Sunday, in the pale April light, that she packed her few belongings and took the almost empty train from Euston to Bletchley Station. She was met by Turing, who accompanied her on the bus through green lanes, bursting with spring, to Bletchley Park. There was the usual charade on the gates with the security guards.

Nervously, as if he was accompanying her to her own execution, Turing led her up to the big front door, where she had not ventured before, and up the stairs. On the first floor, there was a welcoming "halloo", and a large lady of uncertain age, dressed as a nurse, bounded down the corridor towards her like a starched Labrador.

"Hello, hello! You must be Mrs Schneider, our patient. So good to see you, my dear. Let me show you to your room. It's on the sunny side of the house; I do hope that's all right, and you won't get too hot. I know what it's like, well, when you're in that condition..."

"I don't really think of myself as a patient," said Xanthe, smiling. "I'm just having a baby."

"Well, of course you are. Such a silly phrase. That is to say, Mrs Schneider…"

"Oh. please call me, Xanthe."

"Of course – Nancy, so much better!"

*

Xanthe sat on the iron bed frame and the counterpane and looked out at the lawn, where the first games of rounders of the year were taking place. She felt enormous and nervous too about what was coming out of her, and how it was going to get out. She felt very alone. If only her dad could be there or some of her friends from home. Yet again, she wondered a little how she had become mixed up with the affairs of nations that were not her own. Still, that was what had happened and, assuming all went well in the next week or so, that was it. She was going to be a mom…

There was a knock on the door.

"Come in!"

"Could I, um, that is to say, would you…?"

"Alan! Lovely to see you. Where have you been for the last few days?"

"Well, the truth is Xanthe, that we have had something of a coup. I'm not allowed to say much about it, but we have been able to get hold of a codebook and it is yielding fruit. In fact, here it is…"

He produced a crumpled document. "I thought you would like to see it."

It said: "*Schlüsseltaeln M-Allgemein 'Heimische Gewässer' Kennwort HAU. Prufnummer 1566.*"

"So there we are," he said, with the air of a man who had finished his Cambridge tripos. "It's the home waters settings for naval Enigma for February. Can't tell you where we got it. I want to be as honest as I, um, can. We mightn't have got here without your help in Berlin, but we are not hopeless. We are getting there, what with my *bombes* and all."

She racked her brains.

"Oh you know, Xanthe, the machine I showed you that time?"

Xanthe racked her brains again. "Does this mean you can read naval Enigma signals now?"

"Oh no," he said dismissively. "Long way to go, even with the bombes doing most of the heavy lifting. No. Long way still, but we have been able to decrypt a few from earlier in the month!"

He perked up a little.

"We've also got a plan. Again, can't say much about it but it involves using the codes we *can* crack to take a shot at the naval codes. It's worth a try, and one day, I'll tell all."

Xanthe was fascinated but knew better than to ask.

"And I've got more news too," said Turing, turning a little red. "I'm engaged!"

"You're what? Alan, that's amazing – wonderful. I'd just been thinking what a good father you would be..."

There was just a hint of irritation that Xanthe was suddenly aware of. Was it jealousy? Surely not. She really liked Alan, yet somehow there was a spark missing. Yet, also – well, she didn't know.

"To Joan."

"That's wonderful news. She's absolutely lovely. So why," said Xanthe, realising that this was no conventional conversation, "do you look so miserable about it? Have you changed your mind?"

"No, um, that is to say, I was to ask, er, Xanthe. I know this isn't a good moment and you've only just arrived and all that, but I need your advice. You see, you and Joan, and my mother, of course – but I can hardly talk to her about this – are the only women I know at all. I don't really know what to do."

"Well," said Xanthe, a little embarrassed. "I don't know if I can help with this. Despite appearances, I'm not really the woman of the world I seem."

She gestured towards her huge bump, which seemed to swell further moment by moment. Alan guffawed.

"I don't mean *that*. I mean something else."

"Then, sit down, Alan, and tell me. You're making me nervous. Of course, I'll help if I can."

Alan sat on the end of the bed.

"Well, the thing is. I don't want to shock you or anything, but… well, I like men. I know I've sort of said this to you before. I prefer men, I mean, you understand. You *do* understand?"

Xanthe stared. Did she understand? What was he trying to tell her?

"You mean you're a – you mean you're homosexual? Or do you mean you *don't* like women? There's a big difference, isn't there?"

"Right, right. Here's the thing, Xanthe. I like men. I like their bodies. I feel excited by them. I've hardly told anyone this, and I know I'm supposed to be ashamed of it and that it's illegal – and especially in the armed forces. Did I tell you I joined the Home Guard, by the way? But I'm not. I'm not at all ashamed. It's just the way I am. Some people like beans on toast, I like sleeping with men. It's that simple really. But it isn't easy; it means I have to be very careful what I say to people, and if I want to sleep with them. I sometimes need to find a kind of code so that they'll only understand me if they already see things my way. Then sometimes they get cross, but sometimes, well, it's the start of a wonderful night. Not very often though. I told Joan, well, some of this, and she says she doesn't mind. But what do you think? Can a man who likes men marry a woman? What do you think?"

It was a longer speech than she had ever heard from Turing before. It was heartfelt and she noticed that his distinctive stammer disappeared completely when he was speaking from the heart.

"Listen, Alan. Do you love her? Do you love Joan?"

"Yes."

"I mean have you, I mean, have you have kissed her and stuff?"

"Of course."

"And what did that feel like?"

"Good."

"Well, what I think is this. If liking men gets in the way of liking women, then you can't marry her. But if you love her and you want to sleep with her, then there's no reason why you can't be together. And you do, don't you?"

Turing smiled nervously, Xanthe thought.

"Well, I think so…"

"Are you sure?" she said coaxingly. "Well, I can't think of anyone better you could make a life with. I mean, everyone, or nearly everyone, has feelings for their own sex at some point. I certainly have – though I never actually… well, you know…"

She found her mind drifting back some years to a night after a dance back home, holding hands with her friend Pearl, and the powerful feelings of longing, which horrified her at the time.

"Thank you, Xanthe. For your advice."

"I don't seem to have cheered you up much."

"It's just that – I've got a bit of thinking to do, haven't I…"

CHAPTER THREE

Bletchley Park, April 1941

"I'm so sorry, Commander, but that's what I've decided. I have responsibilities now. I simply can't leave my baby after all we've been through together. He's got no father, and I just can't contemplate the idea that he would also have no mother – even for a little while. I can't go abroad again. How can I?"

Commander Fleming looked irritated at this first interview since the birth of Indigo Schneider. She had toyed with the idea of calling him Ralph, after his father. But she imagined that Fleming might say it was a security risk.

"I don't mean you'd have to go *now*," said Fleming with a tetchy edge to his voice. "I mean when you've recovered. In a few months' time perhaps."

"I've got nothing to recover from," said Xanthe, suddenly irritated herself. "For God's sake, I've just had a baby. It's perfectly natural. Yes, I was one of your operational people, and wasn't very good at it, and now I'm a mother. I know there's a war on and all that. But I just can't."

Fleming pursed his lips as if about to say something.

"Mmm," he said. "Pity. Well, I can understand what you're saying. Turing and Twinn and the others tell me you're an invaluable member of their team. You could just stay."

Xanthe began to feel tired. It sapped her energy to resist Fleming's will.

"I'm afraid they're being kind. I don't think I'm being any help at all. I would go back to London, but I don't have anywhere to go and I don't have any money. But the *New Yorker* says I can come back as soon as I'm able."

"Ok fine," said Fleming with deliberate resolution. "It's just that I have a scheme that might just appeal to you and would certainly suit your skills. Let me just leave that idea with you, ok?"

And with that he picked up his white cap, and, with a formal bow, he left though the door in one deft move and returned to Whitehall. Xanthe was left alone in Bletchley.

*

Except, of course, that however isolated she might have felt, she was certainly not alone. And it was really rather peculiar, that wartime, youthful, unofficial spirit of Bletchley, now that hundreds of staff had converged there from all different walks of life: the dusty geographers, dustier mathematicians, who together were busily shaping a culture that combined obsessive secrecy with fun. Even Xanthe enjoyed the occasional game of rounders, in the early summer sunshine on the front lawn, and the endless amateur dramatics at Christmas. They knew not to ask each other what they actually did behind the rickety walls of their huts. So the appearance of a young woman, with blonde hair and her blonde baby, on the lawn on the sunny end of April 1941 – as battle raged in Greece and Yugoslavia – may have raised eyebrows but no questions.

Nor was it true that she was as decided as she had told Fleming. The truth was that she was still in constant pain, from stitches after the birth and in her breasts, which seemed to be coming to terms – rather agonisingly – with the idea that they would not be used for the purpose they were designed for, as the nurses had decided that Indigo would be fed by bottle. She was seeping from top and bottom and kept up so much in the night, that she had moments when she feared she hated the baby, though she recovered as soon as it was light. She dreaded the little air-raid siren she had given birth to and was aware that there was no relief of an "all clear", except a blessed silence, which she filled with her fears about herself and her future.

Despite the staff taking both mother and baby to their hearts, Xanthe was still teetering on the edge of loneliness and misery. But as Indigo grew stronger in the weeks after his birth, she began to take him out in an old-fashioned perambulator, lent by Sister Agnes, the nurse Xanthe knew originally as The Labrador, down the country lanes and to the various pubs to meet Alan and Joan, and whoever else happened to be around.

Both were busy a great deal. It was an exciting time, though they did not say – and were not asked – the reason was that there were now six of Turing's bombe machines chuntering through the clues, until they turned up a possible match. At any moment a missed convoy, or a botched capture, or leak might lead to the Nazis developing new systems which would be beyond the limited capabilities of the bombes. Thanks to the capture of codebooks for March, they were now very close to a solution to naval Enigma. They could also now read much of the Italian naval signalling and the Luftwaffe version.

Indy's first outing, wearing a little hat to keep out the sunshine, happened to coincide with the visit of Admiral Cunningham to thank the girls of Hut 6 for their help in his defeat of the Italian fleet at Matapan, back in March.

"Who is that guy?" asked Xanthe.

"He's the commander-in-chief of the Mediterranean fleet," said Alan. "We just won his battle for him."

"So why are they bullying him?"

She watched as the Wrens mobbed the admiral slightly, until he edged back with his beautiful blue uniform onto a newly whitewashed fence. It caused a great deal of secretive laughter at this jape.

She had ventured out because the week before, she had exchanged letters with Hugh, and they had agreed to meet for a drink, when he came on leave, at the Eight Belles pub, which was an easy walk but still sufficiently far from Bletchley Park. She had, and would, tell him nothing about why she was so far from London. Giving birth seemed to be explanation enough.

Then, suddenly, there he was. He stood and waved at her as she came into the garden, wheeling the pram awkwardly round the garden furniture.

"Xanthe and – what's his name?" said Hugh with triumph. "I've got a little present."

He reached into his knapsack and produced a small toy dog.

"It's off ration, you know…"

"Oh Hugh, you're a darling. He'll love it. Thank you so much, and thank you for coming…"

Hugh was peering nervously into the pram.

"He's absolutely beautiful, like his mother. Xanthe, you've never told me about your – his father. Might I have known him in the RAF, do you think?"

An overwhelming feeling of guilt passed through her.

"I'm sorry, Hugh. I will tell you all about it one day, but not now. Do you mind?"

"Of course not. It's lovely to see you."

An elderly lady went past, beaming at them.

"May I just have a little peek?" she asked. She looked up at Hugh and back down at Indigo. "The baby looks so like his father," she said, patting him on the arm of his grey uniform. He burst out laughing.

*

"That's it. The *Bismarck*."

Xanthe had been surprised by the unexpected arrival in her room of Commander Fleming, one Sunday afternoon. He was carrying a file which turned out to contain some aerial photographs.

"What? That long, cigar-shaped thing? Where is it?"

"You should recognise it, Xanthe. You told me you'd been there. That's Kiel Harbour. This was taken by a reconnaissance plane a couple of weeks ago, but it shows just how big she is."

She felt good being the object of attention, despite her very obvious retirement. It made her feel useful.

"I see what you mean. I was on a battlecruiser called *Gneisenau*, which seemed huge. Is it as big as that?"

Fleming sniggered a little, like a man in the know.

"Bigger by a long way, *Gneisenau* is thirty thousand tons, *Bismarck* is forty thousand tons plus. A third as much again."

"Ok. I understand," said Xanthe, cutting to the chase. "I'm not sure why you're showing me this. I've told you I'm not available for one of your escapades. Not while I've got Indigo to bring up."

"Right, right, message received and understood. I thought you'd be interested. I've already earmarked this for somebody else."

"Really? Who?" she said, feeling a little defensive that she was so easily replaced.

Fleming picked up the shift in tone and laughed.

"Come on now, Xanthe You can't expect me to shut up shop just because my star operative is otherwise engaged in being a mother."

"Hardly a star… But still, I don't see why you're telling me that."

Fleming thought for a moment.

"I suppose because I can, and just in case. You never know. Now, listen – here's the problem. *Bismarck*, when she sails, which is going to be sometime in the early summer or late spring, is going to play absolute havoc among the convoys. It means we'll have to provide at least two capital ships for each convoy in the Atlantic and that means – even if we had enough, which we don't – no more Home Fleet. It is an absolute crisis. Of course, we need to know where she's going, and that's unlikely to be forthcoming, but, above everything, we need to know *when* she's planning to sail. And we still can't read more than an occasional naval signal, as you know."

Fleming opened his file and brought out an artist's impression of what Hitler's fearsome surface raider looked like, with eight fifteen-inch guns and bristling with other weapons.

"See what I mean? If we could read naval Enigma signals, we would know, and we could be ready before she reaches the Atlantic shipping lanes. But we can't and we don't."

Despite herself, Xanthe could not resist the question.

"So what are you planning to do?"

"Well, here's the point, and this is where you come in – I mean me, of course."

Xanthe decided to grin knowingly.

"We can read Luftwaffe Enigma signals, and there are some remarkably garrulous Luftwaffe generals who seem to ask questions which they really shouldn't. So, here's the plan. You know how to operate Enigma, and there are only a handful of people who can – nearly all of them are here at Bletchley. We will use the Luftwaffe code to send a message in the name of a particularly pushy general and ask the basic question – when does *Bismarck* sail? Clever huh…"

Xanthe was staggered.

"You're insane. This could put everything at risk. If it fails, and they work out what's happened, they'll change the Luftwaffe code and then where would you be?"

Fleming walked around the room and stared out of the window, down at the lawn.

"I know, I know – though it's a good deal less insane than some of our recent capers. You're right that there are a couple of important complications."

Xanthe was now sitting on the edge of her bed. She put the baby down, now that he was sleeping.

"I can't believe you've had permission to tell me this. Why are you telling me if you don't expect me to go?"

Once again, Fleming dismissed the question with a wave of the hand. They both stared together towards Indy's cot for a moment, like proud parents. Then Fleming moved back to gaze at the view of the trees, bushes and huts higgledy-piggledy across what had once been formal gardens.

Xanthe felt aware of the outside world again, and fearful of leaving it behind – of withdrawing into seclusion, to be a single mother, alone while the war was fought on without her. Something about the arrival of the impatient Fleming had made her regard the world of nappies, drying on the line, as even more of a threat – drawing her in inexorably until, well, when? Until she was past it and thirty or obese, or all three? And stuck in a room like this one, on the edge of things and events.

She pulled herself together. No. The answer was still no. She knew where her duty lay.

"There are two complications to this plan," Fleming was saying. "The first is that we have to send the message near where the general actually is, otherwise their direction-finding equipment will pick up that it has come from somewhere else – and that would be that."

"You mean, someone has to go to Germany…?"

"Maybe, and the second issue is that we have to use the right Enigma settings for the day."

"Wowsie," said Xanthe. "How would you do that? Well, I can't go to Germany again. That's for certain."

"Ah well," said Fleming, clearly sensing a sort of victory, and making a deft twist out of the room. "Perhaps Greece? My lips are sealed."

And with that, he was gone again.

*

She thought about the *Bismarck* a great deal in the week that followed. At night, she felt she could hear its horn hooting deep beyond deep, in the darkness. This great lowering beast, awaiting the moment when it was to be loosed on the world. Fleming had certainly had an impact. He knew something of psychology, that man, and he also seemed to be prepared to use it – which Xanthe supposed made him a good intelligence officer. Except, of course, that Fleming hardly seemed to leave his desk, apart from the occasional jaunt to Bletchley or Lisbon.

But it sounded as if this uniquely dangerous ship would be leaving soon anyway, and she would miss out on the excitement. And then there was Indigo, whom she loved with an absolutely fierce determination. Nothing was going to get in the way of that. Indy needed her, and although the world might explode in her absence, she knew what came first. What worried her more than the voyage of the *Bismarck*, or naval intelligence, or her career at the *New Yorker* and certainly more than her correspondence for Mollie Panter-Downes, was Indy's paternity.

She felt deeply responsible for her failure to provide him with a father. It was always possible that Ralph would return, chastened and defeated. It was also possible that he would come back to England as a conquering *gauleiter*. But both possibilities seemed increasingly unlikely, and Hitler had so far failed to organise any kind of credible invasion.

She had begun to wonder at what point she might be able to confide in Hugh about Indigo's father. She knew she was bound by the most ferocious oath of secrecy, which all those around her at Bletchley took extremely seriously, but there would come a time when she might be able to tell – at least about Ralph.

She had also begun to long for her own father, so far away in Cincinnati and glued to the wireless and the newspaper for news from London, engrossed in a way that Londoners quite failed to be themselves. Alan and Hugh and her other new friends were lovely and supportive, but they were not family. She had produced a child, she had become a family herself, but that just heightened her sense of isolation and her need for emotional support. She felt alone and vulnerable. The Blitz was heating up again on London, but she needed somewhere to belong.

Camping out at Bletchley Park was hardly a permanent solution, despite the kindness of Sister Agnes. She would have to go somewhere quiet, maybe in the north – but who would talk to her and who would pay? The Bletchley canteen would not be open to her forever and, once she had definitely stepped back from whatever role she had been assigned in Commander Fleming's strange world – when she was in no sense part of the Naval Intelligence Division – that source of pay and sustenance would be closed to her too.

She agreed to meet Hugh Lancing-Price during a brief slot he had, a rare day off, when she went up to London, as promised, to see her employers off Fleet Street. She and Hugh met at a Lyon's Corner House in Trafalgar Square, with the lions mothballed for the war, under huge advertising hoardings for war bonds.

"How are you getting on?" he asked her and, to both of their great surprise, she burst into tears.

"I'm sorry, I'm so sorry," she said, wiping her eyes. "It's the first time I've left Indy. Sister Agnes is good at wielding a bottle, but even so – well, you know."

"Listen, I know what's worrying you. And I'm going to help, if I can – if I survive, and I'm feeling more confident that I'm going to. It's nearly a year since Dunkirk, after all. What's the date today? May the ninth? Yup, things are going well and, if they're not going so well for you, then I am going to step in to help…"

"I don't see how you can, Hugh."

For the first time since Berlin, she felt like folding herself into someone's arms.

"Oh, I can, you'll see," he said munching most of his butter ration for the week in one mouthful of scone. "I'll write to you when I get back."

*

Something about the meeting cheered her enormously. She wasn't sure why – Hugh had hardly explained himself, but perhaps it was that, for the first time in so many months, she felt loved. Also his sheer optimism – perhaps it ran in the Lancing-Price genes. She walked with a spring in her step after she left him, down the Strand, past the battered Savoy Hotel, where she had first met Ralph. It was a beautiful day, and even the London dust and the bomb sites seemed to be smiling a little.

She did not analyse what Hugh had said, nor really what he meant. It was obvious that he had spoken from the heart about some scheme he had to support her, that was drawn from love, not from some calculation about the costs and benefits, economic or social.

She walked a little more confidently to meet Bob, in the *New Yorker* office – a glorified coalhole, as he put it, near the Bank of England.

"So where's the baby?" he said. "I can't believe you came all this way – where are you staying now? – without bringing the baby in to see his Uncle Bob."

"Sorry, Bob. I couldn't bring him on the train really, could I? I'm not sure that the Blitz is the right place for a baby. Certainly not *my* baby," she added defensively.

"Quite right, honey. Quite right. Now the old man in New York's not so keen on the toilet paper piece. Says the idea's disgusting – but liked the way you wrote it."

"Who?" said Xanthe, suddenly confused.

"You know? The proprietor! Ross. And he'd like you to do another. From Greece."

"From Greece? Why from Greece?"

Xanthe's head was spinning. This was unexpected.

"Well, to be frank, I don't rightly know. Because it used to be his policy, once a girl has had a baby, to say bye-bye and thanks. But I've noticed it's changed here now there's a war on. There was never an editor quite so conservative as Ross, but blow me if he hasn't changed too."

"Yes, but Greece? The Nazis invaded there a few weeks back. It's a war zone."

"Sure it is, but we don't have Liebling in Europe anymore and we want something more... I dunno... punchy!"

Something about this offer bothered Xanthe, but she found it hard to put her finger on exactly what.

"Well, it's too kind of him to ask me, I sure am grateful for the offer, but – as you say – I've got a young child to look after now. I'd love to be able to help – and I really mean that – but I just can't."

*

It was only later, as she walked back along the Victoria Embankment towards the underground station, that she began to wonder about Greece. The fingerprints of Fleming were all over this. Greece – that was where he mentioned sending the fake Enigma signals from. That was the place, wasn't it? She was being manipulated into going. That was all there was to it.

On an impulse, she turned left into Whitehall and headed for the Admiralty, past the Home Guard units guarding the ancient doors, and the piles of sandbags.

"Can I speak to Commander Ian Fleming? I've come a long way."

"I'm sorry, miss. Commander Fleming is at sea."

A powerful sense of disappointment gripped her, then frustrated rage. That was their standard response to women or lovers or fiancées, she bet her bottom dollar.

"Could you please tell him, immediately please, that Xanthe Schneider is here to see him?"

She looked fiercely and steadily at the doorman. Wordlessly, and without looking up, the elderly man on the desk gave a message to what looked like a boy scout, who wandered off down the darkened passageways.

Only a few minutes later, an unkempt young man in RNVR uniform arrived and asked her to follow. Once again, she was showed into the room with the bath and, five minutes or so later, the door burst open and Fleming appeared.

"You're too late! Too late!" he chanted. "We go tonight."

Xanthe forgot her rage immediately, and just felt a sense of loss.

"To Greece?"

"Yes, of course to Greece. I hear you've had your job offer. Greece is the place because everything is up in the air there. It's in chaos, as you might expect. Nobody has time for correct procedures; nobody really notices or expects anything. Most of our forces have withdrawn to Crete, and our Luftwaffe man is in Athens. So, yes, Greece it is!"

He must have detected how deflated she felt because he looked suddenly kinder and opened his folder on the desk.

"Have a look at this, if you'd be interested."

Fleming unveiled another couple of aerial photographs.

"Here we are. There's the picture I showed you a couple of weeks ago, with *Bismarck* next to the dockside. Here she is two days ago at anchor in the middle of the harbour. It is time, or nearly time, but we need to know exactly when. Our man is about to fly out, heading for an island off the Greek coast, where he will go on to Athens to meet one of our radio operators. Then hey presto! The game is truly afoot, as they say."

His excitement was almost physical. It was also infectious.

"Now, come with me, Xanthe," he said, high with adrenalin. "I've got some people you're going to meet."

He shepherded her into the corridor and through some more doors, past uniformed young men and women carrying piles of papers.

"Xanthe Schneider, this is Captain Winn, who runs the submarine tracking room. Xanthe is a journalist for the *New Yorker*, researching how we are fighting the Battle of the Atlantic. That's right, isn't it, Xanthe? The 'Battle of the Atlantic'? That's our new phrase, courtesy of Mr Churchill."

Xanthe was taken from room to room, through the strange Georgian building and out into the Citadel and the bombproof structures underneath it, meeting people, nodding, smiling and shaking hands. She felt a little like royalty.

By the time she was back outside in Whitehall, it was evening, and time to meet Moira in Euston. She felt absolutely drained but also buoyed up that Hugh Lancing-Price had been so supportive and that there was a job offer waiting for her if she chose to accept it. Which she had no intention of doing.

It was dark as she boarded the Bletchley train and she laid her head back. As the train drew out, she heard the platform announcement that a raid was in progress. Strange that she had heard no siren. The usual procedure was to run the train slowly through the area where the raid was taking place, reducing the risk of sparks that might be visible from the air, and hope for the best. The train slowed. There was a palpable rising of the temperature and people studiously closed their eyes in the blacked-out carriages.

Some minutes later, and in the distance, she could hear the muffled thuds that were probably explosions. They appeared to be driving towards it. There was one explosion that seemed to kick the carriage and then no more, as the train picked up speed and they knew they were out of the worst, but the thuds continued in the distance. Who was getting it? The tiny *New Yorker* office? Fleming at the Admiralty? Moira, heading home on the crowded underground to Shepherds Bush? She couldn't know. It was pointless trying to imagine, and it certainly didn't help her peace of mind. All she could do was to get home safely to Indy.

*

Hugh's promised letter failed to arrive the next morning. Nor did he call in the evening, as he had promised to try to do. Perhaps that was hardly surprising. Trunk calls were getting increasingly difficult, so she tried not to be disappointed. The news was full of the devastating raid on Westminster and the destruction of the House of Commons. They obviously felt this was not news that could be censored.

It was at teatime the following day, that she was asked to go downstairs because a friend was on the telephone. But Hugh's voice was not on the end.

"Is that Xanthe Schneider?"

"Speaking," she said.

"I'm sorry to telephone you out of the blue. My name is Tug Roberts. I'm a friend of Hugh Lancing-Price…"

"Oh God," said Xanthe. "No… not Hugh!"

"I found a note by him in his diary with your telephone number, and I thought the only way I could reach you was this. I'm afraid I have bad news."

How many times has he had to have conversations like this, she wondered?

"Might he be a prisoner?" she said, clutching at straws.

"I'm afraid not. He was killed in the raid on London. He helped to carry a child in Westminster out of a burning house. I gather he would have been given a medal."

"Why do you say 'would' have?"

"I believe they're a bit reluctant to give out posthumous medals. It's not considered good for morale. I think that's pretty crazy. He was a lovely man and, as I say, my friend too. I'm ever so sorry. He spoke of you many times."

"He did? What did he say?"

"He… well, he said he loved you. I hope you don't mind me saying."

Xanthe stifled a sob.

"He never told me. I'm very grateful to you, Tug, for having the courage to tell me."

*

As she pushed Indigo around the lawn the next day, in his pram, she felt overwhelmed with rage – first with Hugh for being so careless with his life, for not telling her what he felt – and then with herself for not telling *him*, well, anything much about herself.

By the time she had finished a lap of the garden in the sunshine, the rage had turned against the Nazis. For killing the kindest of her friends. For keeping her from her father. For the deaths of so many, every day, and children too, from one side of Europe to the other. She realised this was an anger she felt, not despite the baby but because of him. It was on Indigo's behalf. So, yes, she said to herself. Yes, for Indy's sake – so that he might not take his turn as a Nazi victim one day – she would, if necessary, go back on active service. Next time, she would accept Fleming's offer – if there was a next time – and she would go.

She was not English. She felt so different from them in their cold and damp. She was not, and never would be, one of them. But this had become her war, and she felt she could no longer carry on as if she could opt out. If Fleming felt she had special knowledge or abilities which made her vital, then she would just have to use them.

*

That night was another tough one. Indy would not sleep. Time and time again she thought she was able finally to drift off, only for the siren to begin. So when she got downstairs in the red-brick pile which was still all she had as a home, and Fleming was waiting for her, she had practically made up her mind, exhausted though she was.

"Xanthe, I'm sorry. But I have to make one last request to you," he said.

"How strange. I was just thinking about you. What happened to your man? I assume that's why you're here?"

Fleming looked embarrassed, just for a split second, but she caught it.

"Appendicitis on the plane out. I mean, not his fault and all that. But what can we do? We want to go ahead if we possibly can, but we have nobody else who really understands Enigma. Might you… possibly go? It will be a fortnight tops and you'll be back here."

"Two weeks? You promise? I only gave birth six weeks ago for God's sake…"

"Of course, I can't promise, but that's what we are planning for. Really."

The decision seemed suddenly obvious. She wondered fleetingly if her real reason was because she was so miserable, but she dismissed the idea.

"Ok. Ok, Ian. You've worn me down. For Indy's sake, and if you promise, solemnly, to look after him if anything happens to me, and we can have some kind of contract along those lines between us, then I'll go. So many people are having to leave their children to fight, so why not me? Yes, I'll go, dammit, I'll go."

A wide smile of surprise and delight had crept across Fleming's face.

"I was hoping you would say that. I have a car waiting and promise to have you back in that fortnight…"

"And you'll write a proper contract about Indy."

"I promise. I'll be his guardian – but you'll be fine and back with him before the end of the month. Welcome to Operation Snow in Ibiza."

CHAPTER FOUR

Aegina, May 1941

When Xanthe stepped, in her bare feet, carrying her shoes, up the beach of the island of Aegina, it was the middle of the night. It smelled of figs.

"Good luck, ma'am," said the blacked-up sailor, who had rowed her over, in a stage whisper.

"Thanks, Steve, bye!" she whispered back.

There was a house ahead of her, visible against the night skyline. Xanthe walked over the rocks, onto the edge of a small beach, and behind a bush. She cleaned the camouflage off her face, put on her shoes and sat, waiting for the sun to rise. She would not know exactly where she was until there was more light.

There was a sudden crack to her left. She froze, then ducked down behind a boulder. The last thing she wanted to do was get caught with her replica Enigma machine in pieces. It was one of a number which Hut 8 had used to work out the wiring of the real ones. The pieces looked more like incongruous, ill-fitting pieces of old typewriters, but you couldn't risk it, could you?

The crack turned into rustling, which in turn came close enough for her to hear a kind of saliva-swilling sound, accompanied by grunting. It was a goat, feeding on the olive trees. She relaxed, and the light began to seep into the sky.

Xanthe had been promised that they were sending her to Aegina because the German invaders had not arrived there yet, but as the sun began to peep over the horizon behind her, there was an almost continuous buzz of planes overhead – on their way southwards. If the Nazis had shifted their assault onto the retreating British in Crete, that would make her doubt some of the assurances she had been given in London.

She had set out only four days before, in a converted bomber with extra fuel tanks and some senior civil servants, heading for the besieged island of Malta. She felt sick and desperately unimportant. Nobody took any notice of her. She ached for Indigo and bitterly regretted her decision to take this gamble – for what? Not for these supercilious types, that was for sure. She tried to keep her tears a secret, but nobody even looked. Her stitches ached, her breasts seemed to have rediscovered the impulse to manufacture milk, and she felt exhausted and uncomfortable. Her body yearned for the baby.

There was hardly time to see the rubble that Valetta had been reduced to, nor the smoking ruins in the distance from the airfield, before they were refuelled and in the air again, and heading for Alexandria. With every mile they flew, she felt colder and sicker and missed Indy the more. Why did she leave? Why did she agree to leave so unprepared?

She carried with her some instructions about how to meet up with one of the thirty wireless operators who had been left behind in and around Athens when the British and their allies had pulled out. She carried, not just those telltale pieces of a working replica Enigma machine, but also various versions of the message they wanted to send, written in German, together with details about who was supposed to be sending it and his various call signs and authenticities.

By the time she had left, she had also been fully briefed about General Hans Jeschonnek, the Luftwaffe chief of staff, now in charge of operations in Greece. Fleming had told her that Jeschonnek had been chosen because of his relaxed approach to using the Luftwaffe code, which they knew at Bletchley as Enigma Red.

She had been given a long briefing to read about the *Bismarck*, which she was supposed to have read on the flight and left on the plane. She had forgotten this in her distress and had left with it, but was trying to remember whether she had managed to leave it on the submarine – or whether it was still hidden among her belongings and would need destroying.

She also carried various bits of paperwork to support her identity as a reporter on the *New Yorker*: a US passport in the name Shirley Johnson, a Turkish visa dated in April – to support her story that she had been in Greece, on the island, since before the invasion in April – and a letter from *New Yorker* proprietor Harold Ross commissioning her for a series of articles from occupied Greece, dated shortly after the invasion. It asked those who saw the letter to afford her the facilities of the international press. It felt a little unfair that she should be making use of these privileges for war work. She allowed herself a moment's guilt.

Finally, she carried the tools of her trade – a genuine portable typewriter, her notebooks, assorted pencils, the phone numbers of various *New Yorker* stringers and the offices and addresses of other American correspondents in Athens.

She had a few spare pairs of knickers but otherwise no changes of clothes and felt inadequate, weighed down, miserable and far from home. As indeed she was. She was comforted by the fact that she had managed to write a letter to circumvent Fleming's "contract", addressed to Mrs Lancing-Price, and left with Turing in case anything happened to her, telling her the truth about Ralph and their relationship and that she had a grandson. Turing had strict instructions not to send it until he was certain she had been killed – even if that meant waiting until the end of the war.

She carried in her head the rest of her instructions. The message needed to be sent late in the evening when Bletchley would have had the opportunity to calculate the settings of the day.

Her first task, once the sun was really up, was to find a man called Brown – apparently British – who would, she hoped, arrange for transport to the mainland. But among those elements which she had not been prepared for was more than a smattering of words in Greek – like *kalimera* or *ti kanis*. She also carried no maps and very little Greek money beyond a couple of notes, and she suspected those had been superseded by occupation currency. The Enigma machine would have to go separately or, if she was found with it, it could seriously undermine her status as a journalist.

She walked along the beach in the general direction of north, at least if the sun was anything to go by. The Mediterranean was glinting beautifully in the morning light. Somehow, she would have to make it to Athens and preferably within forty-eight hours or so, but it would be a wrench to leave this beautiful spot. In the distance, there appeared to be somebody in the fields, but otherwise, nobody was about. It was utterly peaceful. Or it would have been if it had not been for the unearthly row going on above her.

She stared thoughtfully at the sky. Hundreds, no thousands, of planes were now making their way overhead and, as far as she could see in any direction, heading south. It was clear that this was not just a squadron of planes, it was a whole invasion fleet of them, bombers towing gliders – whole armies sailing overhead, like swarms of insects.

She had been given no briefing about it, though she racked her brains to remember whether Fleming had predicted any such thing. They just kept coming. Where were they going? Egypt? Surely not so far for gliders. No, there was still no doubt about it. This aerial armada was heading in the direction she had come from by submarine, towards Crete. It was hard to ignore the noise as she made her way across the uneven scrub towards what looked like a small village.

"I was looking for Mr Brown," she said hopefully. There was rather a lot of shuffling and shrugging, and it was clear that the villagers did not really trust her – and why should they, after all? Even if there were, as yet, no Germans on the island, as Fleming had assured her.

"Where should I go to find Mr Brown?" she said clearly, in English.

This time, the shrugging was seriously off-putting. It was not until she was walking out of the village again, via a rutted track that at least headed northwards, that a young man sidled up to her.

"You are American reporter, right?" he said.

"Bingo!" she said. "Right!"

"You want Mr Brown or you want something else? You know this was where the Myrmidons came from?"

"You mean, as in Achilles?" Her crossword clue background had left some knowledge. "I didn't know. Thank you for that information."

The boy smiled engagingly. She began to trust him.

"You want a meal? You want the Germans? They are not here."

I haven't got anything to hide from him, have I, Xanthe said to herself.

"I'm a correspondent for the *New Yorker* magazine in search of material for an article."

The boy looked at her. Did he look sceptical, she wondered. He said nothing. Perhaps he was seeking out the words to ask why she was here *exactly*.

"Well, most of all, I want to go back to Athens. I understood that Mr Brown has a boat."

Trust seemed to seep back into his eyes.

"There are many boats in the harbour. They dare not go out after what happened to the *Ydra*."

"What was that?" asked Xanthe nervously.

"It was a torpedo boat, bombed by Stukas some weeks ago. Many sailors killed."

They had been walking uphill for some time. It was a mountainous place and they were heading in a circuitous route along a small track, relatively level with the sea on their right-hand side. The roar of the planes overhead continued and they could see them disappearing over the horizon towards the south.

They turned the corner, past a large and forlorn bush, and there was the main town before them and the harbour, with colourful fishing boats bobbing by the shore. It could have been a perfect scene from the Greek islands, were it not for one thing. There was a grey military boat in the harbour as well, and – "What is that?" said Xanthe with a jolt. "Is that a Greek ship?"

"Impossible. The Greek navy has been disbanded. Also, look at its flag."

Flying clearly behind the bridge was a Nazi swastika. It may have been a Greek navy ship some weeks ago, but it was now a German one.

For a moment, a feeling of panic swept over Xanthe. Control yourself, control yourself. It's an opportunity, she told herself.

Yes, if the Germans had only just arrived here, then there was no question of her not having the right permits. She would go into town and ask them to take her to Athens. She would say she had been on Aegina during the invasion and had chosen to stay – and that she now wished to return.

"Thank you. I'll go down there." She felt suddenly alone and frightened. "Will you come with me?"

"No, thank you, madam," he said, bowing formally. "My name is Argyris. Perhaps we will meet again, some day, and then I'll be at your service."

She shook his hand and walked down into the town. There remained the issue of smuggling her equipment to Athens – the idea had been to send it via a radio operator or the mysterious Mr Brown. She could try taking it herself, but it would be a serious risk. It was unlikely that most German officers would know what on earth it was – it hardly looked like an Enigma machine – but it certainly looked suspicious.

The small, narrow streets were shuttered, though the sun was now up, and people were locked indoors, afraid of what the day would bring: this was the first sight of the invaders, just as it was for Xanthe. There was nobody hanging around.

She made straight for the dockside. There were now German soldiers in their field grey almost everywhere. They looked nearly as lost as she felt. They seemed to be searching with checklists and looking at buildings, not for people.

"Can you direct me to the officer in charge?" she said, summoning up her confidence. What am I doing? Her heart was thumping.

A young officer bowed to her in the Prussian style and indicated that she should follow. She felt for the time being that it might be sensible to keep her German language in reserve. This was a moment for American English, if ever there was one.

"You asked for me? I am the acting commandant on the island. My name is Helmut Nikolas."

"Hi," she said. "Shirley Johnson, *New Yorker*. I'm trying to find a way to get to Athens."

"My English is small, I am sad. But if you can wait perhaps two days,

I would be delighted to offer you accommodation on my small ship. But may I ask you what you have been doing on the island?"

"I came here a month ago to write a piece on Greece but, since the arrival of your men, people have been reluctant to take their boats out. So I have been prevented so far from leaving. I am very grateful to you, sir."

"Perhaps you could tell me where you are staying."

Why had she not anticipated that question? She kicked herself.

"I have been staying on the other side of the island. I have only just arrived in town."

"In that case, may I offer you some help. Argyris! This young man will find you somewhere to stay on my authority."

Before her, again, was the young man from the mountain road.

"Does this mean you support the Germans?" she asked him delicately, as they walked away, side by side.

"No, I just speak German, so I have become an intermediary. When they arrive, they ask for me. I went to the German school in Athens," he added by way of somewhat coy explanation.

"That must put you in a powerful position."

"I do not think so, madam. This is only the second time they have come, and the first time, they hardly stayed long. But I can find you somewhere to stay, if that would help. I can even arrange to take you over the sea. I have friends on the boats."

"Thank you. I think maybe that I should not go behind the commandant's back, now I've asked him."

"Do not worry. We can tell him later," said Argyris. "He is a good German, I believe."

"There are such things, then?"

"Of course, as in any nation."

*

It was after a good dinner of olives and some kind of vegetable stew, during an afternoon which seemed to have involved sleeping, for everyone except the military – kept busy unloading crates and going house to house with checklists – when Xanthe experienced her first surprise.

There was a faint tap on the window of the house belonging to a friend of Argyris, where she had eaten lunch. So faint that, at first, she thought it must be a cat or something even smaller. She stood up – like everyone else, she had been snoozing – then watched, powerless, as the door handle began to turn on the back door. A moment later, there was a man in the room. Or was it a man? He was dressed like some kind of hedge priest. He had grown most of a beard.

"Can I help you?" asked Xanthe nervously, horribly aware that she was unarmed.

She felt flustered, trying to draft an article in her head for the *New Yorker* about the strange island and the gentle arrival of German invaders, and the incident with the boat that was bombed in the harbour. If she was going to be a foreign correspondent, then that was what she ought to be doing, she felt.

The new arrival said nothing. He moved a little closer. Then, in a cut-glass English accent, he said: "I believe you have been trying to get hold of Mr Brown."

"I'm afraid I have no idea what you're talking about."

There was no point in giving everything away to anyone who asked.

"You know the Myrmiddons came from here?"

Why was she constantly being told this?

"So I've been told."

"Well, I'm Achilles," said the visitor. "I've been waiting for you."

"Then, tell me, Achilles," said Xanthe, excited that things were somehow now going right. "If I was the person you were waiting for, how would I know you?"

"I would tell you about the rabbits in the south of Spain."

"Well, as they say, it never snows in Ibiza," she said, checking for a look of recognition.

He shook her hand with enthusiasm.

"Delighted to meet you, my dear."

It was impossible to work out how old he was.

"How did you know where to find me?"

"You were asking for me back in the early hours of the morning in Pachia Rachi, I believe. You weren't hard to trace. Now, have you got the stuff?"

"I do. Can you take it? Can you get it to the… right destination?"

"Yup. Sooner the better, I think."

She reached into her haversack and extracted the four pieces, wrapped in cloth, that would fit together into an imitation Enigma machine – three pieces plus a make-do set of rotors, rather amateur versions of the one with which she had killed Stumpf in Berlin.

"Thank you," he said, depositing the pieces in a muddy sack. "All will be in place when you arrive. We'll take it over tonight. In fact, you can come too…"

"No thanks. I'm an American correspondent. I can't be too cloak and dagger."

"Pfff, that's what they all say," said Brown, rudely.

"Was that a dig at the foreign policy of my country?" said Xanthe defensively, racking her brains to think of what the US government had done, actively, on behalf of an embattled Europe. "May I remind you of Lend-Lease…"

Brown spread his hands out innocently. "Nothing could be further from my mind," he said.

They both laughed, then he shushed them.

"It's siesta time," he whispered. "No point in making ourselves conspicuous."

"Then next time, don't be rude about my president," said Xanthe teasingly. "The US army is delayed. In the meantime, you'll have to make do with me."

*

When Brown had gone, she reached back into her bag with a great sense of relief and pulled out her portable typewriter again. It was time to begin her first despatch all over again. How would Mollie Panter-Downes do it? She would start as if in the middle of a conversation.

Xanthe imagined herself talking to Turing about her brief time in Greece, how would she tell him? She began to type:

"*The trouble with being invaded is that nothing is quite what you expect and, because of that, almost nothing works. No shopping, no banks, no money – at least no reliable money: you suddenly need to have 'occupation marks', which have to be printed and brought in with the first troops…*"

She had, in fact, already heard complaints about the occupation marks. They were in short supply because, or so she heard, the Germans had not yet brought the printer in yet.

She scribbled the date on her draft – 22 May – and began to fall asleep. It had been a long night and she felt completely drained.

She was woken by a knock on the door. Outside was the young temporary commandant. He bowed and clicked his heels.

"Fraulein, my apologies for this disturb," he said. "My boat is at your disposal. I remain here. But you are welcome to join my men who are on their way to Piraeus.

"I'm quite grateful," said Xanthe sleepily. "Have I got time to pack?"

"We leave in one hour precisely, Fraulein. I will say farewell to you at the harbour."

He bowed and was gone. Xanthe felt a sense of disappointment which she put down to exhaustion. She was leaving the island earlier than she had expected but had already met enough characters to populate a book of collected articles. Yet also, she could think of little except Indy in his cot back home – but what home? She was still living at a secret cryptographic establishment, about five thousand miles or so way from Indy's only other blood relatives outside Nazi Germany. He depended on her ability to get home safe. It was going to be a quick trip to Athens, find the safe house, send the signal, then back out again the way she had come.

*

As she walked up the gangway onto the docks at Piraeus, Xanthe was surprised to get a salute and a wink from the sailors. How very strange life is, she said to herself, returning the salute like a visiting queen.

But the harbour itself was something of a shock, once she was on solid ground. There was rubble everywhere and sunken ships and boats cluttering the sea lanes with their masts and superstructure pointing sadly above the water. For a moment, it reminded her of what she was supposed to be doing. Civilisation was under threat, from the kind of barbarism she had seen in the London Blitz and some of the behaviour she had encountered in Berlin. But at least it meant there was a purpose to this intense risk.

The key question now was how to get into Athens, and she had only just asked herself the question when a young man popped up alongside her and took her arm.

"Madam, if you will permit me. I have been asked by Mr Brown and by my friend Argyris, if I would accompany you today and take you wherever you want to go. My name is Giorgios.

"Giorgios, you are a godsend. Thank you so much. What do we do now if we want to get into Athens? I also need to find a Western Union office to send my article, if at all possible. Oh, and I need to get to the US embassy."

"In that case, we will take this bus."

Xanthe had noticed the mode of transport that he indicated, but it was no kind of bus that she recognised. It was a cart with fruit and another goat, but he helped her up with dignity and she didn't like to complain. After a hurried conversation in Greek, the driver motioned his horse forward with the flick of a wrist. Then they were off.

"I expect this is not your normal bus, madam," said Giorgios, smiling, "but it is the most reliable. There are taxis, but they are jackals, and not very many of them."

"Tell me, Giorgios. What do you know about occupation marks? And please call me Shirley."

Giorgios laughed. She warmed to him. He was not much younger than she was herself.

"They are worth nothing. They bring them in great quantities, and when they run out, they just go and print some more. I have seen them do so. It is strange, is it not, just to make the money you need? Perhaps also arrogant..."

"Perhaps criminal," she said.

Xanthe began to calculate that the cart was averaging about two miles an hour. If she had walked, she would have got into Athens at least twice as fast. But then she would have arrived tired, hungry and conspicuous. On this cart, with its fruit and vegetables wilting in the heat, and with her hair dyed dark to match her passport photo, she looked like every other young woman in Greece – at least at first sight.

An hour or so later, the cart stopped near the Acropolis, and Giorgios shouted his thanks and held out his arm for Xanthe to descend. The planes were still in the air above them, though not quite so many of them. She wondered how the Greek army was managing in Crete, assuming that was their target, let alone the British and their Australian and New Zealand allies. There were many more field grey uniforms in the centre of the city.

They drew up outside an office with an American flag.

"This is the US consulate," said Giorgios.

"Thank you so much, I am so grateful to you."

She felt elated that everything had been unexpectedly easy.

"Will I see you again?" he said. "Perhaps by the harbour for your return?"

"I hope so,9 Giorgios. I'm not sure right now…"

*

The consulate building was crowded, mainly with Americans but there were other, more ragged people who had obviously made their way here through Romania and Yugoslavia, often because they were Jewish families trying to get an exit visa, or perhaps because they were simply refugees, with all their savings in a small bag, desperately trying to escape the war or the Nazis, or both.

"Thank you, Paul," an intelligent-looking woman in slacks was saying to an official, in a loud voice. "At eleven p.m. tonight if you can make it – that's six p.m. in New York? What would I do without your voice, eh – pffff!"

She laughed ruefully.

"Excuse me," said Xanthe as the woman passed by in a flurry of papers. "I wonder if you can direct me to the Western Union office in this town?"

"Sure thing, honey," said the woman. "Say, are you a reporter? I thought I knew all of us here, but I seem to have missed you. Where have you been hiding – and I mean that quite literally?"

"I've been on Aegina for the last few weeks. I'm here for the *New Yorker*."

"Betty Wason, CBS."

"Fantastic to meet you! I know one of your colleagues – Bill Shirer."

"You know Bill! Well, any friend of Bill's, as they say. To be frank, I'm just having a bit of trouble with my bosses back home. They say women don't have the right 'gravitas' to broadcast about the war, and – well, let me show you this…"

She rootled around in her handbag and pulled out a battered telegram. It confirmed her story.

Betty didn't wait for Xanthe to express an opinion. "Honestly – what a *schmuck*!" she said.

Xanthe laughed, outraged.

"The result is, I have to get poor old Paul to actually do the broadcasts for me. It's difficult enough getting to the radio office as well as getting a line out and forcing it through the censors. Then I have to get one of the embassy staff to help me *read* it! Still," she said, drawing breath, "enough about my troubles – what are you looking for here? I'm surprised to see you, I have to say. Pleased though! Delighted, in fact!"

"Oh, colour pieces. You know. *New Yorker* stuff. Joe Liebling's back in the states. Somebody needs to report on the war for the magazine readers of New York City."

Betty was suddenly serious.

"To be honest, I don't think they are going to stand for us much longer. I'm expecting us to be flung out any time. It is hard to be here more than a day or two and stay unbiased. There's only a few of us left here – Wes and George, and me, of course."

Xanthe nodded as if she knew them. As always, she was feeling as if she stood out like a sore thumb in her adopted profession. She was uncomfortably aware that she did not have as much experience as she normally would need, to be catapulted into a war zone as a reporter or feature writer.

"I'm something of a beginner, I'm afraid," she confessed. She liked Betty immediately and wanted to deceive her as little as possible. She also kicked herself. Would an American have made such a declaration? She should have brazened it out with the best of them. She was becoming too English...

"Oh, come on, honey. We're all beginners here. Some of the old-timers haven't been able to take it and they shipped off home months ago. It takes a different kind of guts to report on an occupation and I've only been doing it a few weeks, since the Schmazis arrived."

Xanthe laughed, immensely relieved.

"Say, where are you staying? You don't know? Well, come along with me and stay at my flat. But you'd better register with the censor if you want to stay the right side of the pigs... Sorry, you knew I meant the Nazis, didn't you?"

She guffawed.

*

For a defeated city, Athens was strangely alive. There was almost no food, no real money, no jobs and no transport, but the place seemed to pulsate in an exciting way – especially at night, when the shadowy reality of the city became clear, people nipping in and out, avoiding the Nazi patrols. But there was no sign of any contact from Mr Brown, so Xanthe worried. She sweated profusely at night and felt feverish. She had already gone through her spare knickers.

After a night on Betty's couch, Xanthe sought out the censor at the Stadtkommandatur. She even managed to send her telegram with her first despatch. She was very aware, as she walked past the Hotel Grand Bretagne later in the day, where the senior Nazis had set up headquarters, that the man she had come to impersonate – the Luftwaffe general – was probably inside. Or that he might pass her at any moment.

As she thought this, a large man in Luftwaffe uniform did skip up the steps next to her. He ignored her completely. It was an uncomfortable moment, and the experience reminded her forcefully that she needed to find her contact via the Athens underground. She had made the connection with Mr Brown, and he had said quite clearly that she would be contacted as soon as she arrived in Athens. She was pretty conspicuous – an American woman reporter going about her business – but nobody had made contact.

She kicked herself for not pushing Giorgios on the subject. Had she been supposed to say something to him? Why had she not? She would wait until the following morning and then, she had been given emergency instructions for making contact if all else failed, but she was not keen to do so unless she absolutely had to.

She walked around the block then swiftly towards Betty's flat, as she had told Betty she would. Then she looked at her watch: Indy would be having his lunchtime feed. She ached to hold him again. She had been gone nearly a week already; how stupid of her to get so miserable. There was no point in waiting. Those were her orders, in any case – to make this signal with all speed. If there were delays, she *must* circumvent them.

She turned round and headed for the cathedral.

*

The Metropolitan Cathedral of Athens was looking beautiful, with its perfect arches shining in the sun. Up the steps she went, trying to look more confident than she felt, and found herself in the most extraordinary arched paradise, full of golden mosaics and patterns.

It was surprisingly bright and it felt a calm oasis in the insanity of occupied Europe. She had never been inside an Orthodox church before, let alone a cathedral, and she was fascinated by the icons. She tried to orientate herself. Where were the confessionals?

She chose the confessional nearest to the high altar on the right. She brushed past the black curtain and sat down. There was nobody else there. No, there *was* somebody. She peered through the grill.

"Bless me, father, for I have sinned," she said, tentatively, and using her best Midwestern accent.

"Your name, child?" said the priest behind the screen.

"Shirley. Some call me Snow in Ibiza."

"God be with you, Shirley. You have my absolution. Now, my instructions are to direct you to where they are waiting for you. Go to the right, outside the main door, take the second road to the left. Pentelis Street. Knock once, just once, on the door numbered twenty-six and wait there. Behold, I stand at the door and knock," he said with a little giggle. "God be with you."

"Thank you, father," said Xanthe, wondering as she did so if you were supposed to call Orthodox priests "father".

She wandered, somewhat dreamily, out into the intense sunlight of the day. She was beginning to feel weak again and told herself she must conserve her energy.

As she slipped back down the cathedral steps, a German military patrol marched past in their ubiquitous field grey. She stood still, chastened, and let them pass.

Fifteen minutes later, making sure she was not being followed, she had passed by the address twice – desperately trying to be certain it was not also being watched. As certain as she could be, she took a deep breath and knocked on the door.

The door was opened almost immediately and she was pulled inside, so quickly that she lost her footing and sprawled on the floor, on the old linoleum.

"My apologies," said a voice from the shadows. Xanthe looked up and saw a young woman with curly black hair, attractive but harassed. "Please come with me, quickly if you can. You should not have come to the door in daylight."

"Sorry, but..."

There was no time to finish the sentence. Xanthe was then rushed through the house, through the back door, across a courtyard and into a house across the way.

"Miss Xanthe, we have been expecting you. It is good to meet," said another voice and Xanthe found herself before an older man, his skin raddled by years in the sun. He must be some kind of farmer, she thought.

"And you are?"

"I am known as Achilles. I have a message for you. I'm afraid you will have to be patient. Robin will meet you here in two days. Come in the evening, please, after dark. He will be here."

"Who is Robin?"

"One of our British friends. With a radio."

CHAPTER FIVE

Athens, May 1941

Two days! How could she wait two days? She and Fleming both had their reasons for wanting speed, but it was not clear to her now, how to make things develop faster. If the radio operator was going to take two days to arrive then, well, there was nothing to be done but wait. But she could see a bit more of occupied Athens for her other job.

"Come on then," said Betty. "I'll show you the city." They were in her home at 14 Odos Patriarchou Joachim, and it was Xanthe's first taste of it – the flat seemed to be full of people. "They cancelled me again at Deutsches Athens, where I broadcast from, so there's nothing to be done. I've told Paul. So come on – get a move on: Athens is a beautiful city, as long as you don't look too closely at the swastika flying above the Acropolis."

The two women wandered down to Piraeus, sat in a café there and listened to the stories that seemed to come from all directions.

"It's a journalist's paradise," said Betty. "As long as you don't feel homesick – then you get to feeling kinda trapped."

"Tell me about it!" said Xanthe, but she had realised – if she had time – this was something she could write about, even if it had to wait until she was back in London.

She had been staggered, as they walked down the shopping streets, to find most of the shops open but almost no food on sale at all. Betty told her that the invading troops had confiscated all the canned goods and any farmyard animals. A friend of hers had a cow that was about to give birth. When the soldiers came to shoot it, they begged them to let it live until it had given birth. It gave birth that night, but the next day the soldiers were back – they shot the cow and the calf died too because it had no milk. "It really is a tragedy. The whole thing. Greece will die," said Betty sadly.

As they walked back through the city in the heat, they were passed by lorry after lorry, driving fresh troops down to the docks or the airfield. In the other direction, they saw large numbers of wounded troops going towards the city hospitals. One lorry was emitting groans of agony from inside. Clearly, the battle was now in full fury in Crete.

As for the locals, those who had not been arrested still crowded into the cafés, though they had nothing to supply their customers with. Betty explained that even those who were a bit better off were also suffering because the main effect of the occupation marks was to cause rampant inflation.

The same seemed to be true of some of the new arrivals. They saw soldiers in their uniforms, going door to door, begging for food and alcohol. They saw Austrian soldiers singing *The Blue Danube*, drunk on ouzo. And they saw small groups of Greek civilians, singing instead, their own satirical song, *Coroido Mussolini*.

"Oh yes, I do know what it means," said Betty. "It isn't that inspiring, to be honest. It just means 'Mussolini, you fool'. Infectious tune though, isn't it? You have to try and stop yourself whistling it. It can get you into trouble, though even the German soldiers sing it these days!"

And all the time, the sun baked them and baked the heads of the women dressed in black, praying at the shrines.

"What is this Chicago they're all advertising?" said Xanthe, suddenly homesick also for the Midwest.

"Oh, it used to be ice cream, nuts and chocolate sauce. But there's practically none left. The recipe corroded somewhat before the last hint of chocolate sauce disappeared."

Xanthe liked Betty enormously. She felt she could risk a question about their common profession.

"Betty, can I ask you: how can you find anything meaningful to say in your broadcasts that won't be censored?"

"Well, it's tough. I mean, you could write about Zonars, the popular bar – not so popular now, of course, now it's full of Nazi soldiers. It used to be a gay old place, with the RAF flyers in there. Now, it's – I don't know – sort of humourless. Unless the locals come, but they don't seem to… On second thoughts, you wouldn't get that past the censor either."

"It's frustrating isn't it," said Xanthe, sensing Betty's rising irritation.

"I mean, I'm supposed to be doing serious broadcasts about geopolitics, like Shirer does – or to watch the bombs falling around St Paul's like Murrow. And I'm not allowed to do either. And even if I did, my stupid editor won't let me read it – in case my 'girly' voice somehow undoes the seriousness of the subject. It's enough to make me take up knitting."

They had nearly reached her flat. They were nearly at the door, but Betty held back.

"Oh, shoot," she said.

Xanthe followed where she nodded.

"What is it?"

Up ahead was a good-looking man in a long military-style coat, waiting outside her door.

"It's Jurgen. I don't trust him. He keeps coming round with flowers and other little presents. He speaks five languages and…"

"He sounds lovely," said Xanthe laughing.

"Shhh, he'll hear."

"Ah, Fraulein!" said a voice from up ahead. It was too late. He had seen them.

"How delightful. You have a friend with you. Now I have brought a small gift."

He brandished a leg of lamb. Xanthe knew this was absolutely unobtainable in Athens for anyone except the secret police.

"May I humbly request that I might come inside for a moment?" He shone them a winning smile. Xanthe glanced nervously at Betty, willing her to refuse.

"Yes, come inside," said Betty, somewhat aggressively. "I've been having trouble with my telephone and could do with your advice."

She winked quickly at Xanthe. Then she opened the door and let him in.

"The thing is," said Betty, as they filed up her stairs to the flat, "it keeps ringing and there is nobody there. It is almost as if there was somebody listening in."

"I understand, Fraulein. I have a little influence and will ask to have the line tested. In the meantime, I have bought you a bottle of ouzo. Tonight, we will party and make merry."

Betty was immediately apologetic.

"Oh, Jurgen, I am sorry. My friend and I both have articles to write tonight, to take to the censor tomorrow. What a pity. Another time perhaps."

Jurgen's eyes lit up.

"Ah yes, your friend. Tell me about yourself, Fraulein – um, Shirley?"

Xanthe coloured for a moment. She had not prepared herself for questioning. Or lying.

"Well, I have been here, and stuck on Aegina, for weeks now, writing for the *New Yorker*. I don't have the kind of responsibilities that Betty has here. I just write colour pieces."

"Colour pieces by a colourful lady," said Jurgen, with a little bow. "Ah yes, the *New Yorker*. I am surprised that it has the resources to send a young girl out to cover a war that is no longer happening. You have an interest in military operations perhaps? We have had great difficulties here with the fifth columnists. I would hate to feel that you had any – let me say it like this – had any sympathy with them…"

"I'm just a writer," said Xanthe simply, looking him full in the face. "I've always wanted to write about the world. There were few enough volunteers for this job. It narrowed the field and I was then lucky enough to get chosen."

"I'm so sorry we have to see you out," said Betty with determination.

"That is understandable," said Jurgen, recovering something of his *savoir-faire* and allowing himself to be herded towards the door. They could hear his metal-tipped shoes clicking down the street outside the window.

"Ugh, that man gives me the creeps," whispered Betty as soon as he had gone.

Xanthe burst into giggles again.

"Shhh, Shirley! He'll be listening outside. The man can't see a keyhole without putting his ear to it."

"What do you think he's after?"

"I'll give you one guess," said Betty. "What do you think? He's just highly sexed and has a thing about American women. I'm very sorry I introduced you."

*

Xanthe had experienced London under attack. She had experienced wartime Berlin. But somehow the picture of the Greek capital city, down but not out, invaded physically but not mentally conquered, was moving and instructive. She knew now what she would write, if and when she got home; it was not something that the censor would pass here.

The trouble was that she had already been gone a week – a week away from Indigo at such an important time – and all she had managed to do so far was find herself bundled into a safe house, only to find she had to wait two whole days for the wireless operator. Time must be running out and there were still at least thirty-six hours before Robin was due to arrive. That was thirty-six hours before the occupying forces began to cotton on about who and what she really was doing in Athens.

Added to which, the *Bismarck* would not wait in harbour forever. For all she knew, those fifteen-inch guns she had not really read enough about on the flight would even now be battering British and allied shipping in mid-Atlantic, with all the death and destruction, the burnings and drownings, that would happen as a result.

There was her new friendship with Betty, which was a plus. Betty knew Sigrid Schultz from the *Chicago Tribune*, as it turned out – still reporting from Berlin, though Xanthe did not explain why her name was familiar. Also, somewhere in Athens, were George Weller from the *Chicago Daily News* and Wes Gallagher from Associated Press. Both of them, experienced hard news reporters. What was a feature writer from the *New Yorker*, the gentle magazine that employed James Thurber, supposed to be doing in quite such peril in the war zone? They were bound to ask the question and wonder why she was supposed to have been on a small island, so far from the action, throughout the three weeks of the German *blitzkrieg* on Greece. She was just going to have to stick close to Betty and keep a low profile.

She reminded herself of this as they wandered rather aimlessly though the back streets of Athens, seeking breakfast, the next morning. Betty's broadcast had been cancelled again, and the unforgiving sun was rising in the sky, indicating another sultry day. Just one more night to go and she could do the job and go home. As long as Mr Brown had done *his* job and got her Enigma components to the right place – and in the same number of pieces that she had given to him.

After a siesta, Betty left the flat in the afternoon, to continue what she called her "clandestine activity" – which she defined as asking any Nazi officials she could find how she could get hold of an exit permit. Betty was afraid that there was now no way out for her and her American press colleagues and was terrified of being stranded in Athens, without access to broadcasting equipment, for the rest of her life.

So far, she explained to Xanthe, she had put most of the gentler Nazi bureaucrats into a panic – the whole question of an exit visa had never been asked before.

"It really would be funny if it wasn't quite so depressing," said Betty when she returned. "One of them asked me today whether I was British. Apparently, the only conceivable excuse they can think of for wanting to leave is if I would otherwise be interned as a prisoner of war. I'm not sure it is going to get any easier. Relations between the Nazis and us Yanks are plummeting further with every day that goes by. They're soon going to give us an exit permit to some kind of camp…"

A shiver went down Xanthe's spine. She could not but apply the problem to her own situation. She had assumed, as Fleming had, that leaving would be relatively simple.

"The only thing going for me is that my damned editor is complaining to the authorities too. The last thing he wants is to have to pay me for *not* working for the rest of the war. Though, knowing him, he probably has some kind of insurance against that."

*

It was now dark outside. Evening seemed to fall with a sudden thump in Athens and the nightlife seemed to be shared by little more than a handful of rather humourless Nazi officers, who stomped by below the balcony of Betty's flat – on their way to Maxim's, the only place in the city still with steak on the menu.

About an hour after nightfall, a strange wailing siren disturbed the conversation. Could it really be an air raid?

"What?" said Betty. "How can it be? What's going on? It can't be the RAF – can it?"

They hurried back out onto the balcony. It was a perfect night, warm and still, with bright moonlight everywhere and a great canopy of stars, so much more visible in the blackout. The whole of Athens seemed as if they were on the roofs or balconies. Soon the streets began to fill. Within ten minutes of the sirens sounding, the streets below them were packed. There was a strange, hysterical, carnival atmosphere, except that the crowd was as close to silent as a crowd could be – listening for the slightest sound. Xanthe also knew they were hungry. She could almost feel their stomachs rumbling.

"Come on, let's go down, shall we?" said Betty.

"Shouldn't we go to the shelters?"

"Shelters? What shelters? No, if this is the RAF, they'll never bomb the historic centre of Athens, I betcha. And I can't think who else it is."

The sound of approaching planes was apparent as they made for the door and Xanthe grabbed her notebook and pencil as they swung out. The moment they reached the street, a huge cheer went up. The bombers were completely visible in the sky, with the distinctive RAF roundels on their wings. There were fewer than ten of them and they were clearly making for the airfield.

Xanthe took out the notebook and asked if any of the people around her spoke English. An old lady tapped her arm:

"We don't care if they drop bombs on us," she said, crossing herself. "But, dear God, protect the British aviators. Let no harm come to them!"

"That is some quote," said Betty, who had been listening in. "Did you get it down?"

"Yup."

"Cos if you don't use it, I will. I may do anyway!"

The planes were circling around again, and now the anti-aircraft guns by the Acropolis were coming into action. They could see the explosions in the air, some way from the raiders.

Xanthe looked around her and saw more than a few women fingering orthodox crosses and also appearing to be praying, not for their own safety, but for the safety of the young men so many hundreds of feet above – who had maybe even been based in Athens themselves, and had flown off from the same airport a few weeks before.

"Where do they come from, do you think?"

"Can they reach here from Egypt?" said Betty. "I don't know. Otherwise, I suppose from Cyprus. They certainly didn't come from Crete. In fact, I'm sure they would have been better employed in Crete, where there is actually a battle going on. I suppose they wanted to show they were still in the game."

It was hardly Xanthe's first experience of bombing, after the London Blitz earlier in the year. But it was her first experience of being bombed by her own side – the RAF had only managed to drop leaflets on Berlin while she had been there. It was a peculiar feeling, which she realised was shared by the crowd, cheering the bombers on.

Another great roar went up, and someone began singing *Coroido Mussolini* again, and then the Greek national anthem:

From the ancient Greeks who died
And set both life and spirit free,
Now with ancient courage rising
We will hail you, Liberty!

It was intoxicating, on this tropical night, the two women strolled arm in arm with the warm night air on their legs, with the cheering and singing all around them. It was almost as if Athens had been liberated. May 23 1941 – she would remember the date. She noted it at the top of her open page. She felt like she would remember it her whole life. She would tell Indigo about it when he was old enough to understand, how she had fought the Nazis on his behalf and ended up walking down the streets of Athens while it was being bombed by her own side.

It was at this moment of elation that Xanthe heard the whistles. It was dark, and it was hard to see what was happening up ahead, except that suddenly there was screaming, and the crowd surged backwards and past her. Xanthe could hear the familiar, spine-chilling sound of boots on cobblestones up the side street next to them, and a squad of soldiers emerged from behind a truck, which drove ahead at speed towards the road junction.

The truck screeched to a halt, the back went down and it revealed a large machine gun, manned by two soldiers in field grey, pointing it at the seething mass of Athenians.

"Oh, God," said Betty under her breath, flattening herself and Xanthe against the wall. There was more screaming and what remained of the crowd dispersed in the opposite direction.

They reached the safety of their front door, without breathing, waiting for the shooting to begin. Nothing happened. The soldiers stood to attention and the trucks began to drive away. Almost nobody was left in the street. But as Xanthe began to breathe more freely, she saw a familiar figure in the blackout gloom up ahead, making in their direction.

"Come on, let's get inside quicketty quick," said Betty, reaching inside her handbag.

"Excuse me, please don't abandon us, ladies," said the figure. Moments later, there was Jurgen and with him was another German soldier.

"Hi there, Jurgen. What brings you out here so late?"

"Miss Wason and Miss Johnson. I'm afraid I'm going to have to ask you to come with me."

The soldier next to him drew his pistol to enforce the message.

"Really, honey? Why is that?" said Betty mildly.

For a moment, Xanthe calculated her chances of slipping away into the back streets and heading back to the cathedral. But in the seconds she took to consider it, it was already too late to run. It would also have made her a wanted woman, whereas – she told herself – if she could bluff her way through the next hour or so, then there was no reason why she should not complete the operation as planned. She had, after all, come all this way with a purpose. Her heart was beating faster than it should have been. She deliberately looked innocent and unconcerned.

"Of course," she said. "Why do you need us?"

*

The room where they were held was a small reception room, apparently in the basement of the Hotel Grande Bretagne, where – as both women knew – all the Nazi leaders in Greece and in charge of the Crete operation were staying. They were not alone. As they waited for Jurgen to arrive, through the early hours, they slouched across the old upturned tables and piles of chairs with about ten others. They were, it transpired, a number of leading Greeks from the city, a poet and a handful of retailers. They sat bored, more irritated than frightened, in the stark electric light, surrounded by the smell of stale cigarettes and piles of old table cloths, in great heaps, in the shadowy corners.

"How long has it been, do you think?" asked Xanthe.

"I don't know; two hours, three hours? They'll come. I've been here before. Unfortunately."

"I need to drink something."

"Funny that. There's a well-stocked bar upstairs."

"Oh, ha ha," said Xanthe sarcastically. "I meant a drink of water."

Xanthe got up from the chairs she had been trying to sleep on, under a tablecloth and went towards the door.

The soldier gathered himself together and barred the way. Then there was a flurry of activity behind her.

"No, no, Miss Johnson, we are in fact ready to talk to you, if Miss Wason cares to join us."

She beckoned to Betty and proceeded into the darkened room indicated.

"Thank you, Jurgen. We're coming."

Stay polite, for goodness sake, stay polite, she told herself. It was sweaty down in the bowels of the hotel, but she realised her teeth were chattering. Her scars hurt.

"Yes, hold on a second," said Betty.

They were motioned to sit and found themselves alone, sitting opposite a smoking Jurgen. He had bags under his eyes.

"Now ladies," he said quietly. "We simply want to know what you were doing encouraging that crowd to make that ludicrous spectacle when the British planes came over. They were shot down, incidentally."

"Listen Jurgen, don't be stupid," said Betty. "We are reporters. We follow crowds, we don't call them out."

"Do not, if you please, dare to call me stupid. That would compound your mistake."

He passed the back of his hand across his temple. It had clearly been a long night.

"Sorry, Jurgen," Xanthe intervened. "What we mean is that we needed to find out why all those people were there, perhaps as you did. We are paid to write the news, and when people gather in the street, it's news. You do understand that, don't you?"

"Do not patronise me, I beg you. For your own health."

"Fine, fine, have it your way, then," said Betty getting cross. "How do *you* think we called them out?"

"I do not know. But I do know this. The Greeks have welcomed us as liberators. Did we not end the nine p.m. curfew imposed by the British? Why would anyone gather outside to cheer bombers which are aiming at them in their own city? It makes no sense."

"It's true, Jurgen. There must be a flaw in your inexorable logic somewhere. I wonder where it is."

This was clearly the final straw. Jurgen slammed his fists on the table and stalked, insulted, to the door. When he got there, he turned.

"Very well, I have a great deal of time and I am a patient man. You can both stay here until I have time to talk to you again. By which time, I hope you will have realised it makes no sense to treat me with disrespect."

Finding themselves shut in the dark and listening to Jurgen barking orders outside, Betty and Xanthe felt overwhelmed with the hilarity of it all. They fell about giggling, as quietly as possible. Tears ran down Xanthe's cheeks, when they heard the key turn in the lock.

When the lights went out, they began to think more seriously about their predicament. They were almost certainly there for the night, if not longer.

"The trouble is that I have rather an important appointment tomorrow," said Xanthe nervously.

"So do I, honey. I have a date to broadcast again, from the embassy, with Paul as my voice. If I don't show up, I have a standing arrangement with him that he will report my disappearance and demand the Nazis to return me. It has been a little touch and go for the last few weeks and it seemed to me to be a sensible precaution."

"Still, I'm glad I'm imprisoned here with you and not on my own," said Xanthe. "I don't like people like Jurgen – I've had trouble with Nazis before. I haven't told you about that."

There was one blanket for the two of them, which they had found in the corner, and they huddled together under it as the night grew cold.

CHAPTER SIX

Athens, May 1941

In the pale light of dawn, Xanthe awoke with a feeling of anticipation and worry. This was the day when she would send her precious signal, finish her time in Athens and find a way back to Indigo, waiting for her, though he was too young to know really who she was. She really could not stay here in this darkened room, if she could possibly get out of it.

It was a moment of powerlessness. There was very little she could do but hope.

"Sorry, Betty. I didn't realise you were awake."

"That's ok, honey. I always wake at this time. And I'm due to broadcast at three this afternoon, for the breakfast time news in New York. But I was due to rehearse with Paul first thing this morning, so there's every chance he'll report me missing in the next hour or so. I don't think the Nazis feel like a diplomatic incident with the Americans right now – not until they've secured Crete."

But time, which had dashed by so quickly in the dark, now hung heavy and sluggish in the light. The sun rose through the skylight in the pavement. The heat began to rise too. Xanthe now felt desperately thirsty. She was also increasingly nervous: what if Jurgen thought too much about her name and her story? What if she said something stupid in her increasingly befuddled state – she could bring Betty down with her if she wasn't careful.

Sometime in the morning, there was a knock on the door, and a nervous maid came in, followed by a woman in German uniform. They appeared to be bringing in a change of clothes.

"We will wash your clothes for you. Please change now," she announced.

Feeling self-conscious with her flabby body – how many weeks now since the birth? Six? Seven? – Xanthe undressed down to her underwear and put on the long, light robes she was given. Her knickers were now disgustingly dirty, thanks to the bleeding from her birthing scars.

"They're dressing us like nuns!" Xanthe whispered, giggling.

"It's probably some fetish of Jurgen's. Come on, honey. It's time to recite poetry. I'll start," said Betty, confidently.

"*O, Captain! my Captain! our fearful trip is done,*

The ship has weather'd every rack, the prize we sought is won,

And something, something…

"Maybe a bit premature. Ok, now your turn."

"I don't know, I think I only know English poetry," said Xanthe, feeling a little ashamed. She wracked her brain to remember her literature lessons at Simonetta College, some kind of finishing school in Cambridge.

"I know!…

"*Full fathom five thy father lies;*

Of his bones are coral made…"

"Jeez, Shirley. Not bad stuff. Now I reckon we only need another round and Jurgen will be here. Do you think I'm being overconfident?"

As it turned out, she was. The hours dragged. Xanthe and Betty stopped exchanging poets and began to worry. The door occasionally opened, and they were presented with a glass of water or a bowl of figs. They slept. They got cross, they got scared, they slept again. The sunlight began to sink away.

As the hours ticked away towards ten o'clock, Xanthe became increasingly silent. She could not believe that, by allowing herself out to celebrate with the crowd, she had fluffed the meeting and probably with it, the whole operation. A great wave of shame shivered through her and she wept, unable to tell Betty why she was so upset.

"Because we've been here more than twenty-four hours – isn't that enough reason?"

"It's true, I've not been here this long before, but Paul will spring us. You'll see."

But the time had gone now, and Xanthe, feeling her body wrecked and her mind wandering, felt inconsolable. She had not even *tried* to send the signal. It was humiliating and, once again, all her fault.

*

They slept again and were woken by voices outside the door. The light indicated it was morning again. A moment later, the door opened, daylight flooded in, followed by Jurgen.

"Ladies, I apologise for leaving you here longer than I intended. It would not do to keep the American public waiting. Fortunately, let me say that you are free to go. Your clothes will be returned."

"Thanks, Paul," muttered Betty under her breath.

"But two things before you go," he said, with an air of menace. "First, do not underestimate me – I address myself to Fraulein Shirley. I have checked up on you, and you spent some time in Berlin, have you not – attached to the American embassy. That is right, is it not?"

Xanthe nodded. Was it possible that they had connected the speedy exit of Shirley Johnson from Berlin with the suspicious disappearance of the "murderess" Xanthe Schneider? She held her breath, but apparently, they had not.

"Your time in Berlin. You were not working then as a journalist, were you?"

"No," said Xanthe.

"Yet you are one now? Is that right?"

"I am."

"It is just that your accent is, how do they say it – mid-Atlantic? You have evidently spent time also in England."

Xanthe was clutching the chair in front of her. Where was this going?

"I do not, of course, claim you are any more than you seem. Only, when I see you again, I will know for definite. I have specific orders to check on the past affiliations of American journalists and, believe me, I will check on you."

Xanthe glanced nervously at Betty, who stared straight ahead. She appeared to have escaped, for now.

"And one other thing, before I forget," said Jurgen with a piercing stare. "I believe you have recently given birth. I see by your eyes that I have guessed correctly."

Xanthe looked down. She could not glance at either her questioner or her friend.

"It is true, is it not?"

She nodded. She knew what she would have to say and she did not want to at all.

"Then may I ask who is looking after your baby? And why you came here so soon on a journalistic escapade?"

Xanthe looked up, clearly aware of the lie she must tell.

"Because the baby died and I needed the job to get away from the memory. There. Now you know."

The tears which flowed now were quite genuine. Jurgen stared uncomfortably, unsure how to reply.

"My sympathies, Miss Johnson – or should I give your married name? You are married, I assume?"

"Jurgen! Can't you see you've asked enough questions! Leave her alone, can't you?" Betty was fierce in her defence.

"Nonetheless, and I address this to Miss Shirley, Mrs Shirley – I will check these stories. I will check. Do not underestimate me."

"C'mon, Jurgen. We don't underestimate you. You made your point, ok?"

Jurgen stood tall, took a deep breath and smiled triumphantly.

"And now," he said. "It is not often given to us the chance to tell a journalist the news, but I thought I would share the latest with you. Have you heard it? No, I apologise again for keeping you cooped up. I understand that London radio reported yesterday that their battlecruiser *Hood* has been sunk, early that morning, and another battleship badly damaged. It exploded in action against German surface forces off the coast of Iceland. A great naval victory, against the invincible British navy too! I wanted to tell someone."

*

Xanthe made her way on foot across the city in the late afternoon heat. There was no swastika flying above the Acropolis, as she had been led to believe.

She had been shaking, in the hours ever since she heard Jurgen's news. German surface forces, powerful enough to sink one of the biggest warships in the world – it could only mean one thing. *Bismarck* was already out; it was too late. All that effort had been for nothing. The battleship was now preying on the convoys that kept Britain alive and in the war, and two capital ships had been beaten off. There was no way the navy could equip every convoy with a fleet powerful enough to fight off an attack of that kind. It was a naval disaster all right, and all because she had been delayed.

Or was it? They did seem to have been ready for *Bismarck*. They had pinpointed her enough to intercept, but – by the sounds of it – they would have been forced to split the Home Fleet in two to do so. It was still her fault. If only she had not dawdled so in Aegina. And now she had missed her radio operator too.

Xanthe knew about HMS *Hood* because of her links to Ralph, a political appointee at the Admiralty. She knew what the ship represented. Certainly, there were ships in the Royal Navy which packed a bigger punch. But *Hood* was, by some way, the biggest, the most famous, possibly also one of the oldest, yet the fastest, and perhaps also the best loved. She could imagine her steaming full speed through the freezing ocean and mists off Iceland at dawn, the battle ensigns flying, black smoke pouring from her twin funnels, flashing out orders by signal lamp to her accompanying ships.

It would have been a sight to see. She almost longed to have been there herself to see it, except that – if she had – she also would have been thrown into the icy sea to a quick death from exposure and drowning.

How could the navy have allowed it?

The answer was, she realised again with a pang, because they had no idea which route *Bismarck* would be taking to the Atlantic, and they'd had to divide their forces. With creeping despair, she realised that she had failed. She should have provided that information and she was too late. Those drowned, frozen sailors would be forever on her conscience.

She sat on the steps of the Metropolis, the cathedral, and watched the city still resting, after her exertions of two nights before, and began to think about her other worry. Betty.

Betty had not been pleased with her after Jurgen's speech.

"Was that true, honey? Berlin and England? I mean why didn't you *tell* me?"

"Well, I told you I had been studying in England."

"Yes, but Berlin? I mean, why not? Because listen, honey, if you're something you don't seem – if Jurgen's right to be suspicious of you – then I may be in one hell of a fix. I mean, I really took to you. I think we took to each other. Now I can't – I mean, I will not ask you to be straight, in case you can't. Only I didn't think I had to ask. I mean, really… And why didn't you tell me about the baby – I mean, I'm a reporter dammit, I should have put two and two together, but why didn't you say?"

Xanthe felt an overwhelming sense of guilt. Why should those in intelligence, who believed they were doing something straightforward, be expected to let everyone down – to betray. And she could not come clean now. Too much depended on it. Tears ran down her cheeks.

"Betty, I…" She reached out towards her new friend. "What can I say? I wouldn't do anything to hurt you. I've loved being in your company. And yes, I was in Berlin – and I kept quiet about it because I was called something else then. I had a different name. And look, Betty, there is a story there involving love and shame, and I will, I promise, tell it to you – in full. I just can't right now, partly, but only partly because it is just too upsetting. I can't expect you to trust me, yet that's all I can do."

She burst into tears. Betty reached into her handbag and brought out a hanky.

"I'm sorry, Betty. All I can say is I am what I seem to be. I am."

"That's all very well, Shirley. But I have to get out of here too. I don't want to be collateral damage to someone else's agenda. Now, I hope to see you at my flat later but – just for a while – I'm going to calm down and do some thinking and prepare for the broadcast."

She walked off with dignity and one backward wave. Xanthe watched her go, sadly and guiltily. Then she set her mind on the task ahead.

She had been wondering if there might be a slim chance. What would the radio operator do if she had not shown up? What would she have done in the same position? There was only one thing she could have done – try again the same time the following night.

As she sat on the steps of the Metropolis, she could think of nothing else, continually weighing up her chances. She had to try.

*

It was just dark. There was little traffic, not just because there was so little petrol, but because the blackout was now being fully enforced – after the air raid – and driving was a dangerous business. She had followed a circuitous route to the safe house to make sure she was not being followed. She stopped outside the unassuming doorway she had been shown by the priest only three days before, and she knocked. Once.

Immediately the door opened what seemed like a crack, and she was dragged through. It was pitch dark inside, and she felt the cold, oily muzzle of a gun held to her head.

"Speak your name." The voice was quiet and confident.

"Shirley. Snow in Ibiza."

In an instant, the gun left her temple.

"Shirley! Terribly nice to meet you. How do you do?"

This is very English, she thought. Just like a tea party in Cambridge.

"Hi!" she said.

"My name is Billy and I'm the sparks."

"What happened to Robin?"

"Change of plan, but worry not – I have your package. I've left it for you to open, though. Didn't want to get things too muddled!"

Her eyes were getting used to the gloom. Billy looked like a slept-in counterpane, tatty and crumpled. And unshaven.

"You look dreadful," she volunteered. "Did you walk all the way from London?"

"What did you expect? Brylcream?"

She was surprised he was defensive. Perhaps he liked her.

"Sorry, Billy. I meant it as a joke. You're a sight for sore eyes, actually."

Billy smiled and relaxed as he brought out Xanthe's package.

"I was one of thirty of us, left behind for wireless ops after the troops left and the Nazis came in. You're almost the first Brit I've seen since then."

"I'm not actually British."

"Whoopsie, sorry! Trust me to put my foot in it. Now here we are. I'm at your disposal."

It might be best not to announce myself as an American again, thought Xanthe. It wouldn't do for rumours of a rogue American to reach Jurgen's ears. He would quickly put two and two together, but Billy was discreet enough not to ask.

He gave a little, rather embarrassed, bow.

"Thank you, Billy, for everything you've done. Now let me try and put my machine together."

It had been less than a week since Xanthe had left home, but already the machinery before her seemed unfamiliar. She reminded herself that she knew Enigma machines, and all their various models, as well as she knew anything else in this insane world now. She put the pieces in order. Keyboard first, then the rotors, then the steckerboard, a spaghetti bolognese of wires. They needed a supply of electricity, and the source was going to have to be Billy's battery.

It looked nothing like the real thing, of course. This was a fake Enigma.

But assuming Bletchley had managed to extract the settings of the day and would, as they should have done every night at this time, broadcast them to her – then it would be an effective machine.

But hold on. The lights were not coming on. "Have you plugged it into your battery?"

"Hold your horses! Just doing it now."

Billy put some finishing touches to the makeshift wires attached to his radio equipment.

"Bingo," he said quietly. "Should work now. Bang on time."

Xanthe put her finger on the X button and was delighted to see the B come up.

"Ok, it's on – *we're* on! Now, where's that message for me?"

"Hold on, blimey you're impatient. Five minutes still till we're due."

It seemed like an age. Then at 10.15 p.m., Billy suddenly swept into action and put his headphones on his head.

More waiting.

"What's happening now?"

"I'm just waiting for our call sign. Then…" His face concentrated suddenly, and he reached for the pad.

Again, nothing.

"What's the sign?"

"Can't say," said Billy. "Sorry, careless talk and all that. Wait!"

The air seemed to be filled with imaginary bleeps and dots and dashes. Billy's hand flew across his pad. Then he took off his headphones.

"Well?"

"Well," said Billy, tentatively. "There are three sentences for you, but I don't understand them. '*A bright dark moon the sky. Every joy on your infantile verandah as quiet Kenyan wildebeest has nothing to do for Sundays through May but June.*' And finally, '*Every girl wants one.*'"

"Sounds odd, doesn't it? That's the settings, ok. Let's get on, shall we…?"

"No, hold on, there's more. There's also a message: '*Beast now loose. Imperative know destination. Immediate.*' They must be desperate. They've only coded it once. I suppose they must be hoping nobody makes a connection, but even I can hazard a guess what that one's about."

"Well, if you do, please don't say it," said Xanthe warningly. "Was it broadcast from London?"

"Yes, on Radio London on the English language wavelength. They've been doing the same every night for the past few nights at this time."

Xanthe was thinking as fast as she could. She felt exhausted and struggled to keep herself thinking clearly.

How was it the settings? We can't know everything, she told herself, but these were going to be their best guess in Bletchley at the Luftwaffe Enigma settings for the day – one reason for making the signal at 11 p.m. The minutes were ticking by too. Come on, Xanthe…

"What's the moon got to do with it," asked Billy.

"The first sentence gives me the order of the rotors, I, II and IV, then the ring positions they need to be set in. Those are the letters in the alphabet. It isn't a difficult code, I'm glad to say. 'Moon the sky' that's the – um – thirteenth letter, so we get thirteen, twenty, nineteen. That's not too tough."

She clicked the rotors into their correct positions.

"The second sentence is the wiring for the so-called *steckerboard*. What was it again? 'Every joy' means we link the E and the J, 'on your' is the O and the Y."

She grappled with the spider's web of wires and plugged them in either end.

"Can you read out the rest of the sentence? Thanks, Billy."

The pretend steckerboard was plugged and they were ready to go.

"Oh yes, the third sentence, that's the *kennegruppen* code for the day – 'Every Girl Wants One' which means EGW."

Xanthe was also thinking tactically. Her original purpose was to find out when *Bismarck* was sailing. The ship had now sailed and, judging by the tenor of the coded signal she had just received, they had now lost track of her. There had been a battle, so they had obviously known where the battleship was at one stage, but now the *Hood* was at the bottom of the ocean, their quarry lost somewhere in the Atlantic.

The navy must be taking other measures. They could not conceivably be relying entirely on her. But, even so, the weight of responsibility hung heavily. She must not get this wrong. Somewhere, four or five thousand miles away, forty thousand tons of naval metal was in the ocean spray, waiting for a convoy taking food or families to or from America. If she could possibly, possibly prevent their unnecessary and hideous deaths, by fire or drowning, she would do so.

But then why, in those circumstances, should *Bismarck* be heading *anywhere* in particular? That was the oddity. The purpose of her voyage was not to head anywhere, but to lurk somewhere on the convoy routes, refuelling occasionally from Nazi tankers. If the Admiralty believed she was heading somewhere, then it could only be for one reason: the *Bismarck* was damaged. Perhaps in the encounter with the *Hood* and maybe others. Perhaps later. Perhaps the navy had managed to get an aircraft carrier within striking range before they lost her. Maybe she was even leaking fuel oil across the Atlantic too. It explained the sudden urgency: *Bismarck* was heading for the safety of home ports, either back in Norway or in occupied France. But which one?

Still, none of this was, in a sense, her business. She just had to do what she had been trained to do – and to do what she was told.

"That's right," said Billy, reading her thoughts. "Ours is not to reason why…"

"Tennyson," said Xanthe. "I once had a crossword clue about that!"

"Ours is but to do and die – that's the next line," said Billy.

It was black humour, given their predicament, but it was at least humour. The tension seemed to relax. They were not defined by this poky basement and the smell of long-spilt ouzo.

"Ok, twenty minutes to go," said Billy grinning. "How're you getting on?"

"I've got to write this signal, haven't I?"

She sat down. She was pretty clear in her mind about what she was going to write. She started in English.

"*Chief of Staff to General Jeschonnek urgent message to Luftwaffe staff, Reich Air Ministry, Berlin. Jeschonnek has godson aboard Bismarck. Please advise heading.*"

Yes, that was about it. But was it too stark? Who knows – those were the lines she had been advised to try, basic, obvious and peremptory. It depended, above all else, on Nazi deference to make its mark. If an RAF air marshal of the seniority of Jeschonnek had asked for such information, and on such a flimsy excuse, it would have rung alarm bells everywhere. But, with a little luck, it would not do so in a Nazi Germany now immune to nervousness about such privileges, such immunity to questioning. And *Jeschonnek* – what a silly name too, thought Xanthe to herself.

The main danger was that Jeschonnek or his staff would see the message and repudiate it, but the chances were that he would only know about it when the reply had been made and, by that time, it would be too late. The signal would have been picked up in Luftwaffe code in Bletchley and the cat would be out of the bag.

Still, all she could do was her very best. She wasn't psychic. It was one of those occasions when she must not let the best be the enemy of the good. The signal had to go, now in sixteen and a half minutes. She translated it into German, then she set and double-checked the rotors and fed it through the Enigma process:

"*Jeschonnek hat Patenkind an Bord der Bismarck. Bitte informieren Sie sich auf Fahrtrichtung.*"

She read and re-read it. Is that what a Luftwaffe signal would sound like? Perhaps the mistakes in naval terminology might be assumed from a Luftwaffe officer. Still, there was no way now to make sure.

"Right, then," she said. "Just let me put it into code."

*

First, there was the time, 2300, followed by "*1tle*", to show there was just one message, then the number of characters.

Next, the starting position of the rotors, using a random "trigram" – let's say Xanthe Rose Schneider, XRS. She put the rotors so that those letters appeared in the little holes.

"What's your full name, Billy?"

"William Richard Edwards, if you must know."

Right. She put WRE in that position and it was encoded as ZDF. That was the introductory sentence:

"*2300 1tle-145 = XRS ZDF.*"

Next, the *kennegruppen* code for the day, to which she added her initial to the start, XS, to give XSEGW. Then she used the same positions to encode the message letter by letter, splitting it up into groups of five letters and not forgetting the X for the full stop at the end.

There was no time to check the German and nobody to check it with. Or so she assumed.

"Do you speak any German, Billy?"

"Sorry, love."

Right assumption.

"Ok. Never mind. Here we are then. Still got a couple of minutes to go. Do you know the right frequency? I know, it's a bit late to ask!"

"Luftwaffe general staff, check. Righto. Off in a jiffy."

A couple of minutes later, with a flurry of tappings, nearly silent in the house, and the message was gone. Gathering speed, hopefully, across Europe.

"Off we go, then," he said, packing up his equipment.

In all her preparations, Xanthe had never quite imagined the moments after sending, and, of course, if the Nazis had picked up the message nearby and had been able to use direction-finding equipment, they would not be far away. They must get out as soon as possible.

She imagined her message sweeping across occupied Europe, to be picked up at Luftwaffe headquarters in Berlin. She could picture the very building. She did so, willing it to reach the right junior's desk who would simply forward the request to the Admiralty. She knew these mind-over-matter games would probably make no difference, but she did it anyway. Hopefully, they were also decoding it in Bletchley and they would know she had succeeded – this far at least.

Right, think ahead, Xanthe. Struggling with tiredness and the aftermath of the rush of adrenalin, she tried to wrestle her thoughts into order. First task: put her dummy Enigma machine into the harbour where it could not be found. Her second task was somehow to get out of Athens and back to Indigo.

CHAPTER SEVEN

Athens, May 1941

"Bye, love," said Billy as soon as they were outside in the street and disappeared into the blackout.

Xanthe staggered out into the night, carrying the components of her machine. She was on her own again, unsure even of the reception she would get at Betty's flat – and who could blame Betty for being angry? She had risked compromising her. She had never asked her permission. She would have been more than cross if the tables had been turned. She felt lonely and isolated.

As soon as she was outside, she thought better of the harbour plan. It would take at least two hours to walk to Piraeus, and maybe half that to get to the sea, but she knew she might easily be stopped before she reached either. The wharfs were also guarded well, and it was just too big a risk.

There must be deepish water somewhere near if she could just wrack her brains. Then she remembered, she was only a few minutes' walk to the Kifissos River, which connected – or so Betty had told her – to the ancient underground rivers of Athens that snaked around the Acropolis.

She headed west, and sure enough, there was the muddy stream of the Kifissos. Wasting no time, she looked around her, flung her bag into the river and walked in the opposite direction towards Betty's flat in Patriarchou Joachim, behind the Acropolis, down the narrow streets with the little shops and no food. She breathed an enormous sigh of relief. If she possibly could, she would now get back to her son – if she could just get across the city in the curfew. She should never have left Indigo in the first place.

*

As usual, Betty's flat was filled with people, chatting happily and scurrilously, mainly exchanging rumours about the occupation. There were also conversations that Xanthe could overhear, as she let herself through Betty's invariably unlocked front door, about the battle for Crete and whether or not there had really been an Austrian mutiny. They barely looked up when she came in, another foreigner, student or journalist among so many.

She found Betty in the kitchen. The relief of having dumped her Enigma machine in the river was making her light-headed.

"Betty. I'm so sorry. Please forgive me. I owe you a huge amount and wouldn't hurt you for anything. I'll tell you as much as I can."

Betty gave her a bright smile.

"Hello, darling. I was worried about you. I was afraid Jurgen had got hold of you again…"

On the way there, in the dark, sticking to the shadows, peering ahead and behind, Xanthe had come to a decision. Betty had been wonderful to her. She had to accept the risk of taking her at least partly into her confidence, especially if she was going to find a way out of Greece. She owed her at least some of the truth. But how much, and how far to go?

Xanthe closed the kitchen door.

"What is it?"

"Listen, Betty. I can't say much. But I will tell you everything one day. You've been more than a friend to me these few days, and I am forever in your debt. But I need to leave soon."

"You mean…?"

Betty was clearly struggling with herself in some way.

"My dear Shirley," she said, hugging her. "I know. Or rather I *don't* know, but I don't need to know either. What you're telling me is that you can't wait for me to find a way out the front door. You need to slip out the back door. Right?"

Xanthe suddenly felt tears pricking the back of her eyes. It felt so wrong to say goodbye in such terms, using a false name, but she dared not risk that revelation.

"You're a brick, Betty. I need to get home because… because I've got a little boy… The baby didn't die."

She burst into tears, kicking herself for doing so as she did. She wept for Indigo and herself, and her distant father, and for Hugh and Ralph and all her hopes and dreams.

"Listen, darling. There was a time I believed in journalistic purity, but all I need to know – whatever it is you're doing – is that we're committed to the same side. And if I ever get out of here myself, I'll use whatever skills I have to save Greece, or help Greece save itself – whichever seems most practical at the time. Speaking of which…"

"I know, Betty. This is a kind of intimate request. But could I borrow a pair of your knickers?"

Betty laughed uproariously.

"My pleasure, honey. Now, dry your eyes, and I'm going to get you to talk to Daphne. She's just outside and you can trust her. She works at the photographic shop around the corner. She speaks perfect English. Ready? Right, let me get the knickers and bring her in."

By the time she had returned, with a dark-haired, dark-eyed girl in tow, Xanthe had composed herself and set her face in what she hoped was a trustworthy way.

They shut the kitchen door behind them.

"You need to leave," said Daphne, without bothering with the niceties. "It can be done. I did it a few weeks ago with my friends Jack and Bruce. One was English, one was Australian."

Xanthe nodded encouragingly.

"There is a boat leaving tomorrow. I will find out the details tonight. You can set off tomorrow morning, when it is light. The problem is, you don't speak Greek, do you?"

"No. Did Jack and Bruce?"

"Well, no, they didn't. But they were lucky. I went with them."

Xanthe laughed.

"That's what I call service. Can you go with me, by any chance?"

"I'm afraid I have to be in the shop for the next few days, but – if you can hang on – I certainly can. But I suggest you don't wait. Don't even wait until tonight."

It took a moment for what she was being told to sink in.

"Of course," said Xanthe, flustered. It was true that once Berlin had replied to her signal, then mystery would surround the reply when it reached Athens – assuming all went well. Why were they being told the destination set by *Bismarck*? It would be confusing and it may be that suspicion would be aroused once they heard it was a reply to a signal in Athens. Perhaps, for a while, they would look for an internal culprit, but it would hardly be long before someone like Jurgen wondered about her. She realised how little she actually knew about the technology of signal interception.

She collected her few possessions next to the sofa where she had slept. It was a devastating thing to do, alienating. The curfew was in place. She dared not go out.

She glanced over at Betty and saw her talking to a large man she had not seen before. He had blonde hair; this was no Greek. Betty kept on glancing over at her. Then the man did too, once, twice. What was going on?

Then to Xanthe's horror, they both moved over to the door and left. The tall man gave her a grim glance as he pulled the door behind him.

Xanthe's mind was now completely jumbled. She knew she was physically exhausted. She knew, on the face of it, that Betty would never betray her. Yet should she also not listen to her gut feelings? How easy it would be just to relax and be led into some kind of a trap. But who could she trust absolutely? Was there anybody, if Betty was behaving oddly?

If she could not trust Betty, then she would need to be at least a little careful of Daphne. Was she going insane? Was this what happened to you when you spent too long in the field – you started getting suspicious of the merest look? Or was it what happened if you went into the field just a few short weeks after giving birth?

No, it was no good; she would have to leave and go – where? It was now very late, there was a curfew and she had nowhere to go.

The people in Betty's flat were too busy talking to notice her, as she gathered her few belongings together into a bag that could go on her shoulder. From the kitchen she found, not bread – nobody had bread in Athens anymore – but a pile of raisins, which appeared to be the only food still widely available. She filled her pockets, took a drink of water from the large bottle that Betty kept in the cooler and slipped out of the house.

In a moment, she was outside in the cool night. Not a sound. No movement. And it struck her, at this critical moment, that there was somewhere she could go. Nor was it very far. She would go, if she could get there, to the Metropolis cathedral and pray that it was not locked at night.

She would wait there for daylight and then she would seek out the priest in the confessional, and ask for guidance, geographical as well as spiritual.

*

The dark streets were completely deserted. It was nearly midnight. There were shadows of people slipping around silently, and she could see them once her eyes adjusted a little to the gloom. There were no signs of the crowds of revellers from the night of the raid. She knew which way to go, if only she could find it in the dark. But she was beginning to feel limp and helpless now that the adrenalin of the evening had dissipated.

If she really had been betrayed, then she had precious little time to get under cover where she would not be found. The first turning she took seemed completely unfamiliar. Fighting back the panic, Xanthe retraced her steps and tried again.

This time, looming out of the dark were the arches of the great cathedral.

She peered through the gloom in all directions and made a dash up the steps. There was an ancient iron handle on the door. Desperately, she pushed it down, and to her astonishment, the door swung open. In a moment, she was inside and in complete blackness.

She stood quite still and could see, up ahead, a single candle. It illuminated the transept where she had gone before, where she knew the confessionals were.

Very slowly, she made her way over, gingerly stepping around the chairs. Her hopes were beginning to rise. She appeared to be totally alone.

She slipped into the first confessional and peered through the grill. There was nobody there.

A tiny shifting sound caught her attention. It was so tempting to risk going back outside to see. She slipped out and into the next confessional. She drew the curtain aside and knelt down.

To her surprise, a young woman's voice spoke to her quietly in Greek. Was this really a confessional? She was nervously unfamiliar with the rituals and rules of the Orthodox church.

"Sorry," she said, very quietly. "I don't speak the language."

"Shirley? Is that you? It's Daphne. Why are you here?"

"I lost my nerve. What's your excuse? How did you get here before me?"

"Speak quietly. We have an arrangement with the priest. He signals to me if there is someone asking for help and I skip in here. Sometimes I'm here all night. I try not to think about the ghosts."

"So you didn't see me coming or something?"

Paranoia was beginning to weigh her down.

"Is everything all right? Listen carefully. I have the information I needed. There is a yacht leaving a small harbour north of Rafina tomorrow night, at dusk. You will need to walk there, and it will take five or six hours, so even if you wait until daylight, you should still get there. But it will be tough and hot, and you have not been looking that well, I am sorry to have to tell you. So you need to decide. Can you manage it?"

Xanthe's heart sank.

"I think so. I have to really. Where is the yacht going?"

"It will take you to Egypt, along with some RAF people and a couple of Anzacs left behind. But look, Shirley, the difficulty is that you will be a woman alone, and you will need to dress Greek and be able to speak the language if you are stopped by anyone unfriendly. So, I am sending someone with you."

"Really? Sorry to sound so pathetic."

"You don't, of course. Now, if you are sure, we need to put you somewhere safe for the night, and it so happens that your guide for tomorrow is quite close. So, when you're sure nobody can see you, I want you to go and pray in the chapel of Our Lady, and I will come there in a moment and introduce you."

*

"Where are we going?" said Xanthe in a whisper, as she was led down some ancient steps, blackened with age, below the cathedral. Then again down an old brick passage and into what seemed like a cavern.

It was freezing cold and damp. Daphne carried an electric torch. She swung it around.

"We are heading towards the ancient river which used to flow through Athens in classical times and now goes underground. It also provides us with a safe passage under the city, and we are going to wrap you up down here for the night."

Xanthe shivered involuntarily. It wasn't so much the temperature. It was that the wraiths of Athens past seemed to live here already. She felt lonely and somewhat spooked.

"Don't worry, Shirley. We have many blankets. You should rest here for a few hours and then Giorgios will lead you to the yacht. And I will leave you with the torch. There is a lamp also. Why did you leave Betty's house?"

"I suddenly didn't feel safe. I don't know really. I was being silly, I'm sure."

"Did something happen?"

"No," Xanthe lied.

"Because if something happened, however small, I need to know about it."

She took a deep breath.

"I just got nervous that Betty and that blonde man were talking about me. I don't have any doubts about Betty, honestly. I'd trust her with anything. Really, I shouldn't have panicked."

In the darkness, Daphne grew silent.

"Very sensible precaution," she said. "Now, here is Giorgios and he has another torch and a spare battery, as I do, and a small lamp."

Strange, thought Xanthe. Why did Daphne not ask more about it? Was she so certain that Betty was safe and straight? Perhaps she was. Perhaps – no, that was to let in the madness…

Meanwhile, the shape of a young man stood in their path. The light flicked in his face and he gave her a big grin.

"Giorgios – I'm so glad it's you!"

"I am also glad," he said.

Daphne handed over the torch, fished out another and gave her an unexpected kiss. Then she turned to go.

"Wrap her up warm, Giorgios. And very good luck!"

*

Somewhere on the Atlantic, five thousand miles or more away, the *Bismarck* was cutting through the waves, heading perhaps back around Iceland, perhaps to France.

Somewhere, a desperate British fleet was searching, propping their eyes open with their binoculars, sweeping the horizon for a giveaway flash. Somewhere, perhaps even then, the signals office at Luftwaffe headquarters was sending a message to the German admiralty, asking for an answer to General Jeschonnek's question. Perhaps at that very moment, perhaps not yet, the reply was speeding through the ether, picked up in Athens to the consternation of Jeschonnek's staff and intercepted by one of the listening stations in England on a shortwave receiver. Then it would pop out of the teleprinter in Hut 6, ready for decoding.

CHAPTER EIGHT

Athens, May 1941

Xanthe could not sleep. She was cold and could see her breath in the pale torchlight. She was wondering about her own emotional resilience, let alone her physical resilience for the long walk. She was, she felt, quite unnecessarily delighted at seeing Giorgios again. She felt absurdly safe with him.

He was not sleeping either and kept on looking over to her pile of blankets with concern. He could see she was in pain, even if it had probably not occurred to him that it was the aftermath of giving birth.

"Miss Shirley," he said, with great seriousness, sitting up. "You are cold; I am warm. I invite you to share my blankets and heat."

It was not an invitation she would normally entertain, especially not from a man some years younger than herself. But these were not normal times. In a moment, she was across the cavern and, in the pale lamplight, lying warmer in his arms.

The tension dissolved and she found herself sobbing there quietly. He kissed her gently but insistently on the lips. Despite herself, she found she was kissing him back. His stubble tickled. It felt rough and even a little exciting.

"No!" she kept telling him as his hand crept around. "No, Giorgios, sorry."

"I may? I promised to love you," he said finally.

"You promised what?" She thought of Neville Chamberlain's famous line: *No such undertaking has been received.* "Sorry, Giorgios. I like you, but I can't."

"Ah well," said Giorgios. Then he fell asleep.

*

She woke feeling cold and damp. It was still pitch black.

A whole army of "what-ifs" began to float through her mind. What if Daphne and Betty were both agents for the Nazis? What if they were working together? What if Daphne had been killed and had led them both down to this dank spot to die? What if nobody showed them the way out and she never got home to Indigo? What, in fact, if she had misjudged the whole thing, come to Greece ill-prepared, had messed up the message and the *Bismarck* was still at large in the Atlantic?

For goodness sake, she told herself. You are a foreign agent and a foreign correspondent. You might expect this kind of emotional turmoil – but you can also deal with it. She struggled to sit up, letting the blanket fall to the stone floor, and breathed deeply three times. Giorgios was stirring next to her. She was in with more than a chance if she kept her head and kept going.

Then she prayed for a little more strength of mind and body, and began to feel better. Yes, she really was feeling a little stronger.

Giorgios was dressed and on his feet above her.

"Miss Shirley. We must go. I can only find you a few plums, they are the best I can do. Are you ready to come?"

"Thank you, Giorgios," she said, as she walked slowly on his arm along the stone passage towards the sunlit patch ahead. "I am so grateful to you and Daphne. I was just feeling sorry for myself."

"You should also feel sorry for us. You can go home. We are here for many years of starvation and tyranny, I fear. For how many years? God knows."

"I know. I am so grateful. Honestly."

"I do not mean that. Do you not think we are also grateful to you for coming to our country to tell the world what is happening? Or whatever you came here for…"

Xanthe ignored the hint. They were now back in the cathedral, and in a moment she was outside in the early morning brightness, blinking, as if seeing it for the first time.

"And now we must walk," said Giorgios. "For maybe five hours, if you can manage it."

"I can manage. What do you mean 'we'?"

"Because I come with you."

Xanthe was suddenly overwhelmed with relief. She felt tears, unbidden and unwelcome, pricking the back of her eyes.

"Thank you, Giorgios."

He looked embarrassed and reached into his pocket. Then he unfolded a canvas bag.

"I have brought you this. So you can look… real. As if you go to market. And this hat."

More relief. She badly needed a hat.

"And if you are asked things, you don't answer," he said. "I will talk."

*

The opportunity arose all too soon.

They were walking out of the outskirts of the city, full of overgrown market gardens and empty fields, when a German patrol marched out of a corner. "Halt!" said the officer. Giorgios and Xanthe stopped. The soldiers at the back leered excitedly.

"*Wohin gehst du?*"

Xanthe pretended not to understand. The soldier looked around at his colleagues.

"I go with my sister to our aunt's farm. She is not well," said Giorgios in German. Then he continued at length in Greek.

The officer waved them on. Xanthe breathed again.

"That wasn't too bad. What did you tell him?"

"I told him my life story, starting with our journey to visit the farm of my aunt today, and going back from there. It seemed to bore them."

"I can't think why..."

Although this little escape was a relief, Xanthe was aware she was flagging. Her scar ached. The sun was swelteringly hot and high in the sky, and they seemed barely to have left Athens. Could she do it? Or was she anyway destined for some kind of swoop by the secret police? If Betty had really informed on her, she could expect to be picked up any time now. Or worse than picked up.

"Quick! Off the road!" shouted Giorgios. "Something's coming."

Using her remaining reserves of strength, Xanthe sprinted after her friend and into a small cleft in the wall where she slid down, light-headed, onto the ground.

An ancient lorry was moving slowly up the hill, spluttering and wheezing. The driver appeared to be looking for someone.

Was this it? Was this what betrayal looked like, she wondered, peering out? Why had she trusted anyone?

Xanthe was aware that one leg was showing, and possibly more of her. Sure enough, the driver stopped close to them and stared. He stuck an swarthy face out of the window and shouted something including the word "*patrótis*".

"He is asking: are you patriots?" explained Giorgios, pressed close against her. "Yes," he said, emerging brazenly from their cleft, "are you?"

"Come on," he hissed to Xanthe. "This is our lift…"

"But how do you know?"

They climbed up and squeezed gratefully into the cab. The driver put out an unsavoury, hairy hand.

"How do you do," he said. "Betty sent me. I am to drive you where you want to go."

A great sense of relief flooded through Xanthe, and, for the first time that day and despite her exhaustion, she felt the welcome breeze in her dyed dark hair. So Betty had been true to her. Of course she had. Betty was a brick and a courageous one. And, as the old lorry rumbled over the broken road, there, glinting in the distance, through the ubiquitous scrub and mountains, was the sea.

"You know what, Miss Shirley?" said Giorgios, affectionately. "You are even beginning to smell like one of us."

Xanthe began to laugh, and soon they were all three roaring with laughter.

Then they passed a peasant who made a sign with his hand and the lorry screeched to a halt.

"My friends, you must get out," said the driver. "There is a checkpoint ahead. My friend here will conduct you over the mountain."

"So near and yet so far," said Xanthe. "Look Giorgios, you leave me here and go back in the lorry. I'll be safe enough."

"No, Miss Shirley. Not leaving."

The sun was lower in the sky as they finally picked their way through the scrub and olive trees into the harbour from the north. Xanthe and Giorgios seemed an unlikely couple. He unshaven; she in a strange hat, but looking for all the world like an adopted Londoner on a hike, lagging behind in the heat and dust, almost overwhelmed with exhaustion and pain.

Ahead, the peasant kept a sharp lookout. But although he looked like a man of the soil, he spoke near perfect English.

"Hold her hand," he instructed Giorgios. "Betty has told me to look after Miss Shirley no matter what."

Tears began running down Xanthe's cheeks. These were clearly the hot coals heaped on her head that St Paul promised the faithless. Once more she had failed to judge someone correctly. It was all too difficult. Why had she ever suspected Betty and her friends? How could she have got it so wrong? This one really had to be her final trip. There was no way she would ever go into the field again, she promised herself.

A short while later, there was the harbour, and for a moment, the war dropped away, with the remaining sun glinting on the water and the small yacht, rigged for fishing, beside the wharf. It was invisible from the surrounding area, a tiny port, more like a fishing village, and she could see immediately why it was an excellent place for a clandestine departure.

"You wait here," said Giorgios, "and I must go. When they hoist the Greek flag, it is a signal that it is safe for you to go aboard. Now, Miss Shirley, I kiss you goodbye. I don't know who you are, but I wish you safe home. May we meet again."

She kissed him, tears rolling down her cheeks, for herself, for Greece and its trauma, for her own shattered heart. She watched him go. A minute or so later, he and the peasant had disappeared.

There was not long to wait. She must have cut it fine because only fifteen minutes later, she looked up to see the blue and white Greek flag fluttering in the breeze. She looked around and walked, still in pain, as quickly as she could, to the dockside. As she did so, she was aware of two men, in tattered British battledress, making their way in the same direction.

Two crewmen emerged from deep inside the boat, took Xanthe's arm and helped her below. She was led through a small hole cut in the cabin wall.

"Do not worry. There is little air, but it should not be for long," she was told. "Just until we are at sea."

She curled up on a couple of sacks. The soldiers were clearly being led elsewhere. The door was shut behind her and she was once more in darkness, with the little waves lapping against the side of the boat and shouts from above.

CHAPTER NINE

Alexandria, June 1941

"Miss Schneider? My name is Sub-Lieutenant Patterson, and I am here to conduct you to the airfield."

A slightly crumpled young man in white naval uniform saluted her.

"Well, heaven be praised. Recognition at last," said her friend Frank, the executive officer of HM submarine *Rorqual*, which had taken her from the yacht, together with two British soldiers and three airmen, and ferried them to Alexandria.

Xanthe had been escorted to the submarine rendezvous, just outside Turkish territorial waters, by the consul there, who appeared to be running his own informal navy.

Alexandria had been extraordinary. For all her involvement with the Royal Navy over the previous year, she had never visited a British dockyard – though she had been to Kiel, of course. There was the bustle of men coming ashore, and she could see the dark grey shapes of an old cruiser or two, lying at anchor next to the ancient walls and stones. But the welcome had left something to be desired. Nobody seemed to have expected her. Nobody knew who she was when she and Frank had gone from office to office to arrange her air transport back to London. They were met with blank faces – sometimes downright rude ones.

"I suppose it's the heat," said Xanthe apologetically.

"I'll give them heat," said Frank and proceeded to do so. His stubbled face and dirty shirt, after a month at sea, contrasted with the pristine uniforms of the desk officers they met around the dockyard.

"Listen," he said. "Miss Schneider is an extremely brave woman. I don't know what she's been doing because I'm not allowed to know and neither are you. But my instructions are to deliver her to you for urgent despatch to London for debriefing. If you're unable to organise that, please put me in touch with an officer who can."

Finally, here was Sub-Lieutenant Patterson.

"About bloody time, if you ask me," said Frank.

"My apologies, Miss Schneider. We have received instructions after all, and I've been told to take you to the airfield immediately. Can I offer you a drink? Water? I'm afraid we don't have terribly long."

"Where are all the big ships?" asked Frank as they strode out to a waiting car.

"Oh well, we can't say, of course. But between you and me, they were sent to Gibraltar to replace Force H which has been hunting the *Bismarck*."

The *Bismarck*. Of course! She had been so exhausted and had slept for so long on the submarine, that she had almost forgotten the reason she had come here in the first place. On board the *Rorqual*, she was still in the dark. But here, she could find out the end of the story.

"I'm so sorry, but I have been rather cut off. What happened to the *Bismarck*?"

"You don't know? Oh well, we got her. The Home Fleet sank her last week. She was heading for France and nearly made it. Miss Schneider? Are you all right?"

Xanthe dissolved into tears.

"Excuse me for being a nuisance. But can I sit down, just for a moment?"

Patterson and Frank helped her to a battered chair, and for a few minutes, Xanthe wept uncontrollably.

She cared little whether her signal had made a difference or not. The *Hood* was avenged, Hugh was avenged. With or without her assistance, the navy had done it. The team, of which she was a minor part, had achieved it. They were tears of intense relief, for herself and for Indigo, in a peculiarly uncertain world.

Then she blew her nose, took a deep breath, brushed herself down and got up. The two naval officers offered her a hand and looked a little embarrassed.

"I'm very sorry. Now, if you don't mind, I'm recovered."

Good grief, she said to herself as she headed across the naval tarmac towards Patterson's car. She had felt so exhausted that she had wondered in Athens whether she was suffering from some kind of post-natal infection, but she felt physically better, and now she was pretending to be recovering mentally too. Is my upper lip now stiff, she asked herself? Have I actually become one of them?

*

The homecoming in London was almost as disconcerting. Nobody met her at the airfield in Buckinghamshire. She had been driven into London and was dropped at Euston, where she caught the train to Bletchley.

"Shh! He's asleep," said Sister Agnes, smiling. "Oh, it's you! How lovely to see you, Xanthe. Little Indy will be so pleased to see you too…"

Indy? She thought the diminutive had been hers alone. Why was anyone else using it? She put her small bag down by the cot.

"Do you think he's missed me?"

"Of course he's missed you! He was only just asking, 'When's mummy coming home?'"

For a moment, Xanthe wondered if this could be right. Had she been away so long that Indigo could speak? No, she was more tired than she realised – this was one of Agnes' fund of little jokes.

A moment later, he was in her arms, still sleeping, and she began to sleep too, the sleep of the depths of her relief. "But this isn't home either," she murmured as she fell asleep. "I need to go back to Ohio."

*

When there was a knock on the door, she was unsure whether she had slept for five minutes or five hours, except that Indigo slept on, much as before, giving little twitches as he lay there, breathing deeply.

"Come in?" she said, as quietly as she could.

Whoever it was came in.

"Oh, um, um. So sorry, I'll… I mean, I'll come back later."

"Oh, come in, Alan, for goodness sake. I haven't got a breast out or anything to frighten the British horses."

He grinned sheepishly.

"I know this may be hard to understand, but not everyone shares this obsession with breasts, enjoyed by so many of my male colleagues."

"Really? Oh well, I thought you all did."

For a moment, her thoughts drifted to Giorgios in the cavern under Athens cathedral. What was he doing now?

"Ah, um, well…" said Alan. "Has anyone said thanks to you?"

"No. I haven't seen anyone."

"Honestly, what a shower! Well, er, Fleming asked me to say thanks from him."

"Thanks for what?"

"Because your message got through and it got a reply."

"It did?"

A huge electric charge of jubilation pulsed through Xanthe, and she gave a great whoop of triumph. Then she checked herself – and then the baby, stirring uncomfortably beside her.

"Oh, look, don't make me too excited, Alan. I need Indigo to sleep."

"Yes, amazing, wasn't it? The message from Jeschonnek got a reply, saying that *Bismarck* was heading for Brest."

"So I *did* help?" she said in a whisper.

"Yes, I gather you really did. Officially, *Bismarck* was spotted heading in a circle by a plane from Coastal Command. But thanks to you, we knew far better where to look. The Home Fleet did the rest. Thanks to you."

"Oh Alan, that is absolutely fab!"

"Fab? What's that when it's at home?"

She laughed.

"Just means good, right. Fab?"

*

All that held back her jubilation was the peculiar sight of someone she knew in the crowd on Euston station. She felt absolutely certain it had been Hugh. But why had she seen him? Was she so exhausted that her imagination was playing tricks on her? Or was he actually alive – that seemed impossible, given the descriptions she had been given about his death. Had it actually been some kind of ghost, sent to welcome her home? Yet, if it was, it hadn't seen her.

She had shouted across the heads of the crowd of soldiers and sailors on leave – "Hugh! Hugh! It's me! Over here!" But there had been no reaction. Had she gone completely doolally?

As soon as she had slept, she would contact his friend, Tug and find out if there was any possibility, any mistaken identity that would have allowed Hugh to have survived.

In the meantime, she was going to sleep.

BOOK THREE

THE SWISS APPOINTMENT

PROLOGUE

Bletchley, October 1941

It was a cold, damp and windy autumnal day as Alan Turing and Xanthe Schneider met on the platform of Bletchley station with day return tickets for Cambridge, one hundred and twenty-six minutes of sooty slog up the line. It was Sunday morning, the steam was swirling around the engine and the church bells were silent.

"A bit sad. No bells," said Turing as the train drew in, snorting and puffing.

"Oh, I'm not sad at all," she said. "Indy is six months old today. That's half a year. How can I be sad? It's going to be time soon to leave the nest."

"If you mean leave Bletchley Park, I've never thought of it as a nest," he said. "I'm not sure anyone ever has done before. This may just be a historic thought!"

The train was not as full as it sometimes was, and they managed to find seats next to each other in a smoke-filled compartment, with a couple of obvious cryptographers and two sailors heading – where? To Lowestoft or Felixstowe perhaps. The cryptographers had climbed in at the same time as Alan and Xanthe, presumably going on leave in the same direction.

They fell silent with the rhythm of the train and the telegraph wires along the track as they seemed to swoop up and down hypnotically.

They had been reminded by Fleming that they must not talk about their mission on the way. Careless talk and all that.

"May I?" Xanthe looked at the paper he was carrying. It was the *News Chronicle*. Typical Turing, she thought. The Nazi advance appeared to be getting nearer to the outskirts of Moscow. There was a small item on a new prime minister in Japan, called General Tojo. Otherwise, the usual sports results from the day before. There was even an advertisement for Jeyes toilet paper, and Xanthe remembered how her wartime toilet paper article had offended the *New Yorker* editor, but had persuaded him to agree to her last, rather frightening mission in occupied Greece.

They walked up through Station Road and Hills Road from Cambridge station and down Regent Street. The city smelled of cold and damp. How could she have lived here for a year, she wondered, as they passed the tiny front door of Simonetta College, the glorified finishing school where her father had sent her all the way from Cincinnati back in 1938?

"I think I'd better do the talking with the man," said Turing. "He is rather strange, and I do sort of know him, though he didn't have much time for my contributions to his seminars."

"I don't think that's how I remember it, Alan. I think he needed your conversation to make them fly along. That was where we first met, just before the war?"

"Of course," said Alan. "You know, I'd forgotten that. We've got to know each other so well since. You and Joan are my closest female friends anywhere in the world."

"That's nice, Alan. Only don't treat me like you treated poor Joan."

Turing stopped in mid-flow.

"Oh, come on, Xanthe – I just broke off our engagement. It wasn't as if either of us were exactly in the throes of passion."

"Yes, but by phone? In the hut?"

Turing was quiet for a time, and Xanthe was immediately sorry.

"I'm so sorry, Alan. I was only teasing. You know we both love being your friends, and you've done so much for me. Without you I'd be starving in a garret somewhere with Indy."

"Well, hardly. Still, let's cross fingers for the most important mission so far."

They crossed their fingers in front of them as they walked along.

"It's because of Indy that I can't go gallivanting on active service to Nazi-occupied Europe anymore. You do understand, don't you?"

Turing ignored her as they reached the door of Trinity College and marched purposefully into the porter's lodge, underneath the great four-turreted tower that acted as a gateway to the college.

Xanthe felt the familiar nerves which she always felt when she was out of her depth – most of the time at work – creeping into her stomach. Well, she thought to herself, I've killed a Gestapo man with an Enigma rotor, I've crossed the Mediterranean in a smuggled yacht, but I've never gone and asked to see the foremost philosopher in the world before.

"We are here to see Professor Wittgenstein," said Turing, unfolding a letter of introduction from Commander Denniston at Bletchley but using an address at the Admiralty.

What had Xanthe expected the reaction to be? Fawning agreement or self-deprecating support? Perhaps haughty snobbery. But whatever it was, she had hardly expected the nervous, almost panicky reaction they actually received. There was a great deal of whispering and consultation between ever more senior porters before they were led into a side room while they waited for a personage described as "the Dean".

He had evidently not been far away because, in a moment, a gowned figure like a huge crow, came into the room and greeted Turing like a long-lost friend.

"Mr Turing, how excellent to see you. I do hope you are well." He ignored Xanthe completely. She and Turing exchanged glances.

"Now, you wanted to see Professor Wittgenstein. That's right, isn't it? May I ask whether you had been given an appointment?"

"Well, I wrote twice but got no reply."

"You see, the thing is, Alan… this is a little embarrassing, but not only has he *gone*, but we are not sure quite where he has gone *to*. Of course, one is familiar with the patterns of wartime secret work and all that, but my feeling was that our friend was not exactly suited for that kind of thing. Temperamentally, I mean."

"How do you mean, exactly?" said Xanthe.

"Too cross, I mean. Too emotional. But I do actually have an address – since it's you, Alan: Nuffield Buildings, Guy's Hospital, London SE1. Make of that what you like."

Turing's face betrayed some confusion.

"How strange. Is he doing war work of some kind? I don't suppose it can be an easy time to be in Southwark, I imagine, with the bombs and blitz and blackouts."

"Well, that's what I thought too," said the Dean. "But actually, I find the address is a nurses' home. For some reason, the greatest philosopher it has been my privilege to know, is working, just between you and me, in some secrecy as a hospital porter."

CHAPTER ONE

London, October 1941

It had seemed such a simple request, such a small favour to ask her, that Xanthe Schneider had hardly hesitated before she accepted. But the main reason she did so was that she was beginning to feel uncomfortable that the Admiralty was still paying her when all she was doing was looking after her baby, now six months old. Other people on active service – and on the payroll of the British government – were risking their lives every day. Her position was unorthodox, as an adjunct to naval intelligence when somebody needed to go abroad – it was certainly somewhat unofficial. She had felt for some time that she ought really to be a little more willing.

Her handful of close friends at Bletchley Park knew her role – not very many of them, secrecy being what it was – and told her she was being silly. Had she not ventured into Nazi Berlin and German-held Athens in pursuit of elements of Enigma puzzles, some of them a little fleeting? She had certainly played her part and hardly needed to; she was an American citizen, and the sword of the United States remained resolutely sheathed.

Somehow or other, the struggle against the Nazis had become her own struggle. She defended Roosevelt and her fellow country people in argument most weeks, as soon as somebody heard her accent, but in her heart of hearts she knew her priorities now: first to look after poor fatherless Indigo in his cot, then to help the Hut 8 team in any way she could and then, and only then, to help the Admiralty. They did pay her wages, after all.

That was where the discomfort came in. She had visited Athens when Indy had been just a few weeks old, arriving only a few weeks after the German invaders, ostensibly as an American correspondent. Actually, she had been on a mission to trick the Luftwaffe into transmitting the direction the battleship *Bismarck* was sailing, still on the loose in the Atlantic, in a version of Enigma they could read back at Bletchley. By good luck or good judgement – more the former than the latter – she had survived. But she had returned so nervous, so exhausted, still not recovered from the birth six weeks before, that she had vowed it would be her last mission abroad.

So when Alan Turing had asked her to join him she had said yes straight away. It was just a simple trip to Cambridge. There would be no pretence, nothing undercover, and then it would be done. Back to her old work at Bletchley Park and as an occasional editorial assistant in the tiny offices of the *New Yorker*, around the corner from the Bank of England.

She had been a foreign correspondent in Berlin and Athens and she had loved the work, but she remained haunted by the idea that she had just been acting a role – on the instructions of the Naval Intelligence Division. She still had something to prove, but – oh well, she had tried, God knows.

"We're just seeing a philosophy professor," Turing had said. "I would have gone by myself, but Fleming suggested you come too…"

"What's it all about? What's he want us to say?"

Turing's face had clouded. He hated to be official.

"I'm afraid I'm not allowed to say until you're definitely committed," he said. "You have to say yes first. You know what Fleming is like," he'd added apologetically.

Xanthe did. Lieutenant Commander Fleming, with his somewhat flashy arrogance and impatience, had sent her to Athens on what she feared had been faulty information.

"Ok, ok, but why me? I can't say I'm one of the world's great philosophy students."

"Well," Turing had said shyly. "I suspect that he thinks you would provide a little encouraging glamour for the meeting, being generally more attractive than I am. Actually, my suspicion is that this particular professor is less susceptible to feminine charm than most – but then, Fleming is apt to think that everybody is exactly like him."

He slapped his head.

"What am I thinking of? You know him already don't you? It's Professor Wittgenstein…"

"You mean the strange guy in the bedroom?"

Dimly, Xanthe remembered the incident. She had been invited by an admirer, who had not shown up, to one of the professor's unusual seminars and had bitterly regretted going at all. Turing had rescued her when she could find nowhere to sit except for the professor's scrupulously made bed.

"Oh, for goodness sake, Alan, I can't! I mean, what would I have to say to him? I remember him as the most intense man I ever met, and I never really met him, did I? I don't think he even looked in my direction. He was all Kant and cowboy films, as I remember rightly."

"Oh, come on Xanthe, be a sport. You've braved scarier things than Professor Wittgenstein before now. I don't think he liked me much either. I don't think he forgives people who disagree with him, even in private. It would help to have a more neutral face there. And it would be fun to work together. It's just a trip to Cambridge, after all. I tell you what – I'll lend you his book. It seems to me to be complete baloney, and those are the bits I understand. It'll give you a little background – you don't have to read it, of course."

*

There was another reason why Xanthe agreed to join Turing on the Cambridge trip. She had an idea that meeting a renowned philosopher, who had famously escaped the Nazis from his native Vienna, might provide her with some material for the *New Yorker*, if she could think how she might package it. It would impress Bob in their London office, at least.

But Bob was not impressed.

"Sorry, honey, Joe's got that one," said Bob. It was Bob's role to administer this distant outpost of the *New Yorker* empire. She had heard this infuriating sentence over and over again. Joe had got this one and Joe had got that one – he was covering pretty much everything around Europe, and those elements he was not covering seemed to be tackled by the indomitable Mollie Panter-Downes, down in Surrey. There hardly seemed to be a corner of the *New Yorker* where she could flex her journalistic muscles now that the great Joe Liebling had arrived back from occupied Paris via New York.

Liebling was lovely. He had a big smile and a big heart. But he was also one of the big beasts in the world of journalism, and he tended to trample the undergrowth around him. Good image, Xanthe said to herself – like a rogue elephant – what a pity she had nowhere to use it.

She could not help liking him and his large round face and huge round spectacles whenever he dived into the office in search of his expenses, which were prodigious. But even so, she wished she had more space to prove herself and her talent.

Then, shortly after the trip to Cambridge, Liebling had, in fact, asked for her help. He wanted to write about Colonel Britton, the mysterious figure behind the BBC European Services 'V for Victory' campaign, which had begun that spring and really seemed to be blowing sparks from the embers of the defeated peoples of occupied Europe, nudging them into the state of mind that might persuade them to resist.

"Say, Xanthe?" said Liebling one day when they had coincided in the office.

Astonished that he even knew her name, she swung round. He seemed to have papers in piles across every working surface.

"Bob says you might give me support on this Colonel Britton story. Can you see what you can find out about him? What kind of colonel is he? Where did he serve? That kind of thing. Oh, and the most important bit: will he meet me?"

"Ok, Joe. Leave it with me..."

It seemed, at first, that the identity and background of Colonel Britton was steeped in even greater secrecy than Enigma. Everyone she asked at the BBC either didn't know, or clearly did know and was pretending otherwise. But now she was back in touch with the Admiralty directly, she tried asking Fleming for his help.

Fleming claimed he was powerless but directed her to the Ministry of Economic Warfare at Electra House and gave her a contact name. But even that trail went cold, and she began listening to Colonel Britton's 'V Army' broadcasts late at night on the English language channel of the European Service. He had a suave gravity about him which gave the impression that he had at his disposal a vast army of civilian volunteers, ready to rise up at any moment and carry out some light assassination work. This seemed unlikely.

"Jeez, you know what," said Liebling when they next met. "This guy Britton has about the same budget a small American toothpaste manufacturer has for advertising. Yet look what he's doing!"

Finally, the call came through to go to Electra House, and Xanthe dutifully made the trip. It paid off. Yes, Liebling could meet the colonel, who would talk to him behind a screen. He could also then talk to the BBC executive in charge, Douglas Ritchie.

"Well done, you're my kind of gal," said Liebling expansively. "Tell him we'll take him to lunch at the Savoy... You'll come too, won't you?"

*

There was also something that had been preying on Xanthe's mind and which she felt she could hardly confide, even in Turing. Twice now, she had been convinced she had seen her friend Hugh Lancing-Price, an RAF officer killed rescuing a child, on the night of the big raid on Westminster back in May. She had seen him only from behind, and each time it was in the muffled crowds around Strand underground station on her way to the *New Yorker* office via the Central Line. She could not be certain – how could she? Her friend was dead – but she had still double-checked with Hugh's friend, Tug Roberts, that there had been no unexpected return.

And how could she be certain anyway, when she had been up in the night as much as she had with Indigo and was exhausted as a result?

Nurse Agnes very kindly continued to mind the baby during the day when she needed to work in Hut 8 or down in London at the *New Yorker*. Even with the little work she did, she clearly had privileges as an American in British government service, at least for the time being. But she also knew that Fleming wanted her to maintain her links with the American press, in case they proved a useful cover once again. It was not generosity; it was hard-nosed calculation by the Naval Intelligence Department.

She had not spelled this out, even to Turing, but she had pretty much convinced herself that she would resign from government service and find some way of going home to her father in Cincinnati. She had been held back from doing so, partly by the sheer luxury and comfort of having Nurse Agnes at hand to advise, by having her friends nearby at Bletchley and partly by her sense that she was – or at least had been – playing a useful role, when so many other young people her age were risking their lives every day. Partly also, she was nervous of irritating the man who had managed her career so far, Lieutenant Commander Fleming at the Admiralty.

All of which left her even more confused about why she was apparently seeing Hugh. Was it because she had cared about him? Was it because he had looked so like, and seemed so like a more civilised version of Indy's father, Ralph Lancing-Price, who she had first been sent to watch in Berlin as a correspondent for the *Chicago Tribune*?

Ralph. Whom she had fallen in love with and who had abandoned her for the Nazis late one night, the evening of Hitler's last peace offer to Britain in July 1940.

What had she actually been seeing? It could hardly have been Ralph, who had defected in no ambiguous way and was still, as far as she knew, in Berlin. It was he who had sent her on such a wild goose chase involving ciphers, that it had plunged her into the world of Bletchley. Perhaps she should have been grateful to the man for that at least.

Nor could it have been Hugh she saw, because he was definitely dead, his body in one of those mass graves dug for air-raid victims in the Westminster parks. She was sure that neither of them had any brothers. So it could hardly have been a real person. It must have been her own exhausted mind, unstitching her fatal love for Ralph and her emergent love for Hugh.

She knew that Fleming concealed a continuing nervousness about the psychological health of agents in the field, and any rumours about her seeing people who were not there might lead to some kind of discharge before she was ready and before she had made any arrangements to sail home. So she kept it to herself and brooded on these disturbing sightings, especially in the dead of night, when she was dragged, bleary-eyed from sleep, to comfort her crying child, rocking him gently and subtly as her mind wandered backwards and forwards over what might have been.

She dared not wish her affair with Ralph had never happened because that would have meant no Indigo. But she wished she had understood a little more about Hugh's growing feelings for her, and she wished she had felt able to confide the truth to him. As it was, he had gone to his death without knowing why she held herself back from him – or that her child was also his relation.

*

"Hey, you know what?" said Liebling when they met. "I just listened to the V campaign in Serbo-Croat, and our Colonel Britton was called 'Pukonyik Britonia'. I like that!"

Liebling was searching for notebooks and hats and spectacles, propelling himself around the room, upsetting books, papers and teacups in his wake.

"I think I already know the basis of this piece. Imagine thousands of people huddled around secret wireless sets, in places I've never been to, listening to the voice of *Pukonyik Britonia* coming out of the darkness… Good huh?"

"In blacked-out rooms?"

"Good, yeah!"

Xanthe decanted herself from a cab outside Bush House, the new headquarters of the European Service, and pulled Liebling out next to her – he seemed to dwarf the taxi – like squeezing toothpaste out of a tube.

"They call it the BBC," she said, "but actually it is run by the Foreign Office."

"Right," said Liebling. "My information is that the BBC guys are pretty pissed about that."

Next door, Xanthe could see the burned-out ruins of St Clement Danes on one side and the billboards at the Gaiety Theatre, advertising Robertson Hare in some kind of calamitous farce, on the other.

They were ushered into a waiting room, decked out in marble as befitted the former European headquarters of the advertising agency J. Walter Thompson. Minutes later, they were whisked upstairs to listen to the recording of Colonel Britton, who did not really look like a colonel. They watched him through the glass partition.

"The studio's about as big as my bathroom in Half Moon Lane," whispered Liebling.

Thanks to her persuasive spadework and a nudge from the Foreign Office, which wanted to make sure the news about the V campaign reached the waverers in the USA, they did not have to interview Britton from behind a screen. They had lunch with him afterwards, as Liebling had promised, at the Savoy. Ritchie – the man behind Britton – had never been a colonel, but they had to promise to keep up the pretence. There was also something about his voice which exuded authority.

It was during the starter, while Liebling nursed a glass of whisky, that Xanthe had her third encounter.

She saw him over by the reception desk, looking, if anything, more like the long-lost Ralph than the more recently lost Hugh.

"Excuse me a moment," she said. The two men, Liebling and his guest, ignored her and she raced across the atrium. But there was no trace of the apparition left.

White-faced, she returned to the table.

"Jeez, honey, you look like you saw a ghost," said Liebling.

"The thing is, I may have…"

"You know, it is surprisingly common these days," said Ritchie. "People are so busy, so tired that they think they see people all the time. Who knows what's real and what's not?"

"Like Colonel Britton, you mean," said Liebling with a guffaw.

CHAPTER TWO

London, October 1941

The raids had let up considerably in recent months, especially now that Hitler was driving into Russia on three fronts. Xanthe and Turing had abandoned their fruitless quest to meet with Professor Wittgenstein in Cambridge and had sent telegrams to him, apparently hiding out in the London nurses' home. The business with Colonel Britton was now complete and she found herself back working directly with Turing again.

"Hardly hiding, is he?" said Turing when she used the term on their way to find him in Southwark. "I can't think of a more dangerous and exhausting place to live and work as a hospital in the heart of London, right now – unless it's Leningrad. Especially right by the river. I can't imagine what he thinks he's doing."

"Is there any scope for reading philosophy at Guy's Hospital, do you think?" said Xanthe.

"I don't imagine so, but he's a very practical man, is Wittgenstein. He started by studying aeronautics and designed a house in Vienna before he came here. He's not escaped Cambridge to think, that's for sure. Oh, that reminds me..."

He reached into his briefcase.

"I meant to give you this."

He pulled out a Heffers paper bag and handed it over to her. It was a slim volume called *Tractatus Logico Philosophicus.*

"Heavens, Alan. Do I really need to read this? What do you want me to do? Seduce him?"

"I don't honestly think he's susceptible, Xanthe. Despite your undoubted charms," said Turing.

"Flatterer," she said, opening the book.

"*This book will, perhaps, only be understood by those who have themselves already thought the thoughts which are expressed in it...*"

"This may rule me out," said Xanthe sadly. She read a bit more, wrinkling her nose as she did so:

"*It is therefore not a textbook. Its object would be attained if there were one person who read it with understanding and to whom it affords pleasure...*"

"Oh, for goodness sake, Alan. This guy is... Do I really have to read it?"

"Hah!" said Turing, as he sped off in the direction of the Euston Road. He had another meeting before they were due with Fleming. "See you at the Admiralty!"

For a moment, Xanthe could not imagine Fleming – always so British, so carefully turned out in his blue uniform and his wavy gold stripes – working on a Sunday. On the other hand, she said to herself as she searched for a bus in the direction of Park Lane, she knew he seemed to be there *all* the time.

As she wandered along, feeling a little strange not to be pushing Indy in his pram, she was horribly aware of the destruction and ruined buildings on either side of her, some of them demolished down to their basements and converted to store emergency water for when the hydrants failed. London seemed to be holding itself together like an elderly widow who had seen better days.

Indigo must now be having his morning feed, she thought, aware that her mind was failing to keep quite still. It was probably the influence of the wretched *Tractatus*, now in her bag.

*

"I'm all ears," said Xanthe, wondering if she had passed Hugh's spectre again in the street outside, but aware that actually, she had not. Thank goodness they were not asking her to go abroad again. She wasn't sure she could hack it. Fleming took a deep breath.

"You remember I told you that Professor Wittgenstein might be in a position to help us? No? Oh well, I must have been talking to you, Turing. Well, when I said that, you must have realised that I didn't mean as a philosopher."

Fleming was pacing up and down beside the famous bath, the same one that their boss at Bletchley had spent his nights during the First World War, puzzling out enemy ciphers.

"It's really because his family owns a chunk of a company that turns out, as far as we know, to be extremely important in the development of the coding system that comes after Enigma."

Xanthe felt incredulous.

"But we've only just – I mean, you've only just begun to read naval Enigma. You mean they're going to change it?"

"Well, they will inevitably change it. The issue for us is how to delay that, and we believe – for reasons I'm going to tell you – that the professor can help."

"Really?" said Turing, nervously. "From Cambridge? Or Guy's Hospital? Really? Have you ever met him? He likes cowboy films, but otherwise, he wasn't really built for this world."

"The thing is, as I said... Anyway, never mind that. Have a look at this!"

Fleming flourished a printed paper, like the ones that poured off the teleprinters into Hut 8.

"Now, take a close look. On the face of it, these aren't Enigma codes."

Xanthe read it. It looked like gobbledegook. It was in blue ink on a narrow strip of paper, with a line that wobbled around but with no curves. There seemed to be only two letters possible…

Fleming flicked the paper suavely over to Turing.

"As you can see, this is another animal entirely. Your colleagues are wrestling with it at Bletchley, and normally we wouldn't compromise the secrecy by bringing you in on it. But since you know the professor, it seemed sensible – and Turing suggested you might be able to help too," said Fleming, with a wink that Xanthe could not interpret.

Turing peered at the sheet with deep concentration.

"It is clear the code is different, isn't it?" said Fleming. "Groups of letters or symbols to mean specific letters, maybe even specific words. We're not sure yet. But what we do know, from diplomatic sources, is that this isn't produced by an Enigma machine. It's produced by an ordinary teleprinter. The code would be too onerous for a human to input precisely, especially in action. Which is why we concluded that it was coded to be read and decoded automatically. You don't have to look anything up, but you do have to set the machine correctly."

Turing was fiddling away with his notebook and pencil, staring both angrily and excitedly at the screed. He loved the thought of a new mathematical challenge.

"I need hardly tell you how important this is. As you know better than anyone, we can now read a great deal of Enigma traffic. Even the signals between U-boats. We simply cannot countenance this access being blacked out again at such a critical moment in the Battle of the Atlantic. It would be disastrous, not just to the lives of merchant seamen but to the whole war effort. This shift could lose us the war. We call the new code 'Tunny'. It's one of the new fish codenames we're using, which Turing knows all about. Are you actually listening, Xanthe…?"

Xanthe cleared her mind. She *had* been listening but had also been thinking about whether she was sane enough for this job, however simple it might seem.

"Oh yes, of course."

"I mean, I'd hate for you to nod off because I was being so boring. Because, here's the important bit. Through our intelligence sources, we believe this is the work of a new coding machine called the Lorenz. It is made in Berlin and we have been getting messages in Tunny, along these lines, for the past two months. Our understanding is that it comes from the Lorenz factory there, but that it uses an absolutely vital component which can only be bought in Switzerland and that is made – we believe – by a company in Berne called Scherzinger Verlag, which is contracted to Siemens. There is not much we can do about *that*, and yet, in Wittgenstein, we have a refugee from Nazi persecution who happens to own much of the company."

Xanthe looked at Turing, who appeared to be in his own world, scribbling calculations.

"I don't understand," she said. "I thought the Swiss were neutral."

"They are, but they keep the Nazis sweet by turning a blind eye to some supplies getting through to them – and we turn a blind eye too. So it is a somewhat delicate task for you…"

Fleming suddenly focused on Turing's scribbles.

"Hold on! Turing, what are you doing exactly? For goodness sake – have you heard a word I've been saying? Honestly, what a pair – one of you dreaming of goodness knows who, the other one code-breaking as if his little heart would break. If Denniston has asked you to tackle this one he, no doubt, has good reason!"

"This is a pity," said Turing, oblivious. "Look at this – doesn't compute."

"All right, all right, one thing at a time," said Fleming, fuming. "We need to persuade your professor that he should help us and tell us what is possible and what might *be* possible. My understanding is that you both know the man…"

Turing's head emerged from his figures.

"Well…"

"Actually, I've just been in his bedroom during a seminar," said Xanthe.

Fleming stared at her suspiciously, then a big, knowing smile suffused his face.

"Really, it isn't what it sounds like. I've actually never even spoken to him before."

"Well, you'll know what to do, I'm sure. And remember, he's on a refugee visa, so if he isn't co-operative, you know what you can threaten him with."

*

"I think we can discount that last idea of Fleming's. He really has no idea of what kind of personality he is dealing with here."

Turing and Xanthe were walking along the Victoria Embankment, gazing at the barrage balloons floating high over the Thames and at the busy tugs, belching smoke.

"I can't actually think of anything more likely to enrage Wittgenstein then threatening him with deportation. He is highly moral – moral beyond moral – and he can't stand his own perceptions of the right thing to do being questioned. We just have to proceed a little carefully. No! Correction – we need to proceed *extremely* carefully! I think they have asked you to come because they think you're more of a – I don't know – *people* person than I am. I know I have a reputation for being so completely logical that I can't communicate at all…"

Xanthe knew he was right. That is certainly what people said about him.

"Oh, poor Alan. You can communicate just fine. I think you're right though. I'm here because Fleming thinks that just because *he's* so susceptible to the charms of women, that your professor is going to be too. Either way, I'll do what I can."

As they walked east along the Thames, crossing the river at Blackfriars Bridge, the damage looked, if anything, more intense. Xanthe could see the defiant tower of Southwark Cathedral, next to Guy's Hospital, and her mouth went a little dry.

Come on Xanthe, she told herself. You've done more difficult things than this. Why was she so nervous? Was it because she felt a fraud alongside a real intellectual like Turing? Nonsense, she said to herself. Rubbish. Of course she could manage. Was she not the Cincinnati Under-Fourteens Crossword Champion of 1932?

*

In reply to their telegram, the professor had agreed to meet them in a small transport café, under the arches outside London Bridge station. It was beginning to rain.

"He clearly doesn't want people to know who he is for some reason. I wonder why."

"Oh well, we'll know soon enough," said Xanthe as they picked their way past the bombed warehouses of Southwark, down cobbled streets where the trams never ventured, and up onto London Bridge.

"What I don't understand is, if the Wittgenstein family is Jewish, how come they still have all this money invested in Germany?"

"It's in Switzerland, dummy," she said.

The café looked tiny, dimly glowing in the semi-drizzle.

Turing pushed the door and held it open. He brushed the rain from his hat, and Xanthe looked around. There was only one other person in there, nursing a cup of tea, tall, cadaverous with unkempt hair – and familiar. He was staring in their direction with piercing dark eyes.

"Professor? Professor Wittgenstein?" said Turing tentatively, hoping for his attention.

The professor closed his eyes and put the palm of his hands on the wooden tabletop. He looked exasperated.

"Please, please," he said, with irritation, the moment they reached whispering range. "For goodness sake, don't use my name. I have no intention of anyone here knowing who I am. And there's no point in replying that we're the only ones here. Let me say that I've been here in London for nearly five weeks now and I know how this place works. News gets around."

"Fair enough," said Alan. "May I ask what you *are* doing here?"

Wittgenstein's eyes clouded over. He looked menacingly at Turing.

"Mr Turing, I am grateful to you for coming all this way to see me – we have known each other of old, though I never managed to jolt you out of your somewhat simplistic beliefs about mathematics. It is quite false that – but… well… one thing at a time."

Turing went pale.

"Well, Doctor, er, Professor. May I introduce my colleague, Xanthe Schneider, from naval intelligence?"

Xanthe found herself lowering her eyes. She proffered her hand. Laboriously, he extracted his right hand out from beneath the table and shook hers.

So far, so good, she said to herself.

"How do you do," she said, in her most demure English style.

"You are an American? Or are you Canadian? I find it quite hard to tell."

"Yes, I am. An American, I mean."

"Working for the Royal Navy?"

"I wanted to do something to help."

This seemed to animate the philosopher.

"Listen to her, Turing. She wanted to help. I too wanted to help. That is why I am now at Guy's, working on the wards. That is what appears to me to be the human thing to do. But I don't want to undermine my efforts by broadcasting that I am actually a rather useless philosopher. Like me, your friend wants to make a contribution."

"Sir," said Turing, cutting to the chase. "I've been authorised to talk to you frankly about our problem, which I am hoping you will be able to help with, but I am going to have to ask you to sign these papers to guarantee confidentiality." He reached into his briefcase again and pulled out a foolscap contract.

Wittgenstein stiffened.

"Turing. I am not in the habit of signing papers, especially for people who doubt my word or my honesty. If my presence here incognito does not convince you that I am trustworthy, then I fear signing papers will not help."

Turing stared, defeated and deflated.

"I have considerable sympathy with you, I must say. What do you think, Xanthe?"

"I say trust him. We have no other option."

Turing began to look a little more hopeful. Wittgenstein looked between the two of them, apparently seeking an argument.

"You must understand," said Turing apologetically, "I am, as they say, a man under authority. The processes of that authority are often extremely illogical, but…"

"The centurion…"

"Excuse me?"

"He was the original man under authority, I believe… Matthew, chapter eight."

On an impulse, Xanthe interrupted.

"You should know, Professor, that my friend, Alan here, is ostensibly a member of the Home Guard. He had to sign papers to say that he understood he was subject to military discipline. And he simply wrote 'no'. And nobody noticed – until they complained that he wasn't showing up for parade. He is not the military stickler he sometimes appears."

A small light appeared in Wittgenstein's eyes and grew, until finally he let out a loud laugh.

"Miss Schneider, I understand what you are saying. And I suspect that you have already worked out that nothing will induce me to sign your document, which I regard as wholly meaningless. So you will have to trust me. All I can say is that you would not have to trust me any more if I'd signed the form than if I'd not. May I order you a scrambled egg?"

Xanthe did a double take. She thought it best to say yes.

The next problem which had arisen was around how much they would need to tell the great philosopher before they won his co-operation. They exchanged glances and began to outline the central issue. A piece of German equipment. A crucial component provided by a Swiss company. The Wittgenstein family trusts.

"May I ask what this piece of equipment is?"

Turing reddened.

"I am sorry, Professor, but…"

"It's a chronometer," Xanthe butted in, with an apologetic look at Alan.

"Ah. Of course it is. Now," he turned on Turing. "You expected me to give you my trust, yet you do not trust me. That is a basic paradox, do you not think? A contradiction – and you know all about those, do you not, Turing!"

Turing turned to Xanthe to explain.

"The professor is referring to an argument we had a couple of years ago about the importance of contradictions to mathematics. You know the *Entscheidungsproblem?* All Cretans are liars, as a Cretan once told me: it goes round and round in circles."

"No," said Xanthe, "I don't."

"Bravo!" said Wittgenstein.

"Ah well, I said it was important. The professor said it was just silly. That was basically our disagreement."

The professor smiled magnanimously.

"Don't let us reopen old wounds, Turing. The fact remains that you will have to let me into your confidence a little, or I will be unable to help or advise."

Xanthe felt a sudden wave of sympathy for the poor lonely genius across the café table.

"Listen, Professor. I have twice risked my life to protect the details of the secret, and other people do so every day. It isn't that we don't trust you; it's that we're not at liberty to divulge something that so many others believe – whether they are right or wrong to do so – is worth their lives. I've told you it's a chronometer, and I don't think we can elaborate further. But we do need your help. It is terribly important."

Wittgenstein did a handbrake turn.

"Have you been to my seminars?" he said suspiciously. "I know Turing has, but have you?"

"Many years ago, I did once, Professor. I met Alan there. He found me a seat, which was kind of him. But I'm afraid..." – here was the admission she had not intended to make – "I don't really think I'm a philosopher."

Wittgenstein rubbed his hands together unexpectedly.

"That is what I wanted to hear. Wartime is no time for philosophy. You have, very sensibly in my view, abandoned study and found useful work. I have found it difficult to do so, but I have managed something, exhausting though it is. I am a dispensary porter, and by the time I finish work at five p.m., I am utterly drained. That is real work; so is yours, I feel sure."

Now it was Turing's turn. The smell of fried onions wafted across the room.

"What we are talking about here, Professor, is a system of serious ingenuity, which will give real power to the Nazi war effort, and we want to stop them if we possibly can, or at least delay them. What we are hoping is that you might write to your brother and ask him, beg him if necessary, to find some way of slowing down the production of this chronometer. Since he owns a large proportion of the company that's making it."

"Forgive me, I was under the impression that Switzerland was neutral."

"Our understanding is that they continue to trade vital war materials with Germany as a way of warding off invasion. Sometimes you have to make a temporary accommodation with the devil to prevent a greater evil. You would agree with that, wouldn't you?"

"You are right," said the great man, his eyes clouding over, and a moment later, he was up and pacing around the café with great determination. The greasy gentleman behind the counter appeared unsurprised. Wittgenstein had evidently done this before.

"Professor," said Xanthe hopefully.

"Oh dear," whispered Turing, "I'm afraid I've upset the apple cart."

As he paced, the air-raid siren went. The first for many months.

"Will you go to the shelter?" said the cook at the counter. "I won't be going, so feel free to ride out the storm here if you prefer."

Wittgenstein now had his head in his hands as he paced the room between the empty tables.

"Do you want to go down to the shelter?" said Turing.

"I'm staying here," said Xanthe.

At that moment, the all-clear sounded.

"There we are. False alarm," said the cook. He delivered Xanthe's egg. It looked repulsive.

It also had a calming effect on Wittgenstein. He sat down again and began talking rather fast, with great animation.

"You no doubt refer to my own family, as you mentioned my brother?" he said. "You know that it was I – yes, it was I – who negotiated with the Nazis on their behalf, to save my sisters who still live in Vienna. It was I who agreed to pay the monsters six billion pounds. The majority of my father's fortune. I did so, having long since given up any claim on the money. And yes, you are right, my brother, Paul, controls what remains. I cannot, in all conscience, ask him to do anything with the money since I have surrendered any benefit from it, or involvement with it. Nor will I do so. I have never asked him for money, and I never will. But I will help. I will write to him and introduce you, Miss Schneider, and say that you come bearing a letter from me, and that you will explain what it is you need. That is all I can do. I can ask him to listen to you; I cannot ask him to act."

"And your brother lives in…"

"New York." Wittgenstein finished the sentence. "Would you go there? That is what I suggest you do. If I ask him, he will see you, and he will listen. If you can give me some paper and a pen, I will write the letter here and now."

Turing reached into his briefcase, and Xanthe's mind raced. Could she leave Indy to go to America, even for a week or so? She had left him before without obvious ill effects, and she would love to go – she could not think of anything she would rather do, if they let her. But could she possibly get there and back in less than a fortnight, say? The crossing alone would take a week at least, and possibly more…

Wittgenstein appeared to be writing as if his life depended on it, with a furious intensity, bending the nib to breaking point, leaning forward obsessively. He seemed to be writing in German.

He signed the letter, sighed, looked up and smiled at Xanthe.

"There we are. Did you like your egg?"

Xanthe remembered how much the professor was said to value honesty, above the social niceties.

"Well, to be honest, I don't much care for powdered egg."

Wittgenstein's brow darkened.

"Bosh," he said.

*

"I'll give you two some bits of advice," said Fleming when he heard Xanthe had been given permission to fly across the Atlantic. "First, buy a flying suit: it is freezing cold at twenty thousand feet above the Arctic Circle. Second, if they offer you a sausage, say no. Mine was sixty-five per cent bread. It was like eating a hot dog with the roll inside the meat."

"Where do I buy a flying suit?" asked Xanthe, unnerved.

Fleming was relishing his impact.

"Oh, they supply them and deliver them to the plane for you. But you must ask for one. You know what we Brits are like when it comes to comfort. They will send you off and let you happily freeze to death because they were embarrassed to mention it."

It had been a whirlwind few days. There had been no time to consider things.

"America? Of course I would love to go, but I have a baby as you know, and I can't take him," she had said, as soon as they had left the café. Xanthe and Turing were talking as they walked back to the underground station after leaving Wittgenstein, who had shaken them both warmly by the hand, silently, in farewell.

"Well, I think you pretty much rescued that conversation," Turing had said. "It probably would have gone better if I hadn't been there at all. How did you read the old monster so effectively?"

"I know, but…"

Air-raid sirens sounded again, and it was almost dark, even in the era of British Summer Time during the war. People were beginning to emerge from the surrounding slums and making their way in the same direction. There was the rattle of shutters coming down and the faint murmuring of people who were uncertain and nervous about what was to happen. She thought of the river glinting in the twilight, beckoning in its way fatally to the bombers.

"All I can say is that this is an urgent priority, and I feel sure we can fly you over, if necessary – if you can trust us again to look after your little boy," Turing was saying as they walked a little faster. "Professor Wittgenstein has conceived a trust in *you,* not me, and – if he wants you to take his despatch to his brother – then that's good enough for me."

They had reached the platform of the Northern Line. The south London families had been hurrying to bring their bedding down to reserve a safe spot on the platform for the night. There was a budgie cage and an antimacassar and a number of thermos flasks. As they had descended the stairs, Xanthe had heard the first distant thuds of the bombs.

"And if it's good enough for me, it is good enough for Commander Fleming," said Turing definitively.

She was still a little surprised at how the professor had taken to her. She could only think it was because, actually, she had nothing to do with philosophy at all. It seemed to have done the trick.

Wittgenstein revealed that he had renounced his interest in the considerable family fortune and had promised to give no advice. So it would require a tough piece of persuasion on her part. She was far from sure she could manage it, but since the hint that she might, at last, be able to visit her home again, Xanthe had been increasingly convinced that she should go. She had imagined seeing her father again from the moment that Wittgenstein had set out the problem that needed to be solved.

What had been so odd about the meeting was that the professor seemed to behave in precisely the opposite way that she had expected. She imagined that he and Turing would understand each other so closely that she would have been the miserable outsider, pathetically begging to be let into the inner sanctum of the officially intelligent. In practice, it seemed to have been the other way around.

When they had emerged again, she had been staggered to see the wild eyes of the professor again seeking her out. "Fraulein!" he had shouted across the road. "I have rewritten the letter. I suggest that if he resists you, you mention the name 'Kurt'. I have noted it down for you. It is a parallel case. He will know it."

*

Now, with all the paperwork out of the way, she was on the runway, accompanied across the tarmac in Ayr by a good-looking RAF officer, having travelled up on the sleeper to Scotland. She asked again about the flying suit.

"Oh, I am sorry. Nobody mentioned that you wanted one. I'll try and snaffle one for you and bring it along. Before we take off, of course," he added gaily.

"What, in twenty minutes' time?"

He gave her a hearty wave. But sure enough, after she had begun to make herself at home on one of the mattresses in the bomb bay of the Liberator bomber, he put his head up through the hole in the fuselage and handed over what looked like an enormous sleeping bag with legs.

"Oh yes, you'll need that," said the Canadian captain. "It can get pretty damn cold up there. Surprised nobody mentioned it before."

It was the third time Xanthe had flown that year. She had hitched a ride in a diplomatic bomber on its way to Malta and Alexandria on her visit to Greece in April and come back the same way, each time along with officials and dignitaries who shared few words with her. This time, she was alone apart from the flight crew.

She took with her the thoughts which dominated her waking moments – of Indigo, being put to sleep in his cot with Nurse Agnes singing to him, as she ought to have been doing herself. Of her father, from whom she had not heard since Indy's birth, her fears about him – whether he was angry with her, whether he was ill, or a host of other reasons why he hadn't been in touch.

It had hurt her that her father had not been in contact. They had always got on so well before she had left for her strange experience at Simonetta College, Cambridge, which turned out to be more of a finishing school than a university, and before she had become so unexpectedly involved with British intelligence.

Once they had taken off, she struggled into her flying suit and began to feel warmer, and soon she could see they were over the Irish Sea and climbing.

"All right miss," said the flight engineer. "You can come out of the bomb bay now. You can sit wherever you like in the plane. We'll have sandwiches in a mo, and then I suggest you sleep. We'll be in Newfoundland in eighteen hours, fingers crossed."

He gave a little laugh to show this was intended as black humour.

Xanthe sat, trussed up in her flying suit, in the rear gunner's position as the gloom over the British Isles began to engulf the view, heading towards the sunset and wondering how this particular mission was going to end. Had she really got the skill, all by herself, to persuade the great Wittgenstein family to act on behalf of the war effort? It was going to be tough.

Something about lying there in the padded suit reminded her of the story of the princess and the pea. She felt underneath the seat and pulled out a battered and abandoned copy of William Shirer's *Berlin Diary*. So Bill had made it home. That, at least, was a comforting thought.

CHAPTER THREE

New York City, November 1941

"Mr Wittgenstein?"

"I am Dr Wittgenstein's valet. How can I help you, ma'am?"

She had wondered if it had been a mistake not to make an appointment over the telephone. But she had not wanted to be put off, so she felt the most effective approach might be just to turn up at his home in the Upper East Side. Now she was here, via a yellow cab and a walk along Central Park, on these carefully manicured marble steps, she was less sure. London was hardly an egalitarian city, but something about the Blitz had rendered it more equal – and this very obvious wealth grated.

"I am here to meet him and have come to New York specifically to do so. I have a letter from his brother for him."

"May I take the letter from you, ma'am? He is performing tomorrow and is very reluctant to be disturbed."

The valet was clearly from Central Europe, probably an old functionary from the Wittgenstein Palace in Vienna. He wore a uniform that looked out of place in modern New York, black and frayed. The same with his white moustache.

"I'm afraid you don't understand. The letter is a letter of introduction. I have been sent to see him by the British government, who I represent, and need to talk to him on a matter I can reveal only to him."

Was that pompous enough? It was hard, she knew all too well, to generate the required gravitas to force your way into mansions like this when you are a twentysomething woman from the Midwest.

"Really, *liebchen*? You don't sound British to me."

The man was being so irritatingly patronising that she could have throttled him. You could see the cogs whirring in his secessionist brain.

Then he made a decision.

"Very well. But I must advise you to wait until after his concert tomorrow. If you would like to visit this house at twelve noon in two days' time, I will make sure Dr Wittgenstein is aware of your visit."

Two days? Fine, so be it. There was no point in ruining everything by pushing too hard. Also, two days gave her the chance to hop on a train to Cincinnati to find her father. She might not have another opportunity.

*

It had been thrilling to get nearer and nearer home. First the airstrip in Montreal, then the night train to New York and now the Cincinnati Limited sleeper to Cincinnati, arriving at 9.30 a.m. She would have one day to find her father.

New York seemed not to have changed a jot since she had sailed from there on the *Aquitania* back in 1938, just as the first war scare seemed to loom over Europe. Now, it was wonderful to fill her nostrils with the distinctive smell of an American sleeper, a strange combination of antiseptic, body odour and tobacco smoke, past the ever-present shoeshine boys and the marshmallow stalls.

After the friendly smells and sounds of Union Terminal, nothing had prepared her for being home in Cincinnati. The sheer sweetness of it, the sense of liberty and sheer commercial power of it. And above all, the sense that nobody would drop bombs on you, the sense of civilisation – the absolute lack of sirens, except those of the police.

She took a cab to her home street and, her heart in her mouth, walked up the front drive. The house was clearly empty. She could see the pile of mail dimly through the dirty window, and there was an old, rain-drenched newspaper hanging out of the mailbox. Someone, at least, had transferred the mail inside. There were weeds on the front doorstep growing through cracks in the concrete.

"Xanth?" said a loud voice a few feet away. A large woman in slacks was emerging from the house next door. It was Auntie May.

"Oh wow, honey, is that really you? And looking so grown!"

Xanthe found the tears were rolling down her face. The anticipation and fear had become too much.

"Where is he, May? I haven't got long, and I so need to see him. Is he alive? Where is he?"

May took her in her arms and stroked her hair as if she was still a girl.

"Oh, Xanthe. He is still with us. There's been no passing, but you will find it hard. He has had a stroke and he's in the St Vincent home. You know, on past Madison Road, up towards Evanston. You can walk there. I visit him every day, but usually, he doesn't – I mean he sometimes finds it hard to know what's what."

"Oh, no," said Xanthe, appalled. "Does he know? Does he know I have a child? He has a grandchild?"

"A baby? You had a baby? Did you get married, honey? Or was he a pilot who was killed? We hear such stories, you know. People here have changed their ideas about the war in Europe since the election,

I know. Especially after the *Reuben James* went down last week. And the *Kearsage*, of course."

They hugged, and Xanthe marched off to St Vincent's, her heart now lodged in her mouth.

*

It began to snow a little fitfully, and she felt herself descending into a Midwestern dream as she walked the few blocks to her father's nursing home. She had slept badly on the train, with its curtains pulled over her shelf, and even worse on the flight across the Arctic. Now her tired mind began to blur the prospects of meeting her father with those of meeting Paul Wittgenstein the following day.

How was she going to persuade this elusive, unconventional concert pianist – from a well-known family of wealthy Jewish refugees – to do the British government's bidding with his investments? Neither Fleming nor Turing had given her much in the way of guidance about what might actually be possible. Presumably, Wittgenstein *frère* could not simply march into Switzerland and insist they stop producing this chronometer or at least stop shipping it to Berlin. She didn't know. But she found it hard to believe it would be very effective, even if he did march in. The Germans would hear about it, and there would be diplomatic difficulties, which would presumably lead to them getting the component in some other way. Not to mention putting his own family at more risk than they were already in.

On the other hand, perhaps there were no other sources of supply apart from the Swiss company. If the Nazis could have made it themselves, they presumably would have done.

First, she would have to get Paul Wittgenstein onside, and that would mean negotiating somehow through the complexities of his relationship with his brother, Ludwig, which was evidently not terribly good. Having met the great philosopher, she could well believe in the complexity of the family.

Next, she would have to ask for his help. And only if he agreed to that part could they begin to discuss what might be possible and how to go about it making it happen.

It was a tall order. Her mind went round and round as she pounded the sidewalk to get to her father – she could not help it: it kept her from panicking – yet the stakes were very high. If the Lorenz system went into full production and naval signals began to be carried by a version of the machine, then they would, once more, be in the dark on the Atlantic, and all the efforts of Turing and colleagues – even her own meagre efforts – would have been in vain.

Why was she continually being put in this position? Why, over and over again, was she expected to make decisions in the field which she felt wholly inadequate to make?

She had been thinking so deeply about the Wittgensteins that she found herself inside the nursing home before she had time to focus. And there before her, very obviously from his distinctive profile, looking out of the window in a large armchair, was the man she had come to see.

Then she forgot herself again and just ran. "Daddy!" she said, as quietly as she could. "Oh, my Daddy!"

*

"Cindy Schneider?" said a man at Grand Central Station as she stepped off the sleeper the next morning, feeling bleary-eyed and emotional.

She nodded. It must be her.

"Yup, that's me."

"Can you come with me, please?"

The man wore a brown homburg hat and looked irritatingly smug.

"Who are you, exactly?"

"That will be explained."

Wary, Xanthe followed, aware also that another man walked behind her.

"I'm sorry. I'm not going to get in that car without a bit more of an explanation," she said, intransigent, as a large black Oldsmobile hove into view.

"We're taking you to see the chief. You don't really have a choice. But you will be quite safe, I give you my word. Come on, honey, you have no choice really."

Bowing to the inevitable, she slipped into the car which drove off down Forty-Second Street and turned into Fifth Avenue. It was extraordinary, the sheer weight of people and traffic compared to the deprivations and emptiness of wartime London.

She turned her attention to the two other people in the car apart from herself and the driver. One was the man who had picked her up at the station and the other was much older, in a homburg hat with a large overcoat, smoking and quietly looking out of the window. He looked like a powerful man, in most senses of the word.

As soon as he sensed her attention, he spoke.

"Miss Schneider, I am delighted to meet you. I have heard a great deal about you. Let me come straight to the point."

He flicked ash into the tray beside him.

"You have the advantage of me," said Xanthe, cross now. "I'm afraid I don't know your name."

"I guess that's the way it's going to have to stay. I work with a group of businessmen. We are Canadians. We don't like to advertise the fact that we are supporting the war effort against the Nazis. We call ourselves the

British Security Commission. I'm not actually the chief, but I report to the chief and the chief has asked me to be here. Now, here's the thing. The politics are extremely sensitive here. We can't have British agents on missions here cutting across what we're doing. We have had no proper information about what you're doing, and we just wanted to have a little chat to make sure we don't trip over each other. Understand? That's why we met your train. So how can we help?"

This was not a helpful turn up for Xanthe. Nor was her brain really engaged. It was going backwards and forwards around her all-too-brief conversation with her father.

He had recognised her immediately and they had wept together, but it had become clear that either he had received none of her letters, photographs and cuttings with her byline in the *Chicago Tribune* and *New Yorker* – or he had forgotten them.

Their conversation had still been echoing around her brain even while she was half asleep, in discomfort on the train.

She also knew there was no way she could confide in a man, however well-dressed, on the basis that he claimed to be from the British Security Commission – though she knew that organisation had helped her, at least indirectly, to get out of Berlin the year before.

"Look, I don't want to be difficult," she said. "I am here for only one thing – which I'm not prepared to talk about – and then I am going home. I have a baby to look after. And if you really need to know more, I will have to refer you to Commander Ian Fleming at the Admiralty in London."

She noticed, to her great surprise, that she had used the word 'home' about Bletchley.

"I have done, honey. Like a clam, your Fleming guy. But we know you've made an appointment to see Paul Wittgenstein, the one-armed concert pianist."

One arm? He only has one arm? Why was she never properly briefed? Perhaps Fleming thought this wasn't one of the important details she needed to know.

"You are well-informed. Yes, and when I've seen him, I will have to go – I also want to drop into the offices of the *New Yorker*, who employ me in London."

Even now, during this stand-off, her mind was wandering. What was it her father had said?

"*My beautiful girl*" — that was it. "*In years gone by, I might have questioned you more closely on why you had a baby with no husband...*" He breathed heavily. "*But these days things are changing, and I know you will have had your reasons, and I know what those poor Londoners have been going through. I'm just happy – I am delighted to have a grandson. I hope to see him one day, but I fear I will not live to see the end of this European war.*"

"*Oh, Dad, you will. Of course you will. Here are his snaps.*" She had tears running down her cheeks. "*I will bring little Indigo to see his granddaddy as soon as the ocean is safe to cross. As soon as the ink is dry on the peace treaty, I'll be here with you.*"

She was wrenched out of her reverie by the realisation that this car trip, apparently with well-meaning allies, was actually aggressive. She suddenly felt cross. Who were these men, risking so little, to cross-question her? What exactly were they threatening?

"Listen," she said. "I'm as American as you are – more so, in fact. But if you want me to believe you are who you say you are, you will respect my orders as an employee of the British government, which are to say nothing to anybody about what I am doing. Yes, I'm going to see Dr Wittgenstein, and when I've seen him, you don't need to worry about me any longer."

She caught a look pass between the two men in Homburgs. Strangely, this little speech seemed to have done the trick. Within minutes, they were speeding back towards the Upper East Side and the tiny hotel on the edge of that wealthy enclave, near the Wittgenstein residence, that she had booked herself into. Seconds later, the sidekick was out, carrying her bag for her up the stairs to the hotel. The older man was shaking her hand.

"Goodbye, Miss Schneider. You are, of course, right. I hope you will forgive our little test. My very best wishes for your trip. Perhaps you will allow me to make an appointment for you to see Harold Ross at the *New Yorker* this afternoon. Oh, and just so's you know, the Wittgenstein recital got some iffy reviews last night."

"Thank you, Mr, er… that would be extremely helpful."

It reminded her again, as the black car disappeared around the corner, of saying goodbye to her father.

"*Goodbye, my Daddy*," she had said to him, already with the strange sense that the whole encounter had been like a kind of dream.

Then he had taken her hand, as she rose to go.

"*You know, Xanth – you are the apple of my eye. You are the reason I have stayed alive as long as I have, to see you again.*"

"*Oh, try and stay alive to see Indy, won't you, Daddy? Please try.*"

"Ok, honey, I will. I will. I'm just overjoyed to see you. You've made me happy again."

The nurse took her aside as she left the room. "I'm so glad he recognised you," she said. "Some days he recognises nobody, I'm afraid."

Once Xanthe was up the stairs and safely inside her tiny bedroom, she fell on the uncomfortable bed and burst into tears.

*

"Dr Wittgenstein will see you now."

It occurred to her that this is the kind of thing they said at the doctor's surgery in Bletchley, and she grinned.

As she walked through into an ornate sitting room, with silver mirrors and secessionist art from Vienna before the First World War, she tried to think her way more effectively into the role she was playing – an emissary from a government at war, asking for help from a neutral. It was just that seeing her father had made her feel like a little girl again.

"Miss Schneider. Delighted to meet you." Paul Wittgenstein bowed a little as he held her hand, like an old-fashioned Viennese prince. She searched her upbringing – not exactly small-town America, but Midwest – and found nothing that would prepare her for persuading a European aristocrat.

She also found the missing arm a little disorientating.

"You are looking at my arm. You are not aware that I am a one-armed concert pianist? I am, as a result, an impresario of music. I have commissioned some of the leading composers in the world to write pieces for me. There are those – I know what they say – who believe that losing my hand was the making of me: that otherwise, I would have been a second-rate two-handed pianist, and I am now a first-rate one-handed pianist."

"The competition is not quite so intense, I suppose."

It had just slipped out. She was not concentrating. She looked at him nervously for a reaction.

"Quite so, quite right. But it has certainly allowed me to be, not quite unique, but at least experimental, don't you think?"

He smiled broadly.

"I hear your performance last night was well-received," she ventured.

"In that case, you hear wrong. It fell a little flat, or so the critics informed me this morning. Still, what can you expect of the *New York Post*..."

What was it about these Wittgensteins? So sharp and yet so deluded.

"Now, please sit down, Miss Schneider. May I get you something to drink? You have a letter from my brother, I believe."

"Please call me Xanthe."

Wittgenstein peered at her with interest. "What an unusual name! And, of course, the name suits you – you really do have yellow hair!"

Xanthe fished in her bag to pull out the precious envelope which she had carried across the Atlantic for precisely this moment. He read the letter and pursed his lips.

"He says here that you have a very particular request of me. He goes on at great length to say that he has no right to ask me anything about the family trust since he is no longer a beneficiary – but that therefore I must ask, as he assures me, whether the cause is both just and urgent. One of those is not enough, he says. This has to be both."

"You are a German citizen; is that right?"

"Well, my sisters are, since they still live in Austria."

"But you have no love for the Nazis?"

"Of course. That hardly needs expressing. I was not brought up as a Jew but I am of Jewish extraction. If I lived in Vienna now, in the city where I was born, I would be in great trouble."

Xanthe took a deep breath.

"I need to ask you these things before I trust you with the information, which is highly confidential, that forms the basis of what we are going to ask you. If you could help the allied cause and undermine the Nazis, by use of what remains of your investments, would you do so?"

The pianist became increasingly red and agitated.

"You must know, Miss Schneider – Xanthe – that we will have to trust each other. I have to confess to you that, to secure my sisters' lives in Austria – which they refused to leave – I have paid the Nazis such a sum… such a vast amount, it could have paid for the war effort. I will not say how much…"

"My understanding is that it was around six billion… pounds, that is."

Wittgenstein's face went, if possible, that much redder and – like his brother – he began to pace around the enormous room, from grand piano to grand piano.

"Well, you seem well informed. But what can I do? What should I have done? I fear, Miss Schneider, that I was and am powerless in the face of this great evil."

"I don't believe you are. I don't feel powerless, and I've just got a tiny slice of the power you have."

"No, and I'll tell you why. Any hint, any tiny move from me and my sisters will be in one of those camps, billions or no billions. Do you not understand? I dare not help. I cannot. Now. I fear this interview must end."

Aware that she might manage a second attempt the following day if she acceded to his request, Xanthe hurriedly gathered herself together and was soon back in Central Park, puzzling about what on earth could be done. She longed to ask him about the selfishness of his sisters, and the funding of the Nazi machine – especially when they remained in Austria as virtual hostages – but this was not the moment.

*

"Miss Schneider? Yes, we liked your piece from Greece – hey, it rhymes! Perhaps I should say your despatch from your patch? No? Say, are you busy this evening? There is a new place on West Fifty-Fourth. I've wanted to go to for ages."

It was a frustrating afternoon. Not only had Dr Wittgenstein turned her down in no uncertain terms, but the editor of the *New Yorker* turned out to be busy, and she was seen instead by a young man with verbal diarrhoea, who only seemed to want to get her on a date. She had wanted to thank Ross for his support and to suggest a couple of ideas, but if she confided them to this guy, she would probably see them under his byline in the next issue.

"I am so sorry," she said, in her best English way. "I won't be able to come because I have to catch a plane back home to look after my family."

She caught a furtive look for her ring finger. Then another look of confusion. Was this girl for real? Was she English or American? Was she married or single? Life was sure confusing…

Her attention was wandering as she put all her crossword puzzle energy into figuring out a key to the Wittgenstein dilemma. Of course she understood why Paul was refusing to help. Was there some way she could reassure him that his name need not be involved? Right now, she could think of nothing.

"Listen, are you sure I can't see Mr Ross for a couple of minutes only? I have a great deal to thank him for – and Joe Liebling specifically sent his regards."

"Sorry, honey. No can do. In fact, his deputy quite *specifically* asked me to entertain you."

Something about this exchange reminded Xanthe of the elder Wittgenstein, now dead, who had shot himself – Kurt. Why had Ludwig suggested she bring him up? And she had actually forgotten those aspects of her instructions.

Once she was outside again in West Forty-Fifth Street, with her written proposals for articles still burning a hole in her folder, she came to a decision. She could probably get away with one more approach to the one-armed concert pianist. This time, she would reveal more of the purpose, and she would bring up brother Kurt, as the philosopher suggested she should. But first, she would delay her flight and get one good night's sleep. It would be lovely to see one city lit up at night again after nearly two years of black-outs. Then there would be the lights strung along the trees in Central Park. It was going to be dreamlike and heavenly.

*

To her surprise and some relief, Paul Wittgenstein answered his own front door himself. He seemed flustered.

"Miss, um… I fear my decision was…"

"I am so sorry to disturb you," she said in her best English manner, "I think I forgot my glove."

How sensible she had been to leave one behind, just in case.

"Did we find Miss Schneider's glove?" he was shouting down the hallway. "What colour was it? Where were you sitting?"

There it was poking out of the sofa.

"How silly of me," she said. "You know, the British government was most insistent that I should carry gloves…" She was ad-libbing. The morning sunlight glinted on the chandeliers. Then when he seemed to be relaxing, she made her confession.

"Perhaps, now you are here, you might like some coffee?" He glanced nervously in the direction of the kitchen. Xanthe guessed he had never made coffee himself.

"I have to admit, I did have another reason for coming round as well. I wanted to pass on what your brother told me before I left him in London. He said I should remind you about Kurt."

Paul Wittgenstein looked confused for a second. Then he sat down and motioned her to do the same. They were not slow on the uptake in this family – whatever the uptake was in this case.

"I see what you mean," he said.

Paul stared ahead of him, clearly moved.

"You see, Miss Schneider, my elder brother is dead…"

He began a long story about Kurt's final weeks in the last throes of the Great War. Ignored by his men, who were deserting the cause in their thousands and going home, he had shot himself. "I have to do something," he had told one of their sisters. "We have lost the war. Austria is no more. I have to redress the balance."

"I understand," she said. Then daring to push a little further: "I believe what your brother Ludwig meant was that perhaps your family might feel they owed something to the effort of getting rid of the Nazis – currently being shouldered by young men like Kurt now – to balance all that money you paid to them. I don't say *I* think that, of course."

He carried on staring ahead.

"Something to sort of redress the balance."

The silence continued. Then, still staring like an automaton, he spoke.

"Miss Schneider, as you have guessed so correctly, I do feel – and clearly my brother Ludwig feels the same – that we owe something to humanity in this matter. I will, therefore, help you if I can. But you will have to explain to me why this is so important."

"I am very grateful, Dr Wittgenstein. I will tell you, but you must agree to keep what I say strictly within these walls."

"I will. I promise."

*

Outside, the snow was swirling around in a desultory way, as if deciding whether it dared settle in November. She was making her way across from Port Washington, a few miles from New York harbour, towards the Pan Am Clipper which floated a few hundred yards away from the launch. Those travelling with her were wrapped up warm, but their faces were peculiarly closed in other respects too. It occurred to Xanthe that anyone who needed to fly to Europe at this period of history would hardly be holidaymakers. They must have their own reasons for taking an uncertain flight to Portugal, and they would be serious.

Nor was she keen to go. She had wanted to fly back on the RAF flight home, to see Indigo. But there had been a change of plan.

She had explained to Dr Wittgenstein absolutely nothing about Enigma, nothing about Bletchley Park, though she had hinted at work involving cryptography that was going on somewhere vaguely inside the British armed forces. She explained something of the threat of the Lorenz code – without being able to convey why it was so urgent. In practice, it seemed, she didn't have to.

"You say that this company, which I own part of, is actually supplying the Nazis with war weapons? From a neutral country like Switzerland?"

"I'm afraid that's the case, sir. The Swiss supply the German side in order to complicate the argument about whether the Nazis should invade Switzerland."

"Really? What you say is quite unexpected. Quite surprising. Perhaps I was naïve. I believed there were international laws to protect against such abuses."

Xanthe felt the moment had come to sound judicious.

"I suppose also that an attachment for a teleprinter might be construed as not for military use."

"That would be a lie, would it not?"

"It would, sir. But may we discuss now, what we can actually do?"

CHAPTER FOUR

New York Harbour, November 1941

Xanthe settled back into her chair and looked out across the huge one hundred and fifty-foot wings of the clipper that was about to catapult her into the skies. She checked again the letter she carried, this time from Paul Wittgenstein to his financial manager in Geneva, M. Gruber.

How had she been so diverted, she wondered, thinking again of Indy asleep in his cot at this time? Here she was, listening to the propellers firing into life, and watching out of the small window as the four engines began to move them across the waters of New York harbour, before heaving them into the sky and setting course for Lisbon via Bermuda.

She looked at the other passengers curiously and wondered what was taking them across the Atlantic to a war-torn continent – why would anyone willingly take this seventeen-hour trip? Not that this was in any way the kind of discomfort of a mattress on the RAF bomber. She sipped her champagne with a little guilty frisson. It was, by some way, the biggest plane she had ever flown in, more like a house on legs than an aeroplane, with its huge silver fuselage and four mighty engines.

Of course, it had been inevitable, looking back, that she would be charged with talking directly to the Wittgensteins' business manager. Paul could hardly get away now that the winter concert season was under way, and Ludwig, well, he could hardly go. There would be a short period of some risk as they crossed Vichy France in the train, but they were non-combatants and so, theoretically, was she, with her passport and her letters of accreditation from the editor of the *New Yorker* himself. In fact, it was almost as if the mysterious man with the homburg, who had greeted her at Grand Central Station, had been sent especially for the purpose by London. Thanks to him and his mysterious 'chief", the letter had arrived before she left, together with a handwritten note wishing her luck on her trip.

"I'm not aware that there are any American stringers in Berne or Geneva or in other parts of Switzerland," he said. "But may I suggest you keep an eye out for a guy named Best. I think he's gone over to the other side."

There did seem to be this quiet acceptance by most American people that they had now chosen a side, Xanthe thought to herself. This was not what she had expected, though there was considerable naivety from most of those she had talked to about the war and what it was like.

The plane was now in the air and circling the Statue of Liberty before heading south. Below her, she could see the lights of Manhattan, blinking innocently in the early evening as she set course for Europe again.

*

If Switzerland was now the civilised corner of continental Europe, a small mountainous haven of sanity and warmth, then Geneva felt slap bang in the middle of it. After the long train journey through neutral Spain, battered and impoverished by civil war, and the stop-start journey through non-combatant Vichy France – which seemed brutalised and curmudgeoned by defeat – Xanthe's train drew into the lighted station in Geneva with an exhalation of steam and relief.

There had been no trouble at either border, though she had been nervous as they had approached the French passport control and customs posts in the Pyrenees. She'd used her American passport – it was a relief to be travelling under her real name again. Her other one – in the name of Shirley Johnson – was also in her case, secreted away under the lining of her spare coat, on Fleming's advice.

To be in the Hotel Génève in Geneva, on her *New Yorker* expense account, with its roaring Advent fire and the distant sound of Christmas on the way, felt almost as good as being home again in the Midwest.

Paul Wittgenstein had cabled M. Gruber, his financial manager, before she had left so he'd be expecting her. With a bit of luck, the whole trip would only take a couple of days and then she could write her article and go home. She had only really signed on for the first trip to Cambridge to see the professor. The other assignments had all been added incrementally, but she was at least now glad to be able to see the whole job through. The Wittgensteins were onside, though they did not know the full significance of what they had agreed to do. Paul's decision was that he would simply order the company he owned to stop trading with one of the combatant powers.

There was something a little naïve about this approach which worried Xanthe. She had imagined and would have preferred something more subtle. But if it worked, it would at least have the desired effect.

The only stipulation he had set was that Xanthe should not expose his sisters in Austria to any kind of Nazi response. She knew how difficult this would be, so this was a subtle commission that must not be carried out in public. It would have to be organised secretly. All now depended on Gruber.

In the event, of course, she could take none of this for granted.

*

She arrived at Herr Gruber's office at nine o'clock the next morning and was shown up to a small, dark office, filled with heavy black mahogany furniture. A small bald man got up and greeted her with outstretched hands.

"My dear Miss Schneider. I am delighted to meet you. May I introduce you to Herr Krieg, who as you may know, is Dr Wittgenstein's banker."

For the first time, Xanthe saw they were not alone. This was awkward. She had no information on Krieg. She could really say nothing in his presence, but it would be difficult to say so.

She played for time.

"Herr Krieg, it is very good to meet you and how unexpected. I was not warned that you would be here too."

Krieg got to his feet and bowed. He did not smile. There was nothing for it. She would have to return later and see Gruber on his own.

Then Krieg spoke. He had a deep, gravelly voice which he used to good effect, putting the palms of his hands together like a pompous family solicitor telling you a difficult truth.

"Miss Schneider, I have been in telegraphic correspondence with Dr Wittgenstein in recent days, and he has impressed on me that he wants to make sure that none of his companies are trading with the combatant powers."

It was getting colder as the evening drew in, and Xanthe found herself edging closer to the fire. Or was the cold emanating directly from Krieg?

"I believe so," she said, happy to confirm what Paul had said, given his own warning not to compromise his sisters.

"I must tell you that it would be improper, not to say perverse of us, to remove our contracts from one side and not from the other. That would be to betray the treaty and – well, you can imagine what those consequences might be. We are surrounded by the Axis powers, and we rely on them completely to provide us with the food and energy and other resources we need to live. We have to make some sacrifices, whether these are moral ones or friendships with former trading partners. We cannot, as I have told your – um, client – have the luxury of completely clean consciences on this matter. It would indeed be most dangerous if we did so."

The speech had now become headmasterly, and Xanthe saw that M. Gruber was looking increasingly uncomfortable, but for some reason chose not to say so. Perhaps he was nervous of Krieg. Still, it was all helpful for the *New Yorker* article she would write, even if it was extremely unhelpful for the central purpose of her visit.

On an impulse, she decided to leave – not to storm out but to leave the impression of moral disappointment and to see what would happen. Standing on her dignity, she rose and walked out of the room.

"Miss Schneider…!" said Gruber hopelessly as she left.

*

The hotel was filled with displaced Europeans. Xanthe settled at the bar feeling drained and downcast. Had Paul been a complete fool? Now, if anything was done about the Lorenz chronometer, then the danger was that the Swiss authorities would know, and the Nazis would know pretty soon after that. Or was Krieg, in fact, being quite clever by framing the suggestion that his only concern was one of even-handedness, which gave her a possible new approach to take. It was going to be difficult, either way. Somehow, she would have to find a way to see Gruber without his banking minder and ask his advice. She felt extremely unbriefed, not to say ignorant, about the Swiss political situation. She had never actually thought much about them before. Of course they must fear invasion too. Of course these must be live issues in Switzerland. She should have realised.

What was more, Herr Krieg had done her a favour by warning her before she had put her foot too far in it by displaying some crass insensitivity.

"I don't know what it is, but you look like a fellow American," said a voice next to her. He smiled broadly. A tall, cadaverous, balding man in a frayed suit, shiny with overuse, shook her hand vigorously.

"I'd buy you a drink, but I am temporarily embarrassed in funds, if you see what I mean."

"Don't worry. I have something already. May I ask, are you a journalist? Or a businessman?"

"Journalist – at least until United Press fired me, but I do stuff all over, *New York Times, Herald Tribune*, you name it. I'm here to look for work actually."

It was with a huge sense of relief that Xanthe took his hand. At last, another sane voice, and she could ask him some of the background of the place. He stood up.

"Well, let *me* buy you a drink. I am temporarily *in* funds at the moment because I have only just arrived. Xanthe Schneider of the *New Yorker.*"

"*New Yorker*? Top stuff! Know Joe Liebling?"

Xanthe nodded.

"Never met him. But I'd like to. Boy, that guy can write…"

With a whisky in his hand and a gin in hers, they settled down away from the bar. Xanthe pumped him about Switzerland.

She learned about the great dilemma that faced the Swiss, surrounded on all sides by the "new world order", as he put it. What could the Swiss do? And, in practice, they had to do what they were told, at the same time as they prepared for war. Xanthe heard about the great tussle between the general in command of Swiss forces, Henri Guisan, and his heroic order to eventually call up the whole male population and to militarise the Alps – and the foreign minister, Marcel Pilet-Golaz, who was determined to maintain the balance to avoid invasion.

"It is delicate, delicate," said her new friend. "They have so far managed to hold off an attack from the German side, presumably because they've calculated that they would lose hundreds of thousands of men and might then lose access to some of the components that only the Swiss can supply. They are no longer supplying the British."

Xanthe steeled herself for the main question.

"You don't think that's unfair? If the Swiss are neutral, why are they supplying one side only with military material? That isn't exactly neutrality."

"Well, I can't say it really matters what I think. But it is realistic, isn't it? Frankly, Xanthe, it can only be a matter of months before the British give up and the Swiss will need to come to some more permanent relationship with the Nazis."

She was suddenly aware that she was again out of her depth. This was a completely different attitude to what she had expected.

"You don't think that's a little defeatist?"

"Depends whose side you're on, doesn't it," said the man. "I like to think of myself as a realist, and – now I am facing a little difficulty finding work in my usual stamping ground in Vienna – I am feeling particularly realistic."

You need to be a little careful of this man, said Xanthe to herself.

"But, hey! Ask away – any questions you have and I'll help if I can."

"That's kind of you. I'm here to write about the Swiss at war, so you've already been quite helpful. Is there anyone particular I need to talk to, do you think?"

Hold on – she suddenly remembered she didn't know what he was called.

"I don't think I asked your name. Kinda rude of me – sorry."

"Bob – Bob Best," he said.

"Wow, I've heard of you," she said and then wished she had not spoken. But he looked pleased. This was the man her editor had warned her about.

"My fame's gone before me. Pity it doesn't result in very much work," said Bob. "To be honest, since we're staying neutral back home, I have a feeling I can learn something from the Swiss way. Since the war in Europe isn't going to last much longer, at least in the west, I thought I would offer my services to German radio."

"Oh well," she said, wondering how to reply. "Rather you than me."

Was that too distinctively English a phrase, she wondered? She must not give herself away. She had to be more careful.

"Thank you so much for your help," she said, rising in her seat. "I think I'd better turn in."

"Miss Schneider!"

She turned and saw M. Gruber, pushing his way towards her through the people who had gathered in the bar during her conversation.

"Excuse me," she said, extricating herself from Best. "Herr Gruber, how good to see you. Is there anywhere more private we can talk?"

*

Gruber was sweating when they reached the street and hailed a taxi.

"Miss Schneider," he said again as he settled onto the back seat and gave the driver instructions about where to go. "Miss Schneider, I must apologise in the most profuse terms. My colleague, Herr Krieg, is an upright man, but he gave you a mistaken impression of my country and our attitudes to the future. I was most disturbed at the impression he must have given you. We do not think of ourselves in these terms, except perhaps for a small band of people, most of them running the government. If the Nazis come, we will fight for our country, and it is only by showing them that we are prepared to die that we can prevent them coming at all. General Guerin speaks for us and we are right behind him."

"So why are you supplying the Germans with chronometers? I don't get it," she said, whispering. She hardly wanted to risk the driver overhearing. "Supplying the Nazis, that is? Why? Can you explain?"

"I know, I know – and we are aware of this anomaly. This injustice. Especially since our government has signed an accord with the Nazis that they will continue to supply them to one side and not the other. And for some reason, the British have not protested. It is most strange, Miss Schneider. I want to hear precisely what Dr Wittgenstein's concerns are and then, together, we will find a way to address them. I am here to help."

Xanthe felt this might be the best time – if not to play it exactly – then at least to make people aware that she had a trump card.

"Thank you so much, Mr Gruber. I have to tell you that my understanding is that the damage to the British side from this particular component – if you and I fail to persuade Krieg and his supporters to stop its supply – would be considerable, and precipitate action may follow against the company."

Gruber went pale.

"What do you mean? You mean some kind of violence? That would be most unwise – the Swiss are deeply stubborn people. We really don't want to provoke them."

"Of course, nobody wants it to come to that. We just have to make something happen. That's all."

*

Only forty-eight hours after her train journey through Spain and France, Xanthe was once again on the move. Extraordinary, she said to herself, and exhausting too. She steeled herself and reminded herself that she was feeling determined. She glanced at Gruber sitting next to her on the train to Berne, still sweating, still apparently prepared to go the extra mile to defend Swiss national integrity.

"What we need to do is to give them an excuse to comply," he said. "And I know just what to do."

"Oh yes?" said Xanthe. "What's that?" They had already discussed, then dismissed, the need to prevent the Nazis from sourcing the specific chronometers the Lorenz company needed from anywhere else in Nazi Germany – (they agreed that, if the chronometers were available inside Germany, the Nazis would have gone there first). She had said nothing about why this mission was so important. But she had picked up a defensiveness in his remark, as if the most important item on Gruber's to-do list was to reassure her – as if he feared she would personally plant the explosives if he failed.

Clearly, Gruber had an inkling that she was not just here as an emissary from the Wittgenstein family.

"We will talk to the senior managers today," he said. "And you will find them very receptive. But they will need an excuse to help and so I suggest that we also talk to the key people on the shop floor."

"You mean ferment a strike?"

This was so obviously not what he meant because Gruber went bright red.

"A strike? Certainly not, certainly not. I simply want to explain what we need, and I think you will find the workforce is most sympathetic. You see, Miss Schneider..."

"Oh, please call me Xanthe."

"Thank you," he bowed a little in his seat. "You see, Xanthe, we are not a disunited nation, though it might sometimes seem otherwise. I am a lieutenant in our militia. When we last mobilised, when the Germans reached the French border and we believed they would try to sweep into Switzerland via Berne, I had to get into my uniform and take up my position on the front line. I am prepared to fight. I am not just a businessman. You know, we have the slogan: 'For one Swiss, two Germans'. I remember, as I took my rifle out of the house, my young daughter clung to my hand – she is nine. I was filled with dread; I didn't believe I would see her again. All I could say was, 'God bless you!'"

Herr Gruber was so obviously moved that Xanthe found tears were springing, unbidden, to her eyes. She knew all too well about leaving young children to go to war. With a huge effort, she deliberately pushed Indigo out of her mind.

"Thank you, Herr Gruber. I do understand."

"We might not win," he went on. "But it would be costly for them, and once we were pushed back, we could carry on the fight from the Alps. They would not forget Switzerland."

The train drew into Berne station, a concrete modernist platform. They found a taxi. The city seemed bright compared to London but also somehow constrained, Xanthe felt.

"I tell you this because we all have responsibilities, even civilians. I myself have a list of people that I must arrest – Nazis and so forth – if there is an invasion."

Soon the taxi was drawing up alongside a very ordinary-looking warehouse near the river. The brass plaque on the door read "*Scherzinger Verlag*".

"And now, Miss um… Xanthe. If you would stay here for a few moments, I will prepare the way. I will be like your John the Baptist, *n'est-ce pas*. I shall make your way straight."

Then, for the first time since they had met, M. Gruber gave her an unmistakable grin.

*

Xanthe sat alone in the taxi, watching the snow begin to settle on the windscreen. The driver had disappeared to a nearby bar. She felt she had spent a lifetime there.

"How did it go?" she asked as the door opened and M. Gruber sat back inside. But it was not Gruber. It was a tall man, dressed in a heavy Mackintosh, with wire-framed glasses and a very severe haircut.

"Fraulein Schneider," he said. It seemed to require no answer. This was no question.

Xanthe said nothing but reached for the car door on the other side.

"I advise you not to get out. My colleague is on the other side of the car, and you will not get far. In any case, my purpose is only to give you a friendly warning."

This is hardly the first time you have been cornered by a Nazi policeman, Xanthe told herself, struggling to stay calm. In any case, either Gruber or the driver would return at any moment. Unless, of course, they were in on the same project.

"It is simply to say that we know who you are. You are Xanthe Schneider, formerly of the *Chicago Tribune* and wanted in Berlin in connection with the death of one of our bravest officers and on other charges, including espionage."

Stay calm. Stay calm, Xanthe told herself.

"I am fully aware that you are a citizen of a neutral power. I cannot have you arrested – though if circumstances change, I certainly will do. This is also neutral territory. But it is not far to drive this car over the border with Germany, where we could consult the charges against you at our leisure."

"My colleague will be…"

"Do you understand what I am saying, Fraulein?"

Xanthe opened her mouth, but nothing came out.

"Very well. I shall take that as an agreement. The reason I wished to speak to you now is simple. We know what you are doing here."

Xanthe's mind was racing. Could they know? Is it just intelligent guesswork – or were the British authorities so obsessed with their own cryptography that they had not noticed the other side was also cracking their codes the other way?

"I am here as an accredited correspondent for the *New Yorker*. I'm writing about Switzerland at war." There was her voice. She knew it had been there somewhere.

"I am prepared to believe you, Miss Schneider. On condition that you finish your article quickly and that you immediately abandon your other plans – to disrupt legal trade between a neutral country and the Reich."

"I don't know what…"

Of course, she realised. Paul Wittgenstein's cables had not even been enciphered. There had been no great feat of cryptology – the Nazis had just put two and two together.

"Because, if you continue along the course you are threatening to take, then you will be considered an enemy agent – you will be committing an act of war in a neutral nation – and there will be no need to take you over the border. We will simply ask the Swiss authorities to act accordingly. Now, nod if you understand me."

Xanthe nodded. "But…" she protested.

The door opened and the man was gone. A flurry of snow swirled into the taxi and the door banged behind him.

"Was that your friend? Has he gone again?" it was the driver.

"No, no," she said vaguely, trying to remember the German for "thank you for being patient". Or even the French. She was clearly going to have to trust Mr Gruber.

CHAPTER FIVE

Berne, December 1941

"*Samuel Johnson wrote that when you are being hanged in the morning, it concentrates the mind wonderfully,*" she wrote in her notebook. It was Dr Johnson, wasn't it? She felt sure there had been some kind of crossword clue along those lines many years ago, but she could always check later.

"*No such deadline affects the Swiss, but they are now surrounded by Nazi allies so that their minds are similarly concentrated. And it is not a comfortable experience.*"

She looked down at her handiwork and was not terribly happy with it. It was all a bit wordy – how would Liebling do it? Still, it would do for the time being, as an intro for her *New Yorker* article.

She sipped the glass of wine she had armed herself with. There were shortages of almost everything across Europe, she knew, but apparently there was no shortage of wine in Switzerland. In fact, they appeared to be determined to drink it all before the Nazis arrived.

Yet it was also extremely hard to concentrate, now that the Nazis knew who she was – probably even knew what room of what hotel she was staying in. She had taken the precaution of asking them at the reception desk not to reveal her room number, and she had locked her door and heaved the cupboard against it, but she knew that was not going to be enough.

Two questions kept coming into her mind. First, what did the Nazis actually know about her mission here? Second, in order to answer that, *how* did they know? Assuming there was no leakage from London, they could have intercepted Paul Wittgenstein's unwise letter to Gruber, in which case they would know only the most general things. Or similarly, they could have intercepted the cables between Wittgenstein and Krieg, or heard the basic information through a contact in either of their offices. What details had they included? She simply did not know.

She knew that Geneva and Berne were both stuffed with agents and spies, pretend journalists and remittance men. She had deliberately made no mention of precisely which piece of equipment was important to her since she arrived – or before, come to that. The chances were, she believed, that they knew which company she was targeting – yet she also knew that they made a range of different chronometers for a range of different electronic products. Unless she talked in her sleep – which was not completely impossible – they would not deduce any connection with Lorenz.

And with a bit of luck, she would also be on the next train to Lisbon first thing on Monday morning.

So why was she worrying?

The answer was that the meeting between Gruber and the officials from Scherzinger seemed to have been ridiculously anodyne. They had apparently barely mentioned anything, either about chronometers or about war exports.

"*The correct thing to do in these circumstances*," the general manager had said, "*would be to summon the board. Herr Wittgenstein owns forty-nine per cent of the shares. If he has any support among the other shareholders, then – if we can – we will comply with his wishes. Otherwise, we cannot comply. In the end, the situation is simple.*"

The manager had trailed off. It had all been a little underwhelming, to have such decisions reduced to dull voting arithmetic. Yet Gruber had asked her to be patient, and she had been.

There was a knock at the door of her hotel room. Xanthe froze.

"Come in," she hissed. One of the maids put her head around the crack in the doorway which was all the cupboard allowed.

"Mademoiselle, there is a visitor for you downstairs. He says it is important. I have refused to tell him your room number, as you instructed."

"Did he give a name?"

"My apologies, Mademoiselle. I have not that information."

For goodness sake, she said to herself. She grabbed her notebook and her coat,heaved the cupboard away from the door and opened it a crack. Nobody was in the corridor. Why had she not brought a pistol?

She knew somewhere there were some backstairs, and – yes – there they were, through this service door. Checking first up and down, she went through. On the ground floor, there was a back door out into the courtyard and then onto the street. It was still snowing, a little fitfully now, and she struggled to put her coat on.

There was nobody in the alleyway out the back as she stepped through the gate into the slush and walked quickly to the front of the hotel. A large black car sat by the entrance on the opposite side of the street, but – if they were looking for her – they were looking for a young woman coming out, not going in.

As she walked up the steps, she heard her name whispered behind her.

"Miss Schneider?"

She swung round without thinking. It was Gruber, and there was a large man with him. Both backed into the shadows.

Xanthe was cross. She was tired and nervous.

"What are you doing here?" she hissed as she reached them. "I think I've gone as far as I can today. I've had a visit from a Nazi official, and I must leave on Monday…"

"I know, I know," said Gruber. "My profuse apologies to you. I have someone you must meet."

Xanthe looked around. The big man was gone.

"Where is he?"

"Mr Lalonde is meeting us in a quiet café round the corner."

"Well, I was afraid you blew my cover by calling me just now. Tell me where to go and I will be there in fifteen minutes."

"Good. It is the Café Guillaume Tell and it is on the street parallel to this one, only five minutes from here. Go to the bar, say you are a friend of Max, and they will show you where to go."

She waved to him briefly and watched him trudge off through the falling snow. Then she went back inside. At the reception desk she said loudly that she was turning in for the night, and that she should not be disturbed. She hoped somebody would overhear.

She took her coat off and as soon as she was upstairs, put it straight back on again and slipped back down by the service stairs for a second time. Then she walked quietly out of the back door. This time, she turned left instead of right and found herself in the small, dark street at the back of the hotel where she was staying.

A couple came towards her carrying a small Christmas tree.

"Bonjour, monsieur et dame, pardonez-moi. Je cherche le Café Guillaume Tell."

It was not far away. There seemed to be nobody following her as she walked through the door into the café and asked for Max.

"Ou est M. Gruber?" she asked as soon as she was alone with M. Lalonde.

"He is waiting for you outside."

Xanthe was irritated by these slightly heavy-handed precautions.

"I took care to make sure I was not followed. I hope he is not too cold – or putting himself in any kind of danger on my account. My name is Xanthe. We haven't been introduced, I'm afraid."

How English I have become, she said to herself.

"*Enchanté, Mademoiselle.* My name is Eugene Lalonde. I am, I think you say in English, the shop steward and the foreman at the factory you visited today. Let me fetch M. Gruber and we can get down to business."

No, not more wandering around! Xanthe was losing patience, aware of how little time she probably had before she was likely to encounter the Nazi in the raincoat again.

"I'm afraid we have had too much coming and going already. Let's quickly talk things through and then we can go and find him together."

"That is acceptable to me, Miss Xanthe. I know something of what you want, and I have drawn up this list. You must understand that it is difficult for the managers to stop supplying the Nazis by themselves. They need an excuse, and this is where I come in – I can provide such an excuse. There is a strong feeling among the men who work with me that it is wrong to supply the Nazis with weapons that could soon be used against us."

Xanthe understood.

"Perhaps you don't know what your components are used for?"

"I have guessed that you would not have made this dangerous journey for general reasons, or because of principles, but because there are particular companies that you have concerns about, and maybe particular products. This is a list of the companies we supply in Germany."

He pulled a piece of paper from his jacket, smoothed out the creases and set it on the table in front of Xanthe.

"Now, look down this list, Mademoiselle Xanthe. Do you see the particular client that concerns you here?"

She only needed to glance at the list, and there it was. C. Lorenz AG, Berlin.

"Yes," she said.

"Now, I will tell you what we will do. We will instruct our shop floor not to work on German contracts which could be used for military purposes. But if you will be so good as to indicate the contracts that most concern you – and you do not need to explain why – then I will make sure that if we do continue with that particular contract, that we will do so only slowly and haltingly."

Xanthe looked at Lalonde. He was not good-looking and he had a scar down one side of his face. She felt a wave of gratitude towards him.

"How do I know I can trust you?"

"You cannot, but I am a sergeant in the militia, and I love my country. Here are my military identity papers."

Xanthe looked at them. They could have meant anything. She really had no choice, and she knew it only too well. She should not reveal this particular detail under any circumstances, but she could barely achieve her objective without doing so. She could hardly interfere with the production process in person, even if the managers feared she had explosives in her baggage.

"Ok then, show me your list again."

Once more, Lalonde spread out the list. His hands were long and delicate, those of a craftsman capable of dealing with the intricate workings of watches.

"You must understand, Miss Xanthe, that we are highly skilled.

We are a highly educated workforce, we know what we are doing. And we know why we are doing it."

Then she pointed at the name Lorenz.

"And may I ask, how important is it?" he asked.

"It is extremely important. For reasons I can't say, the outcome of the war may depend on it."

"Very well, then," said Lalonde. "It will be good to take this responsibility. To make our contribution."

"One thing though," she said, suddenly nervous. "It is important that we do not give away to the Nazis that we know about this component. So could you go slow on two or three others too?"

"Very well. I understand. And now, let us go and find our friend."

*

They walked out into the crisp frozen air and down the back street towards the main road. She shook with the anticipation of success.

"Monsieur Lalonde, I hope you don't mind but it may be best if I am not seen in your company, so I will go on ahead."

He bowed his head.

"Farewell then, Miss Xanthe. You are a brave lady, and I salute you."

There was no sign of Gruber by the time she reached the Kochergasse main road and she doubled back, indicating to Lalonde what she was doing. Where was he? Was Gruber the type to just disappear?

She could see out of the corner of her eye that Lalonde was getting agitated too.

What was that? She U-turned and looked down the alleyway from which she had emerged less than half an hour earlier, leading to the back door of the Hotel Bellevue Palace. There seemed to be a bundle of black clothes lying in the snow. She raced over. It was Gruber.

"Is he dead? Oh, don't let him be dead?" she wailed to herself out loud. "He's got a nine-year-old daughter too…"

Then there was a blow to her head, and she blacked out.

*

She came round quickly and for a moment, could not work out either where she was or what was happening. She was on the ground in the snow and aware of a painful cold. Her head throbbed. But all around her were the sounds of some kind of struggle, with the occasional hissed swearwords in French and German. Someone fell on top of her, digging their elbow into her back. She tried to crawl out of the way.

Then there was a shot and the sound of running feet. Then someone was lifting her gently to her feet. To her great surprise, it was Krieg.

"Herr Krieg, what's happened…?"

"Pray, do not distress yourself, Fraulein Schneider. You are a guest in my country, and I will not let—"

"—These gentlemen have bravely stepped in to prevent your kidnap, I fear," said Lalonde. "And now, we must look after M. Gruber."

It took a few moments, and the phrase "these gentlemen", for Xanthe to realise that there were now three men at her side, panting and exhausted. Lalonde and Krieg, but there was a third, Spanish-looking man in a sharp suit and sporting a large Zapata moustache.

He bowed to her.

"Señor Santa Cruz, at your service."

She tried to stand but buckled for a moment and was held by Lalonde. A searing pain seemed to pierce her eyes.

"Sir, I apologise that I seem unable to stand. I am so grateful for your help."

"Miss Schneider. Your courage is commendable, and I salute you. If ever you find yourself in difficulties again, you have only to shout for Santa Cruz."

"Thank you, sir. I hope to repay you someday."

He bowed and walked determinedly in the direction of the hotel. As he did so, the pile of clothes that was Gruber twitched and turned its face upwards. They could see his bloodied and bruised face. He had evidently taken quite a beating.

Krieg shouted after Mr Santa Cruz. "Can you go ahead into the hotel and ask them to call a doctor? We will carry him in."

"Can you stand, Mademoiselle?"

"I think so," said Xanthe. "Yes, I can."

The two men reached down and lifted the inert shape of M. Gruber, while she held his head, and laboriously they moved towards the service entrance. By the time they reached it, Señor Santa Cruz had done his work, and staff came out to meet them. Someone had telephoned the manager.

There he was in a pompous pin-striped suit, clearly of Swiss design.

"In the side room, if you don't mind," he said, sidling up to Lalonde. "We don't wish to alarm the guests."

It was too late. The guests, who were milling around, seeking excitement, gasped as they saw Gruber's bruised face.

"A street accident," said the manager loudly. "No need for alarm. We have called for the doctor."

On a couch in the side room, M. Gruber looked as though he was coming round. He held his head and blew out of his lips in pain. Xanthe knelt at his side.

"Oh, M. Gruber, thank goodness you're alive!"

Some of his teeth were clearly missing.

"Who was the Spanish man?" asked Xanthe.

"I don't know," said Lalonde. "He came to our assistance, just as we came to yours. We may owe him our lives. Those thugs were armed."

The assistant manager brought a flannel and a bowl of warm water, and Xanthe began to delicately wash the blood from Gruber's face.

"I'll do it *really* gently," she said. "Ooh, sorry!"

It was hard to tell what he was trying to say, but judging by some gesticulation, it was clear that Gruber wanted to say *something* to her. He looked increasingly frantic, with the blood congealing on the wounds on his head. She knelt down next to him to hear him. He was obviously still in great pain.

She put her ear closer to his lips. It was difficult to make out anything except that – judging by the effort – he wanted to tell her something important.

"Xanthe," he said. "Listen to me. You must leave. Now."

Then he fainted.

*

Berne appeared to have closed for Sunday, and – given what M. Gruber had said – it made sense to stick to crowded areas. So Xanthe was sitting in the wooden pews at the back of Berne Minster, the great arched gothic cathedral at the heart of the Protestant world, as well as at the heart of the city. She had heard that Pastor Karl Barth was due to preach, and she knew that, as well as getting out of Switzerland the next morning, there was one more task to do, one more duty to perform, and that was for her editor. She needed to research the article she had promised him and which provided her with her cover story.

She had arrived early, taken her place at the back and was able to watch the burghers of Berne file in and along the pews, judging them to be better off – at that moment at least – than anyone else in Europe.

They looked almost well fed, though she knew how tight the rations were, and – judging by the number which was arriving for church that morning – they were also nervous about the future. As indeed they should be, given their predicament.

She had been led to believe that the Swiss were on the smug side, but that was another misconception. This was actually the last free outpost of continental Europe, and that freedom was in some doubt.

"Who is the conscience of Switzerland?" she had asked Gruber when she had first met him.

"There is no doubt," he said. "It is Dr Barth."

Then he had told her the story, how Barth had been sacked from his job in Berlin because he would not swear allegiance to Hitler. How his sermons provided the nation with a theological backbone against Nazism, and how his friends in the Confessing Church were standing up to the Nazis in Germany.

"And he wrote *The Epistle to the Romans*. If you have time to go to Basel, you must hear him preach."

Xanthe felt sure that had actually been St Paul, but she said nothing. And so when Dr Barth had travelled to Berne that very Sunday, she felt – not just that the minster may well be the safest place to be – but that she *must* go.

The words washed over her. It was dour and unimaginative as a service. It kept her mind wandering backwards and forwards over the momentous events of the past few days. She had gone over and over her decision to point to the word Lorenz, and she still kept on coming to the conclusion that she had been right to do so.

Because this had been an unplanned extension of her original mission, she had been given no advice or briefing on the obvious question – what, if they were prepared to do something, could the

Wittgenstein family actually do? And how could they act without some basic information about exactly what it was that needed doing? Yes, Paul Wittgenstein's letter to his banker had been useful, but it had been unexpected. Why had Fleming not thought ahead? It must be the usual English middle-class ignorance about business, which was a kind of hidden snobbery – she said to herself – never acknowledged, which allowed them to claim they didn't know where anything had come from. The result was that she was left without effective instructions. She did not know enough about the world of business to know what to ask.

Dr Barth, in his black robes, walked slowly up the stairs to the wooden pulpit, his untidy grey hair blowing slightly as he did so. There was a rustle of expectation from the pews.

"*Meine Damen und Herren*," he said. Xanthe's German had been getting a little rusty, stashed away, unused, in the corner of her brain for nearly a year and a half. This was going to be a struggle.

"We are called, you and I, to be the body of Christ in the world," he said. "And my text today is the Gospel According to St Matthew, chapter sixteen, verse eighteen: '*On this rock, I shall build my church*'. We do not preach enough, perhaps, in our protestant nation, about the church and what it is, except that we are called to be Christ's body. But let me tell you what bodies *do* – and note that St Paul did not say we were called to be the mind of the church. No, my friends, bodies do not primarily *think*, they do not contemplate, and certainly not when the forces of evil are on the march. What bodies do is they *act*. They *do*. People bear witness with their own bodies. This is the essence of my message today…"

Xanthe looked around her. The congregation was completely focused on him. One man, who risked everything by standing up to the Nazis and survived – and was presumably now top of their list for arrest if they were to arrive over the mountains. He gave the congregation hope, it appeared, helped them feel they were not riding out the war, but resisting.

"When I left Germany, as many of you know, this was the sermon I preached," said Dr Barth. "We cannot hope that Hitlerism, which is such a threat to us, will go away all by itself. We cannot pretend we are somehow neutral in the struggle between good and evil. We cannot expect somebody else to do all the work. That is what we mean by a Confessing Church."

This is good, inspiring stuff, thought Xanthe. She edged out of her pew and along the pillars at the side of the nave, and at the end of the sermon, she made a dash for where Barth was sitting and shook his hand. The sober and sombre members of the congregation clearly felt this kind of behaviour bordered on the crass, but she took no notice.

"Dr Barth," she breathed. "I'm writing about Switzerland and the war for the *New Yorker* magazine, and I was wondering if I could ask you… that is to say, ask your advice? I'm afraid it'll have to be this afternoon because I'm leaving Berne tomorrow."

For a moment, she feared she had shocked him too. But he grinned back conspiratorially. The congregation was preparing to pray.

"And what is your name, my dear?" he whispered.

"My name is Xanthe Schneider."

"Well, Fraulein Schneider, I should be delighted to help. I am staying tonight at the presbytery. Perhaps you could come round before dinner, and we can talk. I don't believe now is the best moment."

She thanked him and took down the address. Then she suddenly felt nervous again. She shouldn't have made herself so visible, even in this crowd. She glanced at the bowed heads of the congregation. There were a number of them staring at her, and it was impossible to read their expressions – curiosity, disapproval, active malevolence? She couldn't tell. There were one or two tough-looking types in raincoats, but really they could perfectly well be loyal Swiss burghers or Nazis as far as she knew. She would have to survive a few hours unscathed, keeping away from the hotel and staying in crowded, restrained places, like the minster, and – if she did that – she might just make it.

The main problem was that her belongings were still in her hotel room and goodness knows who was watching her there. She just needed to get in unseen, barricade the door for the night, then get packed, check out and go.

She had planned to visit M. Gruber in hospital, but perhaps she'd better not.

*

"Tell me, Miss Schneider, do you believe that Jesus wants us to do what we are told by the governments of the world?"

They were borrowing the study belonging to whoever lived at the presbytery. Xanthe did not know who this was because Dr Barth himself had opened the front door.

Wasn't there something about rendering unto Caesar? Xanthe thought. She was feeling emotional and wanted to be honest.

"I'm afraid, Dr Barth, that I'm not a good Christian. I haven't gone to church for some years. Since the war began, I've doubted – I suppose – that God can possibly be active in the world."

"Ah well, I have some sympathy there. You know I lost my youngest son some months ago?"

Xanthe's heart went out to him. To lose a son…

"Was he killed in action? I know there have been incidents, fighting, even here."

"No, it was a climbing accident but no less pointless, or so it seemed to me. I only tell you this because I need you to know that I've also been forced to search my heart as well, to see God's purpose in the accident – just as we all puzzle to see God's purpose in this terrible war. And the truth is that we see darkly through a glass, that is what they say – I'm not sure of the translation in English. We can't know. We certainly *don't* know."

Xanthe stared at the open fire, flickering in the grate and began to feel sleepy. For a moment, she must have dozed off.

"Oh, I'm so sorry, Dr Barth, you're not boring me at all. Only I feel so comfortable listening to you and sitting here, and I'm so far from home and… oh well…" She trailed off.

"Where is your home, my dear?"

"Well, I come from Cincinnati, Ohio. But my home, I suppose, is where my family is, and I have a child in a small town in England."

She could imagine him glancing at her wedding finger to see if she was married, but there was no disapproval.

"My dear Xanthe," he began, but there were noises outside the door and they were becoming intrusive.

"Let me just see outside what the commotion is," he said.

Moments later, he was back with a couple of young men in a state of high excitement.

"Xanthe, you must come and listen to the wireless next door. It seems that the Japanese have attacked the American fleet in Pearl Harbour."

CHAPTER SIX

Berne, December 1941

It was nine o'clock in the morning, and the queues of exhausted and hopeful refugees were gathering, as usual, outside the American legation in Sulgeneckstrasse. Her train had been due to leave for Geneva at this time, but since the borders had been closed, there seemed little point in catching it.

It had been little more than twelve hours since she had hurried into the parlour of the presbytery to find the clergyman who lived there and his family – Dr Barth's hosts – gathered around the wireless set, listening to the BBC news in English on the European Service.

"*The long-awaited aggression threatened by Japan in the Far East has begun with an aerial attack on the American naval base of Pearl Harbour in the Pacific*," said the newsreader. "*Reports are still coming in, but the situation so far is that Tokyo says they have declared war on the United States, and a number of American battleships have been sunk or badly damaged...*"

Then came the bombshell. "*Germany and Italy are expected to declare war on Britain and the United States within hours,*" said the newsreader. "*A communiqué issued by the German Foreign Ministry supported the Japanese action and said that the behaviour of the United States was threatening world peace.*"

As she settled down to listen quietly and compulsively, the gravity of the situation suddenly felt overwhelming, and she burst into tears. The clergyman and his sons were very kind, especially given that they had no idea who she was or what she had been doing in the house. They held her hand and helped her blow her nose and wiped her eyes with great kindness.

Was she upset because her own land was threatened and her own navy had been so severely wounded? Or was it the relief that her adoptive country would probably now survive, given that the mighty USA, with its huge productive capacity, would be fighting alongside them after all? She was not sure, but the occasion felt momentous. Whichever it was, she found it hard to stop sobbing while Dr Barth held her hand.

It soon became clear that the Swiss had responded by closing the border, and it was not long before she realised the implications of that. She had no diplomatic status. She was a member of the armed forces of one belligerent nation and a national of another, working in a neutral country, and would surely, when inevitably discovered, be liable for internment.

"But I'm a journalist. I've got accreditation," she said, hoping it was true. She had already heard unpleasant stories about the Swiss internment camps, and the thought of being separated for years from Indigo, as he grew up, terrified her.

She had calmed down considerably by morning, barricading herself in her bedroom by heaving the heavy wardrobe against the door. It will be just my luck if there's a fire, she said to herself. It made her giggle. Black humour, she supposed. She reassured herself that, as far as anyone knew, she was not a combatant herself. There must be hundreds of Americans, just in Berne, in the same situation. They could hardly arrest them all. Yet the uncertainty unnerved her – she knew her American nationality could only make her more vulnerable to Nazi agents, especially if they knew who and where she was. Why had she come back to sleep at the same hotel, she asked herself.

What would she do if she was purely an American in difficulties, she asked herself? She would beg for help from her own diplomats.

*

Her footsteps on the icy pavement, in this immaculate but nervous city, reminded her with every step just how vulnerable she now was. All the Nazis needed do was to provide the Swiss authorities with evidence that she was the agent of a combatant power and then she would be locked in some camp until the far-off end of the war – or something considerably worse.

What she had not expected was that the embassy would be virtually besieged by refugees, plus crowds of American nationals trying to get home and by well-wishers, hoping to express their sympathy for the Pearl Harbour attack.

If the Nazi agents were hot on her trail, and she had to assume they were, hence her doubling back in the approved way to stop anyone following her, she dared not wait in line. There was nothing for it but to try the Berlin trick again. She marched straight up to the security desk and asked for Uncle Sam.

It seemed to have an effect. The security man stared at her for what seemed like minutes, blinked twice and then seemed to collect himself. She noticed that Americans seemed to be understandably dazed by the attack.

"Will you wait here, ma'am? And can you write your name down for me here?"

It must have been half an hour later when she was greeted by a large, thick-set man in military uniform, who introduced himself as Brigadier General Legge.

"Miss Schneider? I regret to say that Washington's asleep at the moment – at least those parts of the US government I needed to talk to about you. But I know who you are and I understand why you've come here." He smiled benignly, and Xanthe relaxed a little. She let out a small and somewhat premature sigh of relief.

"But I must be frank with you. We have a difficult task here right now, and I will find it hard to give you the diplomatic immunity you need, given that you are already known to the authorities as a journalist."

"But my life has been threatened," said Xanthe, beginning to shake.

"Listen lady, we've all now had our lives threatened. By this Hitler guy. I know something about you, and I have a suggestion. In fact, it's more than a suggestion – it's an order. You're to go immediately to the British embassy in Thunstrasse, and ask for John Lomax. Lomax is your man, and I will telephone him now to say you're on your way."

"Really? Who is he?"

"I have no idea," said Legge, giving a little wink. "I reckon you'll have to ask him yourself."

*

Xanthe trudged through fresh snow, careful always to make sure she was not being followed. It was all horribly reminiscent of her sudden departure from Berlin nearly eighteen months ago, and as she walked to Thunstrasse, the full vulnerability of her predicament became clearer.

She could hardly go to the police in case she was interned. She could not leave the country because the borders were closed. Now that her status had changed, she had to assume that the threat by the Nazi policeman who had virtually kidnapped her in a taxi might be made good – that she would be arrested and handed over to the authorities on suspicion of committing an act of war, not to mention the matter of a dead body in Berlin.

She mentally checked off the people she knew in Switzerland. She could hardly ask Dr Barth for help because she would put him in even more danger than he was already in. Krieg, she did not trust. Lalonde was as powerless as she was. What about Bob Best? No, he had gone over to the other side. The declaration of war might have brought him back, but she dared not rely on that.

It was a fifteen-minute walk across the river to the British embassy, and as she walked, she puzzled over the oddest elements of this latest twist of history. Why did Hitler declare war on the USA when he did not have to? There would probably be internal pressure back home to concentrate on the Japanese first, but why would Hitler run the risk of the British winning the argument and the whole, vast American arsenal being brought to bear first on him? It made no sense – unless he had made some kind of deal with the Japanese. Yes, that must be it, she thought. Even so, it was a peculiar deal to make. Then there was Roosevelt, forced to declare immediate war on Japan, when he had been avoiding anything but tacit support for the war against Hitler. Why did Hitler not simply keep those divisions in place?

She found the British embassy and was shown up to a somewhat unkempt office, occupied by a thin, balding man with a twinkle in his eyes. Papers and what looked like small electronic components were piled on every table top and on the floor.

"Mr Lomax?"

On every flat surface, there seemed to be what you might imagine were sales samples from companies involved in the cutting edge of Swiss engineering.

"Miss Schneider, do come in. I've been expecting you – and, in fact, I had been expecting you even before my friend, General Legge, informed me that you were on the way over. You don't have to spell out your difficulty. I understand it all too well. I don't know what you have been doing here, and I don't need to know either. Suffice to say that I know your work is important to HM Government. I also have a plan which I will shortly outline to you. It involves some risk, I'm afraid, but perhaps less risk than you would run by staying here."

Xanthe felt pathetic but relieved.

"Mr Lomax, I am so grateful to you," she said, taking to the man and his intelligent eyes.

"You see," said Lomax, warming to his theme. "Although I am a career diplomat, trained in the art of caution, I am now seconded to the Ministry of Economic Warfare, which has, in turn, trained me in the art of action. And I know my employers will turn a blind eye to what you might call unorthodox methods. Indeed, that is actually my job, in a sense."

Xanthe could not stop herself giggling at his tone, part mandarin, part little boy.

"You may well laugh, young lady. But it must be expected that, one day, I will return to the Foreign Office, where my misdemeanours are noted and where I have no doubt that my elders and betters will exact a terrible revenge."

Now it was Lomax's turn to laugh.

"Can you drive?"

Xanthe nodded. "But I haven't for some time," she said.

"You're aware, of course, that they drive on the wrong side on continental Europe – as you do back home in the States, of course? Now, next question: do you mind wearing a chauffeur's uniform, if I can obtain one?"

"Of course not. Anything which seems likely to get me home I'll wear."

"Excellent," said Lomax, rubbing his hands. "Then I will tell you what I am planning. It so happens that I was at a party, given by the embassy staff, of a small Latin American country, and I met the man who is now their ambassador to Berne. He is quite an eminent lawyer in his own country, but I digress. He needs to leave in a few days for London to take up his new post as Ambassador to the Court of St James. He has kindly agreed to carry a diplomatic bag for me, in the shape of a box which contains, well – let's just say it contains some crucial equipment that can only be obtained in Switzerland. He has agreed not to look inside the box but to drive it through Vichy France and Spain and down to Lisbon where he will catch the flight to London. Now, I have told him that he will garner the everlasting gratitude from HMG for his efforts and even more so if he can help in one other respect. Some weeks ago, I proposed to him that a man in his position cannot possibly drive himself. In fact, earlier today, I suggested that he needs a chauffeur to drive him and interpret for him. The borders will, I am sure, be open tomorrow – but even if they are not, he has diplomatic immunity."

"But I can't speak Spanish."

"My dear girl, he is from Latin America. He was born speaking Spanish. It is French that he will need a translator for – you do speak French, do you not?"

"Well, sort of..."

"Excellent. Then I suggest that I accompany you to your hotel now and fetch your luggage, and you can stay in the embassy in some comfort, and rather more safety, until you leave in a few days' time."

He began collecting up his cigarette case and other bits and pieces around the room. Xanthe was too fascinated to prevent herself from asking.

"Are you really allowed to do this kind of thing? It seems most unusual for a diplomat…"

"Well, officially, of course I'm not," said Lomax, getting up and walking over to the window, as if to engage the enemy more closely. "I went to great lengths to persuade HM Government that they must make the strongest representations about the Swiss supplying military equipment to the German side which they were not prepared to supply to us, but I was overruled. That said, I clearly made such a nuisance of myself that the Foreign Office seconded me PDQ. Ironically, it is now my task to *obtain* those items, and that is why I have been forced to take up my current position."

"Which is?"

"Oh, sorry, I thought you knew. I am Smuggler-in-Chief, by appointment to His Majesty the King."

CHAPTER SEVEN

Berne, December 1941

"I don't want to alarm you, but I believe we are expected," said Lomax as they descended from the taxi a block away from the Bellevue Palace Hotel.

Sure enough, two policemen were posted outside the hotel steps as Xanthe walked up with Lomax.

"I think it might be wise for you to go around the back. I will meet you upstairs – remind me of your room number? You have kept hold of the key, have you not?"

Xanthe nodded. "It is 276."

"I will meet you after I've gone through reception to settle the bill. I will be paying it out of funds put at my disposal for these kinds of events. I will meet you upstairs as soon as I have paid. But if it is too dangerous by my judgement, then I will meet you round the back, and I will signal like this."

He made a bloodcurdling slicing motion across his throat.

Xanthe went down the back street, past the spot where she had found Gruber injured and where she had nearly been kidnapped. The route was becoming uncomfortably familiar. She glanced around. There was no sign of Lomax warning her off. So it was up the backstairs and along the deserted corridor to her room.

She knew something was wrong the moment she put her key into the lock. It was broken, and the door just pushed open. Inside was carnage. The drawers had been pulled out and overturned and cupboard doors smashed, her suitcase lay in pieces. She rushed over, desperately worried and calculating whether she had left anything incriminating about her identity or, worse still, about the mission. But she knew she had not been so stupid. She had brought none of her briefings with her and no letters, nothing, in fact, except the tools of her trade as a journalist. Unfortunately, her portable typewriter would never work again. It lay, bent and smashed, with the ribbons spewing across the room like intestines. It was clearly beyond repair.

She had brought very little with her. She searched in vain for the notes of her interview with Karl Barth and her other scribbles for her Swiss article, but everything was gone.

A shuffle outside the door brought her to her senses. It was time to get out – and not through the hotel exit. Or down the corridor outside. She glanced through the window. Could she dare to take the ledge for two feet to get onto the fire escape? Hold on – she checked the en suite bathroom window, and managed to slide it up. A moment or so later, she was through the window and down the stairs, on her way to meeting Lomax when he came out again.

By a stroke of luck, he had already emerged from the hotel when they ran into each other in the side street. He was sweating a little.

"My dear girl," he said, trying to catch his breath. "There is a real hue and cry going on about you. The Germans are obviously exerting pressure. There was a policeman by the desk when I asked about you – I thought it best not to pay now – and the man behind the reception desk told me that you were wanted in connection with a murder in Berlin, or some similar cock and bull story."

"That's good to know," said Xanthe despairingly, "because somebody has smashed my room and stolen my things. It sure is a horrible feeling, I can tell you that for nothing."

"Heavens above," said Lomax without obvious emotion. "Look, there's a cab over there. I suggest we return post haste to the embassy, and we can talk there. I have talked to the ambassador this morning and he is on board – at least I think he is. So, with a bit of luck, you will be heading home tomorrow or the next day. The border is still closed. I think it may make sense to wait until it opens rather than pressing the diplomatic immunity message, given that we are not exactly sticking to the rules ourselves. All I can say is that you will not be pursued for unpaid hotel bills. At least, not after I've finished with them on the telephone."

*

"I am sorry. It is with the deepest regrets, Mr Lomax, but I will not do this."

The South American ambassador was audible outside the embassy room where Xanthe was waiting. Her spirits sank.

"May I ask why not?" said Lomax. "I was given to understand that you were willing."

"That was before my discovery that the proposed chauffeur was female. Very distinctly, I heard you describe the person as 'she'. I will carry your box with the greatest of pleasure, but I will not be driven by a woman. I will be a laughing stock."

"Your Excellency," said Lomax. His voice seemed louder outside the room, and Xanthe realised he had risen in his seat. "In my country, as you will discover, all the most important generals are driven by women.

It is a sign of status in warring nations, I assure you. Come, let me introduce you… Miss Schneider, please come in!"

Shaking a little, Xanthe stood there, uncomfortable in his scrutiny, her hair dyed dark again the previous evening. And wearing the uniform with gold braid that Lomax had commissioned overnight. The ambassador looked familiar somehow.

"And she is too attractive. People will think I have chosen her for her looks. It does not make me look sober… responsible."

"On the contrary, Ambassador, it gives you appropriate style."

Xanthe could see that he was now peering at her with a renewed interest.

"Wait!" The ambassador held up his hand, and Xanthe recognised him. How could she have forgotten such a copious moustache?

"Are you by any chance Miss Schneider?"

"I am indeed, Señor Santa Cruz. You are the man to whom I owe my life."

He grinned broadly and proudly. Lomax stood back, astonished.

"Now, I believe I made a promise to you, Miss Schneider. I said, if you needed help again, you had only to shout for Santa Cruz. Did I not?"

She nodded.

"Now, if you do me the honour of being my chauffeur, do I fulfil that pledge?"

"Oh, absolutely. In full."

"Right, Mr Lomax. You were always a persuasive man. I do not understand what I am agreeing to do, but I have promised not to ask. Nevertheless, I accept, on condition that the British government is told when I arrive in London about the part I have played."

"I am deeply grateful and so is HM Government," said Lomax bowing low. "Now, if you would be so good as to provide Miss Schneider with a passport."

The ambassador's face darkened again.

"No, I draw the line there. Yes, one may pretend to be a Bolivian – how do you say it: a cat may look at a king? But citizenship of my country is a great honour, and it will not be thrown away on a convenience for you or anyone else. Even for my esteemed friend, a courageous woman like Miss Schneider."

He bowed to Xanthe.

"Oh, very well, then. I am deeply grateful to you. I believe the borders are reopening at midnight. You leave at dawn tomorrow?"

The ambassador nodded, bowed to both of them and withdrew.

"Right, I will have to get one forged before you go. I will see you later. Now, for goodness sake, practise your spoken French..."

*

"That is correct, Miss Duarte," said the ambassador as they drove haltingly out of Berne towards the frontier with Vichy France.

Xanthe now held a Bolivian passport with the name Maria Duarte. The car was by far the biggest she had ever driven, and she had crashed the gears nervously all the way out of town, having stalled embarrassingly outside the embassy on her way to fetch the ambassador around the corner.

She was afraid she had displeased him already, first by failing to get the car started effectively and then by a series of hops she made it do as they drove past the British embassy again at the start of their journey. There seemed to be nobody about, which was a relief. Fuel was almost as scarce here as it was in England, though not quite as scarce as it probably was in France, so there was little traffic on the streets. She had studied the road map given her by Lomax and tried to memorise the way to the frontier and beyond that to the Pyrenees.

"Sorry, sir. I know you expected a better start than that, didn't you," she said, hoping to jolly along the dour man in the back, reading his official papers.

"That is correct, Miss Duarte."

Oh, stop talking, stop talking for goodness sake, Xanthe told herself. You're just digging a hole for yourself.

Once they had passed Lake Geneva safely and they were only a few final miles away from the frontier, she glanced round at her passenger a few times, and he seemed pretty unconcerned – mainly reading his papers and sometimes snoozing. Lomax had proposed a small hotel in Nîmes, if they could reach there by nightfall, and at the present rate of progress, they ought to do so. It was barely breakfast time, and they were already almost over the border.

Finally, there was the checkpoint. Xanthe had little idea of what the procedure was, but she recognised the uniforms of the Swiss police who were flagging down her car. Her heart turned over.

Looking ahead at the group of police, she was sure she recognised the man in the grey Mackintosh as the one who had accosted her in the cab when she had first arrived in Berne.

She fixed her face into an impassive stare. It was only when she presented both their passports for inspection that the Mackintosh man noticed the car and strode over. "Diplomatique," she said guardedly to the official.

"Halt! Arrête! Stop!" shouted the man, and he and two of his fellows, dressed in macks and mufflers, walked quickly over. Why was a German official working with the Swiss border guards? It made no sense, and Xanthe was unsure whether her French language skills would stand up to a prolonged argument about diplomatic bags and diplomatic immunity.

"Ah," said the man. "Miss Schneider, I believe, and – how do you English put it? – wham on time! You have been expected."

She froze her face into an impassive stare.

"Non," she said. "Je suis Maria Duarte and I am driving Ambassador Santa Cruz to his new appointment. You are in error I fear, Señor."

This was just the kind of altercation she had hoped to avoid with an unwilling ambassador in the back. Especially one so monosyllabic and who would – would he? – be happy to hand her over to the authorities to avoid a difficult diplomatic incident involving his country.

"Non, monsieur. Je suis Maria Duarte et cette voiture est un baggage diplomatique…"

Was that the correct term? She wasn't sure.

"I demand that you get out of the car so that we can discuss this. I think you will find that I have the authority to demand, since I am in pursuit of a murder suspect."

"Non, monsieur. Je regrette…"

She was going to have to think of something new and effective to say. She glanced into the back. Her ambassador appeared still to be reading.

By now, a small gaggle of officials had gathered around them and were in some kind of furious discussion.

A Swiss official came over. He bore himself with some authority.

"I am sorry, monsieur, mademoiselle, but we have received information that this lady is not who she claims to be and that she is wanted for questioning on a serious charge. I must insist that you and she get out of the car so that we can resolve this in an amicable way."

A silence followed this demand.

This was the critical moment. She glanced back again at her passenger, and he was clearly aware of what was going on. This would be the moment he would throw her to the wolves. She knew only too well that ambassadors were not supposed to get involved in tussles like this. With her heart beating even faster, he reached over languidly to the window and wound it down.

"Listen to me," he said, addressing the senior man. "This car and everybody in it is diplomatic baggage. If you insist on delaying us, we shall remain in the car while you contact your foreign ministry, who will tell you the same as I have done. You will also create a major diplomatic incident, for which you will be held personally responsible, and I have to say that my government will not take at all kindly to this violation of international law and the accepted formalities of diplomacy. Now, I suggest you go immediately and get advice from a more senior source. In the meantime, my driver and I will remain here. So, if you would be good enough to return our documents to me..."

With astonishment and relief, Xanthe turned to stare at the ambassador with gratitude in her eyes. The speech seemed to have had some effect on the officials, who now seemed to be in a loud argument with the Nazi officer, who was still shouting and gesticulating in her direction. After some minutes, the senior Swiss official marched back to the car and handed over their papers.

"Miss Duarte, I must ask you to stay here while we refer the matter to higher authority."

Xanthe watched the ambassador in the back seat make a wave of acknowledgement, then sit back, close his eyes and appear to go to sleep. Still, she thought – it was all useful material for her *New Yorker* piece, especially now that her first draft had apparently been taken into custody by some Nazi thugs. She began to pass the nervous time by rewriting the thing in her head.

How did it go now? Something to do with being hanged in the morning?

That's the thing about finding you are wanted for a crime which, in a sense, she knew she was actually guilty of carrying out – despite the circumstances – it concentrates the mind wonderfully. Not perhaps the happiest metaphor right now, she said to herself.

It must have been only ten minutes, as the snow piled up on the windscreen, before the new shift arrived at the checkpoint. The faces all seemed to be unfamiliar. To her astonishment, they raised the barrier and waved the car through.

Xanthe's fingers were cold, and she struggled with the ignition key. Had these border guards made a mistake? Were they taking a risk on their own authority? She had no idea, but she gave them a little salute. One of them gave her a thumbs up. Another motioned them forward and pointed to the open gates ahead.

"I should drive on if I were you, Miss Duarte," said the ambassador.

She breathed a sigh of relief as she managed to start the engine. The car moved forward and the guards came to attention and saluted as they drove by. It was a wonderful example of Swiss resistance to Nazi advice. What a pity she could not use it in her article, but she knew she would do nothing that might embarrass the ambassador, who had now saved her life twice.

She could not help smiling about how angry her Nazi kidnappers would be to find them gone. Perhaps the Swiss guards just felt uncomfortable being ordered around by a Nazi official. Who knows?

She had expected difficulty on the French side, but they seemed completely unaware of the fracas which had taken place on the Swiss side. They were soon driving almost alone down the road to Provence.

"I am very grateful to you," Xanthe whispered to her ambassador. "I think the guards just changed shift, but I know you have taken a risk for me."

"That is correct, Miss Duarte," he said.

*

Once they were on the road in Vichy France, it struck her how miserable the country had become, how dependent on horses and carts, which were about the only conveyances they passed as they shot along the main road towards Lyons and then south towards Nîmes and Montpelier.

The small hotel there appeared to have become pinched and curmudgeonly under the Vichy government. The bitter resentment was palpable there. The manager and his staff and family stared miserably at Xanthe and her ambassador as they disappeared into their different bedrooms, as if regretting that the history of South America was turning out happier than their own.

Nor was the food any less bitter, and the bread was a day old at least. The ambassador asked for an egg, but he was told sadly that none was available. It was a relief to get on the road again after their dawn diet of mean slices of baguette and coffee that tasted like the dust from the road outside. There was no sign of the ambassador opening up.

"What a beautiful crisp morning," Xanthe began hopefully.

"You are correct, Miss Duarte," he said.

She was still feeling light-headed about her escape from the Nazis at the border. It was a wonderful sense of liberation and freedom, and it grew on her. They were not quite safe while they were still in Vichy France, it was still possible that they would guess their direction of travel and the *gendarmes* would wait for them, perhaps at the frontier with Spain. Otherwise, every minute, every hour, they get closer to safety,

Xanthe told herself as she drove, writing and rewriting her article in her head, imagining Indigo in his cot and wondering – something she rarely allowed herself to do – what his father, Ralph, would be doing now, inside the Nazi war machine.

She found it hard to understand how the man she had loved so passionately, albeit briefly, could have thrown his talents away on the bunch of thugs who had been pursuing her.

There was still the chance that her pursuers would be able to arrange some kind of interception at the frontier beyond Perpignon, but – judging by what she saw around her as they drove along – there was no stomach among most of the French population to assist their invaders, except possibly against the British. She remembered what the Royal Navy had done to the French fleet as they passed the naval base of Toulon, where presumably what was left of the fleet lay mouldering at anchor. But for an *American* wanted in Berlin, well – it wasn't clear that anyone would stir themselves for that.

As her spirits lifted, the further south they drove, she took the chance to look more closely at Señor Santa Cruz, perfectly dressed in the early morning as he was late at night. He had a kind of guardedness and hauteur, even while he allowed himself, as a relaxation, to light a small cheroot before turning in for the night.

The miles fell away, and by lunchtime they were in Spain, heading for Madrid. When they reached the outskirts, it was clear that the city still lay largely in ruins left over from the civil war. It was a dismal sight. The ambassador directed her to the Bolivian embassy, where they left the car behind. She carried his valise, evidently the one that was not actually diplomatic baggage, onto a plodding train of ancient design, all the way to Lisbon. He travelled in first class, together with Lomax's precious box.

When they were once more on a train, it suddenly struck her that – her whole time in the USA, Switzerland and afterwards – she had never once encountered the mysterious or ghostly figure of her old friend Hugh Lancing-Price. Perhaps she was finally beginning to recover.

*

They slept the night on the train, and in the morning, there was the River Tagus and the sunny liberties of Lisbon, and the airfield awaiting for the BOAC clipper flight to Poole.

"You must excuse me, Miss Duarte," said the ambassador unexpectedly as they took their seats aboard the plane. "I am usually airsick. I will endeavour to be discreet."

"Please don't worry, Señor Santa Cruz," she said with a suitably discreet smile. "I too sometimes feel unwell when I am travelling by air."

It was when they were in the air and swooping over the patch of water from where they had just taken off, buffeted by an Atlantic gale, that Xanthe realised what the ambassador had meant.

He was immediately and horribly sick. He vomited until he wept and until he was left shaking. And, moved by his plight, Xanthe had the temerity to hold his arm and then his head as he retched and retched again. The other passengers in their compartment pretended not to notice, though to have a man, dressed so resplendently, retching loudly just a few feet away was liable to be upsetting for everyone involved. But for Xanthe, it reminded her of Indigo and his habit of sicking up his meals, sometimes spectacularly.

When there was no more vomit, for a while at least, and the clipper was soaring high over the Bay of Biscay, she helped him – with the support of the stewards – into a recovery bay where he could sleep. And never once did he lose his dignity.

Then she sat back in her chair and stared out of the window, loosening the collar of the chauffeur's uniform that Lomax had rigged up for her, patting the ambassador's diplomatic bag beside her on the seat and relaxed. She let the roar of the plane's four huge propellers lull her into a reverie.

For the first time, she felt pleased with her performance. She had succeeded in getting the workforce to agree to sabotage the production of the chronometers designed for the new Lorenz coding system. She had dodged the Nazi's network of police agents in Switzerland, she had slipped out of the country and – barring accidents – would now make it home rather than spending the rest of the war interned by the Swiss or, worse still, packed off on a train to Berlin to face whatever trumped-up charges they felt like inventing for her. She had not done too badly. She only hoped that Fleming would see things her way.

But really, it hardly mattered compared to what was most important. She would be with her boy again.

CHAPTER EIGHT

London, December 1941

She remembered again once she was back in London, on the way to her debrief at the Admiralty, that there had been no more visions of poor Hugh which had so worried her before she had left. She could only conclude that either she had recovered – or they'd had nothing to do with her own mind. Unless it was somehow the proximity to where he had died that was setting off the memory in her head.

Perhaps, if it hadn't been her imagination, she had really seen his ghost.

She arrived in London early and wandered down Oxford Street, hoping to get into the Christmas spirit, but it was a dismal sight for the third, dour Christmas of the war. No lights, little in the windows – hardly any windows on the boarded-up shops and the burned-out wreck of what had once been Bourne & Hollingsworth. It was sad and depressing.

The debrief had gone well. There had been some consternation that she had revealed her interest in the chronometers for Lorenz, but even Fleming understood that some kind of honesty was inevitable and necessary to achieve the objectives they had wanted.

"Thank goodness we did not come entirely clean with Wittgenstein and his brother," said Fleming, musing aloud. "There's no knowing what he might have taken it upon himself to say. It hardly needs saying how grateful we are to you."

"Thank you, Commander."

Fleming looked a little embarrassed.

"I think we also owe you an apology. We did not brief you fully. But I think," he said with self-satisfaction, "that we had a good excuse. We were not aware of many of the circumstances."

"Is that the case?" said a battered looking commodore, with his single broad gold stripe on his sleeves, next to him around the table. Xanthe did not recognise him. "May I ask, how confident are you in the shop steward? Will he be able to do what he said he would?"

"I believe so, sir."

"Then I don't think we could possibly have done more in the circumstances. All we can do is delay the shift to Lorenz, and if we are to accept Miss Schneider's testimony here, then we have done so. They will inevitably find some other supplier from Switzerland, but if that gives us another six months for Turing's old team to tackle the new system, it may be enough."

Fleming sat back and pushed his legs out under the table, to show he was changing the subject.

"You see, Xanthe, while you've been away, there have been a number of changes at Bletchley. A number of senior staff there, including your friend Turing, wrote a private letter to the prime minister asking for more resources. The letter caused considerable consternation in official circles, but those resources are now on the way. Though, also, as a result, Denniston is out. We are therefore considerably expanding the payroll. That means space is at a premium, and it may mean it is time for you and your child to move out. You can, of course, rely on us to make satisfactory alternative new arrangements. That is right, is it not, Commodore?"

Turing, the quiet troublemaker. It was extraordinary that so diffident and shy a man could cause so much trouble around himself.

"We are also reorganising Hut 8. Turing is being sent to America to liaise with our new allies. So when the commodore mentioned Turing's 'old team', that is what he meant."

"Turing? Are you sure?"

Could Alan cope with her pushy fellow countrypeople?

"Well, he knows the world of mathematics, and I believe he was at Princeton too, wasn't he?"

*

Alan gone! Frankly, Xanthe admitted to herself, she would prefer not to live at Bletchley without her friend. She forgot to ask when he would be leaving and wondered if he would have time to advise her on her burgeoning relationship with her friend, the Bolivian ambassador.

When they had landed in Dorset, he had turned to her and kissed her hand.

"Miss Duarte, Xanthe, I must thank you for your kindness and gentleness. I was not what I expect of myself, and for that, I humbly apologise. You have looked after me all the way from Berne, and I am grateful."

Xanthe was taken aback by this dramatic change of tune, which often seemed to accompany something else which she had learned to expect. The moment a man could see her as a woman – not an operative or chauffeur – she sensed the flickering awakening of an interest in her.

"Señor Santa Cruz. It is I who must thank you. You saved me from the Nazi thugs in Berne. You saved my life outside Geneva at the French frontier. I risked discovery and goodness knows what else, and you stuck by me. I know you were running a risk too."

"My dear Miss Duarte, it was the least I could do. Perhaps you would do me the honour of dining with me at the embassy. I had the great misfortune to lose my wife some months ago – to a U-boat. I have no love for the Nazis as a result. I am, therefore, in need of female company, and I can't think of anyone I would like to see more than yourself."

Since then, no word.

Well, she would take him up on the invitation if it transpired. She assumed this had not been a request to drop by. It would be fascinating to dine in an embassy, and she found she had a soft spot for the old monster, which had grown as they had driven away from the checkpoint to Vichy France.

She had spoken a great deal, and he had said virtually nothing on the whole journey, but somehow, somehow, part of the psychic communication between people which drew them almost unnoticeably together had operated on them both.

*

"I know I shouldn't have done it, but it worked. I'm only sorry it seems to have led to the demise of poor old Denniston – though I don't know what he could have done to prevent that. I suppose the thinking is that we should have gone via him, rather than direct to Churchill himself."

"I know," said Xanthe. "I've got a lot to thank Denniston for. It seems strange that I've never actually met him."

"Oh well, he's secret, isn't he," said Turing with a grin.

They were having a quick scoot around the Bletchley grounds with Indy in his pram. Turing was pushing, and Xanthe was wondering, a little broodily she feared, what he would be like as a dad. Now that she was being actively pursued by the ambassador, she had begun to feel obsessed about who to choose. "It's a big decision," she said out loud.

"What is?"

"Oh, nothing. I was just wondering things, that's all. Listen, what would you think about me getting married?"

Turing looked shocked.

"Don't do it, Xanthe. Not now. Not till the war's over. You can't make a clear-headed decision before then."

"Is that a proposition?" she asked cheekily.

"Oh, ha-ha. I'm not what they call the marrying kind, and in any case, I'm off to your homeland in a few weeks' time."

Xanthe was hit by a wave of sadness, and even as she felt it, she was aware of the irony – strange that she should feel nostalgic about the most miserable period of her life.

"I don't know, Alan. I can see I can't stay married to Bletchley for much longer. It's going to balloon."

Most miserable period? she thought to herself. Also the most intense, the most tremendous – the period of her life she would never forget.

*

"So you see, Xanthe. I am lonely here. In this embassy. I know this is premature, but I have noticed how quickly people make these personal decisions in wartime. Because tomorrow, a bomb might fall, so they might as well get on with it."

Xanthe's ambassador had popped the question over a meal at the Savoy. It is strange how many turning points seem to have happened to me here, she said to herself. Though the poor old Savoy looked battered and unkempt compared to the way it had looked, so splendid in white and gold, only two years before when she had made her first visit. Now, the dust from the raids and the greenhouse glass which had replaced so many of the windows had given the great hotel a second-hand feel.

Xanthe's heart was pounding. There was no doubt that she admired Santa Cruz. She also found him attractive, if she could maybe set aside the voluminous moustache. Their relationship had been forged in that moment of rescue at the checkpoint. She trusted him and believed he could, and probably would, be a good father for Indy – not that he knew about a child yet. It might even be her duty to say yes – but then Indy was hardly the only consideration.

"Ruperto, I have to tell you. I have a child. A child and no husband. Never have."

The ambassador looked serious. He played with his glass of claret – perhaps the last to be drunk anywhere in London.

"That is not a rare thing these days, Xanthe. There are many like you, whose husbands, or rather the fathers of their children were not married. As I say, in wartime, life happens at an accelerated pace."

"You mean you might accept Indigo as your own? I don't mean pretend that he's your son, but to bring him up as if he was?"

"I have done no less before. I have two sons, grown up and living in La Paz."

A silence fell.

"My dear Xanthe – could you tell me some of those thoughts?"

"Sorry, I know you are waiting for my answer. All I can say is that I promise to give it within a week."

"Then I shall wait patiently until you do."

Was she right, she asked herself, as she made her way onto the street towards the last train home to Bletchley? Was she right to have said nothing about Indy's father? She had allowed herself to give the impression that he had been killed, perhaps heroically in the Battle of

Britain. Perhaps she owed him the full truth. Because of the way they had met, the ambassador must have realised that the woman he wanted to marry was not just an aspiring journalist.

She needed to ask him also if he would accept her continuing her writing career. Perhaps he would be one of those Latin American macho types who would want her simpering at his feet. She could not do that – not after Athens, she couldn't.

How stupid she was not to have probed these questions. Could she pop back through the Savoy foyer to ask him? No, she would miss her train. All she could do was to set some conditions and see how he reacted.

Then she heard a horribly familiar voice behind her.

"Xanthe, good lord! How are you?"

She swung round, and in a moment, she understood where these disturbing visions of Hugh had emerged from. It hadn't been a ghostly Lancing-Price at all.

"*Ralph*!"

She could say nothing more. She stared, horrified, into the face of her former lover.

"Xanthe, I was wondering when I would run into you. How are you getting on? How's the writing?"

"I mean. Why are you here? *How* are you here?"

She appeared to have lost the power of coherent speech.

"Me? Oh, I slipped away, and here I am. Home, da-da!" he said, like a conjuror. "Can't say more here, I'm afraid. Listen, why don't we meet up next week? I'm in Westminster most days. Why don't you give me a ring?"

Still gaping, Xanthe nodded uncertainly. There was something dream-like about the encounter. Something she could not quite grasp.

"Auf wiedersehen!" he said, with a little wink.

CHAPTER NINE

London, January 1942

The war had changed. The declaration of war against the United States had shifted the balance in the west – though, of course, the conflagration was now worldwide – or so informed opinion said. Hitler could have prevailed against the British and possibly even against Russia but not if he also had to fight the limitless resources of the USA.

It was no longer a private British affair, however much the British might have preferred that. There were allies to liaise with again, and the institutions of war were becoming less personal. The bureaucracy which had been flung up into the air after Dunkirk had now begun to harden and consolidate again. Xanthe's little arrangement with Bletchley Park had to come to an end. She had said a tearful goodbye to Nurse Agnes, and she moved back into Moira's flat in Shepherd's Bush with the baby and all the detritus of babyhood.

But all the time, she was taking in the implications of these changes around her – and the incredible news of the loss of the *Prince of Wales*, her favourite battleship since it had stood alone against the *Bismarck* while Xanthe had been in Greece – she was also now trying to understand what it meant that Ralph was back in London. Ralph the lover, Ralph the traitor – and not just to his country. He went round and round in her head over and over again.

Clever and wounding ripostes to his final '*auf wiedersehen*' crowded into her head, unmade and unexpressed, things she wished she had said. Other rather vital things she wished she had asked. What was Ralph doing in London? Did the authorities know? If he had taken his Westminster seat again, they must do. Had he finally decided to do the right thing and been welcomed back by the establishment like the prodigal son?

"Look, here is the real point," she said to Fleming, once she had plucked up the courage to talk to the Admiralty about the man they had asked her to watch in Berlin. "Whatever he now says, he *was* a Nazi. He was one of them. I loved him, I lived with him, and I can tell the difference. He was a convinced traitor. I just can't believe you've let him come home."

Fleming wriggled uncomfortably.

"All I can do, Xanthe, is to repeat what I have been told when I made discreet enquiries when you first contacted me. And I have been specifically refused permission to tell you this – so I am disobeying orders to do so, because, well… you know."

Xanthe did know, of course. Because Fleming felt responsible for her predicament, falling in love and all the rest.

"I know! I know you said he was playing a deeper game, on our side. And I just don't believe it."

"I assure you, I…"

"You know what I mean, Ian." She had never addressed him by his Christian name before. It marked a rite of passage of some kind, which had quietly taken place in her soul.

"That, unbeknownst to us, MI6 specifically sent Lancing-Price to

Berlin in a sophisticated operation to convince the Germans that we would make peace, so they would decide that invasion was an unnecessary waste of resources. It seems to have worked. Now, if the reason that you're so cross…"

"Cross? I'm not cross, I'm really mad. I'm *furious*!"

"Fine. If the reason you're furious is that Lancing-Price misled you, then that may just prove that he was effective. Because it misled the Nazis too. And I do have to say this, Xanthe, you were also misleading him. That was the name of the game."

Now she was really incandescent. She stood up and held the back of her chair, shaking with rage.

"Listen! How can you be so obtuse? I don't care if he misled me – well, I do – but what worries me is that he misled *us*. I mean that he misled his country, who is he is working for now. Or so he says."

Fleming stared in silence. "I know, I know. All I can say is that this question is a long way above my pay grade," he said.

"Well, if you can't act, then I *can*…"

She stormed out, pausing only to settle Indigo in his pram, but – as she did so – she realised that Fleming was right. There was nothing she could do: who would listen to her, a junior operative and a jilted lover? She was powerless.

She also recognised that, morally, these issues were hardly as clear cut as she had thought. She was angry with Ralph for misleading her, when it was also true that she had been sent to Berlin by a rival intelligence operation, intent on misleading him. If she felt betrayed by him, he might reasonably feel betrayed by her.

But then again, her feelings were absolutely real. Could he say the same about his?

*

Dear Xanthe,

I do apologise that I am unable to advise you more than I did when we met at the Admiralty last week. We owe you a great deal, not least for sending you on what must now seem like a wild goose chase in your first operation in Berlin.

One of the points you made has struck home, and I thought it right to tell you. I have taken the matter up with the authorities and will let you know, in due course, if anything transpires.

Please give my sincere good wishes to Indigo.

Yours sincerely,

Ian

Cdr I. Fleming RNVR

*

Dear Xanthe,

I was sorry you didn't feel able to contact me after we ran into each other, for a second time, outside the Savoy. I have been thinking about you a great deal and the time we had together, in another place (as they say!)

I hope you will forgive me for doing so, but I have made enquiries and understand that you have a baby, which implies to me that you have met somebody since we knew each either. I can understand that.

What I did want to say is how much I valued our time together, though it is quite reasonable that you should be confused about my loyalties. Especially as I bitterly regret the last time we were together was not the kind of farewell I could possibly have had in mind for you.

Let me say emphatically that I did not, will not and would never betray my country. I hope you will one day be able to accept my word on that because there are matters I must not speak about. But then, nor would I willingly betray you, who remain in my thoughts as a precious memory. And if we never see each other again, you always will.

I remain your obedient servant,

Ralph Lancing-Price

R. Lancing-Price, DSO, MP

*

Dear Ruperto,

First, my sincere apologies for my failure to keep to my promise and give you an answer to your most generous offer within a week.

I am so sorry, because you are a dear man, but I have to say no. I have realised that – as your wife – I would have, and would want, to follow wherever you go, yet I now want to see this war through. I know myself enough to expect that, although I hardly long for action anymore, I am not sure – after I have been through what I have– I could any more be able to be the quiet, biddable, reliable partner that you need and deserve.

This is a difficult letter to write because I have loved your company and have grown to admire you. Yet, since our conversation, I have had an encounter with my own past that was very uncomfortable for me. This would have to be an issue for you too, if you were to join your name with mine. I have met again, very unexpectedly, the father of my child.

I tell you this in strictest confidence. I had given him up as lost to the Nazis, but he tells me he is no traitor – as I had supposed – but some kind of hero. I don't know what to believe, and I owe you a better, more decisive, less battered woman to love you as you should be loved.

I am so sorry and so grateful that you saw something in me worth loving.

Yours truly,

Xanthe

*

Dear Ralph,

I have written some difficult letters in my time, but this one is the toughest. It is to tell you three things you need to know.

First, you misled me in Berlin, but – for reasons I can't explain and you probably know already – I was not quite all I seemed either.

Second, despite this, my feelings for you grew so overwhelmingly that I would have misled the whole world for you if you had let me. It is best I don't pretend that night at the party did not break my heart because it did.

Third, you must also know this. There has been nobody else. When you hear my baby's birthdate, you will know that it is your child. You have a son called Indigo. I do not need anything from you, so please don't put on your very English mask of concern.

I know you will ask me what I want. I have no idea, except that I would like you to know your son. But if you pretend to me anything at all, I will know it, and we will never meet again.

Yours sincerely,

Xanthe

EPILOGUE

London, February 1942

It was a dull, overcast day in February when Xanthe found herself wandering across London Bridge again, towards Guy's Hospital. There was the smell of smoke on the breeze, though there had been no raids for weeks, as far as she knew. Perhaps this is just how London smells, she thought. Weeks had also gone by since she decided to make the trip, Turing had departed for the USA to liaise on cryptography, and Bletchley was expanding very fast. It was a new world, ushered in by the Pearl Harbour attack, and she no longer felt nearly so welcome there.

She found the familiar gaunt figure nursing a greasy cup of tea in the same café where she had met him, under the railway bridge.

"Professor?"

"For goodness sake, please do not call me that!" said Wittgenstein, looking around nervously.

"Sorry," said Xanthe. "Listen, may I sit down? I have something to say."

Judging by the look of dawning recognition on his lined and sensitive face, it was clear that the philosopher was only just beginning to recognise her.

"You are Miss, um, from naval intelligence? Miss, er… I am most terribly sorry that I have forgotten your name."

"Xanthe. Xanthe Schneider." She smiled encouragingly at him.

"Of course! Delighted to see you again, Miss Schneider. Are you here to ask me to write another letter? My brother has not, perhaps inevitably, kept me informed about what happened. If indeed anything did."

"No, no, definitely not. Just to say that I was most enormously grateful for your help a few months ago and to your brother too. I can't thank him directly, but I can thank you."

Wittgenstein took another sip of tea and offered Xanthe her own cup. She shook her head gratefully.

"Well, I can't really say what happened, I'm afraid – in fact, my boss was pretty shirty about the idea of me coming here to thank you at all. But I can say that it seems to have worked – at least, I don't think it could have gone much better. And we have, I hope, shortened the war as a result."

"I am glad. Thank you for telling me, despite your boss." Wittgenstein looked far more pleased than he ought to have.

"Well, I don't think intelligence types are very good at saying 'thank you'. I suppose they're afraid it will lead to 'careless talk'." She laughed a little.

"Miss Schneider. I understand completely. In fact, I believe you have done a brave thing staying human despite your involvement in the war."

"Oh, I don't know. I think I've managed braver…"

She laughed. He didn't. Then she suddenly realised why she had been so determined to come.

"Professor? I mean…" she whispered. "May I ask you something? A question about life. About love?"

Wittgenstein took a deep breath.

"About love, I fear I am a novice. But life, maybe."

In very basic, not to say coded form, she set out before the great philosopher her dilemma about Ralph. A man with Nazi sympathies, who came home again, having been prepared to help them – and she did not know whether it had been out of fear or courage or conviction – but who was the father of her son and who she nonetheless loved. What should she do?

Wittgenstein sat listening intently, as if it was the most obvious thing in the world that this young lady should unburden herself in this way, then he began to pace fast around the café.

"Let me ask you a question, Miss Schneider. Do you love him for what he is or despite what he is? The reason I ask" – he said, racing ahead before she had the chance to come up with an answer – "is that love is about courage. It is not, or should not be, about what you can *receive* through love – it is about what you can *achieve* through it. Do you understand?"

"I think so."

"Very well then, let us come to some kind of arrangement. I am feeling friendless at the moment. If you will come to the flicks with me next week, then beforehand we can discuss the question and see whether it is a real problem or just a confusion of terms. What do you say?"

"The flicks?"

"You know – cinema, movies. Have you seen *Stagecoach*? Because I think life is a little like that. There are terrifying ordeals along the way and challenges and important decisions too. But in no way is it supposed to be fun. Do you understand what I mean?"

Xanthe stared at him, trying to work out what to say.

"You are a serious young lady. I was impressed with you when we met the first time. It seemed to me that you had risen above the narrow dictates of wartime, and you had kept your humanity. I hope you will not be insulted when I say that you have not been educated into uselessness, like so many of the people I have met in Cambridge. You will not understand my philosophy, but then almost nobody does."

"I really can't pretend I'm a philosopher."

"My dear Miss Schneider. That is precisely why I am willing to help. I promise I will think about your problem, and together, we will come up with an answer. Then we will go on to the Picture Palace and see *They Died With Their Boots On.* How about it?"

"Thank you so much, Pro… I mean Dr Wittgenstein. I would be ever so grateful."

www.ingramcontent.com/pod-product-compliance
Lightning Source LLC
LaVergne TN
LVHW041106080826
845145LV00007B/1700

* 9 7 8 1 8 3 9 0 1 1 6 0 3 *